A HOUSE IN THE HAMPTONS

A HOUSE IN THE HAMPTONS

(One Summer Near the End of the L.I.E.)

A Novel by

GLORIA NAGY

Delacorte
Press

Published by
Delacorte Press
Bantam Doubleday Dell Publishing Group, Inc.
666 Fifth Avenue
New York, New York 10103

Library of Congress Cataloging in Publication Data

Nagy, Gloria.
   A house in the Hamptons (one summer near the end of the l.i.e.): a novel / by Gloria Nagy.
     p.   cm.
   ISBN 0-385-30096-4
   I. Title.
PS3564.A36H68   1990
813'.54—dc20   89-77849
                                                  CIP

Manufactured in the United States of America

Published simultaneously in Canada

July 1990

10 9 8 7 6 5 4 3 2 1

RRH

*To Tony Wurman, my darling son, for making me laugh
and filling my heart . . .*

And to the memory of Sy Kamens

I wish to thank Carole Baron for being a great Lady and renewing my faith in the Business; Patricia Soliman for her unflappable support, nurturing, elegance, humor, and gentle brilliance; Alexandra Penney, my darling pal, for everything; Ed Victor for his wisdom, class, enthusiasm, and charisma; Olive Harmantzis for putting it all together and always being there; Dr. Milton Pereira for guiding me deeper; Lisa Roda for being herself; Susan Grode for her counsel, caring, and for "Morgan," the world's funniest dog; and Richard Saul Wurman, my biggest fan and my very best friend. I would also like to acknowledge myself for never giving up.

PART ONE

The highway is called by some, Route 27, and by others, the Montauk Highway, but by most, just "the Highway," because it is the only way in or out of the Hamptons. Leading down to the very tip, the Montauk point—the end of the line. The slender tip followed by sightseers and day trippers for decades, like the Pied Piper's mice and children, ending in the sea.

On this highway between Southampton and Bridgehampton is a deserted Carvel ice-cream store. It has been there, deserted, for years. An eyesore. Inappropriate. Like a bum in a fine neighborhood. Neglected. It stands there. The CREAM after ICE rubbed away. A lost dream. A remnant of hope, of days when hot and eager families stopped on the way east or west. Bare feet flapped across the threshold toward the delights. Swirling soft cream cones. Chocolate sprinkles. Summer sweet. Now it is a tiny ghost town.

Each summer sometime in July, a strange thing happens. Suddenly, there are young bare-chested men in work boots in front of the Carvel store. Trucks with plywood and paint appear. HELP WANTED signs go up. Hope rises among the summer residents and locals alike. Come on, old girl, you can

3

do it. You're not dead yet. COMING IN AUGUST banners in fluorescent green are slapped across the sides. CALL 555-7856 FOR MORE INFORMATION! HELP WANTED! COMING IN AUGUST! The young sun-brown men come and go looking busy. July is passing. Time is short.

Soon the trucks leave and the men leave and the CREAM is never repainted beneath the ICE and the hope dies; leaving only the HELP WANTED! and COMING IN AUGUST! signs as a bitter reminder of dying dreams, passing time and the truth of summer. It is not endless. It is not a dream. It is only a brief and bittersweet passage between spring and fall.

While the boats glide and the lotion coats the ripe young bodies turning in the sun like animals on a cosmic spit; and the wine is sweet cold pleasure and the nights are soft twinkling black, the Carvel stand is waiting in the dark on the Highway; waiting in the midday sun. Deserted and alone. A reminder.

PROLOGUE

"The Disappeared in Argentina," she thought out loud. She remembered it later, because it was the last rational thought she had that week, the last old thought, coming at the end of their old reality, but before the new reality had taken hold. She sat curled up on the sand, looking out into the vast, endless Atlantic horizon, as she had for so many summers before, thinking of a foreign movie. About military coups in distant lands across the sea, where ordinary people, husbands and fathers like her own, vanished from the streets never to be seen again. Lost inside an insanity that closed the mind, stopped the brain, froze the blood in the human heart. Things like this just simply did not happen to people like them.

She smiled. What an embarrassing sentence, even inside your own head. What an officious, elitist, Princess crock. Everything happened to everyone, babycakes. She shivered, drawing her knees so close to her chest, they flattened her breasts against her rib cage.

Vanished. She screamed. One loud, violent scream of frustration and fear. It was not acceptable. "Please," she whispered, tears released with her rage.

Horrible thoughts filled her head. Headless bodies floating in the Hudson River. Cardiac arrest with no ID in his pocket. Or worse. At least from her point of view right now. By far the worst. He had gone off with *Her*. Like that other movie. On cable in the middle of one of her recent sleepless nights. *Hot Spell.* Shirley Booth and Anthony Quinn. Middle-aged man fleeing in the family sedan with his teenage dream girl. Fleeing his desperate sagging wife and the stuporous sameness of his overburdened life smack into the full price of his escape. Well, whatever she was, she was hardly Shirley fucking Booth, now was she? No. No way. He wouldn't do it like that.

She knew him so well. Or at least so she had thought. He was more honorable than that. Or at least more dutiful. Or was he? Was anybody? She was no longer sure.

The only thing she was sure of was that he was gone. Just disappeared. A vanishing point on the summer horizon. A potential headline in the *Daily News:* PROMINENT MANHATTAN MAN DISAPPEARS ON WAY TO HIS HOUSE IN THE HAMPTONS. FOUL PLAY OR LOVE TRYST BEING CONSIDERED.

Well, if it turns out to be love tryst, I'll see to the foul play part all by my very self. She released her legs and stood up, stretching her arms up toward the bright blue, cloudless sky, breathing in the sea smells. All alone on the vast summer beach. All alone with a crisis that nothing in her entire life had prepared her for. "Please," she whispered, "let him come home."

1

Harry Hart is standing at the Oak Bar in the Plaza looking out at the snow filtering down on Central Park wondering if he's supposed to be at a table in the Edwardian Room. Or maybe in line at the Palm Court? Could that be possible? No. Nobody has lunch at the Palm Court of their own free will. Trader Vic's, is that possible? No. He didn't even know where the fucking place was. Pineapple and greasy bacon wrapped around water chestnuts. Mai tais. In Manhattan. In January. No way. Maybe *she* suggested it? She lives in California for chrissakes—God only knows what they call lunch in San Diego. What are those blue drinks? Curaçao. Blue Hawaiis? Maybe curaçao is the winter drink of San Diego.

No, *he* was the host. *He* suggested the Plaza. It had to be the Oak Room. They knew him at the Oak Room. He would only take a woman who had almost had his baby over half a century ago, a woman he hadn't laid a watery blue on since just after high school, to someplace he was known! She was just late. Very late. Or maybe she had changed her mind? Maybe she wasn't coming at all. The ultimate one-upmanship. Or maybe, she was right here and they didn't recognize each other. Twenty-five years, after all. Women really change. Okay. Men really change too. Maybe she saw me and fled in horror. Maybe I should just get out of here while the getting's good and go back to work.

Should I call her hotel? I didn't ask the name of her hotel. Good, Harry. Really good. What if something had come up? You'd leave a woman, who you walked out on, whose heart you nearly broke, whose life you nearly ruined, whose goddamn husband has just died, waiting alone in a strange restaurant in a strange city? What a schmuck. Things come up all the time.

Maybe I'll have another beer. No. Bad idea. Just relax. She probably couldn't get a cab. Maybe she slipped on the ice. Maybe she got mugged. Just calm down. She'll be here.

Get yourself prepared. She wants something from you. That's for sure. (Tell her the line forms on the left.) What could she want? Money? (The line forms on the right.) Sex? Nah. No one wants sex anymore. Too big a downside. Besides, she comes from fucking San Diego, that's where whatever sex is left is going on. The chlorine kills the AIDS virus or something. She wouldn't come *here* for that. (Maybe I'm underestimating myself.) Nah. Too remote. Too . . . prime time.

So, if it's not money (Who said it wasn't money? Nah. She must have money. Martin made a ton of money. It can't be money) and it's not sex, pretty sure on that one, then what *could* it be? Shit. I hate surprises. Why didn't I just ask her on the fucking telephone? Too taken aback, I guess. Too much ego, more like, Harry, my man. Too much curiosity. I mean, twenty-five years and she calls me up like it was twenty-five minutes. Well, why the hell not. It *seems* like twenty-five minutes. If the next twenty-five goes like that, and the first seventeen, who even remembers that—that took about fourteen seconds—so you're eighty years old, you croak and the whole thing is like an hour. The whole birth-to-death number. An hour and fourteen seconds. Plus tax. (There *were* a couple of very long nights.)

You certainly knew who *she* was right away. Since you can't even remember your secretary's name half the time—a half-century-old name shoots right up the gray matter.

Harry ordered another beer. "Amstel Light, Charlie." He felt like a sissy.

How do you tell someone over forty? Just take a peek in the kitchen. Everything's *Light. Light* beer. *Light* cream cheese. *Light* margarine. *Light* Doritos. Was there ever a heavy Dorito? Light as air. Fluffy food. Egg whites. "Lite Cuisine." A continual and desperate attempt to defy gravity. The lighter we are, the longer we'll last. Even clothes are light. Heavy means . . . old. Earth is heavy. Under the earth is really heavy. Stay light, and stay above ground. In 1963 nobody knew this. Young likes heavy. Guinness stout and cheese steaks. Combat boots. Shetland sweaters. Padded bras. Motorcycle jackets. Hair glop. Even our hair was heavy.

His stomach dropped. He was scared. More than scared. He was shrinking. Harry's hands were cold and wet, tears filled his eyes. Suddenly he was not a relatively well-preserved and stable member of the Grown Up and Functioning Club, he was a frightened child. Not even a frightened seventeen-year-old—a little boy. Lost in time. Plucked from his past into the Oak Room by some wicked witch. *I want to go home.* Mommy and Daddy's home. Ancestral home, the WASPs call it.

Jesus. Fifteen years of analysis and I'm disintegrating in the Plaza Hotel for no reason at all. You know better than that, Harry baby. There's always a reason. Al-ways. What are you afraid of here? Get it before she comes, now, boy. Nail it down fast.

What? That movie. *Peggy Sue Got Married?* She's unhappy,

9

she goes to her high school reunion, she sees her old crush, her ex-husband, she has an anxiety attack or palpitations or something and she wakes up in the past. In high school. Oh my God. Oh boy. Is that it? This woman will drag me back into my adolescence and accuse me of all the terrible things I've always been afraid were true about me.

Oh, God! Imagine having to go back there knowing what I know now? Knowing when *he* dies, when *her* head goes soft. And my brother, all that shit. Imagine having to wander around in that vat, again. I'd have to hear all those speeches over and over. And I'd know the endings! God, I hated that movie. And the worst part was, she did it again! She didn't change a thing! Unbelievable.

So, is that it? That's the fear? Madeline Olsen is going to swoop in here and put a spell on me. Doom me to a life of overdone brisket and Elvis Presley? Then why did I feel like going home? Mythical home. An idea of home. Innocence. Safety, is what I want. Protection. Not Melrose Park. Not whining and yelling (I can get that here and now). Not the great and total void of the future. There's a lot to be said for having half the future behind you.

What was that other movie? *Back to the Future*. Making it with your goddamn mother in a Studebaker! How do they sell that stuff? And they sell it as comedy/adventure instead of the tragedy/horror flick it really is. I don't want to go back. I don't even want to be younger. (Now, that really is weird, Harry.) So what am I shaking for. Why are my hands sweating? Come on, unconscious. Cough it up.

A tiny faint little voice inside Harry's head whispers to him. *She's dangerous. She's not in your control. She's a windmill and you are the Nobel laureate of tilting. You have no power over her.*

That fits. I can see that. Harry felt bigger. His hands unclenched the beer bottle. Was it true? He basically trusted

10

that little whisperer in his head. It had taken him fifteen years to tune it in. It was now, to all intents and purposes, his godhead. And it was always right if he listened. Sometimes, he still got cute. I don't have anyone in my entire life I can't control, Harry thought, and then tested it out to see if the idea was sound.

That must be what the fear is about. Powerlessness. Primary castration anxiety. She doesn't need me for anything. Or does she? She sure did then. I had all kinds of power then. She loved me to pieces, then. I wasn't even impressed, then. This bouncing gorgeous little blond yummie. So sweet, you could lick her for dessert. Big tits. Great ass. Crazy mad about me. No one had ever been even mildly intrigued by me. Not even the JAPs. And here's this Catholic pom-pom girl, offering me anything I want forever.

Boy was that scary. It's still scary. Sleeping with her was the scariest thing I had ever done. Okay. So being a virgin didn't help, but it was more than that. She was so, different. Actually, stupid. She was so stupid. Or was she? Maybe that was just my defense. Maybe it was just that she loved me. No one had ever loved me like that. Not even my mother (especially not my mother).

It made me so fucking nervous. Oh, to have a shot at her now, like she was then. Me now, her twenty-five years ago. I'd know what to do with her now! How she came! Momma mia. What a thrill. I made a woman come! She made the craziest sound. Like Minnie Mouse with gas. *Whoow, whoow, whoow.* Real high and sort of screechy breathy. Over and over. *Whoow, whoow, whoow.* Scared the shit out of me. But I had power. I liked that part. I made a Catholic cheerleader lose total control of herself.

Oh, sure, Harry. Sure you did. What a fool you are. You really are the kind of guy who needs a shrink on a twenty-four-hour beeper implanted in your skull. Power! She got

11

pregnant and you had to marry Minnie fucking Mouse! Some power. A few *whoow, whoow, whoow*s, and you almost ruined your entire life! No wonder you're scared. This broad manipulated you out of your socks while your shoes were still on. She *is* dangerous.

Maybe I should call Gina and have her meet us. A wife would help. Oh, good thinking. It would take you three days to explain why you didn't tell her about it a week ago. Donnie, maybe a friend would help. Donnie! Donnie loved her all the way through high school. She *dumped* Donnie for you. It took him *ten years* to get over it. Great, Har. I should have invited Dr. Wexel, he loves shit like this.

No, it would take another three days to explain why I didn't tell *him* about it a week ago. Forget it. She's twenty-six minutes late. Four minutes more and I'm out of here.

Perfume. It surrounded him like a ghost. Spread all over him, enclosed him, filled Harry's winter-red sinuses, drawing out the available oxygen mingling with the steam heat, foul breath, and passive smoke and trapping him. He couldn't breathe. He couldn't move. He was dizzy in it. It was familiar, too. Elevator perfume. The kind that lingers like sulfur and everyone holds their breath until escape is possible.

Femme. Was it Femme? Not possible. The red whorehouse box with the flamenco number on it. So fifties. No one wears it anymore. Not even in San Diego. Arpège? No. Not trendy enough. What did his wife wear? Something clean and crispy. The Virginia Slims of perfume. No nonsense. Charlie. Jake. Ramba. No. This was seduction perfume. This was not a modern-woman-in-Adidas-and-gaberdine-suit-and-briefcase scent. This was *Dynasty* perfume. This was horrible.

"Harry? Harry Hart?"

Harry turned, ever so slowly, sucking in air through his mouth.

"Madeline?"

A blond bunny rabbit stood grinning before him. Complete with red runny nose and white furry earmuffs. A platinum blond bunny wrapped in a bank of white fur. She threw her arms around his neck threatening, for the second time in just moments, his air supply. She squeezed tight, her fur and fifties perfume making him faint with panic.

The furry woman giggled, and removed her white fuzzy earmuffs with one white leather paw. "Oh, jeez, that sounds so funny. No one calls me that. Not since high school!"

Harry signed the check and motioned to the captain. "I was worried. You were late. We'd better sit down now."

"Oh, Harry. I'm so sorry. I hate to admit it, but I overslept. Jet lag, I guess. I didn't even hear my alarm! I'm so used to Martin being with me. This is my first trip all alone in my whole life!"

Harry guided his white rabbitess to a table by the window. He felt dizzy, nauseous and confused. He had no idea what he had expected, but furry and cheerful was not it.

Madeline wiggled out of her coat, revealing almost the same body carved in Harry's memory. The body was also encased in white. Cashmere, he thought. Expensive, but really Hollywood, his wife would think. Tight white cashmere skirt and sweater. Diamond rings. Diamond earrings under the earmuffs. Sonja Henie without the ice. A winter wonderland, he thought. Maybe she had lifted and tucked, maybe it was just good genes, but she looked almost the same. A thinking man's version of her girlhood self. He was speechless.

Madeline smiled a big pink smile. "Fritzi."

Harry tried to focus. He was still lilting, tilting again,

moving in and out, round and round this apparition in a bright vertiginous daze.

"Beg your pardon?"

"Fritzi. That's my nickname. That's what everyone calls me. Martin chose it because I was always on the fritz, he said. Anyway, everyone uses it, if you call me Madeline, I'll feel very weird."

"But if I call you Fritzi, *I'll* feel very weird."

"Better you than me. Ladies first."

"I had a hamster named Fritzi. When I was eight."

"Great!"

"It died a horrible death. If I have to say Fritzi over and over it will trigger all sorts of painful memories."

Fritzi smiled, a slow, wicked sweet smile. "I had an embryo named Harry Junior."

Harry spit a mouthful of water across the table, spraying Fritzi/Madeline's white cashmere chest.

"Are you okay, Harry?" She kept smiling.

Harry sat up very straight and turned on his famous cold blue stare. At least that's what he hoped he was turning on. He was overwhelmed. It was hard to be sure. "I'm fine . . . Fritzi, Fritzi, Fritzi, Fritzi, *Frrrriiittttzzzii.*"

"Great! Harry, Harry, Harry, Harry, *Hhhhaaaarrrryyy!*" She laughed.

He laughed. In fact he laughed very loudly. He laughed and laughed and while he laughed he had absolutely no idea why this was funny or what it meant. He couldn't actually even remember another experience where such a state of mind had occurred. He always prided himself on knowing what was happening and why he was reacting to everything. Anal compulsion, Dr. Wexel called it. Smarts, Harry called it.

"I'll have a margarita, no salt," said Fritzi.

A HOUSE IN THE HAMPTONS

"The same," said Harry, as if inhabited by an alien being. Could Trader Vic's be far behind?

A middle-aged man was losing it in the Oak Room and everyone else on earth was going about their business.

"So, Fritzi? What brings you to New York?" he heard a casual male voice saying, as if from deep inside a Lily tank. He glanced behind him to see who it was. He had separated from himself without a sound.

Harry did not go back to the office after lunch. First, because he had consumed two margaritas and two bottles of beer, which was exactly four times his usual lunchtime indulgence. But there were other reasons. He needed time to think. Fritzi's appearance in the middle of his well-organized daily life was the first spontaneous occurrence in a very long time. Much longer than Harry liked to admit. He was unnerved. When Harry was unnerved or needed time to think, he always did the same thing. He walked briskly over to the Museum of Broadcasting on 53rd Street and checked out one of the Bergman tapes.

Harry had two obsessions. Baseball and Ingmar Bergman. Neither seemed to fit the personality profile of the publisher and owner of the *Duck Hunter's Journal* and various offshoot publications.

But then Harry, who barely knew the difference between a Green Head and a Susie, was not your typical highbrow publisher. Harry, his wife, Gina, liked to say, was really more of an eyebrow. Above low and middle but not above forehead. He liked it like that. He, in fact, got a certain frothy demonic pleasure out of his apathy and ignorance regarding his subject matter. "You don't have to be a goddamn bird to sell bird seed. Fuck ducks! The only ducks I know about are cotton and white! I know selling. I know *ad-ver-tis-ers*. If I published *Psychology Today*, would I have to be Carl Jung?" Harry got off on it.

15

And as long as there were so many thousands of "Eddie Bauer assholes, who want to wade around in ice-cold fish shit, blowing on little whistles and freezing their nuts off for the chance to blast the feathers off some poor pigeon—so be it! It's their party."

He had a point. In truth, he made a living, but what he really wanted to do and knew he never would, was go to Sweden and work for Bergman. Photograph him and publish small, esoteric tomes on his productions. Bergman was Harry's duck shit. Every little syllable. He was fanatical about him.

Harry checked out *Face to Face* with Liv Ullman and Erland Josephson and retreated to a cubicle. Harry loved *Face to Face*. Watching Liv (Goddess Liv—the most sensual woman, the greatest actress in the entire world) come apart at her grandparents' house. Nerves breaking down. A perfectly rational woman, a psychiatrist no less, haunted by childhood dreads at the scene of the crime, coming undone and reforming all within a few days. The yuppie nervous breakdown—have it over Memorial Day weekend, get it out of one's system and back at the desk first thing Tuesday morning.

Harry tried to lose himself in the stark clarity. The Bergman silence. Those eyes of Josephson's, with those tiny black centers. Dead beady, marble twinkling black eyes. Bird eyes. You could never see inside. Those kind of eyes scared Harry. It was like talking to someone wearing reflecting sunglasses. Deflecting your impact. Giving no clues. Bouncing you off and into your own trip. Leaving you powerless. Can't control anything you can't see into.

He was having trouble concentrating. He still smelled of Fritzi. How could he go home anyway, smelling that way. He would walk. Winter would suck her off him. His head hurt. He felt dizzy from the booze and the experience. And he still didn't know what she wanted. From him, anyway.

What she wanted from New York was a change of scene, so she said. He was not, she had told him cheerfully, the only "person from my distant past" she was looking up. And there was real estate involved. A house in the Hamptons that she was "seriously considering." (Money he ruled out immediately. Money she had.) She just felt an overwhelming urge to see him, again. (She said.) Nothing more. Old times' sake. He could deal with that. Or could he? Something had happened to him at lunch that hadn't happened to him for a very long time. What was it?

Liv was now swallowing an entire bottle of some sort of sleeping pills or something—but he wasn't terribly concerned—he knew that Marble Eyes comes over in time. Not to worry.

He did know what it was that had happened to him at lunch. He'd had a good time. That's it. They'd shared old stories. She listened to his success saga with rapt, chipper attention. They'd gotten a little smashed, eaten too much. Passed the double entendres back and forth with the bread and butter. Laughed. He'd had fun. Harry didn't have fun. Fun was not one of Harry's things.

He felt rather guilty thinking about what fun he'd had while poor Liv lay in the fetal position with tubes in her nose in a Swedish nuthouse. But it was really okay. He knew it wasn't for long.

Madeline "Fritzi" Olsen Ferris back from the living dead. Back from the ghosts of high school memories that lived always in Harry Hart's head. Frozen in time, always right under the surface waiting for the code word to plug into his psychic data system. And she, always at the top of the disk. A part of the cobwebbed past—combining reality and fantasy, sadness and loss, hope and despair—and yearnings. Christmas past knocking on the computer screen, Marley's ghost in a skintight bunny suit, smiling a big pink smile and melting Harry's winter weariness. Making him laugh.

What does she really want? he thought again as Liv's daughter appeared to announce, "I know you've never liked me."

2

J*une 1* _____

"The Hamptons," Frankie Karsh, co-owner of Vintage Classics, the fancy used-car lot where everyone who wanted to impress anyone but didn't want to pay retail for it went, was saying to Gina Hart, "The way I see it, is like an intersection. A four-way intersection between . . ." Frankie paused. He had never actually been interviewed before, let alone for *New York* magazine and he wasn't sure how fast she could write it up. "So, like I said, it's a . . ."

"Four-way intersection," Gina helped him out. "It's okay, I've got a tape running, too. Just talk, I'm with you." He was so young. She smiled to herself. He still thought this was a big deal.

"Yeah. A four-way intersection between the Always Had Its, the Just Got Its, the Maybe Next Year I'll Get Its, and the Never Gonna Have Its."

"That's great. Tell me more." Gina took a sip of cold coffee, vowing for the hundredth time that week to cut the caffeine. Her heart was pumping.

Frankie smiled a great big enthusiastic, eager, slightly

19

crooked smile and ran a tan hand through his long curly black hair. "Well, okay. See, almost everyone who comes out for the summer comes by here. I sell a lot of cars, to all four types. I get the old money Southampton WASPs in, like maybe they own the old twenty-acre mansion and stuff, but the trust fund's a little parched—they want like an old Rolls —want it to look like it's been in the family for decades. And I get the yuppies, my age, late twenties, pulling in a hundred and fifty thousand or so. Slobbering over the '82 Ferrari—the Maybe Next Year guy. I'll put him in an M.G. or an old 'vette or something. He'll be back and back.

"Then there's my main men, the investment bankers, traders. These guys *have got it*. Making minimum, a mil. They pick up maybe two cars in a day. Walk out with, let's say, an '84 Bentley and a tasty little '86 Carerra. Write a personal check like they're buying diet soda at the IGA. These guys want everything on earth, today! They're the pace drivers. They set the pace. You can't go around them, over them and you can never, ever, catch them.

"And then, we've got the locals. The folks that live off the other three types. Clean their pools, build their custom cabinets, bake their croissants. Come in to look at the Maseratis, but know the best they're ever gonna do is an '82 Prelude with bad tires."

Gina laughed. "God, Frankie, what a depressing picture. You sound like a feudal landlord or something. Where you are is where you stay and the only thing that matters is money."

"No. No. No! I . . . what I'm trying to say is that's the way it is, not the way I *want* it to be. Just the way it seems to be, here. People I deal with aren't into 'love thy neighbor,' they're into shiny toys, houses on the beach. That kind of stuff. Or they don't come to the Hamptons. They go to Maine or someplace."

A HOUSE IN THE HAMPTONS

"Why, hello, Frankie boy." A very tall, very blond woman in her middle forties stood in the doorway, dressed entirely in bright yellow with a large flower-covered straw hat on her head and one perennially tanned arm, aching for a tennis racquet, on her bony hip.

Gina and Frankie turned toward the intruder. Gina noted that Frankie Karsh was blushing.

Frankie stood up as if the new schoolmarm had just caught him throwing spitballs. "Hi. Mrs. Thomas. Just got it back from the shop! Came out great!"

"I never doubted it would." The tall, tan blonde turned her even pink smile on Gina. Who returned it with one of her own.

She's jealous, Gina thought, having no idea where the thought came from.

Frankie was out of his depth here. "Uh, Gina Thom, I mean Gina Hart, this is my, uh, client, Bonita Thomas. Gina's doing a story for *New York* magazine. I'm, uh, bein' interviewed, so, let me get you to Kenny; he's got the keys. Be right back, Gina."

Gina and Bonita nodded to each other. Gina watched her walk out. Women like that were so far away from her, she always reacted to them with a combination of awe and contempt. As it was, she hardly ever even saw one up close. They seemed to stay buried behind those endless hedges in Georgica, only emerging at night to swoop into the Parrish Museum gala or a quiet dinner for fifty at Charlotte Ford's.

She watched Frankie seeing to her. A handsome, sweaty young mechanic, Kenny, no doubt, had joined them. Something insinuating in the way Bonita Baby talked to Frankie made Gina suspect she had slept with him. Or was it just another idle projection? Gina was never sure.

Still, the idea had possibilities. How far could she go with him? He certainly liked to talk. And he had never been interviewed before. The best kind. He had never had the horrifying moment of seeing what one has said in black and white for the whole world to snicker at.

Her mind wandered. I hope Harry remembered the goddamn corn. How many people did he say were coming? Ten. Ten! What about Janie and Donnie Jamieson? Did Harry count them? Shit. Every Memorial Day it begins again. All I want is a motel room on the beach in Montauk with maid service and paperbacks. This time I mean it. After Labor Day, we are putting that mildewed piece of pigeon shit on the market. No matter what Harry says. Let *him* try four loads of laundry a day for a while.

Bonita Thomas was rubbing Frankie's back. No projection. Gina smiled. Talk about putting your heart in your work. Mrs. Thomas slid behind the wheel of an enormous shiny white Rolls-Royce and pulled out onto Route 27.

I bet she doesn't have to fight with the gardener. Gina made a note about socialites.

"Sorry." Frankie flopped back down behind his desk, glistening with the excitement of all of this attention. "Where was I?"

"Feudal society. Houses in Maine."

"Oh, yeah. Look. I got a great story. To prove my point. That lady that was just in here? Well, she is a very big deal. Husband died and left her a pile of gold. Plus, she's got family money of her own going back to the Indians. Anyway, she's on the board of the Bayfront Club. Know it?"

Gina laughed. "Do I know it? Our claim to fame among the Sag Harbor intellectuals is that my husband Harry was asked to leave the Bayfront Club."

"No shit?"

"Absolutely. He was invited by a fellow publisher for lunch. But my husband, well, how can I say it, he is not the most WASPy-looking guy on earth. He said that when he walked in, he could hear the Jew alarm go off. Anyway, they seated him, and he and his colleague ordered drinks and out of nowhere a very regal gentleman approached their table and quite politely, if such a thing is possible, told Harry that they were very, very sorry but he would have to leave. No reason given."

"And he left?"

"It hardly seemed worth fighting over. Harry's philosophy is more 'don't get mad, get even' than a fist fight with descendants of the Founding Fathers in a public dining room. Besides, the guy was twice his size."

Frankie pondered this information. "That lady, this is off the record, okay?"

Gina nodded eagerly. "Sure."

"Well, she's on the board there and this client of mine, one of the Just Got It guys, this guy is only thirty-five and he's made maybe two hundred million—Rikki Bosco, ever heard of him?"

"Harry knows him. They play Sunday softball together."

"Well, the guy practically kept me in business my first couple of years here. And his obsession, I mean after he had money, he needed something else to strive for, so his obsession became getting into the Bayfront Club.

"But, I mean the guy's from Staten Island. No private schools, Brooklyn College. And Wall Street on top of it. But I figured, I owed him one and Mrs. Thomas, Bonita, she, uh, she likes me—I mean these rich broads—these widows, they're always slipping me phone numbers, sending me presents, asking me to parties. It's a trip.

"So I asked her, as a favor, to have lunch with Rikki, give him an interview for membership. Well, you should have seen the poor guy. Every day he's callin' me up. What should he wear, what car should he take?

"So finally, the day comes and he meets her and they don't

even get past the looking at the menu part and she says to him, 'Well, Mr. Bosco, what clubable—that's what she said—'what clubable activities do you have to present to our board?'

"Well, Rikki was ready for that one so off he goes with his list of stuff, none of which seemed to impress her. So then, she waves the waiter away. Like waves him away before they had even ordered a beer or anything and she says, 'Let's get right to the real point, Mr. Bosco. What do you do?'

"And Rikki, whose dad was a butcher for chrissakes, so he's proud of what he's done. Rikki says, real cocky, 'I'm in stocks and bonds.' And Bonita just like blinks at him. 'Well, of course you are,' she says, *'everyone* is, but what do you *do?'* Poor Rikki. He never had a chance."

"Great story." Gina took a last sip of the poison coffee. "I think I've got enough, Frankie, but I may want to do some more. Okay?"

"Sure. I like this. I got a million stories. You wouldn't believe what I see here."

"The raw underbelly."

Frankie grinned at her. "Yeah, that's right. We see what's under the hood, if you know what I'm saying."

"I think I do." Gina stood up, thinking simultaneously of her dinner guests and Bonita Thomas screwing Frankie Karsh.

June 5, 1988

My name is China O'Malley (I know it's a great name) and I'm almost twenty (in October). This is the first entry in my journal. I'm going to keep this journal for the whole summer and then, when I get back to school (SUNY Stony Brook) in the fall, I can use it in my creative writing course. I think now, that I may want to be a writer after all. Well, we'll see.

So here I am, back in the "fabled Hamptons." Not so fabled the way I've seen it. I grew up here, more or less. My mom (her name's Clovis) is from Levittown originally, but we came out here after my dad died and she's been here ever since. She's a waitress at Jimmy Vale's in Bridgehampton. It's sort of a local hangout. Lots of famous writers used to go there. Capote. Even Hemingway, though I don't really think he's such a big deal. Anyway, it's not one of the chic spots, but the locals and the old money types like it. The ones who see through all of that nouvelle cuisine junk. Anyway, I basically hate it here. Especially now that it's gotten so in and totally out of control. Bridgehampton used to be the nicest. I mean it was mostly farm fields, potatoes and corn and stuff. It was really just sort of a bridge (like its name) between Southampton and East Hampton. But all those Wall Street jerks had to have someplace to go for the summer that wasn't so uptight and snooty, so they ruined it.

The most stupid thing of all is that they built all of these really grotesque new houses in all of these fields and they sort of look like the old-time houses but they all look into each other's windows and stuff. It's like a great big gaudy tenement if you ask me. I mean no privacy. Isn't that what being rich is supposed to mean? Privacy? Not having to see your creepy neighbors. I think they've been in the City so long, they've forgotten what privacy is. Anyway it's a joke. The locals all think so.

And the traffic. I mean you would not believe the traffic! I vowed I'd never spend another summer here with all these obnoxious rich yuppies, but I got sucked in. My mom waits on this couple, the Cowans. They're nice. They've been out here forever and they are really, really rich. I mean her dad owned something like Phoenix. Anyway, Mr. Cowan, he's this philanthropist, and he does all kinds of really important socially aware stuff—like he flies into Ethiopia to help the starving children. That's his main thing now. That and the art collecting. Anyway, they're old. I mean their daughter Jane (everyone calls her Janie. Actually everyone calls her Janie the JAP, but that's another story) she's in her thirties, at least. But about six years ago, Mr. Cowan (everyone calls him Big Ben, he's enormous) brought home this little Ethiopian orphan. They call him Louie. God only knows why. Well, Louie's seven now and his nurse, Mrs. Murray, had to go back to Ireland or something and so they needed an au pair girl. (God, I hate that word. Talk about nouveau! But that's what they call it.) So they asked my mom if I might be interested in doing it for the summer. Talk about an offer I couldn't refuse! Room and board and three hundred a week! And you should see this room. You should see this house. It's right on the beach in Bridgehampton and it must have thirty rooms and two championship tennis courts and an indoor pool and a movie theater. I mean, it's totally awesome. So I said yes. Not that I could have said no and escaped death at the hands of "the Mother."

So here I am. My goal is to get a really superb tan, make a lot of money (and not spend any of it), meet a guy and write about everything that happens here this summer. Especially about the people. I'm really trying to study people. That's the most important thing in writing. So this should be a perfect opportunity. Oh, rats! Louie's at my door. Later . . .

CRACK INVADES THE HAMPTONS; AIDS
CONTAMINATED BLOOD VIALS STOLEN FROM
SOUTHAMPTON LAB PICKUP BOX; TOWN OF
EAST HAMPTON TO FIGHT DUNE LANE
MILLIONAIRE OVER SECOND POOL PERMIT—
THREAT TO DUNES; TOWNSHIP SAYS . . .

A HOUSE IN THE HAMPTONS

Donnie Jamieson shook his head and gathered the local papers around him. No place left to hide, he thought. The local news is now as bad as the city news. Jones Beach had been closed for days, riddled with syringes and broken blood vials, and the threat was moving down the Island. In a fight between man and nature, who will win? Where had he heard that? A play. Somewhere.

Donnie was sitting in the front booth at the Soda Shack. The only really family-like eating place in the Hamptons, as far as he could tell. He loved it there. Every morning of the summer that he was down, he took his morning run, ending up at the Soda Shack, where he bought all the papers, local and national, and ordered a great big "white bread breakfast," as Gina Hart called it. And every morning at exactly ten, he would start his daily bet with himself on whether his wife, Janie, would meet him to drink her coffee and drive him home. Every night they had the same conversation. "If I'm not there by ten-fifteen it means I had a bad night—so don't wait." Janie would pout.

"I'll wait. There's always another paper to skim. I'll wait till ten forty-five."

"Ten-thirty."

"Okay."

He checked his watch. 10:12. Would she or wouldn't she. She had had a bad night. But then, it was the beginning of the season and being back in her parents' house always made her anxious. It used to take a month. But somewhere in the third year of her analysis, she had some kind of break-through about her mother and in the last few years, it was better.

The second pool would go on top of a dune and right in the path where a hurricane would cause the

27

worst flooding, said the defenders of the East End's fragile coastline.

10:13. Donnie felt suddenly lonely. He realized how much he missed his wife even after an hour's separation. Even after sixteen years. Even though half the time she drove him absolutely crazy and he couldn't remember why he had ever wanted to marry her in the first place. They were embedded in one another. Maybe it was because of the scene with Delores last night. Jesus, what a mess. An elegant drunk, his mother-in-law was. But a drunk is a drunk. Poor Janie. Imagine never knowing which mother will show up?

Last night she was as bad as Donnie had ever seen her. I mean, she fell down the damn stairs in front of twenty people! It's a miracle she wasn't killed. Poor little Louie. No wonder Janie's so in tune with him. It's like going back and comforting herself, I bet.

Donnie tried to shake his mind off the depressing scene.

"They just think it's silly to have two pools, but it's none of the town's business whether we need them or not," said Mrs. Lassere.

"Most people are lucky to have one pool," said the zoning board.

"We'll have to sue," Mr. Lassere replied.

Donnie's mind wandered. Maybe part of the loneliness had to do with Harry Hart's call about the new arrival on their summer scene. Madeline Olsen. His stomach tightened. My God. Everything is a circle. Bigger hoops, but the same circle. He'd have to tell Janie. She'd probably be at the Harts' dinner tonight. Could Janie possibly be jealous about someone he'd gone steady with in high school? You betcha.

And he wasn't feeling well. His ulcer again. Damn. If

there was anything Donnie was, it was a health nut. He covered all the bases from Pritikin to vitamin, except for his breakfasts at the Soda Shack, and he *ran* to them. That counts for something. Stress. The *S* word. And worse, it was all passive stress. What other kind of stress could a psychiatrist have? Women were always complaining to him about the responsibility of child rearing, but what about shrinks? All of those needs without end. No place to hide, he thought again, and the pain in his intestine stung. Another goddamn ulcer. No. I'm willing it away.

10:16. Janie came racing toward him looking like an ad for one of those Manhattan health spas. Totally encased in some kind of rubberized black shiny stuff. Stuffed into it. Around her curly auburn head was a bright yellow sweatband, the entire effect being a walking WARNING HIGH VOLTAGE sign.

Janie tossed her Gucci exercise bag onto the seat and plopped her tiny, underfed body down across from him.

"I did it. I am so proud of myself."

"Did what?"

"I made it to a nine o'clock Maddie Evans workout. And I got through it! I'm having coffee, dropping you off, and I'm going back for the noon class!"

"Janie, for chrissakes—there's hardly anything *left* of you. Two hours in this humidity, I'll be living with Thumbelina."

"Look, who's talking. Mr. Marathon. Are you going to do the Bridgehampton run this year?"

"Yeah. I like a group I can intimidate."

"Intimidate. You have to be *alive* to be intimidated. From what I saw last year, everyone running had just raised themselves up from the town graveyard and taken off. I never saw such a pathetic picture. If any of those cellulite cases had seen themselves, they'd drown their Reeboks in Sag Pond. They all looked like they were having a bowel movement."

Donnie laughed. "What an image."

Janie motioned to Millie, their longtime waitress, for her usual. "Well, they did. Oh, by the way. *Your* son gave me a present. A T-shirt." Janie tore into her dance bag and extracted a large black T-shirt with white letters on it. JAPS ARE PEOPLE TOO.

Donnie roared. "So now he's *my* son. He's really on your case lately. Don't personalize. It's just puberty."

"Don't give me that shrink talk. I'm a person, what other *lize* should I do? I defended my heritage rather eloquently, in fact. I may try to do a 'Hers' column based on it."

"Move over Anna Quindlen." Donnie winked at Millie, who raced over with Janie's coffee and grapefruit half.

"Listen, mopey-brained Irish Catholics who have word processor orgasms over snowstorms and grannie's moth-eaten comforter are not the only people who can write about women for *The New York Times*. That crazy woman even did a column about how great she was for not having amnio—whatever it is. She almost sounded like she'd be disappointed if she didn't have a mongoloid. I hate that woman. I'm going to do a piece about a filthy nouveau riche." Janie grabbed the T-shirt and pulled it on over her rubber body suit.

Donnie kissed her hand. His lips moving over her square-cut diamond, a gift from Big Ben on her thirtieth birthday, pausing for a minute at her Italian emerald-and-enamel wedding band, and resting on each of her perfect inch-long red lacquered nails. She lit him up, is what she did.

Whatever Janie was or wasn't, she wasn't boring and she wasn't morbid. She made him laugh. She and Gina together were literally hysterical. Gina. Tonight. Madeline. Janie. Oh boy. Better plan on a nice quiet lunch. After her class. When she'd be too tired to react.

Janie lit a cigarette. "Honey. I need some professional advice. About Momma. Can we have lunch?"

A HOUSE IN THE HAMPTONS

Donnie nodded. Just another day in Paradise. No place to hide. That was clear.

"Please don't let it be a mistake," Rikki Bosco kept praying to whatever it is that he thought was out there listening. He never put a name to it, a name like God. But he sure talked to it a lot. Rikki was standing in his driveway, as he often did, trying to see what his compound might look like to someone arriving for the first time.

I can't believe this is all mine. Thirty-three fucking acres in the absolute prime part of Bridgehampton. Made that little Polish potato farmer a millionaire. The fucker still can't believe it. "Just a piece of earth," he said. So, are they crazy? Or are we crazy? Nah. Not me. The property has doubled in two years. Rikki spread his arms wide. "Mine!" he yelled to his God. "All mine!"

He turned away from the massive house ("the East End Vatican," The Match called it) and walked briskly, or as briskly as an out-of-shape "pool potato," as his personal trainer called him, ever walked. He moved across the sprawling lawns, created out of flat, barren potato fields and now covered with hills and dales and huge full-grown maple, pine, and jacaranda trees "at twenty-five thou apiece," Rikki liked to point out, to his pride and joy. An underground garage—a bunker really. A hideout in case of nuclear attack, but for now, the home of his fleet of classic cars. "Fuck winter." Rikki kept them all snug as a bug, beneath the ground. He wanted everything to be just right for this weekend. I mean, how often do Katarina and Joey Rivers appear as your houseguests. Everything had to be perfect.

Rikki fed the code into the alarm system and the massive silky smooth steel-enforced doors parted and he was inside, with them. It felt like being in King Tut's tomb or the Pyramids. So quiet. So full of secrets. And all that power, hidden beneath those shiny old hoods, carrying their secrets forth from owner to owner, decade to decade. They were all his for now. "Eat your fucking hearts out," Rikki announced to no one in particular. He could just stand there for hours, sniffing, inhaling the polish, the lemony, clean smells of oil and gas and wax. *All mine.* He exhaled, feeling a moment of pure sensate pleasure. Almost sexual, he thought. Almost like a hard-on.

The Match. The thought broke the mood. Why the fuck had he invited her? She was hardly Hollywood Royalty material. She could blow this for him. You never knew with her. I mean what could you expect from a twenty-six-year-old woman called 'The Match'! Did she have another name? He wasn't even sure. What the fuck would The Match and Katarina Rivers have to talk about? I mean, Katarina was the daughter of two of the greatest names in show business. She had gone to schools Rikki couldn't even pronounce and she was married to a famous movie director. Okay, so famous, smamous. The guy was from S.I. I mean, Rikki *knew* this guy. This guy was one of his own. But still. The Match might be a big mistake.

A horn. A loud horn. Shit. There she was. Rikki took the keys to the '39 La Salle, and got in. Gently, ever so gently, he turned her on, releasing her from her ancient slumber beneath the earth. A metal mummy come back to life, offering her warmth and ancient wisdom to him. "Come on, baby." Rikki always talked to his cars as if they were ripe, voluptuous women. Seducing them with his steady hand, coaxing them forward into his control, getting them ready for action. "Ferrari foreplay," The Match called it. Rikki eased the gleaming queen up out of the tomb and into the sun.

There she was. Rikki waved. Shit. She really did look like a match. In the distance, her bright orange hair, greased back in that club scene way, was his masseuse and girlfriend. The

A HOUSE IN THE HAMPTONS

Match stood almost six feet tall, all pure white, never touched by the sun, "I'm a fuckin' vampire or somethin," as she put it. Long, long skinny white arms and endless legs, broken only by two very large round tits. World-class tits, Rikki thought. Full red lips. Long pointed nose and the orange hair. The nickname stuck. She even had a short fuse. Rikki smiled in spite of himself. She was so inappropriate.

Before he'd given her a car, she would bomb in on the Jitney, and he'd pick her up in town. She was always the last one off, always organizing herself, dabbing on one last glob of eye makeup or something. So he'd wait, watching all the fellow travelers with their trim tan bodies, their espadrilles, and their J. Crew boating shoes. Their sun-lightened hair and their attachés. Their Vuitton overnight numbers and their crumpled *New York Times*es. All the same. Male and female pieces of the same puzzle. All fitting in. Smug in this, fitting in. Safe among their flock. Pigeons and gulls of the Urban Centers. An apartment in the Seventies between Park and Madison and a house in the Hamptons. Ralph Lauren Polo shirts and Laura Ashley pillow shams. He hated them. He didn't want to, but he did. He would never be part of that. Not even *that*. Let alone the Bayfront Club. Dead dreams. Fuck all of them.

Boing. Off the Jitney. Looking like a jack-in-the-box sprung loose in the middle of a rare porcelain exhibition. She was the least Hamptons summer–looking person imaginable. He liked it. But he also didn't like it. The part of him that wanted the Bayfront Club absolutely hated it. That part wanted one of those wiry, tan anorexic blondes with the Margaret or Chris names and large white teeth. A toothy, tall Chris-type girl with lots of white linen in her closet. The Match knew this.

Whatever she was—and it might well be that what she was, was certifiably insane—she wasn't stupid. "I got it," she would say, watching him watch *them,* "you're fantasizing one of those White Sandwich fantasies. Turkey with mayonnaise on white bread, no lettuce, but heavy on the cultured pearls."

She had his number. He remembered how he'd met her. That was bizarre enough. Two years ago. Just before Memorial Day. He was stoned. Really, really stoned. This was right before it stopped being cool to be stoned, and everyone was stoned. Even people who didn't do drugs or drink pretended to be stoned. And he wasn't pretending.

He was with, who was he with? Oh yeah, Edmundo, the Eurotrash designer type. They had the limo and Rikki was hungry, so they hit Tiffany's? Or was it that diner on Eleventh Avenue? Yeah. The Diner. They staggered in and ordered everything. I mean junkie-sober-up food. And the only other customers were this really wigged-out redhead, who was all dressed in something purple and very short and wet-looking. With her hair Vaselined up in the air. She's with this tiny little dude. Turned out to be a cool guy. Rikki hired the guy. Jakie the Junkie she called him. Jakie took care of his cars for him, now. Two years already. Amazing.

So Edmundo starts rapping on the redhead, snickering and making fun of her and this broad, she gets up and comes over and she's screaming and yelling something like, "I'm mindin' my own business, pus pecker, can't a person eat in peace," and Edmundo gets very aggressive and then, there she went, that fuse. She climbed up onto the table and started kicking at Edmundo and he jumped up in the booth and pushed her right through the fucking window onto Eleventh Avenue! Rikki threw the owner a five-hundred-dollar bill and jumped out after her. There she was, sitting in the middle of all the glass, crying like a little girl.

"He hurt my feelings," she said. And Rikki was touched.

Stoned. But really touched. "Well, look, miss, if you go out lookin' like that, you gotta expect a little feedback."

"Want a magic mushroom," she'd said, and smiled at him. And he'd taken her home in the limo and they'd made love like two over-the-edge maniacs with nothing to lose. She was a dancing flame, flashing above him through the dawn light, and he was who he used to be—a wiseass kid from S.I. with a high school diploma and a chip on his shoulder.

Two years. There she was. She had a new look now. All leopard. Every fucking thing from her shoes to her panties. Leopard. Half the time he felt like he'd wandered into some African porno flick. But it was better than the wet purple stuff. That was for sure. He pulled up beside her. She was leaning over the Porsche he had given her, licking a spot off the hood.

"What the fuck are you doing?"

The Match looked up. "I'm tonguing off some bird shit or somethin'. It'll ruin the finish."

Rikki jumped out and pulled her off. "Ever hear of Kleenex? Are you totally fucking crazy? You could get a disease. Come on. Leave it. Jakie will get it."

"It was just a little plop of something. I've licked worse, doll baby. So where's the movie stars?"

Rikki was really regretting asking her down. "They're not movie stars. He's a movie director and she's, well, she's sort of like a Hollywood socialite. I mean, she's a society girl, but her family was . . . her father owned a studio. Don't call them movie stars. That would be an insult."

"An insult? If they think that's an insult, they're gonna need resuscitation by the time I get through with them." She smiled. Then she saw Rikki go pale. "A joke, Rikki, doll. Just a little joke. So what's like not insulting to someone who thinks bein' a movie queen is disgusto?"

She stared at him. That long, green-eyed, smart-ass stare

that always let him know, just in case he should have forgotten it for even ten seconds, that she was on to him, over him, and right dead-ass through him.

"I dunno. Think, think refined things. Like those broads in *Town and Country* and *Vanity Fair* type stuff. Horsey stuff. Princess Grace, like that."

The Match tried not to laugh. "Oh. Simple. Just Princess Grace talk. I'm into that. I've done a lot of that. Let's see. I gave a massage to Queen Noor's cousin once. I can deal with it."

"Okay. Okay. Just help me with this. I go way back with this guy. But it's so, I mean I'm rich and he's famous now. It's funny."

"Sounds like a good title for something. Write it down."

"And no mouth. No swearing."

"Fucking A." The Match grinned at him and slipped her long, slender white hand down inside his pants. "Come on Your Majesty, let's have a quickie before the royal couple arrives."

Harry Hart panted up the sagging steps to his beloved Sag Harbor Victorian, trying to juggle two bags of farm stand goodies, his briefcase and his suitcase. It was clear he was losing. The screen door was swollen again. The fucking humidity. This was going to be one of those summers when nothing and no one was ever really dry.

Harry hated humidity. Harry hated anything that wasn't crisp and clean. Part of his Swedish obsession, his wife said. He could feel one of the bags giving way, the bottom wet from the rain. *The corn. Shit.* "Gina!" Harry could hear his wife's voice from the kitchen. He couldn't see over the bag. "Gina!" I need help, here!"

"Got it, Sven!" It was Janie. No one else would dare tease him about Bergman stuff.

A HOUSE IN THE HAMPTONS

"Grab something, quick. The corn's going!"

Janie grabbed the bag and the briefcase and trotted off toward the kitchen. Harry, panting behind. He could hear Gina screaming at the dog, from the back porch. Great, off to a great start, he thought.

"Arturo, you have ten seconds to live. You gluttonous shithead! Get out of here! Go!"

Janie was struggling to empty the grocery bags. Cooking was not one of Janie's things. "He ate a six-pound Brie. Gina's hors d'oeuvre, for tonight. Toasted with almonds."

"Oh, swell. Now it begins. The double kvetch. The house and the goddamn dog."

"Arturo is not a dog. Arturo is some freak of nature. Sort of a bottomless-pit pup."

"Arturo is a good dog. He's just got a hearty appetite."

"Yeah and Hitler just had a bad temper. How many dogs eat wineglasses? Know what he did yesterday? He climbed up on the counter and ate twenty-seven meatballs."

Harry laughed in spite of himself. "That's my pup. Honest to God?"

"Could I make that up? Then he threw up all over the place. Lucky you missed it. Your wife was at her best. *And* she had a deadline."

Gina Hart whirled into the room, her face wet with summer damp and rage. "I'm telling you, Harry, get the insurance up, because we're going to have a mysterious fire! A true human tragedy! The end of a quaint old house and a psychotic mongrel, who melted into a big glob of fondue. What a shame."

Harry tried to kiss her. "This is my greeting?"

"Don't even think about making nice. I have so much shit to dump first, it isn't a possibility."

Harry backed over to the refrigerator and pulled the handle, which promptly came off in his hand.

37

Gina smiled. "Put it on the list, darling. Also, before you find a way to pry your beer can out of there, the gardener hasn't showed up, the dishwasher is making sounds so intimate, I blush when I start it . . . there was another dead *rat*, *rat*, I repeat, not field mouse, as you like to call them, in the skimmer, which isn't working because for some unknown reason, the pool heater shot up to one hundred and five degrees, when it was set at minimum, so now it's more like a swamp with rafts . . . *and, and,* I had to find out from Janie, who found out from her husband, who is thoughtful and sensitive to his wife's feelings, that among our dinner guests this evening (that is to say, if we can open the refrigerator and find another Brie in time) is your *first* wife. Cute, Harry. Actually, adorable."

Janie dropped the eggplant on the floor. Arturo bounded into the room and made a huge, slobbery pass at it, but Gina was faster.

"Oh, no! Oh, no, you whore for food! Not again." Gina chased him out into the yard.

Harry was pretending to be fixing the refrigerator handle. Janie plopped down on a stool, giving up on the kitchen tasks. "I'm going to send Isabel over to help Gina. This is ridiculous. I'd do anything for Gin' except cooking and cleaning. Gotta draw the line somewhere."

"You're a great influence."

"I am what I am. It's not my fault if no one ever let me do anything. Someone has to *teach* you this stuff. It's like reading maps. You don't just know how." Janie eyed him. "So, Sven! Wanna tell me about it?"

Harry was now pretending to be seriously into the refrigerator repair.

"You should see the scene on twenty-seven. Cars are moving about an inch an hour. And all these farm stands filled with these Upper West Side types, couldn't tell a nectarine

from a tomato, lined up in their BMWs buying 'produce,'
'Look at those snap peas!' What a riot. CPAs playing country
squire. I bet all these farm guys go home at night and do
shtick about us until their laughing muscles collapse."

"Are we changing the subject?"

Harry gave up. "Madeline?"

"Umm. Good guess."

"She, uh, actually, she's called Fritzi now. Her, uh, nickname."

"Oh. So now we're into pet names. Anything else?"

"For chrissakes, Janie. It was twenty-five years ago. What's
with you two?"

"Well. Let's see. My husband was so in love with this
dame, that he didn't have a serious relationship for ten years
after she dumped him. His love or lust or both are unre-
quited, which can last centuries, if you read romance novels.
And you, well, you *did* marry her, however briefly. I'm sure
you can understand your wife having certain unresolved
conflicts about her suddenly appearing without advance notice at her first dinner party of the summer season."

"You're right. It's just, I don't know. Actually, I forgot I'd
asked her. I mean, we had lunch months ago, and her husband had died and she said something about looking at
houses out here. And then I got a call last week, and I said if
she was out, come to dinner and then I just kind of forgot."

Janie's dark, perfectly shaped eyebrows lifted. "Lunch. We
had lunch, did we. I see. So. How's she holding up to the test
of time?"

"Fritzi?"

"The one and only. Does Donnie know about the Fritzi
stuff?"

"No. I don't think so. She, uh, she looks good. I mean,
she's uh, how can I put it, she's flashy. Not an Upper East
Side style lady. Very, uh, West Coast, but well, uh, preserved.

I guess. I mean we only had one lunch and it was January. Lots of layers. Ha. Ha!"

Janie was not laughing. "This whole *thing* has lots of layers." She jumped off the stool and grabbed her expensive Italian purse. "I'm sending Isabel. Tell Gina not to worry about hors d'oeuvres or anything. I'll have Isabel whip up some fried chicken and all the goodies. Give her a Valium and a kir or something and make nice."

She gave Harry a kiss on his moist, bearded cheek. "Cheer up. It's hard being a sex object. Can I bring Louie? His au pair's off tonight."

"Sure. Twenty-five years, Janie. Jesus."

"Yeah. But whatever she had, doesn't decompose. It's the fantasy mind fuck. It's hermetically sealed. We all have one."

Harry followed her out, wondering what to do now.

June 9

Well, I know I said I was going to write every day, but things have been kind of slow, so I decided to wait until I had something worthwhile to write about. I mean the season hasn't really started yet. This is really like the second weekend and Louie is still in school, so there hasn't been that much for me to do. But I have been watching, observing people. These are my perceptions so far.

Big Ben. I heard Isabel the cook say he's going to celebrate his sixtieth birthday this summer. They're going to have a really big party. Neat! Anyway, it's hard to believe. I mean he looks really young. Sort of like Clint Eastwood or, who's Michael Douglas's father? Sort of like that. He's very nice to me. Always teases me and he's absolutely terrific with Louie. He's what my mom calls a "man's man." He seems to like to be with men, not women so much. At least not with Mrs.

A HOUSE IN THE HAMPTONS

Cowan. He sails and hunts and fishes. He's got a big boat at the Montauk marina and he's always taking off overnight with his buddies. When school's out, he's going to take Louie and me. Mrs. Cowan doesn't like all that stuff. I can tell.

He's nice to her, very polite, but they don't touch or anything. Not like Janie, their daughter, and her husband, Donnie (they told me to call them by their first names, so I'm not being forward. They're real casual people, for rich people). Anyway, they're always hugging and stuff, but not the Cowans. Anyway, even if he is almost sixty, he's sexy. I could see women still liking him.

He doesn't seem to work anymore. I know he was an architect. He designed this house even, which is totally amazing. But my mom says Mrs. Cowan has the money. So, I'm not sure. He's a great cook, too. He made an unbelievable dinner the other night. His own pasta and he barbecued a leg of lamb. It was great. It was Janie and Donnie's first night, so it was a big deal.

I like Janie and Donnie's son, Owen (I think I'll just call them the Jamiesons to save space). He's really funny. He teases his mother about being spoiled. Like at dinner, Janie tasted her salad and she said to her dad, "The chevre is too cold," and Owen says, really dramatic, "JAP tragedy." Everyone broke up. Even Louie. It's really a trip to see this tiny little black kid cracking up over New York Jewish jokes.

Louie is great. He has these enormous brown eyes and the white parts are so white they almost sparkle and his skin is the most beautiful color. Really dark, but with a red glint to it and lots of incredible curly hair. He has kind of a crush on me, I think. It's really sweet.

Mrs. Cowan. Delores. But, I would *never* call her that. She's so, like, fragile. I mean she's as dainty and small as Big Ben is huge. I don't want to sound gross, but I can't imagine them having sex. I don't think they do it anymore, anyway. Maybe that's why. Maybe it was a matter of a bad fit.

Anyway. I kept feeling that something was not quite right about her. She always seems kind of dreamy and far away. I mean, very nice, but kind of not there. She spends a lot of time in her room or walking on the beach alone. She has a loneliness about her. A sadness. But then every once in a while, she just perks up and she's very sparkly and funny, too. Like Janie, who is really funny. But then she just kind of deflates.

Well, I think I know why, now. I think she gets loaded. I don't know about drugs. But alcohol for sure. Because, at the party I just told you about, well, I watched her and she was tossing down the French wines all night and then she went upstairs for a while and we were all in the game room and she came down the back stairs and she was weaving, like people do when they're drunk, and she slipped and fell all the way down the stairs! It was awful! Thank God, Louie was in bed.

For a minute, after it happened, no one moved; it was like we were frozen. I thought she was dead, but before we could even race over there, she just got up, like nothing had happened! She laughed and said something about being clumsy and went right over to the bar and made herself an after-dinner drink! Amazing. So my writer-to-be's mind is starting to perk up. Big Ben acted like nothing had happened, but Janie was upset and so was Owen, who didn't even make a joke out of it.

Let's see. I've told you about Big Ben, Mrs. Cowan, Owen, Louie and the Jamiesons. Well, not really much about them. Janie is kind of high strung. She seems a little nervous here, even though it's her parents' house. I wonder why she doesn't have her own. I'm sure they could afford it. Her husband's a shrink. But they do have their own town house setup here, with a whole entire separate kitchen and every-thing. It faces the pool and the beach. It's neat. Cozy and really friendly. Janie got to decorate it herself and it's differ-ent from the main house, which is beautiful, but cold, all architect furniture. I get the names mixed up. Corbu some-one, stuff like that. The Jamiesons' part is more country French–looking. Big Ben hates it. He calls it "the Bendel's Wing."

Anyway, Janie is very intense. She's tiny, too, but she told me she can blow up like a balloon, just like that! So she's always dieting and exercising. She said she had anorexia, bu-limia, and chocotoxia when she was young. The chocotoxia, she made up. She just o.d.'s on chocolate. I sympathize with that!

Anyway, she seems a little uneasy here, but I like her and her husband is just the nicest, sweetest guy. He's like a per-fect husband and father. When I fantasize about my dad and try to picture what he was like, it's sort of like Dr. Jamieson.

I think Janie frustrates him sometimes, but he is never impatient with her. And he's so great with Louie, really amazing. Louie calls him 'Dr. J.,' which is just so cute, when you hear it. No sun so far, so my tan goal is in the future, but I got paid for my first week, three hundred dollars! and it's already in the bank. So I'm not hating it out here as much as I thought.

Cool. Silence. Clean, soft sheets. A whole half an hour of it. Alone in it.

Gina Hart rolled over onto her back and stretched. God bless Janie. She could hear Isabel and her slow, sullen son, Ondine, taking charge in the kitchen. Giving her this pre-cious miracle. Thirty minutes to herself.

Tears rolled down her strong, olive-colored face. It seemed to happen a lot, lately. The tears. Since the approach of "the

Fortieth," as she referred to her upcoming birthday. The Fortieth, as in the Wedding, the Bible, the Children, the End. She hardly ever even knew when they were coming. They were just . . . there. Feelings finding their way up from the bottom of her. It was as if she had reached into an abandoned coat pocket and found notes from her past. *Call Ma*— from before her mother died. *Lunch Sarah*, the friend who had betrayed her trust and taken the last of her innocence about friendship. *Dentist Jeremy*, the braces days of her baby boy before she surrendered him to adolescence.

Moments from her past self, piercing her defenses. Tacks scattered on the rug. Unseen. Pricking. Startling her. Tears. Ouch.

Summers brought them out. Like the marigolds and the daylilies. Feelings and memories springing up all around her. She had always tracked her years from summer to summer. Never from January to January. The summer she married Harry. The summer Jeremy was born. The summer she miscarried and they told her she'd never have another child. The summer her mother died. She remembered each summer of her life as well as each birthday (having a birthday on July fourth did help).

Last summer when she took the Jitney into the city every Wednesday to see her analyst. All of July. Two sessions, a week's worth in twenty-four hours. "Mother mourning," she called it. Jeremy was at camp. Harry was in Maine most of July on some advertisers' perk extravaganza. She came home from her Wednesday double session to a silent foreign apartment. She had never been in her apartment like this. No one there. No one about to be there. It almost felt as if she were spying on herself. Alone. Cool. Silent. Healing. She'd take a shower and turn the A.C. on full blast, something that would have driven Harry crazy. She'd throw all her favorite things on the bed. Gummi Bears. Fritos. Magazines. The bed was hers. The house was hers. No one else to think about. A kid whose parents are out of town.

Sometimes she'd just fall onto the bed and lie there doing absolutely nothing. Images from her sessions rolling across her mind like waves. Hot, summer waves. Muffled, moist, heavy smooth images.

"Why do you think you can't remember your mother ever comforting you?"

"Why do you think you feel so alone?"

"Why do you get angry when I ask about your vacation?"

"Why do you think your mother didn't love you?"

Why. Why. Why, indeed.

Lying on her Upper West Side duplex bed. Why on white sheets. The A.C. murmuring. Alone in the afternoon. The traffic down the block on West End Avenue always in the background. Urban Muzak in her mind. Isolated. Free. Not even guilty about not working. The free-lance writer's blessing and curse.

It was a gift she had given herself. Those July Wednesday afternoons; two sessions back-to-back. Why. Why. Why?

Gina sighed. The analysis was hard. She was embarrassed by it. Not because she cared about what people thought, my God, more people were in therapy than in the A&P. It was just, she had always associated it with self-indulgence. Janie's kind of thing. Harry and she used to laugh at the description a duck hunter zillionaire from Texas had given his Baptist bride when she asked him (in a living room in Manhattan in the late eighties!) exactly what a psychoanalyst was for. He had taken a deep, portentous breath and said, "Well, darlin', psych'analysts are kind of doctor types that Jewish people go to to talk about their problems."

Maybe he was right. All the same, she had resisted far too long. "It's as if a part of you, of your feelings, your truth, has been lost to you," the analyst had said, and her heart had nearly stood still. Halfway through and haven't a clue. It messed with her values (okay, what it messed with was her latent sense of superiority over Janie and her group and Harry). Janie had thought all of her angst about it was a riot. "For chrissakes, Gin', it's like losing your cherry. It's time!"

This summer she had decided not to go in. She would be her own therapist. She had three magazine assignments and a life to lead. But, now, she wasn't so sure she wasn't just resisting again. Who would she find out she was? And what would it do to the rest of her life? She felt scared. And of all the whys in her head, why she was giving this damn party was the loudest. Miss Perfect. Earth mother to the end. Maybe I'll find out I'm not a nice person, she thought. Surprisingly, the idea didn't upset her.

She heard Harry on the stairs. Time was up. Maybe she'd practice not being a nice person on Harry's long-lost first wife.

When Gina and Harry came downstairs, Donnie and Janie and Owen, Louie, and Jeremy were all sitting around the long pine kitchen table nibbling some of Isabel's paper-thin crispy fried onion rings while Janie held court. Great, thought Gina, Janie's in full throttle, I won't have to entertain everyone. Harry, who had rigged up a coat hanger solution to the refrigerator, yanked it open and pulled out a bottle of local Hampton rosé. Everyone groaned.

"Jeez, Dad. You're not going to serve that swill to our guests, are you?" Jeremy was making a list of some sort.

"Fifteen and a wine snob. We've created our own yuppette."

"If it ends with *ette* it's feminine." Jeremy stood up. "Okay, you guys. I want to discuss something before your fast-track friends arrive. I've been going over it with Owen, and he supports me in this."

All parents try not to smile.

46

A HOUSE IN THE HAMPTONS

"I want to change my name. And I'd like to start tonight, since I don't know these people. See how it feels."

Gina took a sip of wine. "Change it to what?"

"Okay. Now. This is serious. This is a big thing for me. So no one laughs or tries to do head trips on my fragile male ego?"

Harry grabbed a handful of onions. Isabel and Ondine moved in to hear better. "Go for it, kid. I always hated 'Jeremy'! Your mother stuck it on you. I can handle this."

Gina shot him a look. "Maybe you'd rather wait until you've heard the alternative, dear."

"Okay. I'll just get down to it. I want to change my name to Twain. Twain Hart. Like Mark. I think it works. It's the name of someone unique."

"It's the name of someone who doesn't exist." Harry licked his fingers.

Donnie, always the sensitive one, leaned in toward Jeremy. "Why, Jer?"

"Well, I've got this theory about names. See, names are trendy. Parents stick them on us before we even hardly exist, so they can fit in sort of. Or they give us some really grotesque embarrassing name to create some fake sense that we're special before they even know us. So names are basically bullshit. And my name—I got stuck in that group, where all the parents wanted their kids to blend in. I mean when I went to Walden, there were like six names in the whole school. Jennifer, Matthew, Jason, Jeremy, and Rachel. Maybe a couple of Tiffanys and Ambers, but I mean, *no one* ever even knew who the teacher was talking to. Ridiculous! And it labels me. One, the whole world knows I'm Jewish. Those are Jewish urban names. Okay? Two, they know about when I was born, because those names were in for only a period of, say, five years. The way I can tell just about how old Janie and Mom are because of their names. I mean,

47

no offense, but no one young is named Janie or Judy or even Susan anymore. So that's it. Twain Hart. It sounds literary and serious. And no one else has it. It's me."

Owen and Louie applauded.

Gina was afraid to move because the tears were right there again. The pride in this wonderful, gawky, growing creature who used to belong to her but now belonged to himself.

Harry solved the problem by jumping up and grabbing Jeremy, who was already taller than he was, and planting endless kisses on his still hairless face.

"I love this boy. This is the future! A boy with vision and spunk! My son!"

Jeremy blushed in spite of himself.

Janie lit a cigarette. "You know, Jer, I think you're on to something here. I was thinking while you were talking about it, and I realized I have all kinds of name prejudices."

Gina stood up. Hostess anxiety overtaking her. "Name prejudice? Is this a trend?"

Janie laughed. "Could be a book in it. Come on, guys. We all do. I'll admit something. I always think people named Virgil or Dwayne are dumb."

Gina opened a cupboard and began pulling candles and vases out. "How many people named Dwayne and Virgil do you know personally?"

"None! But if I met one, I'd have name prejudice to over-come."

Harry grinned. Harry loved conversations like this. "I feel that way about names like Smalley and Mooney. And I've never to my knowledge known a Smalley or a Mooney. What about WASP names?"

Donnie poured more wine. "I play tennis with a guy in East Hampton at his club, and his wife and daughter are called Apple and Pebble."

Harry clapped his hands. "Perfect! Or all the Bootsies and

Muffies and stuff, Seven Dwarf names. I never consider them
real people."

Janie pulled her makeup bag out and went to work. "Like
I said, name prejudice. In fact, since Jeremy's well-meaning
but cruel remark about my name I may just join him. Maybe
something tall. A nice sexy, tall person's name like, maybe,
Consuela or Heather."

Gina moved Janie's mascara and put down an ashtray.
"How about Conswether. Why compromise? People will
think you're a giantess."

Donnie got up to help her. "Don't encourage her, Gin'."

Janie was concentrating on her lip liner. Everyone
watched her, fascinated.

Owen, who had been taking it all in with teenage sardonic
detachment, leaned in very close, knowing it drove Janie
crazy when people watched her line her lips.

"Owen, sschtp it."

Owen made a fist and pretended to be talking into a microphone, as if he were a television field reporter. "What you
are witnessing, folks, is the transformation of a kind but
plain Long Island matron, into that most fascinating of
mythical creatures, the canine attack JAP. In just moments,
the she-devil herself will emerge, totally transformed by the
wonders of the Bergdorf Goodman cosmetics department.
Film at eleven!"

Donnie leaned over and stroked Owen's wavy black hair.
"She's going to get you for that. I'd cover yourself."

Janie finished her lip. "Oh, no. I'm beyond that. I've
moved onto a higher plane. What I'm working toward now
is an idyllic future world where all artifice will stop. Women
will declare a moratorium on face-lifts, hair dye, exercise
classes, high fashion, and all forms of cosmetics. All of us
together. A mass, worldwide commitment to growing old
naturally. Getting decrepit together. I'll be the first in line."

"Great idea, Mom. But it's like nuclear disarmament, what's to stop some secretary in Jersey from sneaking in a few leg lifts in the privacy of her boudoir?"

These times before things when they were all together were their favorite times. Two families who knew each other well. Who had thrashed through the ragged uneven edges of all their various quirks and weaknesses and had pushed past acquaintanceship to friendship and then past friendship to familyship. A long, rutted road that had carried them from (in Harry and Donnie's case) grammar school to midage. And in Gina and Janie's case, from first meeting through everything that had happened in either of their lives in the last seventeen years. Through prefeminism and feminism and postfeminism and parenthood and all of the ridges and blind curves of people trying to be more intimate than they had ever dared to be. They had all tangled with one another's personalities and neuroses, fears and blind spots. And the reward for hanging in there together for all those years was so simple. Four adults and three children eating onion rings and talking about nothing very important. Being that comfortable with anyone else on earth. A miracle that slipped by unnoticed.

While Gina, Isabel, and Janie were putting out the appetizers and Louie, Jeremy, and Owen were tossing a softball around out front, the welcoming squad for the guests, Harry finally got Donnie alone. "We're going for ice," he called, and practically pushed Donnie out of the house and into the car. He had been desperate to talk to him before Fritzi showed up, but once he had him alone, he felt uncomfortable.

Donnie watched him fidgeting around. "So?"

So? So shit. So. I, I'm kinda uneasy about this thing. Remember after the lunch? I called her hotel and she had just disappeared. Just left. I don't know. Did she call you, too?"

Donnie smiled. "Why would she call me when she could have you?"

Harry backed the car onto the road and headed for the liquor store.

"Very funny. She never called you?"

"No. She wrote me a letter."

Harry hit the brake. "She did? You schmuck! I tell you everything! You *never* told me that!"

"I just got it. Just before I came down. I didn't want to talk about it on the phone with the stereo-hearing duo around."

"Right. Good thinking. I like this cunning approach. A new side of you. So what did she say?"

"It was peculiar. Passive aggressive would be the clinical term, I guess. She'd had a lot of time since her husband's death to think about the past. Loose ends. Sorry she'd hurt me. How she realized that I was (now, *she* said this, I didn't) I was the only man who had really loved her as she was. How she wished we could go back and start over. But there was a lot of subtext, I think. Stuff about maybe trying to start nursing again."

"She was a nurse?"

"Oh yeah. She didn't tell you that?"

"No. Un-un. Shit. She sent you a love letter. Whaddaya know. Where is it?"

Donnie grinned. "In a safe place."

Harry screeched to a stop, narrowly missing a pink Cadillac sedan with a Jersey license plate, I BRACEM.

"You scum! Some best friend. Make me rear-end a fucking dentist from Newark over this. I'd tell you."

"Seems like we've had this conversation before. Like forty years' worth."

"Okay. Okay. So let's get a grip here. She's back in our

lives. For one night. For old times' sake. For my guilt. For your ego. For our wives' curiosity. Then we're out of it."

"Harry. She just bought a house in East Hampton. She's back. We'll bump into one another on line at the Barefoot Contessa. So what?"

"I don't know. She, I feel . . . funny. Kinda scared. I don't know."

"Is that the man or the prick talking?"

"Why, Dr. Jamieson, how you do go on!" Harry vamped. Donnie didn't smile. "I don't know, Donnie. Boy, she looks good. Almost the same. It's unnerving. And what scared me, I guess, is that draw. I felt, young. Fun. It was kinda fun. And then, there's all that guilt, I guess. I married her and then I left her like the next month. As soon as she miscarried, I was out of there."

"Harry. Trust it. If she's that scary, you shouldn't play around with it. Deal with it and let it go."

"Yeah. Yeah. I know." Harry sighed. "So what about you?"

Donnie opened the door and eased his long, slender body out. "I love my wife. I'm curious. The letter healed a lot. It never really stopped hurting altogether. I want to take a long look and figure out what the attraction was. But I don't feel threatened. So lean on me tonight and we'll see what we feel later. We may completely change places."

When they got back, everyone was there except Fritzi. Norman Gallo, the most successful entertainment lawyer in New York, and his new, very young, very cool, very pregnant wife, Carla; Franco and Esmeralda Cucci, the most famous book-design team in the country; and Max Stiles, preeminent photographer and the only homosexual Harry was comfortable with (though he would never have admitted that to anyone, not even Donnie). Conversation was already whizzing. The third bottle of wine was on its way out and Gina, Harry could tell at a glance, had relaxed considerably.

A HOUSE IN THE HAMPTONS

You always knew when it was going to be okay. Max was in the middle of a Max story.

"So, I'm channel-flipping and I see this aging belle that I went to high school with twelve hundred years ago in Chattanooga and she's being interviewed about this school for teaching young women *manners*. She takes a hundred and twenty of the baby-fatters for ten days at twenty-five hundred per session and teaches them things like tea pouring and how to do a twelve-piece place setting in under ten minutes. It was like the week before the French Revolution on cable."

Gina clapped her hands. "I saw it, too, Max! The girls were so . . ."

"EEG flatline."

"Ages twelve to one twenty-four . . ."

"Yeah, one hooker reject from the Miss America contest!" Janie screamed. "Oh, Max. Soooo bad!"

"They have to bring nine different dinner dresses and one of them, a CAP, no less . . ."

"CAP, what is a CAP?" Esmeralda Cucci frowned.

Louie ran in and grabbed a handful of crackers. "Chinese American Princess!" he imparted, and sped back to his heroes.

Everybody laughed.

Gina stood up . . .

"She's really overdressed and she comes down this antebellum staircase and the reporter asks her what's the most important thing she's learned in the ten days. 'Well, I guess the most important was small talk. I really know how to make small talk now . . .'"

Max is jumping up and down. "Oh, so beautiful. My classmate leering behind her, beaming like the kid's reciting the *Iliad* . . ."

Norman Gallo, no longer able to relinquish the spotlight,

turned solemn. "We're laughing, but, I'm telling you, that kind of desensitization—the breaking down of all semblance of values—it is going to destroy and defeat this country. People are starving to death on the streets of Manhattan and these rich Barbie dolls are paying a poor man's yearly wage to learn tea pouring. Just what Wolfe was talking about in *Bonfire.*"

"Pa-leese—don't bring that up! If I see one more copy or hear one more conversation about that book, I'll puke!" Janie exhaled dramatically.

Norman's wife rubbed her stomach. "Oh, Norman, not the doomsday speech, again."

"What do you know!" Norman was pouting. "You were raised in all of that, Carla. You're too young to understand consequences."

All eyes were now on the young pregnant bride. Gina stiffened slightly, readying the hostess rescue. The bride yawned. Gina relaxed. These new-breed Amazon women. They could give *us* lessons.

"Norman, if you were giving the speech from the Third Street homeless shelter, instead of here, in your cashmere and silk turtleneck, stuffing French cheese and California Chardonnay into your new five thousand dollars' worth of bonded teeth, it would mean more, darling," she told him. "What's that saying? If you're not part of the solution, you're part of the problem? Well, we're not in Tennessee learning how to curtsey, but we're all more or less part of the problem." Carla yawned again.

"Right on!" Janie lit another cigarette, ignoring Donnie's disapproving look. "We're all of us out here, people with *second houses* for crissakes! I mean, I come home from the country from my second house to my main house and I literally step over a guy who's living in a paper bag! Do I give him a room? Do I give him my trust fund? We write a check to the Coalition for the Homeless and unpack the picnic basket."

Franco Cucci was listening so intently, his flaring jet-black eyebrows arched like gulls' wings. "I saw something in the *Time* magazine. It was about this tribe in Botswana. A very primitive tribe. Several endangered species of animals were disappearing. The herds thinning out, and so an expedition was mounted and they went deep into the jungles and found this tribe. These people were hunters. They lived where it was impossible to farm, to live off the land. They killed to survive. When the expedition found them, a choice had to be made. The hunters or the hunted. Man or beast. And it was not even a debate. They chose to save the beasts. The people were replaceable. The animals were not."

Donnie filled his glass. He knew he shouldn't, his ulcer throbbed. Maybe he was more nervous than he wanted to admit. "Are you saying, Franco, that what is happening in New York, for example, is that the rich, the strong, are being saved at the expense of the downtrodden? The replaceable?"

"Yes. I am saying that. Being Italian, it is not so harsh a thing to admit. We tend to have a different relationship to morality. More realistic, I think."

The doorbell rang. Louie went racing. "I'll get it. It's probably Harry's other wife!"

Everyone looked at everyone else. It was so paralyzingly embarrassing that Gina and Harry burst out laughing and moved cautiously to the door. In the background Janie could be heard, quietly explaining this unique piece of ingenuous information.

Months later when Gina tried to describe her feelings standing inside her doorway on that early summer night, all she could say was that it felt like snorkeling. Like she was snorkeling in her living room. That sense of totally eliminating several senses and concentrating on one or two. Breathing like a fish, in an unnatural way, and staring down into a world that did not want you. An alien place into which you had pushed yourself. A world of intense beauty and over-whelming terror . . . of awe and strangeness. Treading water in cold, clear, silence. Floating silently across her hall-way, gaping through her water-filled goggles at the prize specimen in her creaky Victorian hallway. Startling herself with color and light, with majestic, electric mystery.

Fritzi Olsen Ferris was standing next to Frankie Karsh and smiling the whitest brightest smile Gina had ever seen. She was astonishing to look at. Names kept popping into Gina's head. Marilyn Monroe. Betty Grable. Mamie Van Doren. Mamie Van Doren? My God.

Before her stood a woman who did not look like any real woman—any real life in the flesh woman she had ever seen. A glitzy platinum goddess. A body like Raquel Welch, at least. She was all white cream curves. Her hair was blond. Her neck glistened with an enormous white diamond heart. Her nails, finger and toe, were white. Her mouth was pink frosted roses. She positively glowed. No. Not Mamie. Mari-lyn. Marilyn fucking Monroe was not only standing in her doorway, but had been married to Harry. HER HARRY. *Her* Harry had fucked Marilyn fucking Monroe. Before her. *Way* before her. The information was quite simply stunning.

All of her snide sense of superiority melted around her like one of Louie's Popsicles. Plop. Plop. Drip. Drip. Her ego dissolved. This was not what she had expected. She had ex-pected a middle-aged bimby gone to fat. Overdone, and pa-thetic. Widowed and desperate. Not this. Not this, this, bombshell. This illuminated sex goddess. Not *Marilyn.*

This is a woman who perfumes her knees, Gina thought, and everything in her winced. A huge anatomical wince. Her Harry had kissed those gleaming, creamy, perfumed knees. Suddenly her entire physical persona, her careful, Fran

Lebowitz–inspired understated Manhattan style felt like Sicilian funerary attire. She felt like someone's old maid Sicilian aunt. Dried out. Cynical and dusty.

She felt as if her body were encased in concrete; no, gravel. Gravel! As if she were a farmhouse lawn, covered in pebbles, all the grass underneath dead and dry. Her very existence felt threatened. Who was she? Who was this woman? Who was Harry? How could she possibly ever overcome this terrible, overpowering threat? And threat to what?

Marilyn moved forward and gave Harry a kiss. "Gee, Har, what a cute little house! I love old-fashioned houses like this. There really aren't any like this in Rancho Santa Fe. It's so quaint! I'd like you to meet my, uh, friend, Frankie Karsh, he owns the antique car place on the highway? He sold me my car. That's how we met."

Harry squeezed Gina's elbow, trying subtly to bring her back from wherever she seemed to have gone the minute the door was opened. He was really nervous now, now that he'd seen Gina's face. Holy shit, Harry. Really bad idea. He'd forgotten how, fantastic, Fritzi looked. I mean, it was winter and she was so different from what he was used to. He'd been too nervous to really see her. Jesus Christ. She was unbelievable. Linda Evans, at least. How could he have forgotten?

Maybe it was all just too hard to believe. And he'd been discounting her for so many years. Really super cool, Harry. How is it possible for you to be this fucking out of touch. Your wife looks like she just swallowed a fucking ice cube.

Oh shit. Donnie. Janie. You'll pay for this, Harry. You stupid schmuck. Might as well just climb up on the cross right after dinner. Get the nails, the hammer, the thorn cap. Don't even wait for the trial. You did this to yourself! That's it. I am quitting Dr. Wexel as soon as he comes back from his safari. If I did this—something this unbelievably stupid and self-destructive after all those years—the whole analysis sucks! Forget about it! I'm going to spend that money on Thorazine. I'm going to need a lot of Thorazine or something like Thorazine. Oh shit. Gina's *got* to say something. Close your mouth, Gina, read my eyes. Your fucking mouth is hanging open.

"Uh, Gina, honey. This is Madeline. Fritzi is what she's uh, she's, it's her nickname. And uh, Frankie, uh, Kars . . ."

"Karsh."

"Right. Karsh. He sells cars. Ha! What a coincidence. Karsh. Cars. Ha!"

From somewhere Gina found her air supply. "I know Frankie. I just interviewed him. What a surprise!"

Frankie looked puzzled. Something was going on that Fritzi hadn't told him about. Luckily, if there was anything he knew how to do, it was deal with people. No problem. Let it fly. "Yeah. Small world. How's it going?"

Gina inhaled and blinked. The surface. Splat. She was coming to. *My* name is Gina Hart. I am thirty-nine and nine-tenths years old. This is *my* house. This is *my* husband. These are *my* friends. *My* children. *My* life. I am a *writer*. I am a *person*. I am an attractive woman with olive skin and wavy black hair. Albeit with gray streaks fighting their way out. I have worth.

"It's going just fine, Frankie. I may want one more interview. Please, uh, Fritzi, Frankie, come on in and meet everyone."

Harry and Gina stood back letting their guests, who more than anything else resembled the spun-sugar couple on the top of all those Italian wedding cakes, go first. They followed, not daring to look at each other.

They approached the task of introducing *her* with about the same enthusiasm as: telling a young kid his puppy got hit by the UPS truck . . . telling a feeble old woman her husband hadn't made it through heart surgery . . . telling the psychotic cleaning lady she forgot to change the sheets . . . telling Harry's mother they weren't coming for Thanksgiving.

They were both saved from this horrible moment by a very loud but intensely musical squeal, a melody that began somewhere deep in Fritzi Olsen Ferris's creamy chest and moved up her squirmy, embarrassing body like a sexual howl.

"Donnie Jamieson! Oh, my God! I can't stand it!" Fritzi threw her diamond-white arms open and moved toward him. Donnie was seated between Janie and the pregnant Amazon on the couch. He stood up so fast that Janie and the Amazon tumbled toward each other, almost knocking their heads together. Fritzi threw herself around the startled Donnie so that he was wrapped in her embrace like a cocktail hotdog. His arms at his sides. Engulfed by this silky glowing vision.

It was one of those moments that should have been recorded forever on film, but no one ever has a camera at such an event.

The scent, the vibration of something unusual, had made its way around the entire house. Suddenly, everyone was there. Isabel and Ondine stood shyly in the background holding trays of goodies, but trancelike, not moving. Jeremy, Owen, and Louie stood behind the couch where Janie sat, a cigarette, hanging on her lower lip, unlit and forgotten. All three boys had open mouths and eyes as big as if E.T. had just landed on the coffee table. Everyone was struck mute by the presence of a woman like this. A woman no one in their world had ever seen close up in real life. Her perfume made their noses itch. Even Arturo stood still, the remnants of a Bremner wafer crushed on his drooling hanging tongue.

Marilyn Monroe had risen from the grave and returned, on an early summer evening in Sag Harbor.

Fritzi Olsen Ferris jumped up and down in front of the tall, lanky speechless figure of Donnie Jamieson, while a roomful of New York sophisticates sat in a state of shocked, riveted silence. Nothing remotely like this had ever happened at any dinner party any of them had ever been at in all of their adult lives. No matter what, no one ever, *ever,* stopped talking. Social history was being made, but all present were too engrossed with the shining, shimmering apparition before them, to notice.

Three A.M. The Harts' bedroom. Two married people lying side by side in the dark pretending to be asleep. Disquiet.

"Harry?"

"Hmmm."

"I know you're not sleeping, so please don't give me that hmmm shit. I need to talk."

Here it comes. Let me just take a moment, my dear. Get the longer nails, the ones like in the Piero Della Francesca frescoes. "Do we have to do this now? I can't talk about anything this upsetting late at night. I'll never get to sleep, again."

"Oh, brother. You are really unbelievable. You can't talk about anything heavy after dinner because your stomach will get upset. Can't talk before you go to sleep or you'll have nightmares. In the morning it's you don't want to start your day like that. At dinner it's not while you're eating. *Give me a break.* I need to talk. Now!" To prove her seriousness, Gina Hart snapped on her antique brass bed lamp.

Harry gave up. "Okay. Okay. But please turn off the goddamn light."

"No. I want to see your face. I can't trust you otherwise." In spite of herself Gina burst into tears.

"Jesus! What do you want from me? One lunch six months ago? I *left* this woman. I ran away from her. I chose you. Not

60

her. I never would have married her for a second. She got pregnant! I was a *kid*! It's ancient history!"

Gina blew her nose. "Some ancient history. The dinosaur was in my living room turning all the men present into guava jelly. Even Louie. Louie! He couldn't stay away from her. She might as well have been white chocolate. I was sure at least twice that he was going to bite into her! I'm going to be forty years old next month. It hurts! I don't want to be jealous of her, but I can't help it. You made love to her. She was your first lover and she's, she's gorgeous!"

"Jesus, Gina. She's older than you are, for chrissakes!"

That really did it. Gina was gulping sobs. "Great! Thanks, Harry! I needed that. That really helps. She's older than I am and she looks ten years younger! Franco thought she was thirty! Thirty! It was so humiliating. How could you not know me better by now? How could you not know I wouldn't be able to handle it!"

Harry melted. Her crying always tore him up. "God. Gin', I'm so sorry. I'm such a schmuck. Such a stupid, neurotic, insensitive schmuck! I . . . you are always so together, so much more confident than I am. I thought you'd think she was a caricature. You always make fun of women like her on TV. Lonnie Anderson? Remember that show? You always laughed. You're my wife, and I love you. She's history."

"Yeah, so you keep saying. You're right Harry. You are a schmuck. Winner of the second prize in the international schmuck contest."

Harry grinned. "If I'm such a schmuck, why not first prize?"

" 'Cause, you're a schmuck."

They both laughed in spite of themselves. It was their favorite joke.

Harry snuggled close to her and put his leg over her warm long thigh.

"So, what say we use the jealousy thing to generate a little sexual tension. Does it turn you on?"

Gina tried to push him away. "*No!*"

Harry knew her better than she thought he did. He put his hand under her T-shirt. "Yes it does. It does turn you on. Like my thinking of you with someone else turns me on. Come on, Gin', let's do it."

It did turn her on. In the most primitive, masochistic way. "You schmuck, Harry," she sighed, and hit the light with her free hand, surrendering to her fantasies, knowing the pain and the struggle of this new presence was far from over. But grateful for the reprieve and the passion. Always grateful after so many years of the same sex for a surprise. A rush of passion.

Five A.M. The Jamiesons' bedroom. Janie is sitting out on the terrace overlooking the ocean, chain-smoking and eating Milk Duds. Donnie is in the bathroom. He has been in the bathroom for a long time. She waits. Knowing he'll find her when he's ready.

He comes up behind her and rubs her neck. Janie sighs and pats his hand. He kisses her cheek and sits down next to her. She offers him the Milk Duds. Donnie shakes his head.

"You look pale through your tan. I thought that was only a literary allusion. But you do."

Donnie smiled. "Stomach's upset."

Janie plops the last Milk Dud into her mouth and throws the box down in self-loathing. "Well, no wonder. After the way Miss Jiggle Jugs bounced you around."

"Okay. Let's get it over with. Let it all out or we'll never sleep again. Or, you'll solve the sleep problem by smoking yourself to death."

Janie stubbed out the cigarette. "Okay. I'm trying to handle this, okay? I mean it's not easy to hear your son say, 'Gee, poor Dad—could have had that and had to settle for Mom.' "

"That's *not* what he said."

"Close enough. Poor Gina. I wouldn't want to be Harry tonight. She was totally devastated. I've never seen Gina jealous before." She eyed him. "What does Fritzala want, Donnie?"

"What makes you think she wants something?"

"Do you know who this is you are speaking with? Am I born yesterday? Was I not raised by the two greatest game players of the twentieth century? She wants something. And I am telling you, Donnie Jamieson, if it happens to be you, she can just sit on it, because they'll find her bleached blond breasts floating in Mecox Bay before she even thinks about it!"

Donnie laughed and took her hand. "That's my girl. Fierce. A fierce little Panzer division. Fighting for her man. I am deeply flattered."

Janie's lip started to quiver in spite of her resolve. "Donnie, you're too decent a person to be coy. Please don't patronize me. She knocked you off your feet back then and she did it again tonight. And you know it."

Donnie watched his brave feisty wife trying to be tough. It broke his heart, because it was true and he did not want it to be. He did not want to hurt his wife with that truth. He was silent. She knew him so well. The silence held the truth.

"You wouldn't, would you?" She gritted her teeth. She did not want to cry.

Donnie knelt before her and took her hands. The sun was just beginning to find its way out. Silver streaks behind the dark blue sky.

"No, baby. I wouldn't. I never have and I never will. I promise."

Janie nodded. Very fast. Up and down. Her small pointed

chin tight with fear. "I couldn't stand it, Donnie. Because of Daddy. I just couldn't."

Donnie kissed her hands. His ulcer throbbed. It was his fate. Nice guys don't. The lust-filled dream that had never quite died. Brought back in the middle of his life to torment him. Why now? What *did* she want? Janie was on to it. She did want something. And he still wanted the same thing. To plunge his cock as deep inside that giddy, luscious creature as he had ever dared to dream. His boyhood dream, returning to tease him and hurt him all over again. Why now?

Six A.M. Rikki Bosco's bedroom. The Match is licking Rikki Bosco's penis. The windows are open and they can hear the wind blowing the water on Rikki's private pond. Ducks honk. The Match is lying down at the end of the bed, her head between Rikki's legs. Rikki moans. She increases the action. She knows just when. She has massaged every single part of this man's body from his nose to his toes. She knows all his secrets. "Oh, baby. That's fantastic! Yes! Yes!"

The Match is crying, but Rikki can't tell. He presses her head down, making her suck harder. "Faster. Yes! Yes!"

No! No! She wants to bite the damn thing off, is what she wants. She knows what's turning him on and it isn't her flame-hot tongue. It's the Hollywood Pussy. Is what it is. From the minute she walked up the driveway, The Match knew it was trouble. Big trouble. Rikki had barely been able to speak. He had blushed like a fucking tomato. Unbelievable.

"Hello. I'm Katarina. So lovely to finally meet you! Joey has talked about you for so long. I really feel as if we were old friends. What an incredible place! May I have a tour?"

She had gone to help Florencia make tea. Tea! Fucking tea! Neither she nor Florencia had ever even made it before. Rikki had even tried to get Florencia to wear one of those

64

downstairs maid numbers with the gray taffeta and the white lace and the little doily on her head. They had both gotten so hysterical, even Rikki started to laugh. I mean it was hardly Florencia's style, what with the gum chewing and the white socks and the pink shorts so tight around her blubber, her stomach folded over her waist in a jelly roll. "Hey, Match, how's it goin', keed?" That was Rikki's maid's style. They made the fucking tea.

"Yo, Florencia, he said heavy cream! Not milk. Like in England."

"So, it's cool. No problem." Florencia watched her. Florencia was a witchy chick. "So theese guys, some fancy piples?"

"Yeah. Big deal. She's a Scotch tape job, if ya ask me."

"Whas thees? Scotch tape jab?"

The Match was really talking to herself. "I dunno. Something underneath is very fractured. Held together, like with Scotch tape."

"Oh, I gotcha."

Rikki hated it when she talked on an equal level with Florencia. But The Match *felt* on an equal level with Florencia. Florencia was the people. Florencia was real. Florencia didn't say "as if" and "may I" and neither did she. And neither did Rikki. She was scared.

She knew more about this kind of people than Rikki did. She had spent years massaging them. Riding in their private elevators and their private planes. She knew how it felt to be at the end of a fourteen-hour day that included snowstorms and two-hour subway rides and nine hours of rubbing and kneading unforgiving muscles, so knotted that what she really needed was a little shot of plutonium to open them up, listening to rich women bitch. "God! I am *soooo* exhausted! That helicopter ride from La Guardia is *soooo* tiring. We left Aspen at seven this morning! I'm just dead!"

The Match knew this scene. All those phony voices. Every single fucking one of them had a phony voice. A pretentious made-up voice. Even the ones from Ohio or Arizona had this upper-crust, dry, inflected voice. Made everything sound witty. Though they never said anything witty. Made it all sound sort of flip and ironic. Such unbelievable bullshit! She listened to their tales. Impotent husbands. Gay children. Bad haircuts. It didn't much matter. It all droned out in the same brittle, phony-voiced monotone as if it was all part of the same problem. Life's little annoyances.

But this one. This Katarina Rivers. This was the real big league. Okay. She was beautiful. She was. The Match was big enough to admit it. Delicate, classical features. Wide gray eyes. And that hair. A mane. A fucking mane of glossy black hair. And she knew it. The way she tossed it and twirled it, and ran her long fingers through it. She knew all about it. She had that look. That rich girl, Ralph Lauren look. Very understated. Real pearl studs. The kind of makeup that takes an hour to look like you ain't wearing any.

The Match knew the whole scene. Perfect clothes. The cashmere over the shoulders. So, oh, just so, offhand. Sure. Like a life's work. That look. She had it. Spoke French and Italian, at least. Had a little lilt in the voice to make it less like the other phony voices.

She had seen Rikki's face. It was so easy to read. *Pow*. A Dream Girl Fantasy standing before him. Far better than those horsey-faced equestrians and tennis racquet tit jobs he usually ogled. This was the Jew Boy's bitch goddess in the flesh. And he wasn't even Jewish. Well, same thing. His madonna fixation.

Florencia and The Match carried all the tea stuff out to the patio and waited. "Come on, Florencia, sit a minute. Have some English tea." She said it on purpose, knowing Rikki would hate it. Florencia giggled.

A HOUSE IN THE HAMPTONS

"Eh, Match. Meester Rikki, gonna give it to youse. I'm outa here."

She sat. Saved from herself. It was getting late. She could see them in the distance beyond the pool, way down by the pond. The Lord of the Manor. *What can I do*, she whispered to herself. *What can I do.*

The Match was right. Rikki was coming. Rikki was coming like crazy. To his own fantasy. To Katarina Rivers, lying beneath him, moaning in ecstasy, her billowing black hair spread out around her like a Fendi fur.

He had always been a hungry guy. A guy who wanted things. If he hadn't, he'd be in a state prison instead of the Hamptons and upper Fifth Avenue. He was like the only guy who got out of Staten Island. Everyone else was either in jail, in a coffin, or working in some fucking pizza parlor. He was the only one. Except for Rivers. He got out. That was the truth. He got out and became a big-deal director. But he didn't get rich. Not Rikki kind of rich. Nowhere near. Not powerful. Not even close. Rikki could write a check and finance Joey Rivers's next picture out of petty cash. Which was most likely why, all of a sudden, Joey Rivers had reappeared in his life. He wasn't stupid. He knew it wasn't about old times in the old neighborhood.

Rikki had wanted to be rich from the time he was a little boy, so little, he didn't even know he was poor. He had wanted money. And after he had money, he had wanted status. The Bayfront Club was the only thing he had wanted so far that he couldn't buy. Couldn't have. Until today. Until Her. And the way he wanted her was so far deeper and more searing than any of his other wants, it wasn't even a horse race.

If Rikki had a dream of what building his house was about, it had come true today, taking Katarina Rivers around his world. The astonishment on her face when she saw his pond.

The horse jumps built onto the lawn. The stables with his prized quarter horses.

Of course she rode! Of course she played tennis! What courts! What horseflesh! Did he know her brother was a race driver? Of course she knew cars! Unreal. The Olympic-lap pool. She was on the swim team at Vassar! Of course she was!

He led them through the Italian marble bathrooms, the burled wood-paneled library, the waterfall atrium with the Henry Moore nude. They strolled past the Hockneys and Schnabels and Salles and out to the terrace. The sweeping teak terrace, which resembled nothing as much as the deck of a pre–World War Two luxury liner, and from where, as far as anyone's eye could see, every tree and meadow, every flower and bush belonged to him. It was the greatest feeling of triumph of his entire life. "This is the patio," he had said, so humbly, and she gasped.

"Oh, my! It's utterly magnificent. Extraordinary. I've never seen anything like it!"

"Hollywood likes it, Rikki." The Match. The fucking Match. Breaking his spell. Katarina turned. He had lost her.

"I do like it! How wonderful to spend the summer here. Rikki has just made us the kindest offer."

"Want some tea?" The Match tried to postpone the information, knowing she wasn't going to like it.

"Oh, I'd love some. Darling? Want some tea?"

Joey Rivers had, up until this moment, not spoken one word. He was as small and wiry as Katarina was tall and willowy. He wore all black clothes and black loafers with no socks. His hands were pushed down deep in his baggy Italian linen trouser pockets. He seemed to be sulking, but from all the stories written about him, it was just his style.

"Yeah. Fine. No cream."

"Not too English, huh?" The Match poured. Joey Rivers shrugged. Rikki moved in and took the silver pot from her.

68

"I'll do it. It's too heavy."

Oh boy, she thought, but she surrendered the pot.

"So, what's this incredible offer, Mrs. Rivers?"

The Magazine Ad laughed. "Oh, please. *Katarina.* What do I call you?"

"Everyone calls me Match. Or, *The Match.* It's a long story."

"I'll bet. Well, Match. We have this situation in California. We sold our house, because we're building a new one in Malibu, which was supposed to be finished by now, but, of course, it is not. So we find ourselves homeless, for at least two months. We're just like nomads. And Joey has got to have a base to work on his new film. So, we were telling Rikki about it on our tour and he offered us his guest house! Which is just heaven! I've never, ever seen so much Art Deco anywhere. I mean the entire house is quite authentic. That's my ultimate design fantasy. All Art Deco!"

The Match tried to swallow, but a lump the size of one of the English scones before her had filled her throat. She would not cry. "So, uh, who is this guy Art Deco anyway?"

Rikki looked at Joey Rivers. Joey Rivers looked at Katarina. Katarina looked at Rikki. Everyone looked at The Match. Silence. Dead silence. The Match swallowed. She had absolutely no idea what she had done.

A sound. Coming from Joey Rivers. His shoulders still shrugged. His hand still in his pockets. "Ha. Ha. Ha!" He was laughing. "Haaaaa!" The sound moved to his wife, then, seeing it was safe, to Rikki. *"Haaaaa!"*

Joey Rivers took his hands out of his pockets and rubbed them feverishly along the sides of his slicked-back dark hair. "That is the funniest thing I've ever heard! Who is this chick! This is a great chick! *Haaaaa!*"

Rikki put his arm around her shoulders, protectively. "See! I told you!"

He had told them. He had talked to the Royal Couple about her? A great chick? Maybe she was wrong. Maybe it would be okay. But, the whole summer. She wasn't invited for the whole summer. And Rivers had a movie to think about. Her and Rikki, frolicking in the meadows. Still. They were laughing. They were laughing in a not mean way at something she had said. She was fitting in without a phony voice or flowing black hair. *"Hhhhaaaaahhhhhhhaaaa!"* She joined in. She still had no idea who Art Deco was.

Rikki could do no wrong. Dinner was flawless. The wines from his cellar, personally chosen by the owner of the fanciest wine store in New York, so impressive, even Rivers had complimented him. The food, catered by Loaves and Fishes, was fantastic. A pound of pasta cost as much as some people spend on a week's groceries, but so what! They loved it. They loved his house and they, surprise of surprises, loved his Match. Every thing she said made Joey Rivers practically piss in his Armani pants. She was better than a fucking *Vogue* model or any socialite. She was an original. That's what they said. She showed he was a really deep guy. Not into appearances or superficial values. She made him seem more interesting. He could tell by the way Katarina looked at him now. He had taken on another layer. A mystery. This man is not just a street kid with moxie. He has mystery. Things came to a glorious crescendo when, while their palates were purring with lemon soufflé and the finest sauterne, The Match told them how they'd met!

He was so high, he never wanted to come back down. An entire summer filled with Katarina Rivers. And her friends. He would add show biz to his repertoire. He could do anything. Have anything. Maybe even, her?

The Match sat up, her chin still red from sucking him so long.

"That was fantastico, baby. Now, maybe I can sleep."

She looked like a little girl. Her bottom lip was trembling. She crawled up next to him and pulled the satin sheets and feather quilts all the way over her so that only the top of her head showed. A bright orange shock, like a cock's comb sticking up beside him.

"Rikki. I have a favor to ask."

"Sure, babe. Anything."

"I want you to call me by name. My name is Ellen Mary. I'd like that a lot."

"Ellen Mary. No shit. Sure. I mean, I'll try. It may take some time. Ellen Mary. So why, all of a sudden?"

She turned over on her side and drew her long bony legs up, curling into the tightest fetal position a tall skinny person could achieve. "I dunno. I just feel like it." Before she could think of what to say about the Riverses and her fears, he was snoring. Just as well, she thought. She wasn't at all sure she could handle it now, anyway. She closed her eyes. The sun was in them. She pulled the covers over her face and fell into a deep, black, frightened sleep.

3

Louie Manyara Cowan stood at the edge of the sea, his small skinny feet curled down into the wet sand, braced against the cold foamy remains of the surf.

He didn't want to be afraid of the ocean. More than anything he didn't. But he was. No one knew he was except Owen. Not even Poppa. Poppa knowing would probably be the worst. Poppa wasn't afraid of anything.

Owen thought Louie was afraid because he had been born on the African plains in the middle of a drought and didn't have water, especially seawater, entered into his genetic code. Louie didn't know what genetic code was, even after Owen had explained it, but he thought that it made sense.

Anyway, this summer he had to go in the water. He was too big to be such a baby about it. He turned to make sure China was still there watching him, just in case some gigantic wave rose up out of the blue. Just to be safe. She smiled and waved at him. He waved back. Especially, he didn't want China to know he was afraid.

He thought she was the most beautiful girl he had ever seen and the nicest, too. Not that Mrs. Murray wasn't nice. She was. But she had crooked yellow teeth and she always smelled of sour milk. Not like China at all. China smelled like Isabel's lemonade and she had the cleanest, whitest teeth he had ever seen on a real person. There was one girl on a Close-up commercial who had almost the same teeth, but she wasn't real.

Louie took two small steps forward, his teeth clamped together. The tide was getting higher and the waves rolled over his ankles. He dug his toes deeper into the soft grainy sand and tried to enjoy himself.

They were sending him to camp next week. Boy, did he ever not want to go. He didn't understand it. Last year he had loved going. But this summer felt so different. Something felt wrong. he just knew it. But he couldn't figure it out.

Maybe it was because he was seven. He had never been seven before. Maybe at seven you just get kind of weird and you stop liking things like camp. What he wanted was to be here with China and his family. They need me, he thought, and felt ashamed. He was just a little kid. What could they need him for? But he still believed it. Something was wrong with his family. Usually he could cheer them up and make them feel better. They always cheered up when he kissed them or told them stories. But lately they didn't seem even to hear him. It hurt his feelings. Momma especially. She just smiled that funny not happy kind of smile of hers and patted him on the head, like he was Arturo or something. It made him mad, too. He felt really bad about that. Being mad at Momma. He didn't know how to ask any of them about it. Maybe he could ask Owen. He was really smart about the way grown-ups behave. "Psyching the old folks out," Owen called it.

Well, at least Dr. J. was coming down more. He always had time for him. He never just said, "Um-hmmm" or "That's nice, dear," like the other grown-ups. Pretending to be interested. Not ever. He really listened. Maybe he could ask him what was wrong. Dr. J. probably knew everything.

"Louie. Time for lunch!" China moved toward him across the sand carrying his towel. Saved by the bell, he thought, not knowing where he had heard that saying. Now he could put off the ocean until the weekend. He uncurled his toes and turned away from his fear, running up to the safety offered by his lemon-scented savior.

Just south of the Highway between Watermill and South-ampton there is a house that doesn't belong. On the south side of the highway, the closer to the ocean side, in the mid-dle of an immaculate mowed and manicured road, it sits, like a middle finger—an Italian salute.

The porch sags in the center, weighed down by dry rot, neglect, and junk. It is littered with rusted broken lawn fur-niture, empty oil cans, mildewed mattresses. The grass is dead and so is the ancient Chevrolet, collapsed forever in what used to be a driveway but is now just a deader part of the death. The windows are shut and covered with newspa-pers and the shingles are cracked and chipped. The only sign of spirit, of life, comes from the porch walls, which are filled with various versions of the American bald eagle. Soaring toward nowhere; brass, wood, plastic eagles are nailed to the falling wall of this shack. Holding it up. The whole picture is like a mirage, shockingly out of place, and confusing. Even in the poorest parts of the Hamptons, the area known as the Southampton Ghetto, where limos cruise for crack, the houses are neat. Trees grow. People have pride. Here, this eyesore, this obscene intrusion on the pastoral, well-tended landscape, is a reminder. A Billie Boggs. A menacing Squeegie Man, another truth.

Delores Cowan liked coming to this house. She liked it because it was a symbol of who she really was. Not who she

75

was supposed to be or even who she had been. She liked it because it was honest. It fit the act.

Usually, she drove herself here. I mean, it was hardly the kind of place she could ask Ben or Janie to drive her; but today, she had asked Ondine to take her. Ondine, she could trust. Junkie to junkie. Who would he tell—his mother? Poor Isabel. She tried so hard. She had worked herself sick trying to give this punk a good start. For nothing. The luck of the draw. Some kids were born with character and some weren't. God knows, it was true with Janie. She certainly hadn't given her much. Janie had her own supply of strength. Delores settled deeper into the back of the Rolls and closed her eyes. It wouldn't be long now. She and Ondine, shooting up together. Their little secret.

She smiled. Her family had been so pleased that she wasn't drinking. Little did they know, she had added a new dimension to her addictions. The truth was, Delores liked being a drunk. What she didn't like was anyone knowing about it. If she could have stayed an invisible drunk, she would never have branched out in the first place. They had only themselves to blame.

She loved the feeling of floating, of reality hazing over, smoothing out—the overwhelming sense of well-being that booze gave her. She never got mean or sloppy. She just glazed over and floated away. At least until lately.

Now, it was showing. She fell down the stairs! And then last Friday night, when Donnie and Janie and the kids had gone to the Harts' and Ben had gone wherever Ben was going these nights (that, she was not going to think about) she had passed out on the dune. Just pitched right over flat on her face in the sand. That poor girl, China! Coming home from a date and almost stepping on her; must have scared her to death! Delores knew China didn't believe her falling-asleep story. "I was looking at the moon, and it was just so

76

peaceful, I dozed off." Sure, Delores. With your head in the sand.

Something was happening to her. So, okay. Good-bye Dom Pérignon and icy sweet Stoly—*au revoir* for a while. Heroin. Heroine. I'd rather switch than fight. Just for the summer, while the kids were here. In the fall, Ben will fly off to the Sudan or wherever the drought is this year, the family will leave; Mrs. Murray will return to protect Louie and I will drink myself to peace. Drink myself out of the pain. Drink myself out of the despair. Drink myself dead.

"We're here, Mrs. C." Good old Ondine, even now he couldn't bring himself to call her Delores. He was such a strange kid. Sweet and cold at the same time. Manipulative as a saltwater taffy machine, churning the sticky mass of other people's insecurities into candy for himself. Always working the corners, but winking while he screwed you. Sweet and mean. That's Ondine. She paid him well for his services. Very, very well. She figured that by now, after three years of supplying her with every kind of pill, cocaine, smuggled booze, and her newly beloved her-o-ine, she had paid him enough for a house and a very nice car. At least. So, who would he tell?

He parked down the street, where their shiny machine would look more appropriate, and he helped her out of the back. She was woozy. The Valium she had taken to help her through the booze withdrawal made her feel weak and groggy. Ondine put his arm under her elbow and helped her up the rutted driveway and around to the back. Two knocks, exactly four seconds apart. The signal.

The door creaked open. "Hey, yo! Delores. How youse doin'?" Mr. S. took her hand and helped her over the threshold, his big wide greasy face grinning like an Italian jack-o'-lantern. She was his fanciest customer and that said a lot. He had many fancy customers, though she never saw another one. He liked it that way. Mixing the rich and the wretched. He would shoot her up next to a zombie ghetto junkie, but never next to anyone she might run into at Elizabeth Arden. It gave him power. Drugs were the great social equalizer. Like summer clothes. Mr. S. liked to make this comparison.

"Junk is like summer clothes," he would pronounce, his muscles flexing under his skintight tank top. A magician about to do his best trick before a desperate and captive audience. "Youse see a dude out joggin' on Dune Road, let's say. The guy's half bald, got knobby knees and a little gut. Got on a sweaty T-shirt and shorts. So who is this dude? Just another sweaty asshole? Am I right or am I wrong? Cut to same dude the next day waitin' at the Omni for the Jitney in his two-thousand-dollar Savile Row threads, all put together. President of the World! Can't tell it naked. Can't tell it in his undies! Junkies the same. When the eyes roll back inta the socket, who cares if you got your Texas Unit. Am I right or am I wrong?"

Delores picked up all kinds of conversational tidbits from Mr. S. Texas Unit, for example. Ben had really been impressed by that one. "It's someone who has made a hundred million dollars. That's what the players call it. They don't even consider anything money that's under that. So, I guess we're poor. We only have about half a unit. Maybe a Wyoming Unit." He had just stared at her. She liked it. It gave her mystery. Something she knew he had never thought she had.

Mr. S. cleared a trail for her, pushing newspapers and beer cans out of the way as she passed. The empress at the orphans' home. It was right out of Dickens. He led her to the Chair. An enormous worn velvet lounge chair—the place of honor, even if it was soiled and riddled with cigarette burns. Ondine shuffled along behind her. Ondine didn't like Mr. S.

A HOUSE IN THE HAMPTONS

Ondine didn't like white pushers, especially wop white pushers. He thought it took money from his people.

"Yo. Delores. Sit. I got some stuff for youse, gonna take youse to Jesus. To the promised land."

Delores Cowan let him help her onto the chair, smoothing her white linen skirt with queenly grace. Ondine flopped down on the filthy floor beside her like a palace poodle.

"Why don't you clean this fu— this dump up. It's bad for business, man." Ondine never swore in front of her. It was one of his sweet things.

Mr. S. was busy with his magic. The only clean, immaculate, in fact, part of the shack was the back wall of the kitchen where he conducted his business. It sparkled. That he knew was important to the fancy clients. He liked that. To make them come as far down as possible, but not to the point of not trusting his stuff. That part had to look clean. Like his hands. His hands were so clean and manicured, they glowed in the dark. Not with all the AIDS shit. They could see his needles, sparkling and sterile. They could watch him throw each one away, personally. He knew where to draw the line.

Mr. S. ignored Ondine. He was making his magic for Delores. She watched his tattoos move as he worked. She loved his tattoos. She had even told Ben about them. "I saw this . . . workman today and he had three enormous tattoos. On one arm he had a hideous coiled snake with the name Glenda written over its head. On his chest he had Jesus wearing the crown of thorns with a caption that said, 'Granny—rest in peace,' and on his other arm, he had Pebbles Flintstone!"

Ben had almost choked on his veal chop. "Where do you see these things? You must have been awfully close to read the tattoos on his arms, for chrissakes."

"Oh, I was, dear. I was." She had just smiled and glazed

over. She knew she was safe. He never dared to push her or question her too closely. It was their unwritten pact. Because if he did, then she could, and he certainly wouldn't want that. That was why she did it, after all. Maybe someday he'd get so curious or just so frustrated, he'd break the rules and then she'd be free to tear it all open. Pour it all out. Accuse. Pound out the information. Why! Who is it! Free to pounce. To break out of this polite and malevolent cage in which they lived, circling each other like tranquilized beasts . . . vicious beasts, numbed into wariness, numbed by fear into calm.

Mr. S. moved toward her grinning his fat, even white grin. "Delores, this shit is goin' to rush you like a shark chasin' a guppy."

She laid her head back and closed her eyes. She was his now. He had found a place to inject her that didn't show. She was so small, so small-boned, it was very hard to do it. But he knew how and he had taught her and Ondine. She didn't like to let Ondine do it. Only if she was too shaky, would she let him. Up under her skirt. She had stopped wearing shorts.' No one noticed. Ben never touched her anymore. He certainly wouldn't notice.

She was really quite invisible. The only time they paid attention to her at all was when she got drunk. When they suddenly sniffed danger. The danger of Mother making a fool out of herself. She was too little. That was how she felt. Like a tiny kitchen mouse at a table of bears. "Squeak, squeak!" No one heard her. No one saw her, unless she hopped up and ran across their porridge. Otherwise, forget it. She was like a knickknack. They would miss her if she fell down and broke all to pieces, but they didn't really see her, anymore.

In. It was in. Smack. No wonder they called it that. She sighed. Euphoria flooded her. She heard Mr. S. scuffling around, getting Ondine his fix. Talking, talking, talking. He knew she liked him to talk. It made her float better. His voice was like the sea. A sound in her head.

"Youse guys is lucky. I wish I could still do this shit. Gotta take care of business. Gotta be clean. No more booze. That was the hardest. The smack was easy compared to the sauce. Shit. I could drink! Used to buy my booze in gallon jugs. Come home, take a beer mug, throw in a coupla cubes, fill it right up to the top with tequila, gin, didn't matter. Bam. Two slugs. Empty. Never got sick! Never had a hangover. Just got mad. Boy. I was mad. Tried to break my wife's neck with one hand.

"I'd go inta a bar, get loaded and grab a guy, any guy. 'Hey, youse touch my wife I'll kill youse, you fuck!' The guy would go white, like a sheet! 'Hey, I don' even *know* your wife!' I didn't care. I hated everyone. I wanted to kill every-one. I coulda been one of those guys like Larry Davis. Coulda gotten a machine gun and just took a bunch a fucks out. Like that dude in California? The one that went out for a burger and shot the shit outa about thirty citizens munchin' on their Big Macs. Women, kids—he didn't give a fuck—I was like that. Hadda stop all that.

"Jesus helped me. Second time I tried to kill my old lady. Only weighs eighty pounds. This tiny little Greek broad, my wife is built like a kid. Chased her with a butcher knife. I'll kill you, you bitch! Took all three a my brothers to pull me off. Jesus helped them. Jesus saved me. Now I'm cool. I'm so straight, I'm the fuckin' dividin' line. I'm a businessman. Got my life together. Gonna save enough ta get out of this coun-try. Go south and fish my fuckin' brains out. Give my kids somethin' nice.

"Took me a while but I'm cool. They put me away, Delores. I was in the loony bin. Pumped me so full a Librium, I shoulda been Jell-O gelatin. Hardly slowed me down. Couldn't close my eyeballs for three days. Jesus saved me. I am one saved bastard. Haven't touched any shit in three years! Haven't had a fight, neither. My kids ain't scared a me, no more. But I still wanna kill a lot a fucks. Youse see what's out there. Scum. Am I right or am I wrong?"

Delores nodded her agreement. Everything was right. It was all, all right. She didn't even want to die, today. She felt so right. She didn't care that her husband didn't love her and only stayed because he had been so bent by the money—by all the years of the money holding him up, softening all the edges of his compromise, his lies to himself—that he had lost the courage to live without it.

She didn't care about growing old alone, without his comfort, his caring. She didn't care that she had wasted her own life, let her father's money poison her spirit. She had swallowed the poison willingly. Tasting only the sweet warm honey coating. Here, my dear daughter. Have another piece. Umm. Good, isn't it? No one will ever give you anything sweeter. Only Daddy can. He's your golden sweet candy man. Umm. She and Ben, tongues hanging out. Lick. Lick. The doe and the buck before the sweetened salt. The apple in the Garden. Just one more bite. Umm.

She didn't care, now. The shark had swallowed the guppie. She had found a new candy man. One of her own. One she had bought. Umm.

Louie and China are sitting in the kitchen watching Oprah, Louie's favorite show. China is making notes in her diary and munching on a large juicy pear.

Oprah is talking to a group of females who were men and are now women. Louie is laughing. "Boy, that Oprah is a foxy chick."

China takes a deep crunchy bite on her pear. "Louie, stop

talking like that. You spend too much time with Jeremy and Owen. You're not a teenager, you're only seven years old."

"I'm as old as I feel, that's what Poppa says."

Before China could respond, Janie marched in carrying a large Henry Lehr shopping bag.

"Hi. Hi. Give a kiss." Janie grabbed Louie and kissed his scrunched, resisting face over and over. "Is my mother home, China?"

China put down her pen. "Nope. But your dad is. He's out on the beach, casting, I think."

Janie seemed relieved. "Oh. Okay. Oh, by the way. You know we're having a party for Daddy's birthday two weeks from Saturday and I thought, maybe your mom would like to come."

China's eyes widened. "Oh, gee, Janie. That is just so nice of you. I, gee, I think she'd really like that. I've told her so much about the house and all. Are you sure it's okay?"

Janie grabbed a piece of China's pear. "No. I'm not sure." She pulled China's long blond ponytail with her free hand. "Tell her, no presents."

Janie grabbed her bag and headed toward her house. She was always in a hurry. Owen leapt in front of her, blocking her path.

"Ah-*ha*! I gotcha. Thought you could slip past the shopping detector with a Henry Lehr bag. Will you never learn. I'm too fast for you."

Janie was not in the mood. "Owen. Enough. I've had a bad day."

"Must have been to a Clan of the Cave JAPs meeting."

Janie laughed in spite of herself. That was what Owen called her women's group sessions. "Right, as usual. It was very heavy today. What did you do? Did you find a job yet?"

Owen headed toward the refrigerator. The kitchen was so massive, he took special, slapstick strides to make his point.

"I was at Jeremy's. We made four hundred phone calls. Everyone tells us, it's too early, wait till July. I'm not even out of school yet, Ma, give me a break. Besides, we had a family emergency."

"What? Gina never showed up at the group. I was worried."

"Yeah, well. Arturo ate a thermometer and the vet said he could have mercury poisoning, so Gina had to race him over there. It was a mess."

"Did he die?"

"You don't have to look so happy about it. No. Nothing swallowable will hurt that hound. They cleaned him up. He's fine. But Gina wasn't so hot. I'm sure you'll hear all the gory details."

Louie pulled on her arm. "Janie! Janie! Is Arturo sick?"

Janie knelt down and hugged him. "No! No! baby. I'm sorry. I was just teasing. Arturo's fine. He just ate something bad. But he's okay."

Louie clung to her. Anything that remotely threatened any of them was unbearable to him. She was ashamed of herself.

Owen pulled a pitcher of Isabel's lemonade and a plate of chocolate chip cookies out of the refrigerator and held them out for Louie to see.

"Hey, Lou, my main man. Let's take the goodies and toss the ball around."

Louie let go. The freedom of childhood always amazed Janie. The conduit between feelings. One goes in, another goes out. So easily. No rust in their psychic pipes, clouding the messages, tarnishing the instinct.

"Yeah! We're outa here!" Louie ran after his idol.

Janie looked at China. Janie liked looking at her. She was so pretty. So clean-looking and fresh, like her name. Fine China. Not the country, she was nothing like Janie's idea of

84

China as a country, but porcelain, Chinese porcelain, she was like that. So was China's mother. A little chipped in places. A bit faded. She had not had an easy life. But the fineness of feature was still there; face and bone, still good.

Janie had just thought of asking Clovis on the way home. After all, she had known her parents for years. And she had given them China. What a gift. Louie adored her, and the way her mother was acting, it was good to have some backup. After all, they were only there on weekends, at least until Owen was out of school. Louie needed more than that. Much more.

Thinking about Louie reminded her of group. Her mother. Reality. Good. She could get her father alone and try to talk about it. Something had to be done! There was no way she could take one more summer of pretending. No way!

Janie marched off to put away her packages and prepare her speech for Big Ben.

At the same time that Janie was thinking about what to say to her father, Ben Cowan was thinking about what to say to Janie. If anything, that is. The code of silence, or "the elephant in the living room," as some substance abuse counselor had described it, had gotten too large to ignore. He felt them all looking at him. He was the patriarch, after all. If he could fly into Ethiopia and rescue famine victims, why couldn't he help his own wife? Good question.

Ben pulled in his line and rebaited. How could he admit to them that he was scared? He had been stuck for so long. He was weak, under it all. Maybe that's why he needed so much macho stuff in his life. To mask it. He was sure that was what Donnie thought. Not in a judgmental way, Donnie never judged anyone, but professionally, he thought his son-in-law saw right through his defenses.

What could he tell Janie? That he had sold his balls for a

cushy life? That he was too old to start over and without that great big fat pad under his ass, he was afraid he couldn't make it? An architect who had settled for building castles in the sand. How could a man admit that to his only daughter? A daughter who adored him. At least, he thought she did. Jesus. He was too old to change and too young to die. If he didn't change now, that's all he had left to look forward to, withering and shriveling up inside. Death in life. And the loss of the only woman he had ever really loved. She had waited long enough. He would lose her and what good was left in him would go, too.

He had thought of every possible way out. If he took any of Delores's money, he would never be free; but how could he leave Delores like she was now, anyway? Impossible. He figured he had enough of his own assets to live five years. Art he had collected that had gone way up, several spec houses he had financed through his wife and paid her back out of the profits—things that felt like his own. But with nothing coming in, and not enough capital to really live on the interest, or at least, let's face it, to live anywhere near how he had lived, he'd be in trouble. Old and broke and beaten. That was not much of a package to offer a woman twenty years his junior. His stomach turned. God. He was scared.

He had set up a meeting with Rikki Bosco about a developmental deal. A fantastic parcel in North Haven, all woods and a view of the bay from every lot. He had a six-month option on the property and if he could get Bosco or one of his golden guys to back him, he could swing it. It was his best work. Not like all the trendy garbage popping up all over the farmland. These houses were pure. Timeless. Classic. So, that was something. He was counting on that. It got him up in the morning.

But it didn't solve the Delores problem. He had lived with her for almost forty years. They practically raised each

other. Babies. They had been frightened, virginal infants.
Who knew her grandfather would leave her everything?
Twenty years old and they were suddenly rich. And then
later after her father died, it was like the golden goose, for
crissakes.

The first two years had been fantastic. Jesus! The parties
they had! The brilliant young architect-to-be and his pretty,
sparkly, cultured young wife. Kids playing dress-up. The
money they spent! An apartment in Paris. Delores was the
penultimate Francophile and they had spent an entire year
just studying French architecture and literature and having
parties. A penthouse on Park Avenue bought as a lark for
nothing! Or nothing by today's terms.

Delores had Janie in 1950. Just in time for Korea. He had a
wife and a baby. He pulled the strings. He didn't have to go.
He joined the National Guard and went on with the party.

Maybe if he had gone to war, been a man, when it
counted? Spilt milk. Ben hated people who played that game.
But it was the beginning of the softening of his character. So
he hunted. He fished. He rode horses. "I'm a man! I'm Big
Ben Cowan, bigger than life!" Everyone bought it but himself. Even Delores. That was the saddest part. His poor wife.
She had swallowed the whole slimy bait. She needed him to
be bigger than life. So she could suffer his withdrawal. Humiliate herself with her love for him.

If love was what it was, or what it had ever been. He was
no longer sure. Maybe that was just his ego talking, or worse,
his cop-out, his rationalization for staying. How could he
leave this poor, frail dipsomaniac who would not last a day
without him?

Maybe it had nothing whatsoever to do with love, this
maladie à deux they shared. There had been so many terrible
times. The night he found her with her head in the brand-
new Garland range. The night she ran her car right off the

dead end into Mecox Bay. All the scenes, the long nights of hysterical threats. And what did *he* get out of it all? A lot of attention. The thrill of being that powerful, that necessary to someone. And the safety of having the home and family he had never really had as a child.

Her family had been a major part of his attraction to Delores in the first place. A father and grandfather to take him in and pat him on the back. Golf games with his new parents. Family dinners in their mansion outside of Scottsdale. A pretty, delicate young lady from a fine family. For a half orphan with no father and a mother too beaten down by her lot to offer much more than her best wishes? Heaven!

He had raised himself. Educated himself. He found his way to Taliesin and a world of concrete and wood and glass and stone. Powerful, majestic, and solid. Buildings. Buildings to build. And to help him through, a family to encourage him. A family who knew about art and architecture and poetry. A family who could teach him. He had married it as much as her, though, God knows, he didn't know it then.

Ten years, they played and then her father died, and the family died with him and they were left with each other, and more money than any thirty-year-old couple in the last two years of the halfway mark of this century could possibly handle.

He was offered a job on the faculty of Columbia's Department of Architecture and they came east for good, left with each other and a feisty little girl who held them together.

They both liked to drink. He was no saint. But he was a great big half-Jew, half-Irishman and he could handle it. She couldn't. At least after Lisa, his first real affair. He never counted the one-nighters, Jesus, that had started when Janie was born.

After Janie, Delores was terrified of him. She had almost

died. He could hardly get in her let alone an eight-pound baby trying to get out! She cringed every time he touched her. And he always had to be so gentle, when what he wanted was to ram her. A big man, with a big prick and a lot of rage and frustration!

Lisa was different. He was crazy about that kid. Some kid! First-year arch student with a bod like Sophia Loren and a mouth like Don Rickles. Pow. Ram. Ram.

Someone told Delores. He never found out who. And that was that. Then the drinking really started. Or rather, it took control of her, and of them.

So many lost years. He stopped teaching. He stopped practicing. He had lost his fire. And certainly money, making money wasn't necessary. She turned it all over to him. He managed everything. He gave *her* an allowance!

But it wasn't his. It had never felt like his. Even when he built this house. Every single inch of it had come from what was still alive of his creativity, but it had never felt like his.

Janie had gone off to college and they were left alone and so he built them a house so grand and so immense, that they could hide from each other effortlessly. They wandered around their corridors like Banquo's ghost, politely and cordially rattling the chains of their despair. He cooked and they dined, mostly with guests, but sometimes alone. Alone they dined and drank a lot. It made it so much easier.

Until Louie. Ben had found Louie at his last turning point. When his ability to lie to himself had run dry. He was running dry. All the cute young locals and mercy missions into the land of darkness could no longer shield him from himself.

Janie was having a very hard time dealing with her mother, and so she and Donnie and Owen came less and less. He built his daughter her own house as a bribe. Please now be here to keep us alive. You don't have to be too close, just don't abandon us, don't leave us to the empty rooms and each other's disappointment.

When the addition was done Ben flew off once again, to Africa. One morning an infant, one among thousands, was brought in. A baby boy covered with scabs, his small swollen belly filled with starvation's sick little joke: a fat belly on a starving child. The child looked into his eyes and Ben reached out for him and did not put him down for days.

Louie was named after his idols Louis Kahn, Louis Sullivan. Louis Armstrong. Louis was too old. Louie fit better. He had nursed him and brought him home—and brought laughter and light back into their dead house. Louie lit them up. Janie and Donnie and Owen came back and Delores went into therapy. He had found a miracle in the exquisite, grief-filled soul of an African child, come from a land they would never understand; bringing his spirit to save them.

It was a lot for a nine-month-old baby to be responsible for. Even Ben knew that. But it worked. It worked for a while. It worked until he fell in love with a woman. Who would have expected that? At his age and after he had found a substitute—a son to replace himself. A son he could father, the way he had longed to be fathered. No. No, Cowan. No spilt milk. He had met her. And here he was with a woman he wanted, a son he had promised in his deepest soul to do right by, and a wife. A wife he no longer wanted to live with, but was terrified of living without.

He had a bite. He tightened his hold and reeled it in. So deftly. His biceps pumped. He still felt so strong. He was still a man, goddammit. He was too young to give up!

"Hey, Pappy, way to go!" He turned. His daughter was marching toward him with that spunky quick stride; her six-year-old stride. He knew what was coming. What she wanted. They had lost each other to the elephant. Can't get too intimate when there's something that enormous you don't want to talk about.

It was time to find the guts to change that. He needed his baby girl back on his team. What could he say? Nothing. He'd be strong and silent and listen to her. It was easy with Janie. How did two such taciturn people produce such a garrulous kid?

He would listen and he would tell her she was right, and that something had to be done and he was working on it. He wanted to talk to Donnie. Maybe an intervention? He had read about that. If Delores got herself together, maybe she could deal with it. It was really his only hope.

Janie reached him. Her hair was curled around her cute freckled little face. Thirty-nine years old and she still looked sixteen to him. She was out of breath.

"So, okay. Daddy. We gotta talk. No bullshit, all right?"

He smiled. He knew her so well. She was so scared of him, she must have practiced every possible opening line. And chosen street-smart macho. Good choice, Janie my baby girl. He smiled at her. "Okay, kid. Let's get it over with."

June 15

Well, here I am again, better late than never. I feel like such a failure. I promise myself every day, I'll write and then something happens and by the time I get a chance, I'm too tired.

My poor mother! I had no idea kids could be so much work! Not to mention the questions. I mean, Louie must be the smartest, most curious seven-year-old on earth! Today, he asked me why his parents starved to death and we have all this food in the fridge. He wanted to know why didn't we

91

just send all of our food to Africa and no one would starve anymore. You try that one at eight o'clock in the morning!

I think Owen gets out of school today, and the Jamiesons or Janie and Owen, at least, are coming down for the whole summer. That's great! It's much less depressing here when they're around.

Their friends the Harts and their son Jeremy come over a lot and I really like them. I love the way Gina Hart talks to her husband. I've never heard a wife be so, well, I guess outspoken is the word. She's just hilarious. I mean, she tells him just what's on her mind and she teases him all the time. But it's not mean. I think he really eats it up. Everyone laughs a lot. Even Mrs. Cowan joins in. Last weekend Harry showed up for Sunday brunch with six copies of *The New York Times* Sunday paper! I mean, it was a huge pile of paper! No one paid any attention, but I must have looked shocked or something (he just raced around passing them out to all the adults). Gina saw my face and she told me that Harry was so anal compulsive, he couldn't bear it if anyone looked at his paper and didn't fold it back properly, so he finally stopped complaining and decided it was easier just to buy everyone their own copy! I know I can use that for a character in a story someday.

A lot has happened since I wrote last time. The worst thing was coming home from Bay Street and finding Mrs. Cowan passed out on the beach. I thought she was dead. I didn't even see her at first and I almost stepped on her! I talked to my mom about it; I mean, I'm here as an employee and all, but it just seems wrong not to tell someone about it. I just did not know what to do!

My mom was great (my mom *is* great). She said she thought Mr. Cowan was well aware of the problem and so were the Jamiesons and it wasn't my responsibility to caretake her, that I'd just put myself in the middle of something that was probably much too complicated for me to begin to understand. She said I should just lay back. I think she's right. Anyway, after that, something changed, because Mrs. Cowan seems to be much better. I haven't seen her drinking at all and she's more connected. So, I guess I'm off the hook for now. It was real embarrassing for a few days, though. I mean, she knew I knew.

Next Saturday is Mr. Cowan's sixtieth birthday party and Janie invited my mom. I'm psyched! Also, well, really not also, I mean it's really the most major part of this entry, I met a guy.

His name is Kenny and he is so amazingly handsome. He's a mechanic at Vintage Classics. I met him at Bay Street, that's a club in Sag Harbor all the kids are hanging out at this summer. Usually, it's a real geek scene—lots of week-enders trying to be really cool, bopping to reggae bands with their Rolling Rocks clutched in their fists and a lot of Guidos from New Jersey.

I mean the Jersey girls all look totally like prostitutes and the guys drive 'vettes and wear their collars up in back. So gross. I can't stand it when they scope me up. It makes my skin crawl.

But Kenny isn't like that, at all. My mom's upset because he's not in college, but he's really smart and he's a very good mechanic and I know that when he gets enough money to-gether he'll go back to school. He's told me incredible stories about the rich people who buy cars there. I just know I'll get some good material out of it.

Last night Kenny took me to a housewarming party in East Hampton at this lady Fritzi Ferris's new house. She hangs out with Kenny's boss, Frankie Karsh. What a scene! The house is on Georgica Pond and you drive down a drive-way that's about a mile long before you can even see it. It's modern and really big—not like the Cowans', but really big for a single person (maybe she has a kid. I thought someone said she did, but I didn't see one). Anyway, every single thing in the entire house is white. I am *serious*! Everything. Even the flowers! Amazing.

She's kind of amazing, too. I've never met anyone like her before. She looks like that character in the old Little Abner comic strip. Daisy Mae? I think that's it. I mean she's like really gorgeous and she's pretty old, I guess. But you'd never know it, except that she dresses kind of old, I mean stockings and high heels and lots of makeup and jewelry. I think if my mom did herself up like that, she'd look a little bit like her, but my mom would never do it.

Anyway, it was all catered and there were maids in black uniforms and French champagne and all these trendy people. The Harts were there and the Jamiesons and that billionaire Rikki Bosco that everyone at the Cowans' keeps talking about; he was with this couple from Hollywood, the Riverses. I almost flipped out. I read an article on her in *Elle* and he directed *Loose Change*, which is like my all-time favorite movie. She's really beautiful. Really sophisticated. You know she thinks she's really hot and I usually hate that, but she was nice, too. Sort of. I actually talked to them.

Rikki Bosco was with this downtown clubbie girl called The Match. She is a really crazy girl. And really funny. I was sitting with Janie and Gina and she came over and asked Janie for a cigarette and just plopped down and started talking, and we were all just rolling around with laughter. She told us how when she was a kid, she couldn't afford to have her hair done, so she had a deal with this hairdresser in the West Village, she called it "blow-dry for blowjob." He would do her hair and then she'd—you know. I was really shocked. But somehow, whatever she said, it just seemed okay. Kind of innocent. I know that sounds weird, but it did.

She gives massages and Janie and Gina got her card. They

thought she was just great and Janie even invited her to the next Clan of the Cave JAPs meeting. Oh, God, I'm starting to sound like Owen!

She did seem kind of nervous, though. She kept watching Katarina Rivers and every time she was near Rikki Bosco she smoked another cigarette.

Kenny told me Frankie Karsh really has the hots for Mrs. Ferris, even though she's a lot older than he is. She's kind of hard to figure out. I mean, she looks so sexy and Hollywood and all, but she almost stood in the corner all night. She was hanging on to Frankie as if her life depended on it. Sort of unsure of herself. I had the feeling she didn't really know any of the guests very well. Kenny told me Frankie had really put the list together, to help her get into the social swim. Yick.

I hate that part of being out there. It seems so much worse than I remember it. Just like the city with sand or something. Everyone was talking business or real estate, and the men were like comparing status symbols. Who had the newest cellular phone, whose FAX machine had more special features, who helicoptered in (much cooler than the Jitney). The whole scene makes me nauseous. But it was fun to go. I've never been to a party like that before and Kenny was so sweet to me. I had a lot of champagne and he just drove me home, he didn't try to take advantage of the situation or anything.

I don't want to sleep with him yet. (I mean I do oh my God, I really do, but I don't want him to think he can just have what he wants that fast.) I'm trying to be together about this. Besides, my mom is so disease crazy, I can hardly even think of sex anymore without some gross, terrible picture in my mind. Besides, I want to know that he really likes me first and he's spoiled. He's so adorable, he can probably

have any girl he wants. I don't want to be just another conquest. (This love stuff is really hard!)

Well, that's about it. Now school's out, things are picking
up out here. The renters are swarming in and it's already
twice as crowded as last year. My tan is coming along and
I've got seven hundred dollars in the bank (I cheated. I
bought some clothes).

Louie starts day camp next week, so I should have more
time to write and read. I really need to rev up my brain cells.
Well, until next time, I'll sign off.

If anyone had privately asked the individual members of
the Saturday dawn fishing excursion, if they really wanted to
be going out that day at 5:00 A.M. in the summer rain to catch
bluefish, each of them would have admitted they did not.
That is often how it is with plans made in advance. They
become traps. Traps of commitment to the other planners.
Off they went. China, hung over from her date with Kenny
and wanting nothing so much as a Saturday sleep-in. Big
Ben, exhausted from a sleepless night of decision making and
wanting only to be with his woman. Donnie, angry at his
father-in-law for his distance and stressed from his week of
family and patient crises; and Louie, still terrified of the
ocean and repulsed by the mere sight of dead fish.

But once they were out at sea, fortified with strong black
coffee and a pile of Isabel's homemade doughnuts, they
cheered up.

Donnie sat quietly as he always did, fishing in his own
style. Patient and calm. Strong when he had to be, but not
assertive. Janie called him a "Zen fisherman," and he liked
that. It fit. He talked to the fish and he thought about fishing
as a cosmic metaphor.

Louie came up and sat beside him while Big Ben, who

fished like he did everything else, loudly and aggressively, was giving China instructions at the back of the boat.

Louie watched Donnie, holding his small pole beside him, trying to ignore the grisly worm remains on the end of his hook.

Donnie smiled at him. "You okay, champ? Stomachwise?"

Louie nodded. "Yep. So far, so good. At least it stopped raining. That always makes the boat bump more." Louie's small brow narrowed. "How come you just sit still like that when you fish and Poppa runs around so much?"

"Because we think about it in different ways. Poppa thinks about fishing as if it were a sport. He wants to win the game. So he goes after the fish as if the fish were his opponent. He stalks the fish."

"Like hunting. Like they were lions?"

"Exactly. You are one smart fellow. You have that figured out."

"Just like a shrink, right, Dr. J. ?"

Donnie laughed. "Better! Like a philosopher!"

Louie's brow tightened again. "What's a phil-osfer?"

"Well. The way I fish? I fish, *philosophically.* I think about what fishing means. That's what philosophers do. They think about what things mean."

"That's their job?"

"Sometimes."

"How does it work with fishing?"

"Well, I don't think about fishing as a sport. When I sit here I think about the fish as symbols in a way."

"What's a—"

"Symbol? This isn't easy to explain, champ. So it's okay if it doesn't make sense."

Louie nodded solemnly. He always felt when he was with Dr. J. that if he listened very hard and asked enough questions, he would be able to understand everything and he wouldn't be so afraid anymore.

"Okay. A symbol means something stands in for something else. Like when you and Owen play Old Maid and you use matches for money. The matches are a *symbol* for money. They stand in for it."

Donnie watched him to make sure he understood before he went on. He could feel tears filling his eyes. Children in general moved him almost too powerfully, and Louie moved him more than any other child ever had. Even more than Owen in some ways, because Owen's search, his childhood quest for information, his child view of the world and his clarified truth were not tinged with despair. Louie's honesty came darker, filled with primal pain and fear.

Donnie felt responsible to Louie for finding the deepest, most transparent truth within himself.

He had always seen himself as Louie's guide through the darkened attic of his loss. Poppa gave him gusto and the protection of his powerful presence. Donnie saw his role as the hand with the flashlight on Halloween night. Trying to guide this surrogate son through the makeshift fun house, helping him learn where the ghosts and goblins were hiding. Helping him find his own way into the light. Into the kitchen with the candy and the laughter.

Louie grinned. "I get it."

"Okay. So, I see the fish as *symbols* of man. There they are all swimming blindly around in the deep blue sea. Schools of them, *millions* of them in this vast, endless ocean and one, every once in a while, grabs the hook. If the one next to it was a second faster or slower or hungrier or whatever, it would have been him. But it wasn't.

"It was this guy. Why? Why him and not the one next to him? Is it chance? Does God choose? Every time someone is born or dies, does God sit up there with a great big list and

98

say, 'He goes. She stays.' Does he do it for every single ant and plant as well? Do we choose? Man or beast? Do we decide when to die like that? Do fish and pigeons decide? Or is it all just blind luck. Totally random and without a plan. That's what I think about when I fish. Why that one and not the other one. And that's why I throw them all back. Which, as you know, drives Poppa crazy. And when I throw them back, am I interfering with God's plan? Am I God? Or does the fish just get lucky today. That's philosophy. That's why I fish this way."

Louie put his pole down and wrapped his arms around Donnie's neck.

"If I ever stop hating fish, I'm going to fish like you. Don't tell Poppa. I don't want to upset him. But it makes me so sad when he, you know. Kills them. Even before I knew about symbols."

Big Ben came up behind them and swung a huge dripping bluefish in front of them. "While you two girls were sissy-talking, China and I caught us a beauty fit for a feast! Louie, grab that pole. Your Poppa is going to show you how the pros do it."

Louie looked at Donnie and Donnie winked at him, letting him know it was okay to be scared. "Hey, Poppa. Since you and China are on a roll, let Louie throw his back if he gets one. Okay?"

Big Ben laughed and lifted Louie up with his one free arm. "Sure! If that's what you want, kid. But you may be surprised. You may want to mount it on your wall. Donnie never catches anything worth keeping or he'd be carving them up with the rest of us. Right, Doc?"

Donnie laughed. "Don't want to make the old man look bad."

China found them. Her cheeks were red with joy. "My

God! I did it! I caught a fish. I don't believe it! Louie, it's fun. Really! Try with me!"

Louie wiggled, signaling Big Ben to put him down. He didn't want to look like a baby in front of China. If that meant catching a fish, then he would do that, too. Dr. J. smiled at him and nodded his approval.

Louie grabbed his pole and followed China back to her fishing chair. Big Ben put his powerful, brawny hands on his son-in-law's tense shoulders and kneaded the muscles. Donnie sighed. It was Ben's way of saying he was sorry.

"Want a beer? You're tight as a tick."

"No, thanks. Nothing's as good as the hands of the master."

Ben laughed. "Get it while you can, boy. Old age will work its way down to my fingertips any day now." He paused. "Thanks for coming, Donnie. I gotta tell you, I'm feeling sixty. Louie wears me out. I don't think I could do it alone, without you and Janie. I don't want to let him down, but shit; I forgot how hard it was. Maybe I never knew. Janie was different. Girls are, I guess, and I wasn't as involved then."

"No. You weren't. But it's not too late for her, either."

Big Ben's hands stopped moving for a moment. He was not off the hook any more than the poor blind-eyed bluefish at his feet. He wasn't surprised. His son-in-law was a different kind of man than he was. But one thing he had always been sure of, a man, he was. A stronger, more honorable one than himself. Donnie had shamed him by not being bought off, literally or in any other way, since the day they had first met. He loved him, but he was afraid of him.

He pushed his fingers more deeply into Donnie's neck. "Yeah. You're right, Doc. Still got a lot of fence mending to do. Keep me on track, will you?" For a moment, he was afraid he was going to cry.

100

A HOUSE IN THE HAMPTONS

Donnie patted his hand, without turning around. "I'll try, Ben. But you don't need me for that. You've got all the information you require. You're going to do just fine. With both your kids."

"Poppa! Poppa! I've got something. Come quick!" Big Ben let go of Donnie and walked around to face him. Somehow it was terribly important that Donnie believe this. "I'm trying my best. I know it may not seem like it. It may be too little, too late. But please know that I'm trying to do what is right."

They held each other's eyes, and then they let each other go.

"Poppa!"

Big Ben Cowan went back to help his son with something that he knew how to do.

Lady Mariella St. John sighed and closed her eyes. "Oh, dear girl, those naughty neck muscles are practically frozen. Do be a love and give them your full attention."

The Match pressed harder. "It's the phone, ya know. All that talking on the phone. Try switchin' ears." She put more menthol oil on her fingers and grabbed a great big slab of Lady Mariella's glistening fat shoulder and probed deeper. It was getting through all the flesh to the goddamn muscle that was such hard work.

Lady Mariella was one of The Match's 007 clients—"overweight, over sixty, and seven figures in the bank." She lived in a massive Dune Road Southampton estate that had belonged to her third husband. She was only there for June and July, but she kept the house running with hot and cold water and hot and cold servants all year long. It made The Match sick. She could feed all the homeless in Grand Central for what it cost her to heat the damn place.

She was never alone. Sometimes, even during her weekly

massage, members of her entourage—or, as The Match called them, "the fairy godmothers," swept in and out chirping and soaring, creating a sort of human estuary with Lady M, the golden bird-feeder of all time, calling out orders to one or another while The Match probed the depths of her tense yet flaccid flesh.

The Match thought the group this summer looked a little seedy. "AIDS, darling," Lady M had explained. "I keep losing all my stunning boys to that damn disease. Some of them were really quite irreplaceable. That kind of style and elegance can't just be bought or taught and all the best ones are gone now. *Très tragique.* These are pale imitations. I have a scout in London and one in Manhattan and the poor fellow was reduced to cruising the Pines beach at Fire Island to find me a plausible group to interview."

To The Match, Lady M sounded like a slave trader, one of those characters from a Clavell miniseries, *Tai-Pan* or something—but the truth was that the guys were pretty disgusto. This year there were only four (last year there had been at least seven).

They were all very well dressed, of course, and very attentive. But to her ear, they all sounded a tad hostile and bitchy and they were, on the average, at least ten years older than last year. "Guess the ones that haven't been such hot shit for a while, stay healthier," The Match had offered, but Lady M was too depressed by the downgrading of her staff to even respond.

A knock. It was Glenn, the leader of the pack. "Lady St. John, forgive me, but I have been trying to get some lunch into Oswald for an hour now and he simply will not eat."

"Did you get the veal from the butcher in the village?"

Glenn stiffened. "No. He wasn't open yet. I got the veal at the A&P, which should be more than adequate for a fox terrier."

102

A HOUSE IN THE HAMPTONS

"Time to turn." The Match wanted out of there. This was a hundred-an-hour gig, but she was beginning to feel the money wasn't worth it.

Lady Mariella rolled over, her sagging breasts flashing out of the Turkish towels for Glenn to see. Glenn's eyes looked glassy.

"Dear man. When I say veal from the village I mean veal from the village. Of *course* he won't eat it. He's used to the best. Now, please, have Arnold drive you back and get it right." Lady M sighed and scratched her nose with her thirty-carat diamond ring. "See what I mean. There is no quality, no service, no matter how much money you have. I won't go near the First Class section of an airliner anymore. If I can't get on a Concorde or hire a plane, I don't go. First class used to be quite civilized. Now it's filled with engineers with upgrade certificates. I can't bear it!"

Lady M continued, but The Match had disengaged. Her mind was elsewhere—Rikki and Katarina where, to be exact. The Riverses had been at Rikki's for two weeks. She, however, was coming only on the weekends and even then, she was racing around to clients, not basting by the pool like Katarina the Kunt.

Rikki still hadn't said a word about her coming out for August. She was going to have to push it, after all she had clients to schedule and plans to make. Sure, he had given her the Porsche and lots of nice clothes and the diamond studs and the Rolex, but he sure as hell didn't support her. She didn't even live with him.

So, okay. So the guy had an ex-wife and that had been a real greed scene. She could understand his being paranoid. But it had been over for years, before he was even rich. The whole thing was pretty weird.

Two weeks of the Royal Couple with herself as the entertainment. She hadn't a clue what they talked about when she

was in the city. It seemed like they all just hung around
waiting for her to show up and amuse them. The way it was
going she could probably have farted and gotten a laugh out
of Joey Rivers. Was he for real or what?

Whatever, she was getting tired of it. The Ellen Mary idea
hadn't worked. No one could remember, except Joey Rivers.
She had just given it up. She wasn't stupid. She couldn't
make Rikki love her. That was the thing about love. You
can't make anyone love you and you can't make anyone stop
loving you. That much she knew.

She had always thought that all the bullshit people do
about love was a joke. "I love you like a sister. Like a brother.
I love you, but I'm not *in* love with you. What a crock. It was
like cosmetics. All of the ad hype. This cream for your
elbows, this one for your arms, but not for your legs. Give us
a break! Cream was cream and love was love. Period.

Rikki hardly even saw her anymore. The minute Katarina
strolled by, he was like one of those lab rats with the elec-
trodes on his bean, off to Ozland. So far she hadn't been able
to figure out any way to handle it. She cried a lot. But never
in front of Rikki. In front of Rikki she was cocky as shit. Not
that he even noticed all the extra attitude.

But, so far, he hadn't told her not to come. Maybe because
the Riverses found her so fucking funny. So every Friday she
showed up and did her act. Public and private. Yuk, yuk.
Suck, suck. And during the private part, the sucking and
fucking, they were both fantasizing about Katarina Rivers.
Rikki about fucking her and The Match about shooting her.

It hurt. She loved the creep. How could she possibly compete with a *Vogue* fantasy girl? She would have to pay closer
attention to the under-the-surface of this slut. She needed to
think of her as a great big inflated scratch-and-sniff, get past
the jealousy and psych the bitch out.

One thing The Match knew. She was too good to be true.

A HOUSE IN THE HAMPTONS

She just knew it. A Scotch tape job under all the la-di-da. There was something out of whack. One of the hoses wasn't connected to the faucet. She had to find the fucker!

If there was one thing she wasn't, it was a quitter. Jesus H! If she was able to get herself out of Brooklyn and away from the Gargoyle sisters, all those scary aunts that had raised her, or mutilated her to be more accurate—she sure as hell wasn't going to give up now! Not without one seriouso, dirty girl, gutter-rolling fight! Come on Ellen Mary, get it together here!

Lady M droned on while she kneaded her pudgy wrinkled soles with her long slender fingers.

"I had lunch at Charlotte Ford's yesterday and all anyone at my table talked about was how they were protecting themselves against the threat of kidnapping. That gives you an idea of the level of the guests! No one really important has a home on the beach anymore. It's just too hard to secure! That's what they said, and I felt like a bloody fool! I was the only one! Apparently, all the beachfront property is being sold at high profit to Wall Street people. No one would want to kidnap them!

"Charlotte always sits with her back to the wall, like John Gotti or some criminal. That way no one could sneak up on her. It's really quite sensible."

"Yeah. I'll have to try that." She was almost done. Then Bonita Thomas and she was finished. Jesus, she was tired. Tired and edgy. She couldn't wait to get back to Rikki's and she knew why, too. Joey was in the city overnight and she was working all day. They were there alone. Alone together.

"I hear that that Hungarian car dealer Frankie Karsh went through his entire Rolodex and invited all of his better customers to a housewarming in East Hampton for his latest conquest. Everyone but Bonita, I bet. That Frankie has slept with, well, I shan't exaggerate, but I fancy he's had a large percentage of the socialites who've bought cars there. So pathetic! The next thing you know Princess Di will be dining with rock stars. Shocking, really!"

"Oh, jeez, Lady M. It'll never come to that! Those rock stars are far too snooty." She couldn't help it. It had just slipped out. Who did this broad think she was talking to, the fucking Duchess of Windsor? The one who ironed her money? Forget about it!

The gleaming, greasy Englishwoman opened her eyes and smiled, ever so slightly. "Oh. Well, do forgive me. I sometimes forget to whom I am speaking."

The Match was screwing the tops back onto all of her special oils. "No problem." She had gotten off easy, at least, if Glenn was any example. Guess you had to be a fucking fox terrier to get any respect in this zoo.

"Let me get the tub going." She helped the time-worn, towel-draped woman up and led her, like Nero, to her bath.

"Wanna go for a ride? I just got the Lamborghini back." Rikki was trying to sound nonchalant, but his heart was doing double time.

Katarina looked up from her book, and pushed her Vuarnets back up on her hair. "I'd love to!"

It was happening. The way he had planned a thousand times in his head. The Match was giving massages in Southampton and Joey was in the city having meetings. They were alone.

"I'll have Jakie bring it up. Meet me out front in five."

She stood up. She was golden from lolling by his pool, his pond, his ocean. She turned and started down the lawn toward the guest house. "Just want to grab a scarf."

"Sure." He watched her. She was wearing a flimsy little silk minidress. He could see her nipples underneath. God. God, how he wanted her. Be cool, Rikki. Think of this as

106

A HOUSE IN THE HAMPTONS

Wall Street. Think of this as the biggest fucking score of your life. Don't let it show.

She slid in beside him and he started to ease the luscious purring beauty, his handmade icon, his ultimate status toy down the endless drive. He stopped. He had a better idea. She was looking at him, puzzled. A slow half smile on her beautiful face.

He smiled back. "You wanna?"

She stopped smiling. "Are you joking?"

"Naw. If you wanna try. Be my guest."

"I'd adore it!" Her eyes shone.

Good, Rikki boy. Very good move. Steady now.

He opened his door and jumped out. She slid across, her skirt moving up to her panties, panties he had fantasized her not wearing, and took the wheel. Rikki strutted around and slowly lowered himself into the warm perfumy spot that had been hers.

"Just take it real easy. This bitch has a mind of her own. Very, very sensitive. Zero to fifty in a blink. So easy, okay?"

She was entranced. "Okay."

Easy. She obeyed his every instruction. He talked to her. Softly. Gently. "Hold it back. Slow. Head for 114, we can cut through the back way to the old Montauk Highway and open her up. Slowly. Start moving her up now. Get her out of second, that's right."

He was fucking her with the car. Teasing her. She wanted to go faster. She could hardly stand it, but he wouldn't let her, she wasn't going to come, yet; not until he was good and ready. They hit 114 and he let her go a little, then he pulled her back. She was totally under his spell. Her lips moist and parted, her little nothing dress, clinging to her small perfect breasts, her long perfect legs; her hair covered by a soft piece of silk, sailing behind them.

East Hampton, Amagansett, almost. Not yet, not yet.

Now! He let her go. She was good. A little wobbly, but who wouldn't be, the first time in this bitch monster. She loved this. She was excited. It was the first time he had seen her unselfconscious. Unmasked. And he had done it. He had given this to her. Faster. Faster. He let her fly. Let her keep going. His cock was throbbing under his sweats. He didn't care if she saw. But she was oblivious. She was in her own ecstasy. Now.

He let her have the whole ride. All the way back. She was calm now. Depleted. Elated and exhausted. Her dress was moist with sweat. Pieces of her tangled hair stuck to her face. Her breathing was shallow. She had been there.

"Pull it up over here." He pointed to the washing area built up into the sides deep in the back of the garage. She did as she was told. It was dark at the back. Dark and cold and still. King Rikki's tomb. Akhenaton's second resting place. She got out. The cement was raised on the driver's side, and when she stood beside the car, Rikki's face was level with her pubis. He was now in her seat. The driver's seat. She stood, leaning into the car, dazed and open. Not like herself.

"My God! That was fantastic. I've dreamed about driving like that. I, can't even describe how I feel, I'm so, so high!"

Rikki watched her face. Was this the moment to bid? Was this the deal closer or the deal breaker? Easy, boy.

Instinct had always served Rikki well. Instinct answered for him. She was still standing close up against the car. He leaned forward and ever so slowly, ever so gently, he pressed his tongue against her skirt. He waited. She tightened slightly. But she didn't move away. Okay, Rikki, make your offer. His tongue was filled with saliva, and he pressed deeper, using it like a finger, licking her dress up with it. Pushing it over her vagina. Now, she moans. She helps him. She pulls the tiny piece of silk over her pussy aside and lets his tongue find her. "Oh, God," she whispers.

A HOUSE IN THE HAMPTONS

Rikki finds her. He tongues her sweet, shiny black mound. Her clitoris is right there. He knows how to do this. The Match taught him how to do this right. He shares it all with his dream girl. He quickens his pace. It is his turn to drive. And he knows just when, he feels her like he feels his car, faster, faster, now!

He takes her all the way to the wall. She screams. And his tongue is flooded with her. Sweet dream girl juice, all over his tongue. His cock is so hard, it looks like a second gear-shift. But he knows how to close this deal. He knows how to save the bargaining point. He retracts his tongue, a salamander after the big feed. She slumps forward, her hand clutching the side of his machine for support. "I don't believe this. I, that's never happened to me before."

He smiles up at her. Her eyes are still half closed. She looks drugged. This is more than he had even fantasized. Had he awakened the frigid princess? Given her something little swagger-smirk hasn't been able to. Cracked the big nut. Perfect. Unbelievably, fucking perfect.

"Let me walk you back," he says, so softly, so strongly. He takes her hand to steady her and eases himself up out over the back of the car. She looks confused. He presses his erection against her and kisses her ever so sweetly. She moans and moves closer, but he knows what to do now. How to win this game. He steps back just one step and puts his arm around her.

"Not now. Baby," he whispers in her ear, and leads her, like an accident victim, still too stunned to understand what has happened, away from the scene.

4

Every Sunday of the summer a ritual repeats itself in various parks and school playgrounds up and down the Hamptons. The ritual is called softball and it is a very serious one. An epiphany, actually.

The most revered of the rituals, the ceremonies to which the most ambitious and status conscious of the players (players being mostly male and members of certain social tribes aspire), are the Sag Harbor and Easthampton games. The rules for acceptance are hard and fast, like the balls themselves; like the boys of summer.

The aspirant must be somewhere between thirty-five and death and the possessor of a baggy, threadbare, stained, torn, sweaty, and/or completely anti-chic, jocko, color-blind ensemble including, a worn cap, sweatpants, and/or ragged out of style shorts and a T-shirt or faded moldy sweatshirt. The T-shirt and/or sweatshirt should have suitable emblems such as: the name of a sports team, college or pro (L.A. Dodgers, Notre Dame, Yale, etc.), or some clever saying such as "I may be getting older, but I'm never growing up," which actually sums up the entire spirit of the Sunday softball phenomenon.

The aspirants must not have shaved for at least twenty-four hours prior and should, preferably, be a tad hung over or at least have affected the disheveled look made fashionable by Jack Klugman and Walter Matthau in both versions of *The Odd Couple.*

All players must "know the game." Know it from the corpuscles up. Know it as only boys who had traded baseball cards, memorized batting averages, and dreamed of playing for the Mets can know it. Star-struck kids who played stickball and park ball and Little League and high school and dreamed of the majors—of meeting Mickey Mantle and hitting one out of the park. Who knew baseball in the biblical sense. And who were, above all else, one of the guys.

The Sag Harbor game is famous for its players. New York literati, show biz, art, and publishing whiz kids. Mort Zuckerman, Paul Simon, Pete Hamill, Eric Fischl, Alan Alda, George Plimpton, and the like. Being a name brand helps, but it won't get you in if you're faking it. If you can't take a mean dirty slide into second. If you don't love it like crazy.

It also helps if the aspirant looks as if he couldn't walk, much less run, from the bench to the mound. A paunch, a limp, a bad back, really help keep the mood as it is supposed to be. Mean and painful and serious. More Babe Ruth than Keith Hernandez, more old-time play ball and fuck the umpire, Yankee Stadium in the days of a little boy and his dad sharing male magic.

Language is important. It is a short, often verbless or nounless language, learned in junior high school—a clear indicator of the real guys. It cannot be copied. It must come from within and like pig latin, it can only be learned as a boy of summer—a spastic, unconscious response to certain stimuli. To softball. "Play ball!" "Gimme a fat one!" "Way ta protect!" "Save me a bat!" "Way ta go!"

It is a deceptively simple speak. A male shorthand that

communicates volumes. It says: We are still boys, playing as boys, underneath these beards and paunches and graying hairs. We are still boys of summer. Of hope and comradeship. Of life being reduced to one fine point. One diamond-shaped sphere with one set of rules. Rules that can be learned, and understood. Rules that are clear and by which we can define ourselves. We are part of a team; all for one and one for all and we know only that we never want it to end, this game. We never want it to be too dark to see the ball; to be called back home, to grown-ups and pot roast and other kinds of rules. We want only to remain here, with one more time at bat coming up. One more chance to do it right. To hit it solid and smooth and hear the sound of the team roaring behind you, cheering you on. "Way to go!"

Every summer Sunday, these men rise early and throw on their threadbare battle gear, and wait outside for one another to honk. That is part of it, too. Going together, grumpy and tired and unshowered. A team of boys, too young to drive themselves. They converge. Teams are formed. Ritual decisions are made. A player short here; a bandaged knee there. It starts.

In the beginning there are few spectators. This is also part of the ritual. Wives are supposed to be left snug in their beds, while the boys go off to war. Wives and girlfriends may arrive later to retrieve their sweaty, muddy, stiff, and cranky guys and whisk them home in their own cars. Their Mercedeses and Jeeps and Range Rovers. Whisk their heroes back to safety; to cold beer and hot showers and stories of woe and glory.

The boys of summer like their wives and children to appear in the last couple of innings. To sit in support, sympathy (jeez, poor Pop, his back's really bothering him—what a slide) but not to react out loud. They can gossip among themselves (quietly), sip container coffee, or leaf through the

Sunday *Times;* these are all fine. But they are not to wave, shout support or disapproval at a call, or in any way act as if they were mothers (shades of Little League!). They are not to interfere or call attention in any way to their guys.

Those are the rules. Once you have been accepted as a player, you can remain one, summer to summer, until you fall, like Casey at the Bat or grow too old to care. As unthinkable a thought as that is to the boys of summer. A thought as fearsome as impotence, bankruptcy, or death. The same as death. The loss of the boy self—the growing up of the child within the man.

No one wants that. Not even the wives, who roll their eyes and make fun of their little boys, running around in those disgusting clothes, acting as if this raggedy-ass, silly little game was serious business.

They make jokes and cluck their tongues and sip their coffee and wait to take them home and listen to their war stories and rub their sore and throbbing middle-aged muscles; but they would not trade it. No woman really wants a man without the boy inside. What would she have left to do for him then? Without the wry, accepting, waiting-in-the-stands kind of female superiority and support. The support of her fella. The nurturer of that child/man. It feels nice, to offer that. Because with men, especially men like these, urbanized, successful, and defended, there is so little chance to give in so simple and uncomplicated and gentle a way. This is a lullaby between man/child and mother/girl.

The men who are too grown up for such needs have lost something precious in themselves. They have lost the singular spark that only belongs to the male; an ability to throw themselves totally into the play with all of their unbridled, innocent, concentrated energy. To be that clear and simple and focused; to be that young.

It is something that women do not have—their missing

114

link—and so they are able to absorb it through their boy/ men. Without it, there is something lost. Something hopeful and free has died. They offer their men the protection of the waiting arms, the cluck of comfort, and in return they are given the chance to reconnect with their amputated boy selves, without losing their safe and all-seeing place on the bench.

These are the unwritten rules of the game. And how important they are is known only when someone breaks one; an outsider or newcomer who doesn't know the score. And then the retribution, the glaring silent stares, the shouted insult, are as fast and vicious as a spitball on a mittless palm.

Gina and Janie never went to the softball game anymore. They had paid their dues. About ten years' worth. Even Owen and Jeremy wouldn't go anymore. But this Sunday was different. This Sunday, Katarina and Joey Rivers were going to be there, or so Harry said. Rikki Bosco was on the team now and Joey Rivers was his houseguest and they were short a player, so Rivers was on. For that Janie and Gina would get up.

Also, there was the now ever-present topic of conversation, or as Janie called it, "As the Fritzi Turns." Everywhere Harry and Donnie were, they were, just keeping an eye on their holdings.

This summer was already tilted off-center. All of them almost twitched with the sense of something out of balance; some holding pattern before change—before one of life's little pop flies. They were all searching the skies, feeling it up there somewhere, sensing the danger, but not knowing where, when, or on whom it would land.

Gina honked and Janie raced out carrying her bulging Hermès tote bag, into which she stuffed every conceivable thing anyone could possibly need if leaving home for a week. Once Gina had even found an iron in it.

Janie flung the bag, which was almost as big as she was, onto the front seat and flung herself in beside it.

"How can you already be so harried and frantic and it's only nine o'clock on a Sunday morning?" Gina swung the Volvo around and headed toward Ocean.

Janie lit a cigarette. "I was whirling. I couldn't sleep again, this damn thing with my mother has me so freaked out, so I went out onto the beach early and whirled and I got so dizzy, I threw up and then I had to lie there for a while, before I could try it again. You need at least fifteen minutes of it, but that's so damn hard because you get so dizzy and sick."

"Janie. What the hell are you talking about?"

"Didn't I tell you about whirling?"

"Think not. I would have remembered that one."

"It's new. Erica Hess got me into it. It's like the Dervishes in India. You go to this place in New Jersey and there are hundreds of people in a meadow and the Mystic is up on a hill and you all whirl. It frees the spiritual core. The goal is to get beyond the disorientation and really find the center."

"Give me a break."

"I didn't tell you about the whirling?"

"Janie! You are making me so crazy! I thought you were through with all that trendy bullshit. I mean, Erica Hess? The woman spends her time taking Porsche driving classes and polo lessons. The woman is an I-married-for-money space case. *This* is your new guru? Am I losing you? You whirl. You get dizzy. You throw up. You lie down. You get up. What are you talking about?"

Janie put out her cigarette and burst into tears. "Shit. I'm going off again, aren't I? I've been so good. But I got scared. I just did. And you know me. When I get anxious, I get trendy. It's like an addiction. Oh, that too. I ate two one-pound bags of M&Ms last night. I'm in trouble here."

Gina pulled the car onto Mecox and stopped. "Hey, honey, I'm sorry. I didn't mean to sound so bitchy. I'm fairly unglued myself. Maybe it's a full moon or something. I've been feeling completely crazy all month."

Janie blew her nose. "Yeah. Me too. I hate it when my feeling crazy lasts longer than my premenstrual cover story. Donnie says I've invented an entirely new menses cycle that covers a twenty-five-day premenstrual period and a three-day normal emotional state. The sad truth is, he's right."

"No, he's not! That's how they set us up. Their denial covers their stuff so *we* look out of control, when the truth is, we're dealing with it and they're not."

Janie pulled her eye makeup out and started repairing herself. "I like that. I'm using that."

"Fine, send my agent a royalty. Now, before we get there, is there anything really personal you want to discuss?"

"No. I mean, yes. But it would all take too long. I finally confronted my father. He was great. Really sweet. He didn't seem at all surprised. We're going to Southampton together to talk to someone who runs a fancy clinic. They're tough. They use all the A.A. stuff. So I feel better. Not so helpless, anyway. Donnie's going back tonight. Are you staying out?"

Gina pulled up across the street from the Bridgehampton playground. Everyone was well into the game. "Yes, I'm staying out all week. I'm still working on that summer piece. I've got to turn it in by Friday."

"Terrif. We can hang out. I could use that."

Gina checked her hair in the rearview mirror. A Ferrari convertible pulled up behind them.

"Don't turn or make any sudden movements, but Rikki Bosco's girlfriend and Katarina Rivers, who you do not re-

117

ally want to see, trust me on this, we are not up to seeing her this morning; any old how, they are right behind us."

Janie closed her eyes. "Tell me when. I can't stand it. You know how masochistic I am. Can I look now?"

Gina opened the door. "Okay. But no gaping. We're just here because we were passing by after a hard morning of whirling and thought we'd give our guys a ride."

Janie grabbed her bag and pulled out an enormous pair of reflecting sunglasses. "Check this out. I can devour her with my eyes and she'll never suspect a thing. Let's go."

Gina and Janie settled in on the top of the bleacher. They were the first women, except for Katarina and The Match, who were down front. From the top they had a better view of Katarina. The Match waved at them, but kept her place. Good, actual conversation was not what they wanted. They had almost talked to Katarina at Fritzi's party, but if they talked to her and they liked her, then they couldn't dish her, which was all they wanted right now.

Harry was up at bat. Gina really hated this. She lived every second of it for him. It was really as if she were at bat. Norman Gallo was pitching. He actually looked like he was chewing tobacco. Norman. Mister Perfect Dresser!

Norman was wearing a torn, sweat-soaked undershirt and a pair of checked fifties Bermuda shorts that were hanging down somewhere below his stomach, which rolled over them. Norman had a roll! Amazing.

"Strike two!" called Erica Hess's jerky little husband Howie, who none of the guys liked or trusted, but who financed the team, such as it was, and owned a magazine that many of them did business with. The call was a little too gleeful for Gina's taste.

Rikki Bosco stood up in the dugout. "It was over his fucking eyeballs!"

118

A HOUSE IN THE HAMPTONS

No one paid any attention. She had to think of something else or she'd never be able to stand two more innings.

She focused on Joey Rivers. What an arrogant-looking little peacock! He was chewing gum and punching his fielder's mitt with his hand. Way out in right field. Perfect place for a movie director. He had the same kind of small man's cocky energy that Harry had, but without Harry's vulnerability. This guy was totally packaged. Cool. The way they learn it in Hollywood.

Gina had done a couple of stories out there and had found it fascinating in the same way the wax museum or the snake cages at the zoo are fascinating. Viperous cool. Modulated, manicured, color-coordinated, cool. The guys who made it learned how to be that cool. Each one differently wrapped but all obeying the same commandments; all understanding how the game was played. Rivers had that and he hadn't gotten it on Staten Island. It was pure Hollywood.

Gina wondered what a man like that was under all the facade. Was there a fly in the aspic or could you slice right through him and never find anything but cool, gelatinous, perfectly packaged nothing? She shifted to Katarina. God, she really was lovely. In a cold kind of way. Not sexy. At least she didn't think so and neither did Harry (God love him). But then, Harry had Fritzi taste. No, Gina, you're not going to do *that* to yourself today.

She shook the thought away. The thought of Katarina and Joey Rivers fucking was better. Aspic and ice maiden. She could certainly understand his attraction to her, but what did she see in him? The old rough-and-tough throw me down and do it to me, mess my hair and I don't care whore inside the debutante scene? So boring. So . . . Hollywood.

Maybe that was it. After all, she was raised in that mind set and he certainly lived the part. Maybe their whole reality

119

base was one-paragraph movie synopses. Who knew. Who knew why anyone was attracted to anyone.

She watched the game without seeing it. Other wives and girlfriends had arrived. Their conversation floated over her.

"After the game last week, he was complaining so much. I thought I would choke him. How he hurt! His knee! His back! Finally, I said, Nathan, it's softball. It isn't Vietnam, for chrissakes. If you don't want to play, don't play!"

"Did you see that *Current Affair* about the woman who said she was sodomized by a ghost while she was doing the dishes?"

"No kidding. Wonder if she needs someone to dry."

"So now I've done fifteen pitches to the networks on MOWs and I've got six projects in various stages of development. So I'm making some money for a change but nothing ever gets on the air. You know what I'm becoming? I'm becoming a development slut."

"Hi, guys." A flash of orange. The Match slumped down beside them, snapping Janie and Gina out of their tandem reveries.

"Hi." Janie slid over, giving her more room.

The Match looked tired, Gina thought, and nervous. They had just met her really, but they were both mad about her.

"Is this the most stupido, snooze-time event of the century or what? I guess if you're a wife, it's more motivating."

Janie offered her a cigarette. "Are you kidding? Keep a secret, we only came because we wanted to get another look at the Hollywood houseguests."

The Match lit up. "That's a laugh. I'm totally sicko from lookin' at her, I mean them, and youse guys can't get enough. Come on over and feast your eyes."

Gina laughed. "No thanks. We like to watch from a distance, that way we're not being so catty. Want us to give you a quick ride home?"

A HOUSE IN THE HAMPTONS

"Nah. I'll stick it out. Don't want Rikki to think I'm not impressed. Never been before, 'cause I usually work all day Sunday. But I had a late call last night, you wouldn't believe this scene.

"Got a referral from this lady, I mean a real English Lady, client of mine. She calls me at Rikki's during dinner, says, she has this friend, Count something and he's in the middle of a muscle spasm and he'll pay anything. So, shit. I mean it's like ten minutes away and the guy says three hundred dollars for ninety minutes, so I go. Well, it's this great big old spooky house just off the Highway before East Hampton and a real creepazoid kinda handyman type lets me in and no lights on, like a Boris Karloff movie or somethin'. And I go up all these creaky stairs, down this hall and the Count of Monte Cristo is laying on this great big bed with four huge wooden claws coming up from the sides and he's naked as a baby boy.

"So, I unpack my stuff, real professional, and he's moanin' and groanin' and I go to work and it's spooky but it's okay, I mean three hundred cash, I can deal with it. So I'm almost through and this peckerhead, grabs my arm and he says, 'Oh, it would make me so happy if you'd do that all over my body. It would make me feel so nice!' and he's not letting go of my arm!

So I says to him, 'Oh yeah, well, swell for you but it wouldn't make *me* feel so nice, so let go of my fuckin' arm and give me my money or I'll blow your fuckin' head off.'"

Gina and Janie are wide-eyed with awe. "Did you really?"

The Match smiles and takes a deep drag on her red-stained butt. "Fuckin' A. I mean, the dude knows I'm from the Village. Who's to know? Maybe I'm with the boys. Right? Anyway. It worked. He dropped my arm so fast, I almost fell over on him. Gave me four hundred bucks and I was out of there."

Janie beamed. "I think you're my new hero. I think I would rather talk to some pervert like that than win the Nobel prize. To just say it. Just let someone have it. A man someone. Jeez, Match, that's my new favorite story."

The Match blushed. "You serious?"

Gina patted her long bony thigh. "Sure. We're two products of the late fifties, good-girl generation. Be nice. Keep your ankles crossed. This kind of stuff is very exotic for us. Actually my deepest fantasy is to run around as part of a SWAT team with a machine gun and shoot the shit out of bad guys. I would love that. Or maybe do it in a movie, where no one really dies or anything, or like Sigourney Weaver in *Aliens*. I just love that movie."

Janie nodded vigorously. "I want to stand in front of my ranch with suede chaps over my jeans and my Stetson hanging around my neck and a great big rifle in my hands and tell the bad guys, 'Get off my land!' "

The Match wrinkled her nose. "You guys are crazy. You got to come hang out with me some night. I'll take you on a trip you won't believe. We gotta give you some attitude. It's a jungle out there. Where you been?"

Janie and Gina looked at each other.

Donnie and Harry were racing for the same ball. Gina cringed.

"What's this, silent baseball?" Rikki Bosco yelled at them.

"We've been married. Is where we've been." Janie stubbed out her cigarette.

Howie Hess glared up at them. Gina put her finger to her lips. "We're making too much noise, Howie Hess is going to beat us to death with his little L.L. Bean bat."

"I know that guy. Gave his wife a couple of massages. What a schitzy chick. Never laid eyes on the broad before and she told me all about their sex life, how bad he was in bed, how wild she'd been before she married him, how she

122

had a ten-year I.V. drug habit, syphilis, on and on. They live in this house, looks like a French faggot's doll house. He's a mean little asshole. I can always tell. It's in their skin tone. Toxic vibes."

Gina gave Janie a knowing look. Janie ducked into her bag and pulled out a pack of Juicy Fruit gum. They all took sticks in silence. Somehow, as different as she was from them in age and experience, they all fit together so easily.

Janie was amazed. She felt comfortable with this strange young creature. There were few people she felt comfortable enough with to be silent. Gina, Donnie, Owen. That was about it. Not even her own parents. How odd.

The men were all showing off for Katarina Rivers. Janie had seen it at once. How revolting. She watched her behind her glasses. What would it be like to be a woman like that? She had never been one, not even when she was that young. She was never a woman of mystery and presence. A mesmerizer. Before Donnie, she had had boyfriends, but it was always more good old Janie than if-I-can't-have-you-I'll-kill-myself kinds of relationships.

Donnie was the only man who had ever really loved her. Except for her father. He loved her. But he was too remote. He loved her but he had never really known her. Donnie really knew her. Sometimes he looked at her with so much compassion, so much empathy and love, that it stunned her. She saw herself, in his eyes, the way she had imagined as a child that God saw her.

Janie pushed another piece of gum into her mouth and speeded up her chewing. What would have happened to her if she hadn't found Donnie? It made her too nervous to even consider it. Or if she lost him. If he left her. Fritzomania.

She swallowed a glob of sweet saliva. Katarina tossed her hair for the four thousandth time. So many of their friends' husbands had left them for younger women, the whole look of the softball games had changed. It made her sick. It was all so cliché. Fifty-year-old men with thirty-year-old wives and babies. Gonna beat the Big D any old way.

The saddest, most upsetting part of it all was that from what she had seen, the new wives couldn't hold a candle to the old ones. Most of the time they weren't even as good-looking. They were just young. What on earth could they have to talk to one another about? To really share. Most guys that age don't have sex on the top of their every single daily must list. And even if that was the draw, bringing new life into all those aging pricks, it still wore off. After a couple of years, what was left? Someone who had never heard of Dizzy Gillespie or chlorophyll gum.

She just didn't get it. As insecure as she was, she still felt she had so much more to offer than these girls, so unformed they really thought being young was a nonreturnable status symbol they owned forever, instead of the manhandled little library book it was. The one with all of the overdue dates inked in the front. Just waiting for them to keep it out too long. Aching to slap the overdue charges on their arrogance. That's what got to Janie the most. The arrogance.

She chewed faster. She was mad. She had told Donnie after Fritzi's party that if she had a choice between his leaving her for another woman or dropping dead of a massive coronary, she would choose the coronary without a split second's hesitation and she had already informed God, so he had better watch out. Her teeth crashed into her tongue and the pain brought tears to her eyes. Shit. She had to stop thinking such angry morbid thoughts, even her analyst was getting impatient with her.

She just kept feeling such a permeating sense of hopelessness. It was the countdown to forty, Gina said. Maybe. But she had felt it for years. There was always this sense of living in a bubble that could be popped at any second. Fine. That

124

was called life. She knew it. But her bubble was always so visible to her. She put on a good show. Spunky little bitch that she was. But she didn't really believe it. What she really believed was that it was all a great big setup, all the good things she had been allowed. And the pin was following her around, just waiting for her to let down her guard for a microsecond. No wonder she was so nervous! Jesus, what a worldview!

Erica Hess, dressed to the nines in Ralph Lauren equestrian wear and accompanied by her matching four-year-old daughter, slid in front of her. Gina was right. Where had she been?

"Mommy. I'm a pig." The child grunted. Erica looked around quickly to see if anyone had noticed. Thank God for the reflecting sunglasses, Janie was safe.

"No, you're not. You're a lovely little girl," Erica purred.

"No. I'm a pig." More grunting.

"Girl." Erica's grin seemed a tad fixed. Janie and Gina exchanged looks. The Match tuned in instantly.

"Pig."

"Darling. Why not be a horse, at least they're prettier."

"Daddy says I shouldn't ride horses. That Jews don't ride horses."

Janie's elbow was in Gina's side.

"How about a kitty cat?"

"Nope. I'm a pig."

Erica twisted her enormous diamond ring. "But why a pig?"

"Because I act like a pig."

The Match leaned forward. "Yo. If you wanna be a pig. Be a pig. Be Porky, though. Be a great big, ugly, fat, smelly, giant pig. Be a world-class pig."

The little girl giggled. Erica shot The Match a look that would have dried fruit.

"Game!"

It was over. Katarina called out to The Match. "Hey, Match! Rikki and Joey want some Pellegrino. Where's the cooler?"

Erica froze. Lucky for her. Janie smiled. She could just imagine what The Match could do to Erica if the Count was any example. Erica was too impressed to mess with The Match, maybe she was somebody social.

They all tromped down. Harry and Donnie looked as if they had an hour to live, maybe less. That meant they were really pleased with themselves.

"I'm a great big, fat, ugly Porky Pig," chanted the little Ralph Lauren clone, while her mother pretended to be alone.

Harry Hart was pissed. Of all the days for Gina to show up at the softball game, it would have to be this one! Shit. So, okay. So he'd be late. He had told Fritzi he wasn't sure what time he'd be through. So, he'd go home with Gina, take a shower first, clean up, and then find some excuse for getting away. But what about Donnie and Janie? They'd want to have brunch, they always had brunch on Sunday. Shit.

They were all waiting by the car. What to do? So, okay. He knew. Harry limped over to them. They all watched his slow, gimpy, overly dramatized walk.

"Hey, Sven, we're going to our house. Looks like you could use a little Jacuzzi action. Fix you right up." Janie patted his hunched shoulder.

Harry winced. "Boy! I really pulled something. You all go on. I just want a shower and a nap. Some Nuprin."

Gina watched him. Shit. She knew his every little trick. "Harry, for you to pass up brunch at Big Ben's you'd have to be clinically dead. What's with you?"

"Nothing. It fucking hurts. I want to lie down."

126

A HOUSE IN THE HAMPTONS

Donnie to the rescue. "Hey, come on, ladies, give the man a break. He's our hero of the day. You go on. I'll drive Harry home, pick up some fresh oranges for the Mimosas and we'll just have to forge on without the star player."

Janie hoisted her bag onto her padded shoulder. "Fine. Come on. I'm starving. That softball really brings on an appetite." Gina was still watching Harry. She knew he was lying and he knew that she knew.

Donnie put his arm around Harry and helped him to the car. Donnie was quiet. They drove down Main Street, turning at the monument onto the Sag Turnpike without talking. Harry was making sore muscle noises. Donnie smiled.

"Okay, Harry. Cut the shit. This is me. What's going on?"

"Jesus Christ! What the fuck is this? The National Socialist Party? Can't a man want to be alone for an hour a week? I hurt my leg. I'm tired. I want a little peace and quiet."

"Harry. You hurt your leg or some other body part every single week. You never want peace and quiet afterward. You want a couple of Bloody Marys, a dip in the Jacuzzi, and a lot of time to moan and get sympathy for how tough the game was."

Harry ripped off his sweatshirt. "Okay. Okay, Mr. All-seeing Asshole. I have a date to see Fritzi. She called yesterday, sounding very mysterious. She said she had to see me, she had waited as long as she could, whatever that means, and we made a date. The fucking SS hasn't showed up at a game in years! I thought I'd have plenty of time to run over there, find out what's going on and then meet you all. In fact, I was going to leave in the seventh, let what's his face, the alternate, in, but there they were! Unbelievable!"

Donnie laughed. "Well, well. A bit of intrigue. Have you seen her since the party?"

"No! Have you?"

"No. Harry? Be cool, okay?"

127

Donnie pulled up in front of Harry's house. Jeremy was chasing Arturo down the front steps. Arturo had a large piece of fabric in his mouth.

"Dad! Dad! He ate the front of the couch! He just tore it all up and ate it! Mom is going to shit!"

Donnie laughed. "Pretty glamorous. Canceling a rendezvous with a beautiful blonde because your dog ate the couch."

Harry grabbed up his sweaty baseball gear and slammed the car door. "Oh, no. I'm going. I feel like I'm living in a fucking hamster cage. Every move I make is being observed. Don't you see how they're hovering over us? And it's all my fault. What an asshole!"

"It would be indelicate not to support you in your working through. Just go. I'll take Jeremy back with me so he doesn't know you're not here."

"Good thinking. Tell Gina I'll buy her a new couch. She hated that one anyway."

Donnie motioned to Jeremy. "Better take Arturo with you. You know what happens when he's like that."

Harry raced up the stairs, quite nimbly for a crippled athlete. "Yeah. Good thinking."

Harry raced through his shower, throwing on his clothes. He stopped. He went back to the bathroom and brushed his teeth. He stopped. He went back to the sink and put on deodorant and aftershave. He combed his hair. He stopped and checked himself out in the bedroom mirror. He tore off his T-shirt, put on his J. Crew athletic shirt and his Mets cap. Did he look like he just came from the game? Casual. At ease? Shoes. Couldn't wear cleats. Too obvious. Sneakers. Old sneakers. Harry ripped off his loafers and rummaged in the closet. He found his old ratty sneakers. Clean fresh socks. Old ratty sneakers. He checked himself out again. Okay. It would do.

128

A HOUSE IN THE HAMPTONS

He grabbed the car keys, put Arturo on his leash, and pulled the stuporous beagle down the porch steps and into the back of his rebuilt Austin-Healey. Arturo loved driving with the top down. Off they went.

Okay, Harry. This is risky. You know this is fucking risky. So, why are you doing it like this? Why didn't you just sit Gina down and tell her. I had a call. I gotta get to the bottom of this. I owe this woman some common courtesy. So back off. So why? Hmmm. Here you and Donnie are again. Two boys, one girl. Is that it? Only this time, it doesn't seem like you're the one she wants. First, she's balling that Hungarian car creep and second, from the moony-eyed looks she casts at Donnie, it would seem she's here to find out if she made a mistake all those years ago.

In fact, the truth is, you were shocked when she called. Flattered. Yes. Intrigued. Absolutely. But certainly not expecting it. So, why are you lying to your wife and going off like some crazy adolescent? Do you want to fuck her? Oh Harry. So scary, ain't it? The truth is, you're all talk. The woman still scares the shit out of you. And so does your wife. You have never cheated on Gina and if you're going to, it doesn't make sense to choose someone from the distant past with whom you have complex memories and of whom you are still terrified, now does it? Not too aphrodisiacal. Is that a word?

Okay. I'm drawn. It's unfinished business. She's still so, so fluffy. Fluffy? Ducks are fluffy. And you hate ducks. Fluffy? Oh my poor schmucko. I can hear Gina splitting open with hysterics. "He just couldn't help himself. She was so fluffy."

Okay. It's fun. Not fun in the traditional way most people think of as fun. More Bergman fun. Lots of mixed metaphors and soul-searching. Tension. Sexual and psychic. It was out of the ordinary. A conundrum. Why was she here and what did she really want. *Jules and Jim? Fatal Attraction?* My body? My soul? Donnie's? What.

He was there. He would know soon enough. He climbed out, dragging Arturo behind him. Arturo was not at all happy to be along. He expressed his displeasure by lying down on the white stone driveway and refusing to move. Harry yelled. Harry pleaded. Arturo just closed his eyes and pretended he wasn't there.

Harry pulled on the leash. "Get the fuck up!"

"Harry?" A soft giggly voice behind him. He straightened up. Arturo straightened up, wanting to make a good impression. Fritzi stood in the massive terrazzo entry in a white bikini and some sort of clear high heels. They were high, but they were transparent, so it looked as if she were standing on her tiptoes. Her hair was piled on her head like cotton candy. Jesus. What was he getting himself into? Arturo trotted on in front of him, as if he thought he had a shot at her himself. Gina was right. The dog was a fucking psycho hound.

"Hi. Sorry. The, uh, our dog ate the couch. I mean the front of it, so I, when he's like that, it's best not to leave him home alone. Hope you don't mind."

Fritzi moved toward him. She was wearing a new perfume. Thank God. This one was more like roses. Softer. She bent down to pat Arturo, revealing what was left to reveal of her beautiful breasts. "Oh, no. This is a good pup. He wouldn't do anything naughty like that at Aunt Fritzi's house, now would he?"

For a moment, Harry actually thought Arturo was going to answer her. Whatever "it" was, she had it. Arturo's tongue was hanging out of his fucking mouth. Canine porno. Well, why not. Arturo had certainly eaten a lot worse than Fritzi Ferris. Harry laughed.

Fritzi stood up and smiled at him. "What's so funny?"

"Oh, nothing. You, uh, Arturo seems to like you. That may not sound like much, but Arturo doesn't usually respond to anything he can't swallow, or at least chew on."

Fritzi met his eyes. Gina was right. Marilyn. That was the smile. Marilyn in *River of No Return*.

"Well, maybe Arturo and I can work out a little something." She turned. There was no back to her bathing suit. Was that possible? Harry could feel his entire body turning red. He didn't dare look at Arturo. No, there was something. A string, a little string thing. A thong, that's what they called it. He had heard Owen and Jeremy talking about some girl on the beach wearing one. But that girl was sixteen. A thong barely covering the crack of her beautiful, perfect, ageless ass. Oh, shit. I want this. Okay, God. I admit it. I want this. Before it's too late. Just once and I'll never do it again. Let me have this.

He followed behind her holding on to the leash. He wasn't even sure his tongue wasn't hanging out of his mouth like Arturo's. He felt like he had felt all those months ago at the Plaza Hotel. Dazed, disoriented, suffocated.

They were in the snowy living room. Her flesh, the only off-white color in the room. Her flesh and her pink lips.

"What can I get you to drink, Harry? I was having a Tequila Sunrise."

"Great. Fine. Whatever."

Harry sunk into a massive white cushion. Arturo curled up on the floor beside him, patiently waiting for his goddess to take his drink order.

"Arturo, baby, come with me. I bet I have something for you in the kitchen."

Arturo pulled at the leash and Harry released him. He was off like a shot, the fastest the lazy fucking mutt had moved in years.

Harry watched her go. He felt like a boy with the new

131

schoolmarm. What would Donnie think? What would he tell him? Fuck him. Why should he have to tell him anything? Donnie was always Mr. Sphinx and he was always Mr. Pour-the-Heart-Out. Forget it. This was nobody's business.

She was back with their drinks. Arturo was not with her. She wiggled over and set them down, revealing her nipples when she bent over. Harry reached for his drink so fast, he almost dropped it on her tippy-toed foot.

Fritzi giggled and settled down beside him, taking her drink and holding it toward him. "Cheers."

"Cheers." Harry took a deep gulp, feeling the sweet warm magic move down him. Great. This was going to be great.

Fritzi sighed, her moist, lightly tanned chest heaved. "Oh, that tastes good. Now maybe I finally have the courage to tell you."

Harry took another huge gulp. With the softball and the anxiety and no food, he was already getting loaded.

"Tell me anything. That's why I'm here."

"This is really hard. Because it's been a secret for so long. So long." Fritzi took a dainty sip of her drink, paused; took another, put it down and leaned closer to Harry, resting her hand on his knee. "Harry, there's someone I want you to meet."

Harry stiffened. He was confused. "Sure. When?" He was responding to two different stimuli at once. One was the woozy, erotic rosy-smelling creamy, luscious presence of his briefly possessed first wife and her fingers on his sore but happy knee, the other was the old fight-or-flight neuron raising its periscope.

"Now." Fritzi stood up. "Finish your drink. I'll be right back."

"Sure." Harry tried to sit up straighter, but the couch engulfed him. Now his calf muscle hurt for real. His whole body was starting to stiffen up. He longed for a bath and some aspirin. He finished off his drink. What could she possibly be up to? A ménage à trois? None of this was making any sense. Was it a surprise party? Someone else from their past? He closed his eyes and surrendered to the couch. Calm down. You're already in it up to your horny little neck, so go with the flow, as they said in the seventies.

He was almost asleep. He smelled her reenter the room. A rush of roses. "Harry. I want you to meet . . . Aaron."

Harry opened his eyes slowly. He didn't have his glasses on. She was all the way across the room. He tried to pull himself up off the couch. It took him two attempts, but he was up, on his feet, woozy with Mexican hooch and too many stolen bases. Fritzi had put on a shiny white shirt, covering her beautiful body. She looked crisp and serious. There was a small young man about Harry's size standing next to her. He looked familiar. Very, very familiar. Harry put out his hand and moved closer. Familiar. Shit. He looked like, he looked exactly like himself!

He knew before she could say it. "Harry. This is your son."

An hour later Harry Hart came to a screeching halt in Ben and Delores Cowan's driveway. He was hyperventilating. He grabbed Arturo's leash and pulled the pooch across the seat and onto the ground. Arturo gave him a long slow stare, sizing up his options. It was clear he was dealing with a man who was not following Kennel Club guidelines. It was best not to make him crazier than he was. Arturo moved.

Harry raced up the steps and rang. Fucking security. Ondine always took forever. He could hear them all on the back terrace, carefree and relaxed. Janie's voice soared over him.

"I'm not kidding. I had this dream that I was eating a salad and I asked the waiter what it was and he said, "It's a penis salad with balsamic vinegar and Coltibuono olive oil on a bed of radicchio and I put down my fork and said, "I can't eat this." Now what does that mean? Come on, Donnie, give me a clue."

Owen was laughing. "Mom, it means that you eat in too many of those trendy weird restaurants when you should be home taking care of your man."

Laughter rolling over Harry's frenzied brain stem. Ondine peeked out through the leaded-glass door.

Slow, so fucking slow. Passive aggressive hostility. Harry hated Ondine.

He was in. He raced across the living room and out onto the terrace where lunch was set. Everyone turned.

"Well, well. It's a miracle. Those Nuprin really are wonder drugs. The man is practically flying." Gina put on her glasses and gave him a slow steady stare.

Donnie knew at once that something was terribly wrong. He stood up and made his way over to Harry.

Ben Cowan came out of the kitchen carrying an enormous platter of freshly grilled seafood. "Hey, Harry! Just in time!"

"Yeah. Gee. I, got a, not really hungry. Got a lot of pain. Thought Donnie might have something stronger. Couldn't get to sleep."

Gina started to say something, but changed her mind. Jeremy was watching both of them. Donnie took Harry's arm. Come on, Harry. I've got some muscle relaxants in my bag. Let's get you in a tub and I'll give you an injection."

"Great! I'll be fine. Save me some shrimp!"

Donnie and Harry limped off together, all eyes on them. Jeremy picked up a knife and held it as a microphone. "And there he goes, it's Mighty Uptighty. By day the mild-mannered publisher of the *Duck Hunter's Journal,* by night the fearless star of geriatric softball!"

Gina grabbed the knife. "Enough. He's not to be teased

when he's like that. Just get Arturo and muzzle him or something, so we can eat in peace."

"You're hyperventilating. Lie down, for chrissakes, I'm going to give you a tranquilizer. Your heart is going like a conga drum. What the hell happened to you?"

Harry paced. He sat down on Donnie's bed. He got up. Donnie pushed him back. "Lean forward and breathe into this bag for a minute. I'm getting the shot."

Harry leaned over and breathed into one of Janie's shopping bags. "I can't. Jesus. You don't know."

Donnie rubbed alcohol on his arm. "Shut up for a minute." Donnie took his time. Firm and gentle. That was his friend. Harry felt better almost immediately. He dropped the bag and fell back on the French linen–covered pillows. "Jesus. I love drugs. I can understand why people get into this. What a relief. I thought I was fucking dying. Arturo almost had to drive."

Donnie sat down beside him and put a cold cloth on his forehead. "Okay. It's all over. Take three long, deep breaths and then tell me what happened."

Harry obeyed. He felt fantastic. He never took tranquilizers. He had never even known you could feel this calm. What an amazing discovery! Were there really people who walked around feeling like this without drugs? Or were the drugs invented to try and create a sense of peace that was impossible any other way. Amazing. This was an entirely new feeling. Like the first orgasm. Different, there you were thinking you knew all of these feelings and then, pow. A new one.

"I feel great. Jesus. Do people feel like this without this stuff?"

Donnie laughed. "Not the ones I meet. But it's what we're all working on."

Harry's eyes were closing. He was suddenly totally and completely exhausted. "Donnie. You're not going to believe this. I went there. She was wearing this bikini, this almost naked little number, so fucking erotic. I thought, okay. Go for it, Harry. For old times' sake. Right? She gives me some California booze—Sundown, Moonrise, something—and then she says, 'There's someone I want you to meet.'

"Donnie! Donnie! I have, she brings out this kid. Kid! A twenty-five-year-old man! Aaron. His name's Aaron. And it's me! Looks exactly like me at that age. She didn't have a miscarriage. She lied. She said she couldn't take it when she realized I didn't love her. That I'd only married her because she was pregnant. She knew that being a nice Jewish boy, I'd never leave her pregnant, so she faked it. She married Martin when Aaron was six months old. He was the only one who ever knew. When Martin died, Aaron found his birth certificate in some of the lawyer's files and flipped out. He wanted to meet me. That's why she came east. Donnie! What the fuck do I do with this! He looks, just like my, shoon." Harry was out.

Donnie sat beside him for a long time. He was incredulous. There they all were, smack in the middle of these planned and smug little lives, where the changes and shifts were so subtle, like the waves on the sand, changing always, but without sudden effect. Bam. A hurricane. Or was it only the first alert, only the first turbulence before a much larger, more damaging storm?

Donnie sat beside his oldest friend. The way he had when he was ten and had his appendix out. When he broke his arm playing football. When he had strep throat. He had always felt it was his job to watch over Harry. He felt it not in a superior way but just as a fact. It gave him strength to help Harry. He envied the way Harry engaged in his life, mouth first, feelings first. It was something he did not know how to do, but that by watching Harry live it and watching Janie live it out there in the open, it helped him through, too. It was his pleasure and his responsibility and he took it very seriously—this loyalty to Harry. What was the right way to deal with this?

Harry was snoring softly. His face was as pink and relaxed as a child's. Damn. He was supposed to go in a couple of hours. He had a completely crazy week. He couldn't leave him like this. He would cancel the Jitney and drive back with Harry. They would figure it out together, like they always had.

Donnie put away his bag, covered Harry with a hand-woven afghan and ever so quietly made his way down the stairs and outside. Janie was still holding forth, her voice sounded happy and a little tipsy. It made him smile to listen to her.

"No. This is the truth! Erica Hess was on this fox hunt with Max and his group and she got thrown and they were all ahead, so when they heard her screaming they all turned around and went back, and she comes running out of the woods yelling, 'A snake, oh my God! There's a snake in there!' And Max, who knows snakes from his southern childhood, he says, "Now, calm down. What did it look like. What color was it?" And Erica says, "It was, well, I guess it was sort of a Mercedes cobalt blue!"

Ben Cowan's eyes sprang open like those of a victim in a horror movie. Sweat, cold and sticky, covered his back, his chest and neck. What time was it? He sat up and reached for his neon designer clock. 5:00 A.M. That meant, he was sixty.

Ben stood up too quickly and the blood raced around his tall, powerful body, trying to find its way. He was dizzy. He was scared. Sixty. He looked over at Delores, sound asleep, curled up like a tiny sparrow, hardly making a dent in the bed. Sixty.

Ben grabbed a robe and made his way down the hall, down the stairs and across the main house to his office and gallery. The only place he felt safe. Everything in there was of him. His taste, his books, his ideas, his collection. He paced up and down, stopping before his favorite paintings and drawings.

The Lautrec he had found in a Paris thrift shop thirty years ago. The Klee from the Swiss flea market. The Van Gogh watercolor, the Picasso Imaginary Portrait, the Johns, the two Rothkos, the Dine skull series, the Bacon. He had chosen well. He sat down at his desk. He had never let himself try to be a painter. He loved art. But he hated artists. They all thought they were the only ones with talent, everyone else was derivative shit. He had never met one who was generous about any of the others. Not one. Me. Me and only me. Gigantic egos and mean spirits. He had rejected the world. He liked to be in the position of power. The buyer rather than the seller.

He smiled. He remembered a dinner at some prominent collector's when the hostess had gushed on about how delighted she was with their new gallery because now they wouldn't have to have "all of those art people traipsing through the house." She had dismissed them all, from Jasper Johns to Leo Castelli, with a wave of her rubied wrist. He loved the work. But he did not like the workers. Or was that just another cop-out? So that not having ever tried wouldn't hurt so bad?

Sixty. Jesus. How was that possible? He was born, he went to school, got married, got rich, bought a co-op, built a summer house, went to a few dinner parties, took a few fishing trips, screwed some women, drank some bourbon, played a

little tennis and it was almost over. Certainly the good parts
were almost over.

He was cold. The sweat hadn't dried. His body was shaking with wet, cold fear. Sixty years of dancing in the dark.
Of cowardice. No more. There was no more time. It was
now or never. If change was possible for him, he would have
to do it, now. His insides ached. He had to talk to her. He
had to see her. He needed her. She gave him strength.

He opened his safe, hidden in the bookshelf behind his
desk, and took out her picture. God, how he wanted her. It
was too early. He'd have to wait. He sat down and flipped on
the radio.

"Welcome to New York Christian radio, where you will
always hear God bless you, but you'll rarely hear a sneeze."
Isabel had been cleaning in here. He smiled.

"Today's sermon is entitled 'Blaspheming the Holy Spirit
—the Unpardonable Sin.' The Bible says, oh, so clearly, that
if you blaspheme your fellow man you will always be forgiven, but if you blaspheme the Holy Ghost you will never,
ever be forgiven in this world or the next . . ."

Ben shut it off. It wasn't even funny, the idea was so unnerving. What did it mean, anyway? After sixty years of god-
dammits and Jesus Christs he was damned to hell for eter-
nity, but all of the other not so terrific stuff, the adultery and
greed and cowardice and lying, would all be washed away
with a couple of deep knee-bends and amens? Then it almost
didn't make any difference, did it? They're going to get you
one way or another. He might as well just go the distance. Be
the patriarchal bad guy. Just cool the chrissakes and he was
covered? Sure.

He held her picture to his cheek. Tears covered it. He
closed his eyes. He could smell her. Feel her soft warm skin.
See her sad tired smile. Hear the low steady moaning when

he fucked her. The sound of a woman suffering from love. Suffering from wanting it, from losing it, from finding it.

A woman's moaning—a sound as human and powerful as any on earth. Women's love noises were masterpieces. Tender, erotic, wise, and wonderful works of art. Men yelped or groaned or shouted or were silent, teeth bared, gritted, jaws tight, then slackening like butchered bucks. But women, their love sounds held heaven—held the horizon of the universe. Moaning pain, pleasure, fullness and emptiness, power and passivity. Taking and being taken. Woman sounds. Her sounds.

His cock was hard. He couldn't stand it. What time was it? He checked the radio clock. Five-thirty. He couldn't do that to her. She worked too hard. He couldn't stand it.

What the hell. It was his birthday. Every erection might well be his last. He opened his robe and covered himself with his thick callused hand. He thought of her. He saw her breasts, her belly, her wide sweet hips. He was coming. *Oh, holy Christ. I want you. Oh God. Let me have this before it's too late.*

When he opened his eyes, his wife was standing in the doorway and the look on her face told him what he already knew but had refused to admit. This was no longer his hand. The cards had been reshuffled and he could not control this game. The other players had gotten a new deck and he would no longer be able to fake them out. He closed his robe and slipped Clovis O'Malley's Polaroid into his pocket.

PART TWO

5

Fighting continues in the Palestinian areas of Beirut. Living conditions in the district are said to be so appalling, an appeal has been made to religious leaders for an edict to permit the eating of human flesh to help save the starving.

A computer programmer for Metropolitan Life Insurance was killed yesterday when a 200-pound air conditioner fell on his head from a midtown office window. According to bystanders, the 37-year-old bachelor, who was on his lunch break, never knew what hit him.

Today is the last day to see fashion plate Lyn Revson's magnificent collection of Hermès handbags. The goodies include a pink crocodile shoulder bag and an aubergine lizard cylinder, which Lyn absolutely adores because it's deep enough to carry her portable phone . . .

A 49-year-old electric company executive was killed by lightning while hiking in Aspen, Colo.

Gina threw the newspapers onto the deck beside her lounge chair and took a big gulp of coffee. The first Monday morning of summer. It had brought the sun. And she had surrendered. Arturo lay snoozing off the ten pancakes he had retrieved from the garbage can and Jeremy was doing laps in the pool, which had now, by some miracle of self-healing, cooled down to a frosty ninety degrees.

She kept waiting for the summer elation to kick in. Every summer of her conscious life she waited for that high when the first real summertime feeling hit. The first morning with glistening sunshine and the smell of cut grass and lemons and peaches ripening and sprinklers sprinkling. Each year a feeling of pure sensate pleasure, of joy, filled her. She counted on it. Summer always felt like beginnings. She was prettier, stronger, more hopeful. Anything was possible. Romance was waiting.

When Jeremy had been a baby, long before summer houses and easy access to the Atlantic shore, it had meant time at her parents' house. Small price to pay for access to a pool or the beach. Out to the Jersey shore she went, filled with summer zest. She could sit for hours on the sand watching her fat sweet-skinned baby boy play. Year after year, she greeted the summer with innocent glee.

She liked everything about it. Sea stink and sunburn and sand in her toes. Jersey corn and ice-cream cones and never wearing shoes unless absolutely necessary. She even loved the city in the summer. The long warm nights. Strolling across Broadway after the movies. A.C.s murmuring, people's faces opened up, thawed of that winter pinch. Summer had always been time out. Even when she was still working full-time. Somehow, it felt different. People worked with the weekend dangling in front of them like sugarplums before Christmas orphans.

When she was first in the city after college, the weekends

were mythical in possibility. Every summer she rented a house on Fire Island with a group of friends. And each weekend rose to her as "The One That Could Deliver the Man of Her Dreams." The *one* with her name on him. The *one* for forever.

She practically flew through the week, so great was the reward for getting to Friday. Those were the summers of deep tans, before wrinkles and skin cancer warnings, before anyone knew anything about the sun except, possibly, that the earth revolved around it and it was hot and made you feel and look good. They basked and basted.

That was also the time before overachieving, when they could just loll, without guilt. Young women, lazing in the sun, minds wandering pleasantly. Thinking of young men, real or imagined, sea breezes gentling their hair. The sun penetrating their dreams, taking them somewhere else.

Those were the summers of being young and single, before aerobics and nutrition awareness, and surgeon general's warnings. Before the dangers of promiscuity, aerosol sprays, medical waste, toxic dumping, softening flesh, and hardening hearts.

On her fourth city summer, when her beach sleeps had just started to be clouded with doubt, when the hope of Prince Valiant or even Irving Valiant, had begun to dim, Gina went to a party in a cottage being rented by ten gay art directors. Harry Hart, in a frantic effort to convince the only attractive single woman present that he, too, was hetero, and falling prey to the "Thou protest too much" school of self-promotion, had marched right up to her with that nervous, duck-footed little strut, and pushed a glass of sangria into her deeply browned hand. "Hi! What's a nice girl like you doing in a place like this?" he said, confirming her first impression that he was an obnoxious little creep.

She laughed because in those days, young women did not

145

confront men, even obnoxious creepy ones. "I might ask you the same question," she replied, feeling powerful and in charge of the situation.

And then a strange thing happened. He looked her straight in the eye and smiled. A Harry smile. Slow and devilish and sweet. A little boy's smile. The kind of little boy's smile that is smiled when the little boy has just been found out.

He smiled and she looked back into his eyes, which were bright and twinkly and the clearest grayest blue she had ever seen. Beautiful, bright eyes. Eyes that saw things. Eyes that would always be clicking, recording, revealing.

"Touché. Look. I'm not gay. Really. Ask anyone. I'm down for the weekend, I work with these guys. I, to tell you the truth, I was lonely. And also hungry and thirsty and I hate to eat and drink alone and so I thought what the hell. See, my date and I had a little misunderstanding and she went back to the city. I told you I wasn't gay! So, I paid for the weekend—so I, you wanna get some dinner? I think it's that time, they look loaded enough to start dancing together or something. Okay?"

They had been a couple ever since. But still, every summer, she welcomed the fantasy of new romance in some teenage way. Just out of reach, behind her conscious mind, beyond Harry, her mate, with his funny walk and his self-obsession and his neuroses and chinks. Beyond the real man, to the time before him, the endless summers of waiting for the One. The phantom lover who would cover her like the sun with an oily glaze of fantasy.

She had not felt the click and sitting on the deck, the psychosis of the daily news strewn around her, the layer of Sp 25 blocking the sun, her thighs crossed at the top revealing a new set of ripples, gravity's little guffaw, Gina knew that this summer, she wouldn't feel it. She knew it in a flash of

146

the most profound despair she had ever felt. A second of surging, hollowing breathlessness. She gasped out loud.

She was surrendering something. The tears again. Jeremy climbed out of the water. She watched him. All feet and long bony limbs. A few straggly hairs forming on his upper lip. The rest was hidden from her forever. No more dressing him, bathing him, watching his mysterious male parts grow and change.

Longing filled her. *Take it back, God.* Yearning. Unbearable yearning for her baby boy. The way his hair curled over his fat butter-soft neck. His little pudgy pink toes. The two teeth, one on top and one below; the way she held him, his chubby legs straddling her lap, warm, sun-naked body wrapped around her, feeling their hearts beating together. Every day a new miracle. Yearning, flooding her.

I want to go back. The thought hit her like the palm of a hostile hand. The tears sprang. Jesus, Gina, people in Beirut are eating their dead, a guy goes out for a Blimpie and gets his head smashed in. Those are problems. This is just self-pity. Be grateful. It didn't help. She was beyond irony. Beyond looking at her own process with detached amusement.

What is this world in which one woman is displaying her handbags and another is hoping to cut a piece off a dead man to keep her family alive? What would a Martian think if we beamed up a copy of the *Daily News*? What is any life but a daily hide-and-seek with death. This is what all of those grown-ups were talking about. Now it belongs to you, too, my dear. Middle age. Men hardly look at you anymore. Too many hairs in the comb, too many creases in the smile. Better than an A.C. on the noggin, but not better than getting to just stop right here. For a while anyway.

Summer keeps coming around faster and faster. It's Christmas and then it's summer again. Nothing in between seems real anymore. Spring and fall just seem like a holding pattern between the real stuff. Winter hits and we all start planning for the summer. Maybe all that's left of real life is held in those three months of the year? She shuddered.

I am not special. The tears came, again. Somehow the thought had never occurred to her before. I was never special and I never will be. I'm just another suburban East Coast girl who grew up in a mildly disturbed traditional family, went to college, got good grades, went to work, met a guy, got married, had a child, became a magazine writer of journeyman but not extraordinary talent, achieved moderate affluence through marriage and a certain cachet based on doing interesting work in an interesting place, having a sense of humor and knowing a lot of overachievers. I have a nice life-style. But I'm not special. Not Jane Goodall, Jane Fonda, or even Jane Pauley.

I don't have one special interest, hobby, or physical attribute. I am not going to make my mark on the universe.

When she was thirteen, a very beautiful girl, slightly older than herself, had moved next door to her and she had been consumed with envy. One day her aunt Ida, who was very wise and pulled no punches, saw her staring at the girl while she washed her mother's car. Ida seemed to be reading her mind. "Gina, darling. Let me tell you something that will save you a lot of grief. Around every corner is someone prettier, smarter, richer, you name it. That's the way it is. So don't waste time with envy. It'll just drag you down with it."

She had known right then, that Ida was right, but the reality, that she would not somehow overcome all competition and rise to the top, had never quite taken hold. Until this first real Monday morning of her fortieth summer. Like a lightning bolt to the Electric Exec—it got her where she lived.

She closed her eyes, the tears catching at the corners, burning into her sun-protected cheeks. I've got to get to work. She felt drained. She knew herself well enough by now to know that that kind of enervation had nothing to do with being tired. Estivating. That's what it was like. A word she had written down once. *Estivation.* Summer sleep for reptiles. They slow their heart and respiration down, fill their bellies with water, and wait out the dry spell. Just lie out till the rainy season, conserving their energy. Okay. So, I'm estivating. I'm one of Lyn Revson's former handbags. Lizard in the sun. She let her mind go, knowing that the only way out of this familiar but dreaded ennui was to find the feeling she was so adeptly fielding.

Harry. The trouble with Harry. He kept popping up at her like the body in the old Hitchcock flick. What was the matter with Harry? Sunday had been ridiculous. Harry had finally emerged from Donnie's room, all Valium mellow and Nuprin dreamy and he and Donnie had taken off for the city.

He wanted to get away from me as quickly as a guilt-ridden middle-aged man can ever get away from his wife. He never even made eye contact. And he was lying. I know it. So, what about?

Gina lowered her lounge chair and turned over, giving up even the pretense that she was not wasting time. Fritzi. Was that it? Was he having an affair with Fritzi? Her stomach tightened. For weeks she had fought the spectre of Fritzi Ferris, using every psychobabble technique she knew (and that was saying something). Nothing worked. The green-eyed duo, jealousy and envy, filled her soul, wounding her with a truth about herself that she hated. She wanted to be a person who was above such base emotion. Why was she jealous of an Orange County bombshell instead of Mathilde Krim or Sandra Day O'Connor? It shamed her.

Unlike Harry, Gina had actually been to Orange County on one of her L.A. assignments. Where was it? Newport Beach? Yes. She had felt like a blind person who regains her

149

sight without any warning. Blondness. Overwhelming blondness. Everywhere.

She had been taken to some gigantic glitzy new mall, feeling completely out of place. Black, she was wearing black in the daytime, which was perfectly hunky-do in Manhattan, but in Blondsylvania, she felt as out of step as if she had shown up at a February funeral in Boston in her underwear. Nothing was black. Anywhere. Black had not made the color spectrum in Newport Beach.

As far as her East Coast eye could see, everything and everyone shimmered in shades of white/blond, yellow/gold, cream/beige. The floors, the furniture, the hair, the clothes, the skin, even the sky was blond. Even the orientals and black people were blond! It was truly astonishing. She had to close her eyes and refocus. She pulled out her sunglasses, squinting against the glare, and made a note on a napkin. "If you buy a house in Newport Beach, you must sign a form swearing to keep everything in it neutral, including pets, children, and appliances."

Most fascinating of all had been a certain type of woman Gina saw everywhere she went. A blond chirpy type of the Farrah Fawcett school, which did not exist, to her knowledge anywhere outside of the West Coast. It must be, she thought, that if one of them ever leaves and goes to Philly or New York, they undergo some organic chameleonic process— some sort of cosmetic photosynthesis or something—because there are no people on the East Coast who look like this, talk like this, dress like this, or act like this. Or smile like this.

The smile was unique. It was a smile of people who have a lot of time to spend on their teeth and feel no ambivalence toward anyone or anything. It was a truly egalitarian smile, flashed with equal intensity at fox terrier and Big Mac flipper, mother or lover.

She had wandered around in this glittering blondness for

two days. Everything and every place and every person was new. New and clean and bright, fresh and crisp and white; nothing was broken or chipped or dark. Dark was death. Death was not real here. People don't die in sunshine, on the tennis court or shopping for tank tops.

Gilded blond matrons glided from silver beige Mercedeses to buy fresh yellow fruits and chilled white wines, whizzing off to their pale pink New Southwest–style condos where their gray-white husbands with their taupey beige tans were waiting with blinding yellow diamonds for their platinum-haired wives.

"This is what the whole entire world would be like if Hitler had won the war," Gina had written, and hopped on the next plane for home.

So she had a sort of prehistory with Fritzi. And Fritzi won the Mrs. Orange County contest hands down. Fritzi played into her deepest, most shameful fears about her husband and all her husband's friends. Deep down inside they were all Philip Roth fuckups. Champagne wishes and shiksa dreams. Why was Robin Leach mixed in all of her metaphors? Now, that really *was* troubling.

So, Harry had fled, leaving her feeling abandoned, isolated and paranoid, another set of not unknown, but certainly unwelcome feelings. But were they *the* Feeling? The one draining her energy, making her want nothing so much as oblivion. Sun and sleep. No thinking. No coping.

Arturo farted. Maybe in her next life she would come back as a flatulent beagle. Just eat and sleep and fuck everyone. The thought cheered her. She dozed. When she woke up, she would call Harry and make him deal with it. Whatever, or whoever, *it* was.

"Mom. Mom. Psycho Sink is here. She wants to know if she can throw out that noodle glop from last night?"

Gina struggled to consciousness. "Uh. Huh. Sure. Tell her

I'm outside if she needs me, I'm trying to stay out of her way."

"Sound thinking. I'll be back."

Gina rolled over, and looked at her watch. Half an hour. She had been hoping for a world-class, time-wasting snooze. She was still tired. Jeremy strutted toward her, a big goofy grin on his dark handsome face. "She is such a trip. She's wearing a baseball cap backward and boxers, like Owen wears, and she's got her portable TV on top of the stove. She's watching one of those your-father-would-have-been-so-proud-of-you movies and she's smoking a cigar."

"Psycho Sink" was Jeremy's name for Ethel Smith, who, though probably harmless, resembled no one so much as Anthony Perkins in drag in the original *Psycho,* a fact Harry never failed to point out to Gina, even though it only fueled Gina's case for selling.

In ten years Ethel was the only cleaning person she had ever gotten to show up more than twice. However, in true horror movie fan paranoia, Gina tried never to be home or have anyone else home when Ethel was there. Ethel didn't take direction well. As long as you kept out of her way, didn't interrupt her TV viewing, and left the check on the sink, she was fine. Even Arturo stayed clear of the kitchen when Ethel was there.

Jeremy flopped down beside her and opened a container of yogurt. "I just watched the weirdest movie."

Gina sat up. It was so rare that he sought her out for conversation anymore, that when he did, she tried, no matter what was going on, to pay attention.

"There were these ancient vampires and they suck the life out of these young girls and then the old vampires become these babes, beautiful, stacked, and young."

Gina reached for a spoonful of yogurt. "I wonder if that works better than Oil of Olay."

A HOUSE IN THE HAMPTONS

"God, Mom, you really are warped." Jeremy reached over and grabbed a T-shirt and pulled it on. The shirt had faded images of James Dean on both sides and various holes, tears, and pins pulling it in different configurations.

Gina watched him, debating whether to make mother noises. She decided against it. "So, what's new, kid?"

Jeremy slugged down the last drop of yogurt and handed Gina the empty cup.

"Thanks."

"Think of the calories I'm protecting you against."

He watched her in that way that teenagers watch their parents when debating whether to reveal something for which they could be lectured. "Something really bad happened to my friend Allison's sister."

"Allison from school?"

"Yeah. She just called me. It was on the news, but I missed it. Her sister was like sixteen and I guess she was messing around with drugs and stuff, anyway she was found in this really perverted drug dealer's apartment and she was stabbed to death and then set on fire."

"My God! How horrible! Poor Allison. Her poor family." Gina bit her lip, she would not follow with an evils-of-drugs lecture, the event, God willing, held enough information.

"Yeah. She sounded kind of down."

"Jeremy you are a true master of understatement. I wonder if Janie knows. Owen used to go around with Allison. Janie knows her mother."

"Yeah, she knows. Owen called me. That's how I heard it first. But something was going on over there. Everyone sounded really uptight."

"Really? Just this morning?"

"Yeah, while you were zonked. Owen said his mom had a call and raced out of the house like there was a fire sale at Bergdorf's."

Gina laughed. "Owen is so bad. I wonder if I should go over there."

"I'll go with you. I don't want to be here alone with you know who, especially after the vampire movie."

Gina stood up too fast and felt the blood leave her head.

"Please! If Ethel was sucking on young flesh, I think she'd have her act a little more together, kiddo."

"Yeah. Unless she's in disguise so's we won't suspect her real identity. Something really twisted like that."

Jeremy fell back on the deck and screamed. "Ow! Ow! My back! My back!"

Gina crouched down on her knees, "What is it? What?" She rolled him over.

A safety pin from his T-shirt, which held James Dean's hand against his nose, had opened into Jeremy's shoulder. Gina pulled it out.

"What was it?" Her son, for a moment, was vulnerable.

"You have just become the first teenager to be stabbed by his shirt."

"Gina Hart!"

It was Ethel. Gina and Jeremy jumped like Laurel and Hardy caught loafing by the new foreman.

Ethel always called her by her full name. She called all of them by their full names, no one had ever dared asked why.

"Yes, Ethel?" Gina poked Jeremy to keep him from snickering or in any overt way antagonizing Ethel, who had, in fact, chased him and Arturo around the house with a toilet plunger for laughing when she sang along with Kenny Rogers on some talk show. Actually, Arturo had not laughed, but he was with Jeremy and that was guilt enough.

"Telly phone. That rich friend of yours. You're outa bleach, so don't blame me if the wash looks grayish."

"Fine, Ethel. Thank you."

Jeremy two-stepped behind her into the kitchen. Gina

picked up the phone, turning her back on her overly curious son and menacing cleaning lady, both of whom were poised for eavesdropping.

"Janie?"

"Gina? Are you alone?"

"Surrounded."

"Okay. Oh boy. I'm at the Southhampton police station, can you meet me right away?"

"Uh. Sure. Of course. What. . . . ?"

"Keep a blank facial expression at all costs. My, oh, God, my mother's been arrested. Just come!"

"Fine. Bye." Gina felt her face fighting her like a rubber band in a slingshot. Four eyes burned into her back.

"Well, Janie wants to have lunch. Want me to drop you at the beach, hon?"

Jeremy watched her with teen cunning. Psyching her out, they called it. "Hon? Where did this 'hon' stuff come from? You been sniffing room freshener, or something?"

Ethel snickered, which was the closest she ever came to a laugh.

"Too much sun, smart-ass. Come on, Ethel has work to do. Get changed and let's go."

Gina followed Jeremy up the stairs. So much for a fine summer morning. Her feeling of dread, of the absent click grew stronger. This was not going to be like any other summer. The thought of Delores Cowan behind bars flashed across her mind followed by Harry. Harry. Shit. Harry would have to wait.

While Gina Hart was racing down the Montauk Highway to Southampton, Harry Hart was reclining in a chair at the "various Varinofskys," as Gina called their dentists. The Varinofskys consisted of the very old and eminent Dr. Vladimir Varinofsky and his three aging-hippie sons, who all sported black motorcycle boots, ponytails, and noses so Rabelaisian, hooked, and chiseled that they were not only certainly un-dentistlike, but seemed to have been cloned from the original version of the Three Musketeers. To the Harts' knowledge, they were the only father and triple son act in modern dentistry. Harry could never tell the junior Varinofskys apart, thus the various tag.

Harry was compulsive about many things, but dental hygiene was not one of them.

Ever since his senior editor had gotten a viral infection around the sac of his heart after having his teeth cleaned, Harry had been panic stricken at each long overdue dental visit. To make matters worse, the Varinofskys had a new hygienist, who was German and, so far as Harry could tell, on first impression (she had stuck him in the chair and marched out to get his file), looked to be old enough to have escaped after *the* war. *Great. On top of everything else, I'll probably get mutilated by Marathon Woman.*

Harry closed his eyes. Poor Donnie. He had taken care of Harry, driven him, listened to his breast-beating, run a bath for him, practically put him to bed. He had stayed at Donnie's and Donnie had slept beside him in Owen's extra bed, the way they used to do as kids. Donnie had a patient at eight and had made him coffee and left him a Valium and a glass of fresh-squeezed orange juice before he went. *I'm at the office all day if you need me,* he wrote on the napkin.

What a friend. What they had not come up with yet was a decision on how to handle the Aaron situation. Harry moaned. An entire new person, dropped into the middle of his life like a human grenade. A son. A second son. My God!

After Fritzi had unveiled the hidden past to Harry and given him a while to recover, she had left them alone together.

"So?"

A HOUSE IN THE HAMPTONS

"So?"

"Jesus. It's like looking in a mirror."

"Yeah, but you get to look back, I've got to look forward. Not such a pretty picture. I was hoping to keep the hair."

"Yeah. Well, that's not the worst of it. Two bridges. Three root canals, astigmatism in right eye. Nearly blind in the left. Gingivitis. Expanding waistline. Arthritis in the left elbow and not a lot of sex drive."

Aaron smiled. Harry smiled. They sat facing each other. Neither of them knew what to do next.

"You sound just like me. I mean your speech rhythm. Of course the humor is a little, underdeveloped. A little young. But now that you have the role model. . . ." Harry burst into tears. He moved forward and clasped Aaron to him and held him tightly in his arms. "My God. Son! Son! I'm so fucking sorry! All those years we could have—I could have given you. Please don't hate me. I didn't know! I never knew!"

They held on to each other. Aaron spoke into Harry's ear. "Don't feel bad. I had a great dad. I got a lot of love. I'm okay. I mean this is really a gift. My father dies and I find out I've got a brand-new one waiting in the wings. It's okay, Harry."

Harry let go and moved backward. "Can you call me something else? I mean, I don't know what, yet, but something else?

"Sure. I guess so. I don't know what. I mean, I'm not quite ready for Daddy. Are you?"

Harry pulled out a crumpled Kleenex and blew his nose. "No. I don't know. Let's leave it on the table. Harry for now, but with something else in the works. Maybe it will just come to us."

Aaron shook his head. "It's funny you would think I would hate you. If I felt anger at anyone when I found out, it was at my mother. She told all the lies. To you and to me. I accept it now. I mean, I can see her reasoning, but in many ways it wasn't fair. I think my father . . ." Aaron hesitated at the word and looked at Harry. "My father was really quite a guy. But it's kind of like finding out you were adopted. I really lived a lie. It was hard on them, too, I bet, because I look just like you. After I found out, it fit. The way she used to look at me sometimes. And sometimes she was kind of distant. I mean, she's not your typical mom, right?"

Harry laughed. "Right." He was fighting an almost over-powering urge to tell this man he loved him. It was the myth of Narcissus come to life. It was like loving himself.

"Aaron. This is going to take a little time. I have a wife and child who know nothing about any of this. I . . . Well, I wish I could just take you home with me now. But, if you don't hear from me right away, please don't think it's because I'm not there for you. I have to figure out how to approach them. I'm a little fuzzy-headed right now."

Aaron tensed slightly. Harry could feel it. "Sure. I understand. I've known about you for months. You're new at this."

Harry blew his nose again. The reality was starting to sink in. "I'd better go now. I . . . I'll call you soon. I want to spend time with you. I want to try and make it up to both of you. I just don't know how."

"Sure. Me too. I mean, I don't know either. It's okay, Harry."

Harry shook his head. "I don't know. I just hate you calling me that."

Harry reached out and Aaron came closer and Harry put his arms around him again and held him. For a moment he saw what his life would have been like if Fritzi had told him all those years ago, and he shuddered. He had gotten off easy. And for that above all else, he must atone.

The Nazi hygienist reappeared holding his file before her

158

with a look of such profound disdain that for a moment Harry feared that she had seen something in an old X ray, some fatal mouth virus, just what he probably deserved.

"Mr. Hart. It has been two years since your last cleanink. Dis is turr'ble. Very bat! Please open your mout'!" The Nazi slammed down the file and slipped into plastic gloves, face mask, all the post-AIDS safety paraphernalia.

She snapped on the operating-like lights, picked up the mirror and torture tool, and leaned in. "Vider!"

Anxiety flooded Harry's every corpuscle. *I gotta get out of here.* His mouth filled with saliva.

The Nazi withdrew, shaking her masked head fiercely. "Dis is not goot! You are a secreter. De saliva builds de plaque. You got so much plaque! Turr'ble! Do you floss ant brush tvice a day?"

Harry swallowed, fearing reprisals for the truth, but determined to go to the oven with dignity. "Brush, yes, floss, no."

"Sure! Sure! Two years vit no scraping! Your gums are receding. Do you have other self-destructive tendencies?"

Harry came to. "No. I've chosen to destroy myself the slow way, through poor dental hygiene."

No laugh from the Nazi. "Vell, I speak to Dr. Varinofsky. Maybe he can deal vit you. Find de best approach, to make you take your teeth seriously. Sometimes guilt ant fear work, sometimes positive reinforcement. I do not just treat de mout, I treat de entire mind–body relationship."

One of the junior Varinofskys appeared in the doorway. "Hi, Harry, long time. How's it going?"

"Fine. Until about fifteen minutes ago."

The Nazi ignored him. "Doctor. Dis is serious. Such plaque. No flossing. Two years vit'out cleanink!"

"Well, do your best. Harry's a very busy man."

159

The Nazi marched out of the room. "I get my special pick."

Harry sat up. "Where did you find that one, Buenos Aires?"

The Varinofsky laughed. "Yeah, not much bedside manners, but a genius with a gumline. Relax, Harry. She won't hurt you."

"Sure. Easy for you to say. Can you have her cool it with the Freudian interpretations? I am not really interested in the relationship between my flossing habits and my psyche."

"I'll try. She's a little, uh, touchy. But Jesus, it is so hard to find a good hygienist anymore. They're all becoming computer programmers."

"Great, next time I'll go to IBM for this."

The Nazi stormed in wheeling the largest water-driven cleaning instrument Harry had ever seen. Harry grasped the sides of the chair, desperately wishing he had taken that Valium Donnie had left.

The only release from mental anguish is physical pain. Where had he seen that? Some gallery opening. Well, he was about to test the theory. He closed his eyes and opened his mouth without even being commanded. He deserved this. At least. He would meekly accept his fate. He could see all of those evil little viruses poised at his gumline, waiting to slide down around his heart muscle.

"I promise nutink," the Nazi said, and closed in.

The next thing Harry Hart knew, he was lying on a day-bed in Vladimir Varinofsky's office with the entire clan peering down at him. *Now I know how newborn babies feel when the relatives come to view,* he thought, and then immediately panicked. I died? I had a heart attack? I'm paralyzed?

A junior Varinofsky, Vance, Harry thought his name was,

put a hand on his shoulder. "You're okay, Harry. You just fainted. Take it easy. Don't get up too fast."

"Fainted? I've never fainted in my life!"

Vladimir snickered. "So be glad for a new experience. Something to tell your grandchildren. How you became the first person to faint having their teeth cleaned."

The various Varinofskys found this very amusing and all chuckled politely at Harry's expense. Harry made a mental note to change dentists.

"It was the Nazi sadist. She must have hit a nerve. I'm fine. Just let me out of here!" Harry tried to sit up and was overcome by a wave of nausea. His pulse raced, then slowed, he felt himself growing cold and clammy. *I'm having a coronary. I'm gonna die surrounded by sadistic dentists.*

A second junior put a stethoscope to Harry's wrist. "Your blood pressure is still low. Can your wife come down and take you home?"

"I'm having a heart attack! I'm dying!"

Vance put a cold compress on his head. "Relax, Harry, your heart is fine. I'd say it's just anxiety. I'd give you something, but your pressure's still too low. Who can we call?"

"Donnie Jamieson, 555-7869. If it's his service, tell them it's urgent." Harry closed his eyes, trying to breathe deeply like Donnie had told him to. Thank God Gina wasn't here, how perfectly humiliating to have your wife see you reduced to whiny embryonic terror by a group of Hassidic gum cutters.

Somehow his life had turned a corner while he stood watching from another car. He dozed off, feeling his blood pumping him forward. *Come on blood, keep moving. Get me out of here.* He moved in and out of consciousness. He could hear two old men talking in the waiting room.

"So, you know how my wife is always finding new restaurants? Well, she drags me last night to this new place, way the hell down in the Village. An Abyssinian restaurant. So we sit. On the floor. My back is broken. We wait. We wait. Finally these two, whaddaya call them, Abyssinians, Ethiopians? Is that a race—is that a country? Maybe not, anymore.

"Whatever they are, they come out with this huge platter of unknown substances. A plate full of brown stuff, looks like from one of those vegetable horror movies. Like mounds of greasy vomitlike Jell-O and stale bread. That's it. With our fingers, we're supposed to eat this stuff. Stick our fingers right into it.

"So I look at my wife. I say, "Look, forty years you've been dragging me to new restaurants, when all I want is a little lean pastrami on rye. A little pickle. A cup of noodle soup. I go. I go, because I love you. But, this is it. Enough. I will not put my fingers, worked to the bone for fifty years to put food on our table, into that hozzeray! Make your choice. The Carnegie Deli or the Galloping Gourmet. Took two of the waiters to get me back on my feet."

"So, did she come with you?"

"Ha! You bet ya! Not a peep. Went uptown. Had a Reuben with extra Russian dressing. Sauerkraut dribbling down her mouth. She says, "You know, Sam, I had a terrible thought. That's what the Ethiopians eat, when they're *affluent*. No wonder they're starving! Went home, wrote a check to Save the Children. My troubles are over."

Harry smiled in his sleep. Old Jewish men talking always made him smile. His father's face swam before him. Poppa. Always a laugh. Always an opinion about everything.

Poppa and Momma in their Miami condo. Surrounded by their peers. Old Jews in the sunshine. "Miami is God's waiting room," his father liked to say. He was right. But there was something comforting about it. Every day his father

162

played cards. One by one his partners died. Finally he was the only one left, so he played with the widows.

When his wife got sick he cared for her himself until her mind softened into mush and he had to let her go. Terror in Harry's heart. It would happen to him. That look in his mother's eyes near the end. Screaming eyes, pleading eyes. No way in. No way out. The day before his mother died, Harry went to Miami, some primitive instinct moving him. He woke up that morning and went to La Guardia. When he got to her hospital room, he saw a sight that was etched in his memory forever. His mother lay in bed, dressed in a pink silk nightgown that his father had insisted on. "She always kept herself nice," he had told her nurse. Harry's father stood at the foot of her bed, holding one of her shrunken callused feet lovingly in his hands. He was polishing her toenails.

Harry stood watching him, tears falling from his eyes. Tears that had more to do with his love for his father than the pending loss of his mother. He prayed that he would be capable of the same devotion to Gina. God forbid.

His father lived two years longer, but his heart wasn't in it. He stopped playing cards. He watched the news and philosophized. Harry called every day.

"What's up, Pop?"

"What. I just hopped off the water skis and I'm making lunch for Liz Taylor and Loretta Young. Then, a few sets of tennis, maybe I'll take the jet to Vegas for dinner . . .

"What's up. The nightly news! The maniac of the day! 'Description, five feet eight, black male wearing sneakers and a black leather jacket.' No wonder they never catch anyone. The description fits half the East Coast!"

"How ya feelin', Pop?" Harry asked simple questions since they didn't really matter, his father was so lonely. He just loved the chance to talk.

"It's relative. Everything's relative. I'm feeling fine for a Jewish altercocker, but pretty lousy for an Olympic pole vaulter. Listen to this. Remember your mother's friend Mrs. Rosenberg? Well, she got sick. Pneumonia. So I went with her to the hospital and they put her on one of those stretchers with wheels . . ."

"Gurneys?"

"Gurney. That's a word? In English? Gurney, shmerney. Anyway they wheel her into this room and leave her there. We wait, we wait. Finally this doctor, looks like one of the Marx Brothers, comes tearing into the room, so busy, so fast, the dust is blowing, looking at some chart, doesn't even say hello, how are you. So he says to poor Mrs. Rosenberg, in an accent from Elmer Fudd cartoons, 'I'm Docta Tuma, where's da carcinoma?' And Mrs. Rosenberg gets very upset.

" 'No. No! No carcinoma! Pneumonia!' And they go on like that. 'No carcinoma?' 'No! Pneumonia!' I'm thinking, this is meshuggener. So I come forward. Is this a joke, Doctor. Tumor? 'Tuma, Tuma.' He says. I says. So, *Tuma*, no *tumor*. No *tumor*, *Tuma*. *Pneumonia*. Now get out of my face before you make a sick old man with a weak heart hit you.' "

"So what happened?"

"So? I found a nurse, who found a real American doctor, who took nice care of Mrs. Rosenberg, who thinks I'm a hero, who is falling madly in love with me. All in a day's work."

Harry loved this. "So, this Mrs. Rosenberg, not bad?"

"Eh. Not bad. Not good. Listen son, take it from me, when the crotch cools, the mind clears. Well, my crotch is freezing cold. That's why my head works so well."

It did, too. When Harry got the call that his father was dead, it felt like he would die, too. It was simply unbearable. It was all gone now. All that was left of his past, the last person who knew him from the beginning. Maybe the only

164

person who had ever totally and completely loved him as he was. And whom he had loved without any expectations or conditions. He had loved his father. He had loved his mother, too, but he had never liked her. Not really. She picked on him. She disapproved of so much about him.

She was too much like him, too. He looked like her. He hated that. It was almost like seeing himself in drag. His father evoked noble feelings in him, feelings Harry was proud of in himself.

Harry did not have many noble, pride-filled feelings about other people. Gina, most of the time. Jeremy, most of the time. Donnie, most of the time. But his father, all of the time. Maybe he had mythologized him. He was a pretty ordinary man. Filled with frustration and compromise and ego and Jewish angst. It didn't matter. Harry worshiped him and when he died a part of Harry died with him. A part he mourned every day. A missing piece he secretly longed to replace.

"Harry. Harry."

Harry opened his eyes onto Donnie Jamieson's smiling face. A most welcome sight. "Thank God! I thought I was going to check out here, in a dentist's office. What a way to end it. Get me out of here."

Donnie reached out and put a hand on his chest. "Okay. I've checked your pulse and respiration. You're fine, but sit up very slowly. I think you had a panic attack, didn't take the pill, did you?"

"No, Mom. I know. No dessert. Believe me, I regret it."

Donnie helped him up. To his surprise he felt fine, better than he had all day. "I'm okay. Let's get a cab."

"I've got the car. I thought I might have to carry you home. Come on, let's get some dinner.

"Dinner? Dinner? What the fuck time is it?"

165

"Six-thirty or so. You slept for over an hour not including the fainting part."

"My office must think I've lost it."

"I've called them. Relax, everything's under control." Donnie led him out. The night was warm and surprisingly dry. Harry felt revitalized. "Donnie. I feel, really much better. I mean, I think we can work out this Aaron thing. I mean in relation to how we deal with Gina and Jeremy. I feel much more in control."

"Good. Though I think you've bought a little time." Donnie helped Harry into his car and slid behind the wheel.

Harry watched him. "Whaddaya mean?"

Donnie smiled. "Don't tense up again. This has nothing to do with Fritzi Ferris. This is *my* family drama."

Harry relaxed. "So, what?"

Donnie took a deep breath. "Now, bear with me, because for some probably deeply unconscious set of reasons, every time I think about this I start to laugh and, believe me, it is not funny. Okay? So this is the first time since Janie called me that I've said it out loud, so I have no idea what will happen."

Harry grinned. "And we both know how little you like that feeling. Raw, uncontrolled emotion."

Donnie nodded. "Know it well. Okay, here goes. My mother-in-law was arrested today. She's in jail."

A moment suspended in space. Neither of them moved or breathed. Donnie broke first. A loud, raucous laugh, picked up by Harry and carried over the top into hysterics. Tears burst forth from their eyes. They screamed with laughter until their stomachs hurt and Donnie was unable to drive.

"It's not funny, Harry."

"I know! I know! What for?"

"She was, ha! Ha! She was nabbed by the Southampton police in a raid on a drug den. Ondine was with her."

"Ondine! *Haaaaa!*" They were gone again. By the time they calmed down they were at their favorite Italian restaurant and into their second bottle of wine.

They were famished. Released. Purged. Why this badly needed release of tension should be at the expense of poor frail Delores Cowan, was something neither of them had a clue about. Something about the absurdity of it, of their lives, of the smack of tabloid reality on their oh-so-manicured and well-tended and neatly arranged lives. First there was the long-lost sex goddess reappearing, then the miscarriage who turns out to be a son, and now the elegant dowager in the clink with the junkies.

This was not the kind of thing that happened to guys like Donnie and Harry. It made everything else about their imaginary defenses against life, or death or fate or whatever they called it at the moment, most patently hysterical. It freed both of them, for a moment, from the burdens they had placed on themselves. The endless voices in their heads, organizing their behavior into socially responsible and acceptable patterns.

They were such good boys. Members of professional organizations, attenders of school activities and sporting events, payers of taxes and husbands of faith and loyalty. They did it every day the way they had been raised to believe they were supposed to and the fantasy was, that would keep them safe from the fates of those others they read about in the *New York Post.*

They were getting drunk and having a very good time.

"We should call, Donnie. Gina and Janie are probably certifiable by now. Did Big Ben get her out?"

"At last call, Big Ben was nowhere to be found. I called Norman Gallo, I knew he'd taken a long weekend. He posted bail. They should be home, by the time we're home. We're okay."

167

Harry and Donnie were settling in to what Janie called one of their "Alfie conversations," where they grappled with the meaning of their lives. It had been a long time since they'd had an evening all alone together like this and they were both loving it.

Two sexy full-of-attitude young women strutted by and sat at the next table. The women lit cigarettes, crossed their legs, and checked out the room to see who was watching them. The list included Harry and Donnie.

A seriously inebriated middle-aged man with aviator glasses and a drink in his hand moved in on the two beauties. "*Bonsoir*, Mademoiselles. May I join you?"

The sirens barely acknowledged his presence, allowing him only half-raised lids to show the depth of their uninterest. How dare he! Who did he think he was talking to, some man-hungry secretary? "No!" one of them said, and turned her head, tossing her long blond hair and blocking him from view.

The man's face reddened as if he had been smacked. He seemed to shrink. He stood there for a moment looking dazed. The two ignored him. He was already invisible. He turned, his head down, as if the possibility that anyone had seen his moment of rejection was more than he could bear, and disappeared into the bar crowd.

Donnie watched him go. "He reminds me of one of my patients."

Harry laughed. "Only one?"

"Well, if we're talking about middle-aged men hung up on the conquest of young women as a way of fending off the *D* word, no, but that kind of really self-deluding behavior. Not having a sense where you belong, who will receive you. I've got one guy who does things like that all the time."

"What a schmuck! And this asshole is wearing a wedding band as big as a fucking Timex. It's pathetic."

Donnie smiled. "It's only pathetic when it's someone else doing it. Just because we don't, doesn't mean we couldn't."

Harry poured more wine. "Did I ever take you to see a tape of that Bergman play, *The Lie?* He did it for the tube? With George Segal and Shirley Knight?"

Donnie sipped. "No. Must have been the only one you left out."

"Jesus. I can't believe it! That's one of my all-time favorites. They have this marriage. I mean, it's like the perfect marriage. They're rich. He's a hotshot architect, she's this beautiful educated lawyer or something, they are terribly polite and loving to one another; the kids are always clean and well mannered; only she's balling his best friend, the whole center of the relationship is as hollow as a malted milk ball.

"It's the weekend that Martin Luther King is assassinated, and it's on the news all the time, but no one cares. No one connects to it. They're all too gauzy, too superficial. Something happens and he has a major ego killer setback at work and then King gets it, and he gets a migraine or something and he goes to see his doctor. Well the doctor isn't there, but the nurse likes him. She's warm and sexy and she hears him, she validates him, and he ends up making love to her, realizing that something is really wrong with his marriage. But he has never been unfaithful, he fucking worships his wife! She's perfect, absolutely perfect all the time, even at seven in the morning—no unshaved armpits, no morning mouth, nothing.

"Anyway, he goes home and, they have separate bedrooms, which tells you something. God, I love Bergman, he finds those details, says so much without any words! Anyway, somehow he tells his wife who he thinks he knows so well; he starts to confess to her because he feels so guilty and all she keeps saying is 'Don't tell me, don't spoil everything,

I don't care, I just don't want to have to know about it,' and this tears him up. It's like, who was that masked man—who is this woman? And then she gets mad and tells him, I think that's how (God my memory is so fucked!) she tells him about her lover, George Grizzard? Yeah. And he's just gone. The whole thing, his whole life has been a lie. It just blows his mind."

"And?"

"I take it you are waiting for me to make a point. Well, the point is, I had a point, somewhere. Fuck. I lost my point." Harry refilled their glasses.

They were quiet. Thinking. One of the sirens is saying to the other, "I wasn't designed for long-term use."

Donnie pushed his plate back. "Harry, Gina is not Shirley Knight. Your life is not going to blow apart and send you off into the madness of the middle-aged singles scene. This is workable. Aaron is twenty-five. You're innocent. She'll deal with it."

"Yeah. I know. But, Jesus, Donnie, this is hard to admit. Part of me, not a major part, but a little part of me is fantasizing about her *not* dealing with it and throwing me out. I'm free to run back into a meadow full of flowers with my aging arms spread wide, pluck, pluck, and it's not my fault or my decision. Out of my control. I didn't leave my wife for a midlife fling. A chance to one last time drive a woman crazy with lust and passion, a new woman who has open admiration and sex in her eyes. One last burst of freedom. I can't say I haven't thought about it and it scares the shit out of me."

"Of course you've thought about it. You're alive. You're a middle-aged man and you're human. It's okay to think about it. Think about it as much as you want, trying not to only makes it worse."

"Do you think about it?"

170

Donnie laughed. "Jesus, Harry, give me a break! Who do you think I am? The archangel? Of course I think about it. Fritzi. I've thought about it with Fritzi. So there. Don't say I never open up to you. I've thought about violating her, even."

Harry's whole body lit up. He loved this. "Really?"

"Really." Donnie leaned back in his chair and took a long deep breath. "Harry, let me tell you something that happened to me years and years ago. I never told you and I don't know why or why I'm thinking about it now. I was going through a period, right after medical school. I was in my internship, my mother was dying. I had just married Janie and she was pregnant and I was trying like a son of a bitch to meet everybody else's needs. And I was having paralyzing migraines because I was so damn angry all the time.

"So, I went to see my training analyst and we worked on some of this 'Mr. Perfect' stuff and I left and got into the elevator at Bellevue, thinking, I don't have to be the goddamn bar mitzvah boy every minute of my life, maybe I can even be a selfish asshole like all the guys around me all day.

"Anyway, I always had this thing about elevators. I was always the person that everyone else in the elevator asked to push their buttons. I always hated that. It was like, somehow they knew I would do it for them. So, I got into the elevator, and I'm feeling very rebellious, regressed, one might say, and there's an older man already in the elevator, he's very well dressed and he says to me 'Would you please push three for me.' God, I even remember the floor!

"Well, I was enraged, I mean he was in there first and yet not only did he not offer to push the button for me, but he waited until I got in to have *me* push it for him! So for the first time in my life, I asserted myself. I said, 'Push your own damn button!' And the man just stood there for a minute, very dignified, and then he said, 'I can't. I'm blind.'"

Harry choked on his wine. "Jesus!"

"My point is, Harry. I knew something about myself and the course of my life then. Right then. I knew that for whatever purpose God had put me here, I was supposed to try to be a good person. I was not going to get away with any bullshit." Donnie patted his hand. "You, too. My friend. You, too."

"You're right. Fuck! I hate to admit it, but it's true. Maybe that's what Fritzi is about. What the former Madeline was about. We got our oozing Delicious, our big fat Granny Smith, and the garden snake out of the way early on.

"You know, Donnie, when I went over there, yesterday? Was it only yesterday? Feels like months. Anyway, I told you, she was wearing like nothing, and I had this moment when I thought, 'Fuck everything, I'm going for it.' What a joke. My fantasy adultery is interrupted by the appearance of my long-lost son! I mean if that's not akin to the blind man in the elevator. If we were Catholics, we'd probably have been priests."

Donnie laughed. A sleek young waiter appeared and they ordered Sambucas and double espressos and crème brûlées, knowing they would pay dearly, but exerting the only form of rebellion left to them.

"Tell the truth, Harry. Do you really feel monogamy is a scrifice?"

Harry smiled his wide, bad-boy smile. "The truth or The Truth? *The Truth* is, no. I dunno. I mean, I like sex. I like sex with Gina. I *know* sex with Gina. Gina is the ultimate safe sex. I mean she's clean. I know where she's been; I know how she feels, smells, the noises she makes. I know what she wants, needs. I know she loves me; it's not a performance or a test. She's passionate, I mean it's not like she's a phone-in or anything, but she's, she's sweet and passionate. There's a kindness, an elegance. I know how I sound, I sound like

172

Gina's aunt Ida or some fucking faggot, but I think you understand.

"Remember those days, being single? And this was before it really got heavy. But God! I went home with women, wanted me to beat them with belts, tie them up. Wax globs in the ears; funny smells. One girl, I liked her. She was well educated, pretty, great body. Fun to be with. First time we did it—I know how disgusting this sounds, only you would I tell this to—but her pussy smelled like Kitty Litter.

"I couldn't tell her! 'I really like you, but your cunt smells like cat shit.' I (quite ingeniously, I may add) suggested we take a long bubble bath to heighten the experience. Raced around, lit candles, rolled a joint, got her in the tub, and I was like a housewife on one of those fucking kitchen cleaner commercials. I scrubbed her, bubbled her, rinsed her, powdered her. Back to bed. Same smell! After that, I was always thinking about it when I looked at her. Jesus!

"One woman wanted to do it with her and her sister. One girl screamed hysterically, blood-stopping screams when she came.

"There was this copywriter from Barnard, she had so much body hair, I never knew whether to caress her or pick the fleas off her. Jesus, it was fucking scary! And that was before all the sicko stuff and all the diseases! Even Fritzi was scary.

"Gina was like a miracle. Sweet and clean and sexy. Just right. We fit just right. Do you hear this? I should tape this and send it to her! I've just recommitted to my marriage for another hundred years!" Harry beamed.

The waiter reemerged and placed their indulgences before them. Donnie was quiet. He took a bite of the crème brûlée. Noises swirled around them. Lusty Manhattan restaurant sounds, ebbing and flowing like sea sounds, gentling them, protecting them from the ears of others.

Two overdressed and angry gay men at the table behind them rose to leave. "Well, I'm not worried about it, because I never let *anyone* come in my mouth."

Harry and Donnie's eyes locked. "Me either," Harry whispered.

Donnie laughed and blew him a kiss. Harry attacked his crème brûlée, relieved of his conflict. Of the guilt of it as well. He knew what to do. It was easy as long as his goal was in sight. The goal was to keep his marriage alive and healthy. Period.

Donnie watched him, struggling somewhere with his own need to finish with something. Something, un-Donnie-like. He was just drunk enough to risk it. "Can you tell me about Madeline? Without compromising her. I mean, it's been a long time. Can you tell me what it was like?"

The question was as unexpected as Donnie knew it would be. Harry put down his coffee cup and watched him. His whole body relaxed. This was not funny. Harry knew him so well. This was from the bottom of Donnie's private well of longing.

"Nice. She was, well, we were both so young, neither of us had any experience or anything. She, has, as you well know, the most beautiful body. I'd close my eyes and run my hands over her and it was just like magic. So sensual. Really soft. Very sexy. Hot, too. She liked it a lot—a little giggly, but that was nerves. To tell you the truth, most of the time we were in the park, the backseat of a car. I never even saw her completely undressed until we eloped and then it was in my old bedroom at home. Talk about a turn-off! I think I was too terrified of her to ever really have the experience. But definitely an A. Christ, Donnie. I always forget you never slept with her! It should have been you instead of me. I've never figured that one out."

"Yeah. Well, we probably never will. I've always wanted to ask you that. I don't know why I never could."

"Did I make it better or worse?"

Donnie sighed and took a long sip of his Sambuca. "Better, I guess."

"Would you have preferred foul odors and hairy tits? It's not too late, I can change it."

Donnie smiled. "No. No, thank you. That would really be depressing. If I'm to go to my grave with that one zipless fuck still on my mind, better that I should have chosen well."

"Well, there *is* one thing I left out. Didn't want to make a joke of it. But, I think it might be helpful. She made a noise when she came like, well, like Minnie Mouse with gas. That's what it reminded me of. Squeaky."

"Squeaky?"

"Squeaky."

"Much better, Harry. I can return to my wife now, a cleansed man."

They exchanged slightly red-eyed groggy looks. Their wives. "Get the check, Harry. I'll get the car."

Janie Jamieson lay on her French antique bed curled in a ball under layers of white linens. Her windows were open and she could hear the waves in the distance. She breathed with them, trying to unlock the tension just under the exhaustion, so that she could sleep. She had stayed up waiting for Donnie's call, but by the time he did, full of Italian wine and himself, she was too angry to get much comfort from it. No. That wasn't fair; he wasn't full of himself, just a tad less patient and supportive than usual. Give the guy a break. Imagine having to cancel an afternoon's worth of patients because Harry passed out having his teeth cleaned. She laughed in spite of herself.

175

God, what a day. Sort. Janie. Come on. Sort. A picture of her mother being led out in handcuffs by two enormous, sour-faced deputies flipped into her mind. She shuddered. If Gina hadn't been with her as a witness, no one would ever believe her. Her mother in a tank full of black junkies! Heroin addicts! Her mother was no longer a quiet genteel dipso —she was a streetwise momma.

The look on her mother's face was the worst part. It was a look Janie had never seen before. It was worse than despair. It was, what exactly? Arrogant? No. More defiant. "Look at me! I don't care." It was almost as if she was gloating. As if she was gaining pleasure from Janie's shock and pain. It was as if her mother hated her.

I don't know her at all, Janie thought, and the tears finally came, unlocking her. She rocked, holding herself, the sea breeze rolling over her, soothing her, cradling her. The pain came from so far down, Janie knew it was a wound she had been carrying forever. The look on her mother's face was not a new look. It was just one she had never let herself see. *I never had a mother*, she thought and the sobs shook her, rattling her like a baby's plastic toy, shaking without purpose. Senseless.

All of my life I have been running away from the truth about her. About them. About myself. She couldn't protect me. She couldn't guide me. She couldn't *see* me. I reminded her of what she'd lost. Him! After me, she lost him! That's when it all started. I certainly heard that in the middle of enough drunken fights.

She had been their dancing doll. Cute little Janie with the smart mouth and the answer for anything, always so eager to fill all the holes, dance on her broken little toes to keep them happy. They used her and she hid in them. Unwilling to confront and give up her illusion. JAP Tragedy is right, she

176

thought. "Please God, don't let me fail my son the way she failed me."

There, she had said it out loud. Failed her. Her mother had left her untended long ago. Neglect. Neglect of herself. She had never allowed such a thought. What a selfish greedy child! With everything she had been given! That was how they trapped her, kept her away from the truth.

Her mother was frail and kind, the myth stated. She did not hit her, verbally abuse her, or deny her things. She just simply was not present. My mother is obsessed with my father. He's the only thing that's real to her and she can't have him. That's why she's doing this, sinking this far. That's in the look, too. "If I can't get to him, I don't care." I've never been enough to save her. I never will be enough.

Janie rocked. The rattling loss shaking her small little-girl body, holding herself in her slender freckled arms. Holding on to whatever love of herself she had patched together over the years. Like a tiny sparrow rummaging in the snow, gathering a bit here and there, she had formed a raggedy little nest of self-love; mother love, carried each piece in her tight little beak, up and up. She needed it now, that homemade little pile. Needed it to be strongly crafted, strong enough to cradle her through the night and the coming summer days—strong enough to fight off the huffs and puffs of the big bad wolves who were waiting below in the dark. She couldn't see them, but she knew they were there. Waiting.

Her father was still not back. Gone fishing, said his note, but Janie didn't believe it. Rage filled her, heating her heart.

She doesn't want me. She doesn't need me. The whole time Norman and Gina and I were bailing her out, talking her out, taking her to the clinic, she wouldn't even speak to us. Just that look. All she wanted was for him to know. That's the only thing she asked me. "Tell your father."

Let him take care of this! I'm sick of turning my life inside out for them! There's nothing I can do. It's their mess! I'm halfway through my own life and I've never even lived it. I'm still living theirs.

Another shot of truth hit her, blinding her with despair. Okay, Janie. Okay, babe. Hold on. I love you. I may not show it much, but I do. I'm here. We're going to be fine. Count our blessings, now. Donnie. Owen. Louie. Gina. Curly hair. See, made you smile. It's okay, babe. Go to sleep now. Go to sleep.

She held on. This was something she must see through by herself. Donnie had protected her enough. Mothered her enough. She had to do this for herself and her family. Tomorrow morning she would find her father. She would go to the clinic and deal with the doctors. Norman was handling the police.

My God. The police! This is real! It was a raid! The dealer was shot! Ondine was in jail. Isabel had refused to let them bail him out. "He do wrong. He pay the price." Poor Isabel. If only it were that simple for her mother; she didn't even know what the charges would be. Hopefully, Norman would keep it out of the papers. That would just be great.

Owen didn't know the truth yet. Not really. He sure knew things were weird. He had tried hard enough to get her to tell him.

"Grandma's sick. We had to take her to the hospital."

Not enough for Owen. "What hospital? What kind of sick? Where's Big Ben? Where's Ondine?" Louie just stood beside Owen, his eyes as big as coffee cups, holding Owen's hand. God! She couldn't even have pulled herself together for Louie!

Another thought. That was part of her mother hurting her father. She moaned. It was so ugly. She had always thought of her mother as so kindhearted, so gentle. What a crock. This was prime-time ax-murderer stuff! Okay. I know. She's sick. It's not her fault. Shit. Some of it is! Not trying or caring is! Wanting to punish innocent people who love you is! I hate her. I wish she would die!

Janie gasped. She was always sure God heard her thoughts and would make them come true. She always took the wicked thought back. See this, God. I am taking this back. Forget all about it. I wasn't here, I never said it. But she didn't. She held on to her right to the thought. She really didn't know if she meant it or if what she meant was, she wanted to escape from them forever and death seemed the only way possible. Easier for her to die than for me to grow up, she thought, and held on tighter.

She must tell Owen the truth in a way that he could handle. And then, when Donnie came back on Friday, they would talk about moving out. She swallowed hard. Yes. Out. No more velvet trap. It was time to find their own summer place. Maybe somewhere else. And Louie. She wanted to take Louie with them. Oh boy, it's not going to be easy.

A new thought appeared. She let go of her legs and sat up, icy-cold under her heat. The *party*. Oh, my God, I forgot about the party! Big Ben's sixtieth birthday party. Saturday night. Three hundred people!

This is a joke. So? So, they'd have the goddamn fucking party! Her mother could sign out for an overnight and they'd just have the stupid thing! Why not. She could wait until Sunday with all of her bombshells. It would be a perfect ending to a perfectly wonderful family circle.

Janie rolled over and let the breeze float across her sun-red back. Pretty spunky, babe. Pretty hard-core. The Match was a good influence on her. She sighed. She'd call and invite The Match and her crew to the party. The hell with all of them! She was the one who'd been working on the damn party for months! She'd have anyone she wanted! Janie curled into her ball and hugging tight, she fell asleep.

6

In an unusual warning, doctors have reported the case of a man who injected cocaine into his urethra to heighten sexual pleasure and then, through extreme complications, suffered gangrene that led to the loss of both legs, nine fingers, and his penis.

Helpful hints expert Mary Ellen Pinkham offers this handy tip: you can give hair ribbons a quick "ironing" by drawing them across a warm light bulb or toaster.

Not so easy, Mary Ellen, with nine fingers missing, however. Gina tore the two items out of the paper and put them in her folder. Her "Hope and Absurdity" file, she called it. But the absurdity certainly outweighed the hope. Her *hope* was to someday publish a book of the most horrifyingly absurd newspaper items she had ever read, positioned next to the most airheaded and ridiculous. She took out her pen and notepad and tried to concentrate. Seven-fifteen. She had the front booth at the Soda Shack all to herself and it was still quiet. Janie was meeting her there at nine, which meant

181

nine-thirty, so hopefully she could get some work done. Of all summers for her to have serious deadlines, this was shaping up as the worst. She tried to concentrate. Conversations around her kept seeping into her head. Workmen came and went. She loved the Soda Shack first thing in the morning, the earlier the better.

Six A.M. was the best. That was when the real people or, as Frankie Karsh had so eloquently put it, "the Never Gonna Have Its," came in on their way to or from work. Construction crews, the contractors always sitting in a booth, their "men" at the counter. Fishermen, night workers from the police and fire stations, locals and old-timers, nodding to one another with the tacit unspoken understanding of the insider. The resort town equivalent of Town and Gown, an ancient barrier never to be crossed or forgotten. Forgetting or not understanding its presence was a mistake for which either or both sides paid dearly. Gina knew her place. She was the summer folk. Employer and invader and so it had always been.

Jack Reed, tall, handsome, and the most successful pool contractor on the South Shore strolled in. "Cup of brown water, Millie."

Gina waved. Jack took his coffee and came over.

"How's things, Mrs. Hart?" It bothered her that he never called her Gina. He had spent weeks at their house when they put in the Swamp. It made her feel old and unimportant.

"Fine, Jack, how about you?"

"Can't complain. This place is really popping. Everyone keeps saying the bottom is going to fall out because of the Wall Street mess, but I'm not seeing it." He stood over her sipping, Gina thought of what would happen if she were suddenly to lean forward and unzip his fly. She blushed, as if he could read her thought.

A HOUSE IN THE HAMPTONS

"I heard about Mrs. Cowan. Would you tell Mr. Cowan if there's anything I can do to help, just give a yell."

Gina was speechless. Jack Reed smiled and took his leave.

"Give my best to Harry." Harry and Mrs. Hart. She felt left out of something. What, was unclear.

How could Jack Reed know? It *just* happened. Don't be ridiculous, Gina, of course he knows! He hangs out at Jimmy Vale's with half the Southampton P.D. My God! Every time someone's barbecue overheated the whole town knew about it. This was no place to keep a secret, even a far less juicy one than one of the primo landowners of the entire area and a noted philanthropist and fund-raiser to boot being nabbed in a drug raid. Oh, God. Poor Janie. Who knew what would come next?

Two well-preserved men in sweaty jogging suits puffed in and sat behind her. Gina reflexively patted her hair. Old habits die hard, she thought, ashamed of herself and guilty about her Jack Reed fantasy. Was this to be her fate? One of those aging women desperately seeking reassurance of their dwindling charms. One of the candidates for "surgical recontouring," as a recent ad for some plastic surgery mill had called it.

The thought made her mad. It was starting all around her. Friends and acquaintances, disappearing for weeks, only to show up with noticeably different eyelines, jawlines, and bustlines. Who are they kidding? If they all did it, then it wouldn't even make any difference? She hated it. Somehow it made her feel bullied.

If I choose not to, which I will, considering how horrifying I find the thought of anyone, doctor or mugger, coming at my face with a knife or, what did they use for those face peels? The ones where you look all shiny and unreal. Acid. Yes! They pour acid all over your face and it literally burns off layers of your skin! My Lord. No way! But if she refused and everyone did it, what then? She would look older and they would all look younger and younger? Could she handle that? Hard to say.

This was all part of the article she was trying to write. Sort of postfeminist treatise. Women and illusion. How she and so many others had bought into this whole bullshit myth that feminism had turned all women into friends. She had, in her own life, turned women not just into men's equals but into gods. It was quite simply insane. She had made more mistakes in judgment and had suffered more hurt feelings and betrayals in the last ten years than in her entire life. She bought the whole thing. It became essential to reveal deep personal information to every woman you had lunch with. To trust totally all their intentions as if some feminist fairy godmother had waved a magic wand over all of them, eliminating competition, jealousy, and personal flaws of character. No woman would ever again want another's husband, job, or bustline. Poof! Gone.

She had changed all her doctors, lawyers, and agents. Women, women everywhere. And what was the truth? If women were really equal, not tokens, then they, like blacks, Jews, and other minorities, should take their lumps as human beings with the rest of the chickens. She had had her brains (not to mention her heart) bashed by several of her sisters. They were still just folks, after all. Including Gloria Steinem who was dying her hair and cavorting with millionaire bachelors at Manhattan charity balls. Give us a break.

Anyway. It had hurt a lot. She felt as if she had turned her life over to strangers. At one point she had so many "friends" and had told so many personal things and listened to so many *really* personal things (there was only so far someone as private as herself could go) that she could no longer differentiate one plight from another, one life from another. Sometimes she almost forgot what had happened to her and thought it had been told to her by someone else! She had overinvested in many not so selfless and well-motivated people. It was like being in eighth grade (the nadir in most females' social development) only with a far greater downside. And her husband and son had suffered. She had become a friend to all and thus to none, including herself.

Now she was in recovery. A dry drunk. Not a consciousness-raising group in sight, except Janie's; because Janie really was her friend and really needed her there. *But,* she never talked. Almost never. And she had put Janie on notice that attending was threatening her sobriety, so if she felt, at the next session, an overwhelming urge to talk about her sex life, she was out of there.

Women, she now believed, were pretty much what they had always been. Some of them were nasty, jealous, manipulative witches and some of them were divine and most were everywhere in between. But to live in a place like New York City surrounded by the most narcissistic, competitive, and driven human beings on earth and think that they had all taken their NOW pledges to heart was not only naive but downright self-destructive.

All the years of *Cosmo* pap, *Ms.* diatribe, *Vogue* intimidation, and the rest of the women's magazines self-serving reshaping of reality had left her and hordes of others angry, confused, and somewhat lost. She felt like one of those old guys who wander the Jersey shore with a metal sweeper, trying to find the silver in the sand. She was trying to find the truth about herself and her peers, amidst the rubble.

She made notes. "Many women still have an adolescent idea of female friendship. It often prevents us from seeing our mate as our best friend and most trusted ally. There is still too much of the teenage twitching limb—boys as outsiders. All of the most painful betrayals of my life, beginning with my mother, have come from women; not men. What does that mean? What is a real friend and how many can anyone have in a deep and reciprocal way? Have we all read so many stories of old widows and their card groups, that we start collecting our protection against the ultimate humiliation of old age and aloneness, earlier and earlier? Men die, it is other women that we will be left with?

Needy women see me and others like me coming. We have been the bottomless fuel pump of the wounded and needy. It became our raison d'être. "We have been blessed with good men, children, work and decent lives; we owe the less fortunate." Our sisters. What we never saw was that unevenness does not breed gratitude and mutual support. It becomes a giver and a taker. We led with our guilt more than our hearts. Not always, but often. We owed every woman something. Often the result was their contempt and abandonment. On to the next pump.

I have done spring cleaning of my friendships and cleaned out the cobwebs in my relationships. Now I know who everyone in my life is and why they are there. Better one good cashmere sweater than a lot of junk, my mother always said. It still feels kind of scary. Lonely. All of those thoughts of who would be there if you needed someone, pop up and zap me. But what I have learned so slowly and painfully is that none of those people were really there for me anyway and I was there for them more out of fear of not being there than of really wanting to be.

Gina sighed. She had sold this idea, but what was she writing? She'd probably get lynched. She sipped her coffee and chewed on a cold hard bagel. A man behind her was telling a story. "So I tell him, well, I don't have that cat anymore. I don't have that apartment anymore and I don't have that wife anymore!"

Gina looked at her watch. Eight-thirty. She couldn't believe it. She always concentrated better in coffee shops, they

186

were her favorite places to work. Anonymous and no interruptions.

Kurt Vonnegut wandered in and headed for a booth in the back. Martha Stewart and her former brother-in-law, a tennis pal of Donnie's, strode in and bought all the papers. Gina smiled. Last summer Christie Brinkley and Billy Joel had come in to get an ice-cream cone for their daughter and nearly blew the cool of even the most blasé Soda Shackers.

This was the Hamptons, after all. She forgot sometimes, that this was a big-time, big-deal place. Whatever you know becomes humdrum and familiar. It was very much like hundreds of beach towns, only its proximity to New York had turned it into something more. And, as she had said in her summer piece, the More was becoming More madness.

There was less and less left of the charming, low-key place she and Harry had fallen in love with. Granted Sag Harbor was a different scene than Bridgehampton, Southampton, or East Hampton. Thank God for that! But they were all within spitting distance, and the Scene aspect of the summer had infiltrated even the funkiest Sag Harbor literary barbecues.

Town snobbery abounded. Even block snobbery. Bay versus ocean. Village versus woods. New construction versus old Victorian. Everyone had their shtick and their prejudice. Only now, with all the megamoney, glitz had been added. Now we were talking Rodeo Drive East rather than conservative, subtle one-upmanship. Designer shorts and makeup in the morning. Where would it end?

Two attractive women, tall, blond, and tan, glided in, clearly coming from a Maddie Evans workout. Gina recognized them from *Dan's Paper*, the local news and gossip sheet. They were divorced wives of two prominent men, one a publishing hotshot, the other an actor. Gina watched them while pretending to take notes. They moved quickly to the back, nodding to someone here, someone there. She had watched a lot of women like these, the discarded wives, living sometimes forever on what was left of their lost glamor. Living on their former names and the attraction of the less famous or renowned to anyone who had been more so. These women always moved with a kind of forced urgency, as if they were really doing something terribly serious or interesting, even if it was just entering a room. It was a defense, a posture. There was a nervousness, almost a desperation, about them, as if they knew that their inclusion in the life they had led was being held together with invisible tape and that the illusion of belonging must be maintained at all costs. Gina made a real note about them.

She refocused. Women in the nineties. What would happen next? My God. The nineties. It didn't seem possible. The century was winding down. The ride was almost over. The century would end, taking with it their youth and tantalizing them with a beginning that they would not see through.

Gina sighed. Her coffee was cold. She looked up, trying to catch Millie's eye. Someone familiar was coming in. A young man in shorts and a Princeton sweatshirt. He leaned over checking the headlines on the piles of papers on the front-window ledge. Why was he so familiar? Friend of Jeremy's? Two people entered behind him. Frankie Karsh and Fritzi Ferris. Oh, great! She averted her eyes, hoping they wouldn't see her and would pass her by. This she did not need right now. She still hadn't talked to Harry. No. She was not going to think about that.

"Gina? Is that you?"

Shit. Gina looked up and managed a smile of surprise. Fritzi was wearing an all-white sweatsuit and no makeup, blowing Gina's last defense. She looked even better without makeup. "Oh, hi! Hi, Frankie! Nice to see you."

A HOUSE IN THE HAMPTONS

Fritzi looked at her strangely. Or so Gina thought.

The young man came toward them carrying several papers. Gina thought he would pass, but he stopped by Fritzi.

He was close enough now for Gina to see him clearly even without her glasses. She gasped. It was like flying backward in time. Harry. It was Harry, the way he looked when they first met. What was happening?

Fritzi watched her with a strained, puzzled look on her face. "I don't think you've met my son, Aaron."

Gina's throat closed. They all stood over her, waiting. The young man's face tightened. She couldn't move. Harry's son. No one had to say anything. She couldn't breathe. There was absolutely nothing she could think to do or say. She was trapped. Her eyes caught Fritzi's, pleading, in spite of herself, for a way out.

Fritzi moved forward and leaned down closer to her.

"Oh, God. He didn't tell you? I'm so sorry. This is terribly embarrassing. Please forgive us."

Gina held her eyes, unable to move. *Someone, please, help me.*

"Hi, guys!" Janie bounced in dragging her tote behind her. All eyes turned, grateful for the diversion. Janie was fast. Thank God for Janie. She clicked on Gina and then on the young man, who stood rigid and grim beside his glowing mother. Click. Click. She got it.

"Gee, sorry to intrude, but, we're late Gin', come on, I'm in a tow-away. We gotta go, now!"

Gina rose, blindly gathering the papers and notepads, and practically pushed Harry's son out of the way in her effort to escape. "See you later," Janie cooed, and shoved Gina forward out of harm's way.

189

July 2

So, here I am, again. After weeks of having hardly anything to say (except about Kenny), all of a sudden, intrigue;
cloaks and daggers, who only knows what lies in store!

I am definitely learning a lot about families. I guess because it was really just my mom and me all those years, I
never really learned much about other people. I mean, in an
intimate way. Well, that is certainly changing!

So, here is the latest. Tonight is the big bash. Big Ben's
party. There must be thirty people running around up at the
house (I am on the beach with Louie and Owen).

You have never seen such a production! Tents and dance
floors to cover the pool and heaters for the entire outside.
Fish and pelicans made of ice and an entire bandstand for
the orchestra. A real, live orchestra! There must be a zillion
flowers and whole trees in pots everywhere. I'm psyched.
I've never been to any party like this! So that's the good
news. Everything else around here is really kind of upsetting.

First off, last Monday, Mrs. Cowan and Ondine went out
on some errands and never came back. I mean, it was really
weird! Janie got a call and left and didn't come back until
late and she told us all this story about Mrs. Cowan having
an asthma attack and being taken to the hospital, but Ondine
didn't come back either. Isabel has been crying in the
kitchen; Janie hasn't taken her sunglasses off all week; Owen
and Louie are really upset and Big Ben, who was gone fishing or somewhere when all of this happened, has been really
uptight. He hasn't even joked around with Louie, which is
like totally unusual. If you want my opinion, I think that

they put Mrs. Cowan in a detox. Owen won't talk about it (not with me, anyway) but I know that's what he thinks.

Anyway, it was pretty weird and then, on top of that, Dr. Jamieson hasn't called in two days! I can tell that Janie is freaking out. I mean they always talked every ten minutes. He calls her all the time or she calls him, but with all of this going on, she can't reach him.

I eavesdropped. I know that's really bad, but I just couldn't help it. I was in the kitchen and she was on the patio on the cellular phone and the door was open. Anyway, I heard her talking to his secretary, who told her he had been called to Washington for some consultation and he said he would call in as soon as possible. He was supposed to be here yesterday (the party is tonight!). Mrs. Cowan is arriving from the "the hospital" any minute now. What a mess!

And then Gina and Jeremy and Arturo (God, I hate that dog) moved in! Harry Hart keeps calling and Gina won't talk to him and *she's* wearing *her* sunglasses all the time and she and Janie are locked in these heart-to-hearts every other minute. I mean, I'm almost out of it with curiosity, and no one will tell any of us kids anything! It's worse, of course, because I'm not even a family member; but they've all become like my family. It feels really bad.

And on top of everything, I went home yesterday to try and talk to my mom about it and she burst into tears and ran and locked herself in her room, and *she* wouldn't tell me anything! And she never keeps secrets from me! I know it sounds chauvinistic, but maybe they're just all on the rag or something. Anyway, Louie's been really loving and very needy. Janie is trying, but they're all so busy with all of this intrigue, that I know he feels it. Last night he came in, in the middle of the night, and asked if he could sleep in my room. When he's scared he usually sleeps in Owen's room, except now Jeremy's there, but I think he came to me because it's mothering he's missing. Anyway, no one seems to be in much of a party mood, so the evening should really be interesting, writerwise. People are coming from all over the world! I'm psyched for my mom to see this. I mean, photographers from magazines and everything are staked out at the gates and security people to make sure they don't get in! It's really *Dynasty on the Beach*. I should have a lot to tell tomorrow.

No one, arriving at the Cowan estate that evening at eight P.M. would have known anything was amiss. From the entry portico, luminous with flaming torches, to the receiving line of family members, all was perfection. Shining smooth perfection. The way those kinds of parties are created to be.

Big Ben Cowan, in white dinner jacket and ruggedly handsome joviality, greeted the flora and fauna of his life. Fishing buddies, bush pilots, art dealers, civic and city leaders. Diplomats, former ambassadors, and Gerald Ford. Movie stars and even a few rock stars gathered on Ethiopian excursions.

Beside him, dressed in sea blue Givenchy and diamonds, stood his lovely wife, Delores, looking relaxed and dainty, chic, smiling, her clear blue eyes welcoming the world. Down the line celebrants passed. The tall, scholarly son-in-law, Dr. Donald Jamieson, just flown in from Washington. The vivacious, adorable only daughter, Janie, aglitter in Donna Karan evening wear, her wide brown eyes sparkling, her hair filled with summer flowers. The charming children, Owen and Louis, in matching dinner jackets, bright pink roses in their lapels. Perfect!

The privileged invitees wandered, French champagne in crystal goblets clasped in every hand as they oh-so-reverently invaded every nook and cranny of the Cowans' lives. Wandered through Big Ben's private gallery, grazing before paintings and family photos; wandered through the bedrooms, poking into cabinets and closets to see the inner workings of these oh-too-good-to-be-true people. The Haves at Home! The night was warm. Even the sea breeze had quieted enough to let the candles, twinkling everywhere, giving the stars a run for their money, do their magic without strain.

Women in evening gowns and bare legs, women who would have such gowns at the beach, who lead lives where ball gowns and nights like these are part of their daily routine; danced alongside fishermen's wives who had never before tasted caviar or seen real emeralds, except in magazines. Everyone was having a wonderful time. What a perfect celebration of such a wonderful man's life!

Janie had done her work well. On a projected screen behind the bandstand, an elaborately compiled photo montage flashed scenes from Big Ben Cowan's bigger-than-life life. Ben fishing with Lyndon Johnson. Ben with Frank Lloyd Wright. Ben teaching architecture students at Columbia. Ben loading food containers into his plane for the first drop into the Sudan. Ben holding starving orphans in his strongly muscled arms. Ben with the mayors of half the cities in the U.S. Ben with Carter, Reagan, Bush. Ben and his I Have a Dream Foundation board. Ben with his family through the years, hunting, riding. Working for Save the Children. Working to Save the South Shore Coastline. A man's man! The envy of all!

This was, in its way, an old-fashioned kind of party. The kind that was still given as part of a personal odyssey. The Cowans were too liberal and, at the same time, too personally conservative (call it guilty if you like) to ever give a party like this, as so many others of their wealth and stature did, just for the hell of it. A hedonistic show without reason.

That was part of the very old or very new megawealth. Lavish parties for no reason at all.

They had never had such an affair. Janie's wedding, Owen's bar mitzvah, and this. Delores shunned the very mention of a party on her important birthdays or anniversaries. The spotlight belonged to Ben; they had agreed on that in some unspoken way, long ago. And on Ben, this night, it remained. He embraced it. It loved him and he loved it. And, maybe because he knew he was most likely saying good-bye to its cozy, flattering light, he relished it even more.

Janie was her father's daughter. When the show had to go on, on it went. Everything in her life was changing, but first things first. This had been the week of Gina and her mother. If Donnie Jamieson had to choose a week to throw her the first fast flying curve of their marriage, he had chosen well. She had not had the time to dwell on where in the hell he had been for two days that didn't have a telephone. Next week.

At four this afternoon her father had gone to bring her mother home and her husband had called and told her he was flying from Washington and would explain everything after the party. He arrived, fully dressed and looking, she thought, a little pale, just minutes before the first guest. Unbelievable! But she was dealing with it.

Her parents had returned somber but in control and she had helped her mother get ready. Ironically enough, her mother looked better than she had in years. Her head seemed clear, she was on some medication, but to Janie's knowledge she had not touched a drop of anything but bubble water, so far. If this was a circus, it was at least Barnum and Bailey. Center ring with all the lion tamers ready to perform. She had one more duty as M.C. before the tributes started, and then she was going to sit down with the biggest piece of chocolate cake anyone had ever seen a single person eat and go for it.

Donnie was sitting at their table talking to Owen and Louie. He was most definitely not in the mood for this, but he had given it a fair shot and made the rounds.

Harry had made up for him. If Harry had ever been more manic, she had missed it. Mainly Harry was chasing Gina around the party and Gina, who looked ravishing, was dancing it up and flirting it up with every man under seventy (and a few over) who came within range. Poor Harry, she really, actually felt sorry for him.

He had made a hell of a mistake racing off with Donnie instead of going home and telling Gina about Aaron, immediately. He had obviously freaked out, but she didn't for a minute believe he had known about Aaron and lied to Gina. Not in his character. But to find out like that, in the goddamn Soda Shack! She certainly saw Gina's side. They'd work it out. In a way, it was kind of romantic, making your husband chase you all over the Hamptons begging for forgiveness.

Maybe she should try it on Donnie. She watched him. Naw. She couldn't. He looked too tired and too sweet. Besides, with everything going on, he was certainly going to be the house shrink to the masses, so this was not the time; on the other hand, where in the hell had he been?

"Hey, Jane, whaddaya think? Will I make it as a social-*eat* or what?" The Match. Janie turned. The Match, Rikki Bosco, and Katarina and Joey Rivers, fashionably late, at least, stood behind her. Janie could feel the eyes all over the darkened tent-covered terrace following them. New blood in a too familiar world. The Match was covered in bright red satin. One long, skintight slip of satin with enormous dangling red crystal earrings. She looked fantastic. Her hair was growing in and fell in soft tendrils around her pure white face. Katarina Rivers, standing beside her, looked almost drab in comparison. The thought cheered Janie. Even Katarina can have an off night. Janie went back to her lions, ready for the fiery hoops ahead.

Clovis O'Malley sat alone at a small table near the corner of the dance floor, sipping a Scotch and water and watching her daughter dance with her first serious beau.

China took her mind off Ben and made it almost bearable to stay. There she sat like Stella Dallas or some Fannie Hurst heroine, wearing her five-year-old party dress like a middle-aged Cinderella at her Prince's ball.

She would never have come if it hadn't been for China. She was so excited at Clovis's inclusion in this exotic new world she had entered. What possible excuse could she have given. She didn't even work Saturdays.

Besides, if she was going to be really honest, she had been agonizingly curious. Everything around her was a part of him that she knew nothing about. Their life together was spent in her small Hampton Springs cottage, mainly in bed. There was nowhere they could go together. They had both been in the Hamptons for so long, they knew everyone.

Five years. She sighed. *Five years, God, I must be mad.* She watched him. Vital and handsome and in command, making his way from table to table like a visiting head of state.

China whirled by and waved. She was so lovely! Her face pink and moist with sun and excitement. Kenny pulled her close and kissed her, his mouth open wide. Clovis cringed. He reminded her so much of China's father, she could barely look at him. It wasn't just his appearance either, it was the phony bravado, the easy charm.

Oh, God, she's heading for the same mistake I made and there is nothing I can do to stop her. She took a long sip of her drink. I can't even tell her the truth, not that she'd believe me now after all the lies, all of the years of allowing her

196

the fantasy. How do I tell her that I made her father up. He was not a kind, decent, brave man who died so young and so tragically. He was a weak, drunken, womanizing failure and that's how he died. Broke, drunk, and with a woman.

She could still see herself, standing behind the firemen and police, while they tried to pull what was left of her husband and his lady friend out of her flaming car. Would it have been better to tell her daughter that? Maybe so. Maybe then there would be no Kenny. But then again, maybe there would be something or someone even worse.

All she had ever wanted was to protect her baby, but now, watching her wiggle and whirl in all her powerful, fresh sexiness, she knew she had failed. When they're out there, they're out there. And if Ben meant what he had said last week, China was going to have a whole lot more reality to deal with.

Last week. He had not been alone with her since Delores was arrested. It could all have changed. Maybe it would be for the best. If it was final, she could let him go and try to get on with her life.

Her stomach dropped. He had sounded so sure. His real estate project was going ahead and he felt more secure in himself; he seemed ready to act. Maybe he had told Delores and that's what the arrest was about? But how could it be. It was a raid. She wasn't involved, she was just caught in a nightmare, a nightmare, that so far they had managed to keep private.

Ben was dancing with Delores. Clovis watched them with envy. There was a way that a man and a woman who have been married for a long time danced together, that could never be duplicated. An ease. A sense of the other person's body and rhythm; an intimacy.

She had such empathy for Delores. She knew how it felt to love him—but to love him without his loving back, would be simply unbearable. She wanted to comfort her, as absurd as that sounded. The last thing she had ever wanted was to hurt Delores Cowan or Janie or anyone. She had adored them all, long before she had let Ben into her life.

It was all so cheap, so immoral. It had humbled her, that was for sure. She was much less quick to judge anyone else's actions. Would any of them be able to forgive them for falling in love? Well, it might all be a moot point now, anyway.

Dance with me?"

She turned. Ben towered over her, smiling down, bringing tears to her eyes. "Do you think?"

"Come on, you beautiful broad, let the bastards eat their hearts out. I've danced with every goddamn female in the house to make this look kosher. Up!"

Clovis took one last sip of her drink for courage, and let him lead her onto the floor, where her daughter spun, smiling with the joy of having her mother a part of this fairyland that had opened its magic to her.

"Gina! Gina! For chrissakes! You're gonna give me a fucking heart attack! Enough. Stop or I'll shoot!"

Harry Hart had cornered his wife on her way to the powder room and she had taken off, leading him on a less than merry chase down the private walkway across the dunes, and out past the NO TRESPASSING and FORGET THE DOG, BEWARE OF THE OWNER signs and onto the beach.

Gina tripped on her hem and fell, Harry flopping down beside her on the sand, both too out of breath to speak.

Harry, who was highly motivated, gasped out his plea, not waiting for his second wind. "Jesus, you are one tough cookie! I, just let me try to, tell you why . . . I mean . . . I didn't have a Chinese clue! Not ever! All of a sudden, here is *me*! I mean, this grown man, just like me! It was like walking into one of those fucking teen body-switching flicks! You know what I mean? The son's body, the father's brain, trading places, sort of crap. I felt like such a bastard that she left and lied and never felt like she could tell me! I . . . I . . ."

Gina dabbed at her sweaty face with a cocktail napkin. "Harry! Shut up. Just please, shut up! If you do any more breast-beating you're going to need reconstructive surgery. Please, spare me."

Harry stopped. He knew her well enough to know talking was not going to do it. He swallowed. The fear that maybe he was not going to be able to woo her back, clutched at him for the thousandth time since her call on Monday.

She watched him, almost seeing his wheels turning, her eyes narrowed with hurt and anger.

"I've finally figured you all the way out, Harry. I really get it. Want to hear? Okay, here it is. Harry Hart in a nutshell. Harry Hart is a little piece of shit—at the *center of the universe!*"

It was good. Harry had to give her credit. She had him. He smiled at her in spite of himself.

"Don't smile at me like that!"

"Like what?"

"You know like what. Like a bad little boy caught with his fingers in the peanut butter. That's how I got into this whole damn mess to begin with."

"Mess? You mean sixteen years of marriage?"

Gina sighed. "You know, Harry, one of the real reasons I could cope with not being able to have another child was because I had you. A perennial three-year-old. Well, guess what. *I* grew up! I'm tired of it. I've outgrown my need to 'mom' the planet. I want an equal. Equals don't run away with the kid next door. I love Donnie, you know that, and I've never resented your friendship, but you should have come to me, first. I should come first. *We* should. That's what hurts so bad."

For once in his life, Harry Hart had no idea what to say. He put his head down and started to cry.

"Gina. I love you so. I can't lose you! Please don't give up on me. I made a terrible mistake. But I learned from it. I'm ready to change, too. I'm even ready to stop seeing Dr. Wexel. Please help me through this. I owe this boy, this man, something! And for Jeremy, too. Jesus. He has a brother! Please give me another chance. Please come home. I need you so much."

Gina watched him, feeling her resolve melt. She leaned over and stroked his balding sunburned head. "I never should have married you, Harry Hart. I should have adopted you."

Harry looked up and grinned, tears running down his face. He knew it was going to be okay. She still loved him. Gina handed him her napkin and he blew his nose.

She stood up and shook the sand off her dress. "Come on, Janie needs us for moral support. We'll talk tomorrow."

Tomorrow's softball, he started to say, but caught himself in time. That would really be pushing his luck. Donnie probably wouldn't want to play either. Harry stood up sheepishly and started after his wife, puffing across the sand.

"A little piece of shit at the center of the universe. That's not bad, Gin'. Not too shabby."

Gina turned and watched him scampering puckishly behind her. She laughed. "I bet you were one of those kids who cried when he had to flush. If it came out of you, it had to be valuable. Jesus, I wish I had your ego."

Harry caught up to her and put his arm around her waist. "Actually only for number two. Number one was never a biggie. Maybe a sniffle or two. A little salute. Poo-poo, I wanted bronzed."

A moan. Then a scream. The Harts stopped dead.

200

Shhh!" Gina put her hand over Harry's mouth. "What was that?" she whispered into his ear.

Harry shrugged.

Again, a soft scream, then moaning.

Gina's eyes widened. "Someone's hurt!"

Harry grinned at her. "You've been married too long. Listen again."

They bent down. Moaning. Air sounds. Gasps.

"It's called fucking, my bride. Remember? We used to do it, too."

"Are you sure?"

"Wanna go ask them?"

"Shhh!"

In the distance behind the Cowans' private walkway, two shadows could be seen. The man had the woman against the underside of the stairway, her legs wound around his waist. There was no way the Harts could get up the stairs without being seen or seeing and certainly not without interrupting.

"Can you see who they are?" Gina squinted.

"No. But they're under forty, or at least he is. No one over forty would risk what that does to your back."

"We're stuck." Gina plopped back down onto the sand.

Harry followed. "Great. Beach porno and no rewind charge. And we miss all the speeches."

They were quiet. The sex noises rose and fell. The sea sounds rose and fell. They were exhausted with their own spent emotion.

"Oh, God! My God! Fuck me!"

Gina blushed. As much because it was turning her on as for any other reason. Harry slid his hand up her leg.

"I know you, you wanton old slut. Wanna join them?"

Gina pushed his arm down. "Get serious. Stop that!"

"Oh. Oh. Harder. Harder. Ohhhhhh! I'm coming! I'm coming!"

Gina could feel the giggles starting way down in her stomach. She put her hands over her mouth and buried her head in Harry's lap.

"Why, Miss Jones! I never knew you cared!" Harry was aroused, and Gina's laughing into his lap made their situation even more preposterous. He put his hand over his mouth and laughed into his sweaty palm. He refused to lower his head, though. He still had hopes of seeing the lucky couple.

"*Awwwww*. Ohhhhhh!" Silence.

Gina raised her head. Her mascara was running down her face. "Shit. I ruined my makeup."

"You look beautiful. You are beautiful." Harry kissed her. She kissed him back.

They looked up just in time to see the unmistakable figures of Katarina Rivers and Rikki Bosco, climbing up the stairway back into the light.

The Match sat on the Cowans' Italian porcelain toilet seat with the lid down and the fan on, smoking a joint. She alternated each hit with a sip of champagne. Outside in the waiting area, two women fixed their faces and talked, unaware they were being overheard. She felt bitchy and powerful and ready for a fight.

Her old street self, coming back, comforting her. She needed good old reliable Ellen Mary, the scourge of Bensonhurst, tonight. She'd been hanging around rich people too long. She was losing her perspective. She didn't even sound like herself anymore, thanks to fucking Katarina. The recycled cunt had messed with her self-esteem.

So now, she felt rebellious. Infantile, no doubt, but more like her old self. The self that had gotten her through thirteen years with the Gargoyle sisters. Four-year-old Polish orphan taken in by old maid aunts. What luck! Seven ugly

202

sour-breath broads, pile them all on top of one another, they didn't reach her chin. Stooped and bitter.

In fifth grade she had seen a picture of Notre Dame in a history book and had almost shouted to the class, "Those figures on the top! They look just like my aunts!" They did, too. She had written down the word. *Gargoyle.* Once she had even yelled it at them in the middle of one or another unending fight over her misdeeds. They had no idea what a gargoyle was. Her aunt Winnie had taken a shot at it. "I don't gargle. You crazy girl! Just Colgate and a little peroxide."

She had raised herself in the alleys and the streets. Taught herself to be tough, never let them see her sweat, as the ads now said. She had survived by knowing that someday she would be big enough to leave. It would not be forever. She had worked after school and every summer and saved every cent and learned enough about people and herself to escape.

So. She was free. Big fucking deal. All the feelings she had so carefully stuffed back down for all of those years in order to survive a childhood without joy or laughter or kindness— they were coming up at her now. She was not going to give in. She was not going to let fuckhead Rikki and the Kunt see her lose it. She inhaled. No one had knocked. Just let them try to get me out of here before I'm ready. The women were oblivious.

"I knew he was gay when he was ten. 'He's going through a phase,' my husband keeps saying. Phase! Four hours a day, the kid's vacuuming. Give him flowers to arrange, he's in heaven."

"There are worse things. He could be crippled, blind. He'll be okay."

"I know. I should look on the bright side. My therapist says I'm always looking down at the ground instead of up at the trees. Fine, but the trees are *planted* in the ground."

The Match flushed the butt down the toilet and emerged,

startling the two partygoers, who had thought they were alone. She stared coldly, intimidating them. They quickly closed their purses and left.

She winked at herself in the mirror. "What a bitch, pickin' on a couple of innocent matrons." Tears started moving up into her heavily made-up green eyes. *No.* She wouldn't. She picked up her glass, feeling stoned but back in charge, and walked out into the party.

The band was playing "Moon River," which The Match would usually have found ridiculous, but the pot and the emotion took her inside the words. She refilled her glass and slouched against a tent pole watching the dancers and listening to everything around her.

> You dreammaker. You heartbreaker.
> Wherever you're going, I'm going your way . . .

Bits of conversation buzzed into her head.

"Mammogram, my ass. "It's like a duck press for tits! I'll never think of my boobs as sexy again."

"All I know is, I got on the train at Forty-second Street and I got off somewhere between the Williamsburg Bridge and Puerto Rico."

"I tell her. 'Leesa, your problem es de young cock. Stop looking for de young cock.' "

"Did you know that in one year the average person receives enough junk mail to stretch all the way to the moon and back fifteen times?"

> Two drifters off to see the world,
> There's such a lot of world to see . . .

"I look like an old hooker in this dress."
"You're always putting yourself down."

A HOUSE IN THE HAMPTONS

"I didn't say it was a *bad* look."

"You know the kind of group. They all have the powder blue American Tourister luggage."

We're after the same rainbow's end . . .

"They had guards at Treblinka, with dogs trained to attack male prisoners and rip their genitals off. The last word the men screamed was always the same. 'Mother!' "

"What, are you crazy? You got a bankrupt business, a bad heart, and a lousy marriage. A baby! How do you even know it's yours? You're drunk all the time. You got a wet noodle. Get a sperm test. Don't take her word!"

"A blood test. You get a blood test."

"Whatever they test. Test it!"

My huckleberry friend, Moon River, and me . . .

The Match floated. She could feel the tears again, but they were okay. Softer. Jesus, had it come to this? Weepy over Henry Mancini? She smiled. The grass was good. She felt tuned in to the universe. From what she could hear, they were all in the same sinking canoe.

"I found this incredible crystal boutique on the West Side. I'm drinking water with crystals in it now. The vibes move up through the liquid and charge my system. They call it a crystal hit. It's heavenly."

The Match picked up a fresh glass of champagne from a passing tray and made her way around the dance floor and out toward the beach. She had lost Rikki and Company hours ago, or was that weed time? It seemed like hours. In between the conversations and the music she glided, feeling invincible. Eyes followed her. Tonight she was glad she looked the way she did. Glad she was so tall, so red and white; so different. Most of the time she hated it, but tonight she claimed it. She was a giant dancing flame. Cold and hot and untouchable.

> I've got you under my skin. I've got you
> deep in the heart of me . . .

"I went through a period when I thought about suicide obsessively. But there was no way I could find to do it without pain or the chance of botching it and ending up a vegetable. So I gave up and bought a NordicTrack."
"They don't pay me enough to fire me."

> So deep in my heart, you're really a part
> of me . . .

"AIDS has completely flipped morality. It used to be, we'd see old movies and snicker because they were so tame. Well now, we'll look at movies from the seventies and early eighties and it will be totally the opposite. But not like a new innocence; it's like the sobriety of reformed debauchers."
"How did Jesus Christ ever get so big, anyway? I mean, it could have been any modern myth. Superman or the Tooth Fairy. The whole Christian concept is based on the most incredible arrogance."
"I told her, 'Listen, you got a roof over your head. You got food and I fuck you good. That's enough.'"

> I've got you under my skin . . .

The Match had reached the walkway to the beach. It was quiet here. The black night sky was encrusted with stars. She raised her arms over her head, breathing in the sea smell, her glass catching the light above her. She closed her eyes and let her head float. She was stoned. Nice stoned.

Someone was coming. She opened her eyes and slid down into one of the Adirondack chairs set off to the side. A couple was walking up from the beach. She heard low laughter and two voices. She crouched down and curled her legs up in front of her. They were moving closer. They stopped a few yards away and he kissed her.

"No. Rikki. Someone will see."

"Fuck 'em. I want you again, already."

"Me too. It's unbelievable."

"Let's get some bubbly. I want to dance with you."

"I'd better find Joey."

"Let him find you."

They disappeared into the lights. The Match uncurled her legs. She shuddered. No stopping the tears now. Better the truth, Ellen Mary, than all your suspicions. So the good news is, you aren't paranoid. The bad news is, everything else. So okay. So do we just wimp out or do we fight back?

The Match tossed her wine onto the sand and opened her purse. She blew her nose and repowdered her face. War is war.

Now the truth had found her. She knew exactly what to do next.

Joey Rivers was locked in conversation about the use of symbolism in the German experimental cinema with John Irving and Dick Cavett. As far as The Match could tell, none of them seemed to know much about it. She came up behind him and leaned down, watching the effect her full, round breasts, tightly shadowed by her dress, had on the trio.

"Yo. Joey. Wanna dance?"

Joey turned and smiled at her. "Sure."

She turned without acknowledging the stellar group and

led Joey away from the table—and away from the dance floor.

"Hey, Ellen Mary, the dance floor is thataway."

The Match turned and smiled at him. "You don't think I really mean that. Can you see me bopping around to that shit? It was just a ploy. I've got some fantastic weed. Perfect party shit. Very connecting."

He followed her, his hands in his pockets, looking laid back and very cool, but she felt his self-consciousness.

She knew this house well now. She had been coming for weeks to massage Janie, Gina, and the Cowans. She led him down an endless black marble corridor to the guest room that was used for massage and exercise.

He followed docilely. She smiled to herself. A macho kind of guy being passive was always a dead giveaway. Little by little, she was coloring in the pieces of Joey Rivers' real personality. He was less dense than the Kunt. She was still so cloudy.

The Match locked the door and turned the dimmer very low. She kicked off her shoes and flopped down on the massage table and took a neatly rolled joint, carefully packed into a filter-tip cigarette, out of her purse. She lit it and handed it to Joey, who looked, she thought, scared.

He took a long hit, coughed, then took another one. It was clear he didn't do a lot of this. She had counted on that.

"We should find Rikki and Katarina." Joey's eyes were glazing already. An easy high, she thought.

"Let them find us." She felt the irony of her response and her hand trembled as she took the joint from him.

She took a deep hit and threw her head back.

It was quiet. In the distance the music sounds and the buzz of conversation rose and fell, insulating them, creating an illusion of absolute aloneness. The intimacy of the stowaway or the stranded. People stuck together in an elevator; strangers on a night train.

The Match stood up and walked over to the small refrigerator in the corner and took out two cans of beer.

"So, Joey, you go to a lot of parties like this?"

Joey flopped down on the huge Italian leather couch behind the massage table, his eyes already red and half closed. He watched her cross to him. "Yeah. Some. Mostly Hollywood, though. This is a kind of different scene. There it's business, even if it's a fucking wedding. It's all business."

The Match handed him his beer and pulled him up off the couch. "Get on the table. I'll give ya my special quickie massage. You look real tight."

"Yeah. This preproduction shit is making me crazy. My financing just fell through, this is off the record." He was opening up. Joey never talked about his film.

He climbed up and rolled over on his stomach and The Match started working on his neck. He moaned. She could feel the knots under his shoulder. She knew just where to press. She could feel him letting go. The grass working its mental magic on both of them.

"Oh, Christ. That feels so good. I can't tell you."

"You got a lot of junk in there, Joey. Gotta break up that shit. It makes you toxic. Let me get it out. Take your shirt off." She helped him. He offered no resistance.

It was clear this was a service the Kunt did not perform. She kneaded. She went deeper and deeper. Slowly she let her hands move farther down his back, reaching ever so casually down under his pants, kneading his buttocks. She leaned over him letting her breasts brush against his naked back.

"So, why don't you ask Rikki for the money? He's always lookin' for investments. He really digs the whole show biz scene."

Joey's breathing was changing. She let her fingers move farther down, around the sides of his pelvis, teasing him.

"Yeah. I'm thinking about it. I don't want him to feel like I'm using him. I mean, after staying at his place and everything. It was easier before we got tight again."

Joey Rivers pushed himself up on his arms and rolled over. He looked at her as if he were about to film a scene. He was stoned and aroused, but he was trying to figure her out. "What the fuck are you doing, Ellen Mary?"

The Match straightened up and undid the skinny slip strap that held her dress together. It slid down her body in silky silence. "I'm seducin' you, Mr. Hollywood."

For the first time since she had known him, he looked vulnerable. Like a boy. Young and awestruck.

Before he could say anything she climbed onto the narrow table, straddling him, bending over and kissing his mouth, covering his lips completely.

"You're the only one who calls me my name," she whispered. "Let me do this for you. I'm very good at it."

For a moment he just lay beneath her, not moving. And then he reached behind her, grabbing her buttocks in his small warm hands and pushed his erection against her.

"Oh, Jesus. I've wanted to do this." He moaned. The first complete sentence he had ever said to her.

When it was over, he slept. The Match cleaned herself up, put on her dress, put the remainder of the joint back in her purse, and sat on the couch, drinking her beer and watching him. She had learned a lot. One thing was clear, Katarina was not getting it on here. He was like a baby. He knew absolutely nothing about making love. Or at least not until tonight. She smiled. Now, he knew. He also knew what he'd been missing. Whatever worked between him and Miss Tiny Tits, sex was not it.

Boy, did you learn about a guy in bed. It never failed to

210

amaze her. Too bad you could only learn it the hard way (or sometimes the soft way), but that was the only way. Joey Rivers was a puddle. A very sweet, insecure, lovable guy in bed. Out of bed, he was a pretentious package job. Who would have thought that. And he knew zip about sex. All of those sexy, witty movies! What a joke. She would have figured he was Mr. Bedman.

She had known different the minute she started the massage. She could always tell. She could tell who was gay, who was a premature shooter, who couldn't get it up. She could feel it in her hands. He had great potential. He'd just never had a good teacher.

She finished her beer. Well, well, well. She had taught Rikki and now Rikki was teaching Frigid Rivers and she was teaching Joey. Somehow it wasn't fair. She should get some kind of credit line. Anger flooded her. The fucking Kunt was benefiting from her expertise. That part she didn't like at all.

Joey opened his eyes and smiled at her. "Wow," he said, and reached for his silk Jockey shorts. She smiled at him. He stood up, pulled on his pants and walked over to her, cupping her face in his hands. "Jesus, baby. That was the most incredible thing that has ever happened to me. You are fucking unbelievable."

She took his hands and gently removed them from her face. She was not used to tenderness. It embarrassed her.

"Thanks. You inspired me."

He laughed. "Yeah. I still don't know what this was about." He watched her. She kept her eyes on his, trying to look innocent. He was no fool. His face darkened.

"I want you to know something. I've never done this before—I mean been unfaithful. I never thought anything like this would happen. You're so fucking hung up on Rikki. I'm not blind. I know Rikki is sniffing around Katarina. So if this is a grudge fuck, I'm hurt. But, the truth is, I have feelings for you. I really fucking like you. I like you better than my wife. So, what do we do with this?"

The Match swallowed a hunk of air. This, she had not counted on. This, she was not expecting. Tears again, falling down her freshly repaired cheeks.

"Yo. Joey. I dunno what to say. Gee, thanks. I never thought about that. I was getting even, I guess. Look, let's get some air. We're stoned. This is very heavy, here. Gee. You made me feel good. Thanks."

Joey kept his eyes on her. She hoped he wouldn't ask her the next question. She was a bitch, no doubt, but she did not want to drop the atom bomb on his marriage. She did not want to tell him what she'd seen. And she had no idea what to do with what he had just told her. This had not come up on the streets of Bensonhurst, Brooklyn. She was not used to being the object of first choice. She was used to fighting. But, the sad truth was, she was not used to winning.

"We better get back." She grabbed her purse and started toward the door.

Joey Rivers took her hand and looked up at her. Now he was in charge. He was clear and she was confused. He kissed her, almost standing on his toes to do it. "You're so fucking transparent. I scared you, didn't I?"

"Who, me? Get real. I live in the East Village. I don't scare easy."

He took her hand and led her to the door. "I never said you did. There's nothing easy about this shit."

When Joey and The Match reached their table, Rikki was regaling Louie, Owen, and Jeremy with minutely detailed descriptions of his car collection and Katarina was doing the samba with George Plimpton.

Joey went off to get a drink and The Match slumped down next to Rikki, trying to decide what to do next. Anger flooded her. Helpless, frustrated anger. Rikki was smoking an enormous Havana cigar, which he dipped compulsively into a large double brandy. The Match took it out of his hand and puffed on it, making Louie giggle.

"Yo. Louie. Want a puff?"

"Sure." He reached out his small dark hand, his eyes bright with hope.

"Forget about it. Wanna stunt your growth? Come on. Let's dance."

Owen and Jeremy nudged each other as Louie got up and stood, seriously waiting for the blazing, bright lady to take his hand. Off they went.

Everyone moved aside to watch them. If there was anything The Match could do well, it was dance, and taking the spotlight away from Katarina made it all the more fun. Louie jumped and twirled, not wanting to let her down, overstimulated by the honor bestowed on him.

The music ended and Louie, feeling the self-consciousness of center stage, ran off to the protective lap of his family. The Match was left standing on the floor alone, her dress clinging to her sweaty lean frame. Rikki was watching her. She motioned for him to join her.

He stood up, somewhat reluctantly, and crossed to her. She reached out to him, feeling her anger soften with grief. He held her slightly away and they danced. It was like grief, she thought—loss of hope.

All her life she had felt as though someone or something was chasing her, trying to take something very precious away from her. She could never see the enemy, never see its face, but she had kept running, holding on to some gossamer treasure within her. She had made it this far without losing this fragile, hot ember inside her. It held her love, her trust, and her faith. She had kept her chin up and her fists low, ready for the body blows and the sniper fire. She had kept this special part alive and unhurt. But now, she felt the damage to it.

She did not know what to do now to protect this part of herself, that no one had ever seen . . . that only she knew was there beneath the tough, smart-ass fierceness of her facade. But she knew it was endangered and she knew that if it died, the best of her would die with it.

Rikki looked at her. "Having fun?"

"Get real! It's amazing how boring interesting people can be. I have overheard some weird fucking stuff tonight—toked a bit and the airwaves just lit right up."

"Hey. Match. Behave yourself. These are nice people. They don't know from your kind of parties."

"Oh yeah? Don't put money on it. Chill, Rikki. I'm cool, they think I'm the fucking Madonna of Krakow. They love me here. I'm like conceptual art."

Rikki laughed. "Yeah, well, don't get too carried away. We're here because I'm helping Big Ben Cowan finance his development, not because they love redheads."

She was hurt. "Hey! Janie invited us. She's my friend. *That's* why we're here. She likes me."

Rikki danced her over toward Katarina, who was now dancing with Gerald Ford.

She watched him watching Katarina. "Hey, Rikki. Over here."

He looked at her. "What?"

"Don't even think about it."

"What?"

"Cuttin' in on Fancy's pants. I'm not dancin' with a fucking Republican no way, no how."

"He was president of the fucking country! You could tell your grandkids. I thought you'd dig it."

"If it's such a big fucking deal, you dance with him."

Rikki led her away. Not trusting what she might say in

front of Katarina to embarrass him. "Okay. Okay. Let's sit down. My back hurts."

She snickered. "I bet it does."

He took her arm and half led, half pushed her along back toward their table. "Maybe later you'll give me a good long rub. Acupressure. With the eucalyptus oil."

She stopped. He may as well have punched her. Tears filled her eyes. He turned, looking at her with a puzzled impatience. The way she had seen him look at one of his cars when they were not responding well.

"A nice long rub. Acupressure? Want me to walk on your spine and do the whole reflexology number, too?" He could see the tears. He did not understand. "Great!"

She pulled her arm away. "Yeah, Great Bosco. I wouldn't pee in your mouth if your guts were on fire."

She left him standing there and made her way back through the crowd of dancers, zigzagging in and out of the tables and partygoers like a bouncing ball in an old sing along cartoon.

Out the enormous bronze doors she went. She kicked off her shoes and walked barefoot, down the endless drive and away from the place that had opened her to the truth and left her, for the first time in her life, unable to zip herself back up inside. Her vulnerability was oozing out around her and she could not risk having Rikki see any more of it. She padded along, making her way in the thick blackness, from one palace of the Haves back to another. How had she gotten into all of this glitz shit to begin with?

"Fuck 'em," she said, to God or whoever was listening. "Fuck 'em all."

Janie was dancing with her father. Donnie was dancing with Delores. China was dancing with Louie. Owen was dancing with Gina. Ondine, who Big Ben had insisted on

215

bailing out, was dancing with Isabel. The countdown to the cake had begun.

Big Ben and Janie moved awkwardly, self-conscious with each other after a week of such intense and unpleasant emotion. It had been obvious to her that when he returned to the "news," he had not been fishing. Or at the very least, not with whom he'd said he'd been fishing with. That she had left alone. But it was right there between them. The loaded gun in the middle of the table.

"It's a magnificent party, baby. Thank you."

"Anytime, Pop." She saw the bandleader waving to her.

"I think it's getting close to cake time. We're supposed to change partners now."

Big Ben stopped dancing and looked at her, holding her firmly in his arms. "Janie. Do you know that I love you?"

She blushed. He had never actually said the words out loud to her before. "I guess so. Nothing that has to do with either of you is really very clear right now." She surprised herself. Such a response was not like her. She had found something new in herself, curled on her bed these last nights in the dark, alone and afraid, whimpering with every new truth.

He relaxed his grip and let go. "Know it," her father said, and they turned toward their life partners as they had rehearsed. The band started the final song, and Janie and Donnie danced together for the first time that evening.

"How're you doing?"

"Fine. I'm just holding on until the chocolate cake. Then I'm losing it. I can feel it coming, Donnie. Chocomania. You may have to pump my stomach later."

Donnie kissed her forehead. "With pleasure." He held her closer and buried his face against her flower-covered ear.

"I love you, Janie. And I'm very proud of you."

Janie pulled away and looked up at him, her freckled nose

wrinkling slightly. "First my father and then you. I don't quite understand all of this sudden verbal validation. Sounds like kiss-off talk to me."

He did not smile and he did not answer her. Her stomach tightened. She bit her tongue. She would not ask him where he had been. In the back of her mind all week had been the tiny, sordid thought, So, if Fritzi is not after Harry in the biblical way, is it Donnie? She would not start that now.

The band stopped. There was no one on the floor now except the family. Drums started. Lights went out. Then, from the house, an enormous circle of light. A gigantic chocolate cake shaped like Big Ben's sailing yacht was wheeled in. The guests cheered and the band played "Happy Birthday" and faces grinned and hands clapped and Big Ben Cowan towered over his family, saluting them and himself.

Isabel came forward with a gleaming sterling silver knife and Ben Cowan raised it over the cake. Poised over the shiny dark chocolate prow while cameras snapped and sparklers sizzled.

An immaculate end to a splendid evening lay suspended before them all, seconds away, when out of the darkness, moving faster than he had in years, Arturo came running, bounding up in a flying unbeagle-like leap and landing flat in the middle of Big Ben's $2,000 birthday cake.

For a moment, everyone froze. Silence. Faces stopped smiling. Hands stopped clapping. Many were unsure what had happened. A time bomb. A raccoon? Some horrible, tasteless prank? Then Jeremy Hart screamed, "Arturo, get off of there!"

The room exploded. Arturo leapt down, his entire fat, stubby body encrusted with chocolate cream and icing like a living mud pie. The frosting covered his eyes and he raced blindly around the room, smearing himself against tuxedo leg and chiffon hem, while Jeremy and Owen gave chase.

217

The room rocked with mirth. It was better than anyone could have hoped. A spontaneous moment!

Big Ben and Donnie were splattered with chocolate. Even Donnie's glasses were caked. Delores and Janie had globs of frosting in their hair. It was, quite simply, hilarious. The band broke into "Black Bottom" and people raced onto the dance floor as if released from prison. As if the strain of social form, relieved only by food and wine, but never ceasing, never ever ceasing so long as they were in the company of others, had relented. The gauntlet of amenity that was never laid down until the shoulders grew weary and the arms weakened, sending them home for release, had been dropped. The burden of good behavior had been lifted by one crazy, totally oblivious mutt, freeing them all of their personas.

People crammed the floor bebopping to twenties soul music, slipping on turds of chocolate and laughing hysterically. Laughing like naughty children jumping into rain puddles on their way to Sunday school. The more evolved, the more they let go. Thus, the duck hunters and fishermen were less raucous than the membership chairman of the Met and the ambassador to Uganda.

Twirling, bouncing, whisking, twisting. Shimmy and shaking. A mass pirouette, set in motion by one original and unexpected act. A canine in the cake was all it took. Free. They were free.

They had been extraordinary guests. Grateful, but not cloying. Lusty in appetite, but not gluttonous or gross. Tipsy, but not stuporous; gay, but not boisterous. Attentive to their tablemates. Polite to the help. Complimentary to their hosts. Properly attired and elegantly behaved.

They had performed well and they had been rewarded beyond their wildest dreams with a lion bursting through a fiery hoop. A canon exploding with tumbling clowns. Boom! A moment of fresh air. Freedom from form.

And Janie Jamieson knew, as she licked a hunk of the mast off her fingers and helped Isabel salvage what she could of Janie's favorite thing to eat on earth, that this is what they would all remember. Long after the speeches and the fancy folks had faded from mind. This would remain. Arturo, the Whore for Food, had stolen the show and freed the prisoners from themselves.

7

Gina Hart sat on Georgica Beach, notebook on her lap, feeling the sun heating the grainy white sand between her toes. Her head hurt and her mind was blank. What was it Raymond Chandler said? "When in doubt have a man come through the door with a gun in his hand." Great. If only she could think of a way to work it into an article about postfeminist relationships. What about a radical lesbian feminist coming through the door with a gun in *her* hand?

She yawned and picked up her thermos of coffee and poured a refill. The beach was still quiet and she savored it, knowing this was the end of it. Tomorrow, the Fourth of July holiday began and from then until Labor Day, forget it.

She sipped and watched the gulls circling and swooping, landing so gracefully, pecking in the sand for breakfast. Two gulls waddled toward each other, making her smile. What odd birds. Actually, what they had always looked like to her were middle-aged Florida retirement residents. More Saul Seagull than Jonathan Livingston. She had written a little cartoon article about them once. Shlomo and Sammy Seagull, two old men; sort of the Audubon Odd Couple. Harry had run it in one of his magazines and had taken a lot of flak from someone. Birds' rights or Jewish rights, someone had been offended, she couldn't remember who.

Okay, Gina. Focus. She checked her watch. The Cave JAPs were going to join her in an hour. This was the last one. Of course, she said that before every meeting, so maybe she should just stop resisting and relax about it. So much had happened in all of their lives since the last one, who could tell what would be needed today.

Big Ben's party had been only a week ago, but it already seemed like months.

First, there was Aaron. Aaron. She smiled. It really was almost incestuous. It was like having another shot at Harry. The thought made her blush. Amazingly enough, it had all gone rather smoothly. The day after the party, Harry had called and invited him for dinner. Just like that. Jeremy's entire response had been, "Wow. Cool! That's fresh (which meant nice). Does he have a car?" As was so often the case with teenagers, whatever you thought would freak them out, had no effect and vice versa.

Aaron had arrived in his brand new Corvette (which Jeremy said was a Guido car and seriously uncool). Gina loved him instantly. He was so much like Harry. Not as manic, but with the same timing, humor, and body language. He had just finished law school. He was so sweet, and comfortable with them, and they were as different from his mother and the way he had grown up as if they were aliens. It was a great case of heredity over environment.

The hard part for Gina was, of course, Fritzi. She felt competitive. She hated it, but she felt it. Every time Aaron said, "My mother," her whole body tightened.

Harry was so overcome with gratitude that she had not only come home, but was cooking dinner for his long-lost son, that he could hardly keep himself from running in circles. He served. He did the dishes. He told her how great she

222

looked at least fifteen times. Well, she would just have to deal with it. What helped was, it was clear that she was his choice, so maybe all that bombshell stuff wasn't everything it was cracked up to be. One thing she had refused to do, however, was include Fritzala in their new "extended" family.

They had had one phone conversation and thank God, Fritzi did not seem any more interested in that kind of arrangement than Gina did. It would be polite and friendly, period. Gina's horror of being compared to "Marilyn" and found wanting was for her and her shrink to deal with.

She watched the gulls sunning themselves. In her mind, she had them lying on tiny chaise longues, holding cream sodas in their little wings, claws crossed, polarized glasses set firmly on the middle of their beaks, talking about their prostate surgeries.

Janie, of course, was not getting off so easy. The day after the party, she and her father had taken Delores back to the hospital; though not willingly. There had been a rather ugly scene. Delores had refused to leave and had accused Ben of cheating on her (which, according to Janie, he did not deny). Delores had gotten so hysterical and abusive that Donnie had to sedate her. What a horrible mess for all of them.

Janie had been at the hospital every day and Ben had been with the lawyers. So far they had kept it out of the papers, but everyone knew about it anyway. The party had gone so well. No one had alluded to anything. If it hadn't been for Arturo, it would have been a totally proper evening. She smiled. The goddamn dog had finally done something worthwhile.

At the moment, it looked as if Norman Gallo had worked out a deal with the D.A. and charges against Delores and Ondine would be dropped. Thank God. But even without jail as a possibility, there was a lot more ahead for the Cowans. And though Janie was not saying much, it was clear she was upset with Donnie. He had gone right back to the City and left her with the whole scene. Granted, he had a practice to run, but Gina could tell Janie was hurt. Also, there was the matter of the two lost days, which he had never properly explained. Spectre of Fritzi, rearing its head.

Janie had half-jokingly suggested hiring a private detective to follow her father and her husband, but knowing Janie, Gina wasn't so sure she was kidding.

There were distinct advantages, Gina thought, of coming from a family with one dead parent and no money. At least she was free from this kind of aggravation.

"I'd better get my body back to Maddie Evans quick, I almost didn't make it from the car over here." Janie threw down her overstuffed Hermès tote, kicked off her thongs, and sank down under Gina's umbrella.

"You're carrying a thirty-pound bag. No wonder you're struggling."

"Necessities. Part of my life-style. I brought the dregs of the chocolate cake."

"It has dog hairs in it."

"Shhh. Everyone will want some. Don't make me feel any guiltier about eating that disgusting mess than I already do. It's nerves. I've gained seven pounds and the end is not in sight. Owen says I'm going to end up like one of the Porcinettes if I don't watch out."

Gina laughed into her cup. The Porcinettes was Owen's name for a group of distant relatives, led by Delores's second cousin who had not been seen since his bar mitzvah. They had arrived from Scarsdale in a giant white limo, all dressed in gold-sequined sweaters, sable coats, diamond necklaces; all sharing the same overdyed blond hair, pot bellies, and facial rearranging. Nose jobs, chin jobs, face-lifts, eye-lifts, cheek implants. In addition, they were each accompanied by a tiny yappy dog.

A HOUSE IN THE HAMPTONS

Gina leaned over and gave her friend a kiss. "Have I told you lately that I love you."

"Sounds like a song title." Janie kissed her back. "I'm not complaining, but you're the third close person to say that to me in a profound way in the past week. You don't know something awful about me that I don't know? Fatal disease? Visible panty line?"

"Certainly not. Maybe all this turmoil is making you extremely lovable."

"Always a downside. Better eat my cake before it melts."

Janie tore into her bag, extracting a large foil-covered package, several napkins, and a fork. Gina watched her setting herself up.

"Since when do you bother with a fork?"

"It's purely ceremonial. I packed it before I found out Erica Hess wasn't coming."

"Great. Who's coming?"

"Just you, me, The Match, and Esmeralda."

Gina sighed. "Janie. I'm not up for this. Writing this article has convinced me I have nothing left to say about my life or my feelings to anyone new. And I don't want to hear about theirs either. I don't even want to have to listen."

"Bullshit! That's like saying, I'm giving up Milky Ways forever. You give them up right after you've had one. When you need one again, you need one. Talking to other women about your problems is genetic."

"Talking to you, yes. To 'other women,' no."

"Yeah. I hear you." Janie's mouth was smeared with chocolate. "I hate to admit it, but I'm just about there myself."

Esmeralda Cucci waved and moved toward them across the sand, a huge picnic basket in one hand and a bottle of wine in the other. She moved with the fluid, easy stride that seemed to be the birthright of northern Italian women. Gina and Janie had spent years trying to copy it, to no avail.

Janie watched. "Look at her. How does she do it? She makes it look easy to schlep that stuff across deep sand."

"*Buon giorno, care.* I'm sorry, I'm so late. I stopped at The Gourmet to pick up the lunch and the pasta salad wasn't right."

Gina and Janie exchanged looks. "What was wrong with it?"

Janie crumpled up her cake remains, trying to avoid Esmeralda's disapproval.

"The tomatoes were *canned.* Do you believe it? In Milan they would be shot. What is that junk, Janie? Are you eating that?"

Janie licked the chocolate off her lips, like a naughty child caught in the cookie jar. "Not anymore."

Gina and Janie had decided long ago that Esmeralda was the most grown-up woman they knew. She was always herself. Always in command with no need to prove anything to anyone, ever. She worked very hard and with great success, babied her husband, spoiled her grown children, and ran a very elegant and tight ship, all without noticeable strain.

Gina's favorite Esmeralda story was about going through airport security with her on a weekend trip to Maine. The metal detector had seen something in her shoulder bag and she was asked to empty it. It contained her own risotto rice, pecorino romano in a slab from Dean and Deluca's, a large *metal* cheese grater, and several packages of dried *funghi* from Tuscany. "But, I always bring my basics," she had explained to the security force. "Who *knows* what they eat in Maine."

Esmeralda spread a cloth and serenely went about the task of picnic preparation. They watched her with respect bordering on awe.

"When I grow up, I'm going to be you, Esmeralda," Janie said, and stuck her fingers right into the pâté.

Esmeralda smiled. "No. No, Janie. You are an original. You must never copy anyone else. It only leads to misery."

At that moment, as if a karmic hot line had connected Esmeralda's words to The Match's psyche, The Match appeared before them looking extremely self-conscious.

They all stared at her, speechless.

The Match was dressed in what seemed to be Ralph Lauren Polo attire. Beige linen slacks. Espadrilles. A white linen shirt and a little straw hat. She wore tiny pearl earrings and her nails were clipped short and unpolished. She wore no visible makeup and her hair, peeking out from beneath the hat, had been toned down to a pale strawberry blond. She was transformed.

She watched them watching her. The only sign of her former self was her cigarette, which she tossed into the sand.

"So, do we have a problem here or what?" She put her hands over her hips, vulnerability and defiance fighting for the upper hand.

Esmeralda, who never lost her composure, kept pouring wine. Gina and Janie remained speechless.

Esmeralda, who had met The Match only twice, but had been very taken with her, handed her a glass, drawing her into them.

"Sit. Have some lunch. We'll discuss it."

The Match sighed. She dropped her purse and lowered her long, narrow body, keeping her eyes away from them all.

"You hate it, huh? I look disgusto, huh?"

Gina and Janie shook their heads, wanting to relieve her embarrassment. "No! No! You look beautiful. It's just so . . ." Gina floundered . . .

"Different." Janie finished for her. "What's it, I mean why did you do it? It's a whole other image. I think it's great that you can change that way. No matter what I do, I always look the same."

"I dunno. I got bored. Besides, this is the look. It's what all the men turn on to. It's in all the mags."

Gina got it. "Are we talking 'all the men,' or . . ." Gina paused. She did not want to reveal what she had seen at the party. She wanted to help, but she did not know how far to go. She hadn't even told Janie. "Or Rikki. It's the Katarina syndrome, isn't it?"

The Match's face reddened. "So. Okay. I blew it. I thought, if he thinks it's so hot on her, I'll give it a try."

Esmeralda finished her serving and looked at The Match, her perfectly shaped black eyebrows raised slightly.

"I know this Katarina. I photographed her for *Vogue*. You are much more interesting to look at. Why would you want to be like someone you're not? This is so American. So disturbing. In Italy, men love a woman for her uniqueness. Here it is all, cakey cutters."

"Cookie cutters," Janie nodded, slugging down her wine.

"Yes. Exactly. You never keep a man like that. You must change this. It is nice, but it is not you. If he wants someone like her, then you do not want him. This is wrong! Wrong for your soul."

The Match took off her hat and put on her huge black sunglasses. It was clear she was trying not to cry.

"See, I had this really spacey week. I mean, first I found out that Rikki the Fuck is *really* doing Katarina the Kunt and then I go back to the city, to try and make some money, pull myself together, and the whole week is like spaceland.

"First, I got this patient, been coming to me for years. He's a Puerto Rican lawyer from Queens. All of a sudden in the middle of the massage, the guy grabs me. 'I can't stand another minute of this, I want you!' He's sweatin and slobberin and he's trying to force me down on the table. So I get a little strong with the guy. I tell him to knock it off or I'm callin the cops. Well, he's a lawyer, so he hears cops and he goes apeshit. I mean hyperventilating. He pees on himself. I gotta drag the guy to the john, give him Valium, smelling salts. That's why I never do the Puerto Ricans, I hate that PRH shit."

Gina spread goat cheese on a piece of whole wheat Italian bread. "What's PRH?"

"It's documented. Medically." The Match shrugged.

Janie leaned closer. They loved listening to her talk and they knew she was taking them somewhere, asking them silently to take this ride with her around and outward as a way back in. "But what is it?"

"Puerto Rican Hysteria. Jesus. You guys don't know shit about New York! Anyway, I had to let him stay there like for hours. First, he almost rapes me, then I have to take care of the creep. Finally, I got him dressed, put him in the elevator. Never even got paid for the fucking massage."

Esmeralda refilled all their glasses. "Unbelievable. Was he attractive at least?"

"Ain't no oil paintin'."

Esmeralda's eyebrows arched again. "What does this mean, 'Ain't no oil paintin'?"

"I know!" Janie jumped in, eager not to look like a sheltered Upper East Sider. "It's what the ghetto women say when someone has an ugly baby. Isabel told me."

Esmeralda smiled slowly. "I like that."

"And then I lost one of my richest women 'cause I opened my big fucking mouth and told her the truth."

Esmeralda frowned. "But you must always tell the truth."

"Get real. Only rich people can afford that kind of shit. Service people like me, forget it. My clients want to hear good news. Good bullshit. 'You look so young.' 'You? Cellulite? Naw.' Forget about it. Truth is death to people like me. But I got this one *social-eat* and she's just moved into this town house on Seventy-seventh Street and Lex. And I'm still

wiped out from Rikki and the PRH scene and she's leadin'
me up and down and around this joint like I'm the editor of
House and fucking *Garden* and she says to me, 'So. Tell me the
truth. Does it look like five million? Can you see it?'

"So, I'm trying not to blow it. I say something like, 'Well,
gee, I'm not the best judge. I mean, my people came over
steerage. We're working types. We don't go to Martha's
Vineyard, we go to Pittsburgh, if you catch my meaning.'

"But, she pushes me. She says, 'No. I want an innocent
eye. You have no basis of comparison, so you would know if
this is stupendous. I mean, does it take your breath away?'

"Well, something just snapped. I guess I've just done one
too many of this kind of Twat Brain. I mean, every other
week they've got some new disease. First, they're all hypo-
glycemic. Then that's out, and it's Epstein-Barr, everyone's
cryin' and sleepin' all day (which they do anyway), now it's
some kind of weird fucking yeast infection and they're all
gettin' these five-hour vitamin injections and only eating lettuce. On and on it goes. And there is nothin' wrong with any
of them except dry cunts and hot wallets. So anyway, I lost
it. I told her, 'Look, the place sucks. It looks like a fucking
fag's attic. I wouldn't live here at gunpoint.' "

The audience applauded. The Match finished her wine.
"Thanks. But she threw me the fuck out. And I'll probably
lose all of her friends, too. Somethin's happening to me that I
don't get."

She put her head down and raised her knees. Hugging
herself. They all reached out to her but she held tighter, not
used to this kind of comfort.

"I love the bastard. I thought we were okay. I got spoiled. I
got cocky. I never let myself, ever, count on any peckerhead.
How could this happen to me? I thought we'd get married,
even."

A HOUSE IN THE HAMPTONS

They were all quiet, feeling her despair. They waited for her to show them how to help.

The Match's shoulders arched and the tears came. She had been holding them inside for so long, she was not quite sure what would happen to her, but suddenly she didn't care anymore. Somehow, sitting here with these almost-strange women, who had lived lives as far from her own as she could imagine, she felt safe. She felt their kindness and she let them in. Let them mother her in a way she had longed for all her life. Longed for in so deep and unknown a way that the need had no shape, no name. They were all mothers and they knew how and she allowed them inside her pain.

When Frankie Karsh made love to Fritzi Ferris he left himself behind. Not even in his cherry-red Ferrari, soaring down the Highway, the wind in his face, feeling free and potent and totally in control, did he leave himself. He always knew who and where he was—always had one eye on the rearview mirror and one part of his brain on business. But with her, he was gone. Moon-bound. Floating in the silky haze of her being, like an eyeless embryo. Mindless. Thoughtless. Disconnected from the planet.

When she had told him Aaron was going to stay at the Harts' for the rest of the summer to get to know his real father and half brother, he had been ecstatic. He would have her all to himself. They could wander for endless nights through the pure white cave she inhabited. Alone in an erotic wonderland. White heat crackling between them. Aaron had left and he was here giving her all of his love, leaving reality behind on the threshold, his steps disappearing in the thick snow glow of her lair, like footprints in a blizzard. But something was wrong. She was not with him. It was different.

Having her not all there was still so much better than

231

having any other woman that he wasn't even too concerned for a while and also, he was deeply into his lovemaking and not at the moment of high concept. But he did sense the change. A slight shift of focus. A pulling back.

He was still, however, not in any way prepared for what happened next.

When they finished, sated for the moment and satisfied, she stood up, rather than rolling into his arms and sleeping beside him until they found the energy to start again. She slipped into her white satin robe, pulled the sash tight around her tiny waist, and crossed her sun-brushed arms, hugging herself tight.

"Frankie," she said, her eyes clouding, "I'm very, very sorry, but I can't see you anymore."

He tried to sit up, but it was as if someone had stepped onto his chest. He was struck dumb by the blow to his ego and his heart.

"You're kidding."

"No. I don't kid about things like that." She sighed.

He managed to raise himself up on his arms, feeling somehow that if he could move closer to her, he could take it away.

"Why?"

"I can't tell you."

If he had been older or had ever been in love in this way before, it is likely he would have demanded an answer— stormed around, cajoled, threatened, pleaded, wrung his hands and pulled his hair. But he had no experience of this sort. Women had always come easy. They had been like his cars. Fast, sleek, and always available. He did not know what to do and so he put on his clothes, said good-bye, and left her standing, arms holding herself together.

Without so much as a whimper, Frankie Karsh stumbled into his fancy foreign car and pulled out of the long white

232

pebbled driveway of the first woman he had ever loved, so outdistanced by his emotion, he did not even understand that he had just hit the wall.

"Marianne, you can't go through life discussing *everything*. There just isn't time!" Harry Hart lay on his bed replaying *Scenes from a Marriage*. He had played it so many times, the tape was worn and grainy. He would have to get a new one. Now that Aaron was with them, Harry had an entire, unspoiled new audience to introduce to his Master.

Gina came out of the bathroom, all made up and dressed in a white jersey off-the-shoulders sundress. Not their usual Sunday-night-at-the-beach attire.

"You sure you don't want to come with me?" Gina picked up her notepad and pencils and stuffed them into her briefcase. She had agreed to cover the Hampton Library benefit auction for *Newsday*, but now that the moment was at hand, she regretted it. She was supposed to meet Harry and the Jamiesons for dinner at The Palm afterward, a special treat they all felt they had earned. Janie and Gina loved the people-watching and Harry and Donnie loved the lobsters.

"Are you kidding? I'd rather have an enema."

Gina laughed. "Who knows. Maybe someone's donating one for the silent auction."

"Yeah, sure. But it would probably be administered by Peter Jennings on Christmas Day at the Rockefeller Center ice rink."

Gina sat down beside him. "Oh, come on, Harry. It's not that bad. Some of the prizes are really fun."

Harry hit the stop button. "You're just trying to talk yourself into it, because you're going to have to bullshit your way through the place and tell polite lies about everyone there."

"Not true. They said I could be irreverent."

"All editors say that. Then they just cut all of the libelous stuff out."

"Okay. I'll go alone. Shall I just meet you all at The Palm?"

"Yeah. Donnie and Janie are picking me up, so we can drive home together."

"Is he staying out until Wednesday?"

"I think so. He'd be a schmuck not to. How many times do we get a Fourth of July on Tuesday. The entire city of New York has been gone since Friday at noon."

"This'll be the first dinner we've had alone together just the four of us in weeks." She bent over and kissed his cheek. She knew he was anxious to get back to Bergman.

"See you."

"Don't bid on anything!" Harry flipped on the tape.

When Gina arrived at the Windmill on Ocean Avenue, the site of the annual charity auction, the yellow-striped tents were already jammed with people. The auction was usually held in August, but the long July fourth had moved it forward.

Gina showed her pass and moved inside, feeling shy and ill at ease. She hated things like this. Anything that involved more than ten people had lost all of its appeal to her. Maybe she was just getting old. It used to be fun to dress up and mingle with hordes of strangers, wandering through gallery openings, first nights at MOMA, book parties; plastic wineglass in hand, smile in place. Now, it just drained her.

She picked up an auction booklet and strolled around, past the Horse People and the available celebrities, trying to get her bearings.

Peter Jennings was, in fact, standing by the photographer's area talking with an enormous blond woman, with blue feathers in her hair and a pink and yellow sequined sweater set. She smiled. Maybe Harry's enema fantasy would come true, on camera. Gina opened the booklet and scanned the auction entries.

Play eighteen-hole golf with author Michael Thomas.

Have dinner with *60 Minutes* producer Don Hewitt and his wife, Marilyn Berger of *The New York Times* . . .

Jill Krementz will take a black and white photo of your child . . .

Tennis for four with George Plimpton . . .

Gina made a note on the catalogue. The idea of paying to star-fuck was so absolutely American late eighties. Unbelievable!

Gina found the whole idea of anyone wanting to participate in such a forced and unnatural social experience fascinating. It was really just a more sophisticated version of the fan syndrome. People waiting all night in the cold to catch a glimpse of Princess Di on her way to a day-care center. "I saw her. I touched her."

She walked over to the bidding area and saw who was bidding on what. The whole idea was so brutal. Some items had a slew of names under them, while others stood blank and forlorn, undesirable at any price. It was a great metaphor for society in general, Gina thought, and turned to the nonhuman offerings.

Firescreen in the shape of a dog
Inlaid mahogany muffin stand

Complete oral health examination
A truckload of manure (delivered)

Gina scanned the lists. There was something for everyone, depending on bankroll and taste. One could sign up for iceboating lessons, surf-casting class, trips to Egypt, Thanksgiving turkey dinners; box seats for the Mets; shiatsu massages; seascapes galore by local artists; opera tickets; aerial flights; clambakes, the possibilities were endless.

Three locally famous horsewomen strode in, still dressed in their formal riding clothes. Gina made a note. This was obviously a new form of reverse snobbery. They were so above the silly world of "caring about social events"; so above the good pearl and silk sundress set, that they arrived sweaty and unmade-up, horse shit still attached to their boots (symbolically at least) from a hard day on the show circuit.

The clothes were their own status. The clothes, showing that somewhere, maybe, even just outside, was a *horse*. A very expensive and unnecessary for human survival *horse*. This was not *Wagon Train*. This was not the century of Horses for Survival, when a horseless carriage would have been the ultimate status symbol. This was the century of Celica and Hyundai necessity, when the *horse* was the ultimate status symbol.

After all, with the advent of replica costume jewelry, Taiwan rip-off Vuittons, fake Rolex watches, and Fred the Furrier, anyone could look rich. It was harder and harder to stay in the lead, to be sure people knew you *were really rich*.

So far, at least, there were no imitation Thoroughbreds. No Korean knock-off Arabian stallions; so horses were in.

Tennis had lasted awhile, having a tennis court put one up there; but the costs went down (as incomes rose) and it infiltrated the middle class so the attire lost its meaning. After

236

all, one couldn't carry a tennis court into a restaurant! Granted, one couldn't carry a horse in either, but the clothes were object-specific. The clothes alone were ten times as costly as even the chicest tennis attire. Horses were in for now.

The three women cantered to the bar and ordered vodka on ice. This was also new "in." Real drinks returning. Real drinks for real women. Women who Rode.

Gina moved along behind them, trying to overhear their conversation. Their only acquiescence to upper-class materialism was three identical sets of diamond stud earrings.

"I'm so nervous about the show tomorrow I haven't slept for a week. My God! I rode so badly today. I may not be able to take this terror. My whole body is rigid."

"Brigit, for heaven's sake. It's just a horse show, it's not brain surgery."

"You don't understand what it means to me."

Gina ordered a spritzer and lingered behind them. The rigid one turned slightly and glared at her. Gina turned her head, picturing the tight, trim, tan, cement-stiff body flying over her horse's head and shattering into a thousand pieces.

"Let's go," said the third one. "No one's here."

Gina watched them stride away, wondering what it would be like to be one of them. She wondered as objectively as if she were considering what the experience of being a dolphin or a firefly would be.

There was a kind of arrogance about women like that, that upset her. They made her lip tremble. Somehow, they brought forth a very-small-child part of herself. They seemed so immune, so capable of inflicting pain. They were the teasers, the scorners, the wearers of cashmere sweater sets—captains of the teams for which she was always chosen last—they were the tormentors of the sensitive, the odd man out, the alone.

237

She didn't want to judge them, but she did.

"Hey. How's it goin'?"

Gina turned, feeling a tap on her shoulder. Frankie Karsh stood behind her looking, she thought, sad and out of place.

"Fine. How about you?"

He shrugged, his tight pink silk shirt wrinkling slightly.

"Can't complain. You here alone?"

"Yep. Couldn't drag Harry on a bet. I'm doing a story."

"Cool. Want some inside info? I donate a week of a Maserati rental every year. I know this scene."

"Sure. That would be great. When's a good time?"

"How 'bout now?"

Gina looked at her watch. She still needed press kits and an attendee list and she had to talk to the benefit chairman. "How about tomorrow? I know it's a holiday weekend, but we can do it on the phone."

"Sure." He paused, looking uncomfortable. Gina smiled at him. He looked so young and a little lost.

"Is Fritzi with you?"

He lowered his shiny dark head and shook it slowly. "Nope. That's all over."

Gina was surprised and, for some unknown reason, disappointed. Maybe it was simply knowing Fritzi had a handsome young lover, made her and Janie feel safer.

"Oh, gee. I'm sorry, Frankie. I didn't know."

He looked up at her and their eyes locked. She was afraid he would start to cry.

"Just happened."

"Well, maybe you'll work things out. Romance is always a roller coaster. That's what makes it fun." She was trying to lighten the mood, feeling maternal and protective. She knew he did not want to burst into tears here.

"Naw. Don't think so. I think she's got someone else."

Gina's stomach tightened. "Really?"

238

"Yeah. We were doing good. That's gotta be it. I mean, a woman like that, she can have anyone. What would she want a punk like me for, anyway."

Gina put her glass down. Her palms were sweating. Poor Frankie. All of his bravado and charming self-promotion had melted like so many ice pops.

"Hey, Frankie. You're young. You've got lots of terrific women to look forward to. It'll be okay."

He smiled. A droopy, sad smile. "Yeah. Sure. But not like her. There's no one like her. Call me. I'll be at the lot all day," he said softly and, head down, moved slowly through the crowd of noisy silent bidders back out into the evening light.

Most of our lives pass around us, under us, through us, time disappearing without notice. Days and years lost to us, not remembered, not recapturable. Moments are held. Moments out of years, out of decades.

A picnic on the beach when you were five and a family still happy and playful together; driving the Anti-Atlas Mountains singing "When Sunny Gets Blue," seeing *Lawrence of Arabia* and losing your mind for Omar Sharif, a night at the opera, a day at the races, a terrible bronchitis, an expired passport not discovered until check-in for a long-awaited journey. Moments good and bad. Large and small. A death. A laugh. A perfect meal. A perfect orgasm. Freeze-frames of a life.

Most of these moments are not keynoted at the time. We do not usually pick them out of the line-up of endless events and say, "This Kir Royale on this terrace on the Rhine, I will always remember." They just stay. Would our lives be better if we could pay closer attention? If we knew with certainty what we would carry with us into old age, into death?

So it was only much later, in hindsight, that the Harts

understood the importance of that dinner at The Palm. Knew it would be with them forever, part of their retrievable memory bank of experience. Part of their emotional history.

Gina was late, weaving through the jam of summer diners, good cheer, and pungent smells of frying onions and garlic wafting over her. When she reached them they were deep in conversation, and well into their second drinks.

Harry was holding court on Ingmar, his passion revived, no doubt, by his four-hundredth playing of *Scenes from a Marriage.*

"See, it's all in his autobiography. Everything he used in *Fanny and Alexander,* for instance. How the adultworld, by its very nature, destroys the childworld. The construct of society, which he says (and God knows he's right!) is set up so that everyone tries to humiliate whoever is beneath them. Why don't we accept that? I mean, all the knee-jerk liberals and the communists and the humanists run around thinking we can change human nature. It's so absurd!

"Don't these guys ever watch *Nova*? I mean, you don't have to be a fucking rocket scientist to get the point. There has always been strong and weak, rich and poor, good and evil, and there always will be animal or man. Why doesn't everybody just accept that? Until they do, how can it possibly get any better? Nothing's based on the way things really are, but on some fucking fantasy ideal that never was and never will be. Not on this planet, anyway."

Gina slid in beside Harry. "Well, I'm glad I missed all the small talk. I like to take on the universal order with my appetizer. It's good for the digestion."

The waiter arrived with platters of crispy fried onion rings and potatoes. Gina ordered a glass of wine and settled in, relaxing into the company of the three other adult people in her life by whom she felt totally accepted.

A HOUSE IN THE HAMPTONS

Donnie was quiet, musing over what Harry was saying. His brow furrowed, with more than usual intensity.

"When Janie and I were in Amsterdam last year, we went to visit Anne Frank House. We went because, of course, all the guidebooks tell you to and because we had seen the movies, read the diary, etcetera. And also because, (according to the guidebooks) the area is now 'one of the chicest boutique shopping sections of the city.' An all-around worthwhile excursion."

Everyone was plunging into the platters, licking salty remnants from their lips, washing them down with their drink of choice, the noise from other tables like white noise or the inside of a conch shell, pleasant and protective.

Donnie sipped his Scotch. "Anyway, you go into this little entry room and pay your fee and then you climb up this very steep narrow stairway, not having any idea what lies ahead and all of a sudden, there you are standing right in front of the fake bookcase—the one we've all read about and seen in films and documentaries, but there it is. It's real. It's right there in front of you and you go through it, the way the Franks and the van Pelses went through it and you are in their nightmare.

"*Five hundred thousand* tourists a year go through it and walk around the shabby little rooms, look at the model that shows where everyone slept, furniture, every detail. And I wondered what they would have thought if they had known that fifty years later German tourists in Bermuda shorts would be tromping around their pathetic hiding place, taking snapshots of the crapper and the kitchen. I cannot tell you what it triggered in both of us. Tears just kept running down my face. You were in it. All those endless days, creeping around with shades drawn. Not being able to sneeze, to flush a toilet, to jump, to yell. Children, reaching their puberty, without any privacy to explore their feelings, let alone

241

their bodies. It was staggeringly powerful. Much more affecting for me than the entire Holocaust Museum.

"In one of those rooms, there is a window facing the street and I went over to it and it was a bright, cold spring day and I looked out into this pretty little street, a lovely serene canal lined with delft china shops and fancy clothing stores, and it was quite simply impossible to believe that in our lifetime this same street was filled with evil and fear, storm troopers and guns!

"When I collected myself, we moved into the exhibit area, where the writings and other memorabilia are and I was looking at some book reviews from when her diary was first released and one of them said, I can't remember it exactly, but it said something about what the Nazis symbolized was that the monster inside of man had for a time won and that it would win again. 'It will come again and it will win again, because it is always there, it is part of us.' It took me two days to recover. Ask Janie. I think, Harry, we tend to deny human nature because that may be at the bottom of it."

The waiter came and they ordered an enormous amount of food and a very expensive bottle of champagne, as people often do at a moment of understanding their good fortune and the tiny distance that separated all of them from the banana peel on the pavement of random monstrosity. They were pensive for a while, checking out the room, noting the especially chic or absurd. The movie star in the corner, the Mafia types by the kitchen. And when they were all ready, they changed the mood.

They reconstructed the party in minute detail with Harry and Gina delivering a slightly exaggerated and hilarious rendition of their beach porno experience. Much was made of the Katarina and Rikki affair, though Gina and Janie kept The Match out of it as much as possible.

Janie delivered all the current data about her mother, who

seemed to be doing well at the clinic, though she was clearly still depressed. Donnie had spoken with her doctors and they were working on antidepressant medication. Delores had told Janie she hated the group therapy and refused to say anything.

They all laughed about the boys' awkward quest for summer love; the increasing time spent in the bathroom, the hair, gel globbed, the new vocabulary emerging every day, non-words that made no sense to any of them. "She's stupid cool." "I really dissed him." They empathized with Janie's anger at once again being caught in the middle, expected to run between her parents like "Navajew," as she called herself, the cheerful Indian scout serving two masters but not her own.

Donnie, who would usually have encouraged her and offered support, was quiet, which Gina noted, on the ride home. But otherwise, it was just an enormously freeing evening filled with the infinite joy of one another's company.

Would they all have done anything different if they had known it would be the last evening of its kind they would ever share together? Would she have announced Frankie Karsh's broken love affair so blithely? The main regret Gina had later was that they didn't take a picture.

Fritzi Ferris stood in line at the East Hampton Beanery, patiently waiting for Erica Hess to decide which vegetable steamer to buy. Fritzi didn't know her, though she had seen her at various Hampton functions, but she knew two things for sure. She was spoiling her daughter and she wasn't being sexually fulfilled. Fritzi smiled to herself. She thought Erica Hess looked like a ferret. All buggy eyes and self-conscious nipping little movements. Her daughter, who was being left to her own devices while Erica examined each French steaming pot as if it were a Ming vase, was quietly, but seriously, rearranging the gourmet coffee beans.

"Is this one really the best? I mean, can you do corn as well as mustard greens? I want the absolute best." Erica frowned, her Ray-Bans pushed back on her long blond hair making her look like an ad for Florida time shares.

Fritzi had gotten so used to being snubbed by women like Erica Hess, she no longer bothered to be polite. Her revenge came in the number of their husbands who followed her around parties and called her up late at night.

The little girl was now grabbing handfuls of water-processed decaffeinated espresso and dumping them into Swiss almond mocha. Fritzi giggled, almost out loud. All of the huge burlap bean bags, so carefully arranged and protected with their own little signs—*Caf. Decaf. Colombian. French Roast*—had now been contaminated by the Little Darling.

Erica remained oblivious. Fritzi waited, skittering her basket of purchases onto her other side. How crazy life was. Whenever you had a remote thought that the system could be beat, the odds lowered, the road mapped, up ahead came the switchback. She had come back east filled with feelings she could barely comprehend. From her girlhood, she had hidden in Martin, hidden herself behind a flamboyant facade because it was the surest way of fending off the others. The more exaggerated and unreal she looked, the less her chance of being uncovered and the real Fritzi Ferris, née Madeline Olsen, whoever she was, having to come forward.

For twenty-five years she had been haunted by the ghosts of two living but remote men. Harry Hart and Donnie Jamieson. Haunted by the rejection of one and the guilt of another. Haunted daily by one because of the presence of his son. A boy who grew into a man, so unlike her and so like him, she could barely look at him without wincing.

Her husband had died and she had been cast out of her

hiding place like a biblical heroine. Cast back into a world she had stopped knowing entirely, so protected had she been, from herself. She knew nothing of greed, betrayal, jealousy, and cruelty. These were emotions that were foreign to her. The closest she had come had been with Harry, whom she had loved and who had rejected her love and so it was back to him that she had gone. She had an ace to play, after all. Aaron. How ironic to discover Harry was no longer a source of pain or love or anything. He felt like a fond old friend. She shared a child with him, though he didn't know it at the time. But that's all.

It was all so old. So cold. How ironic for her that it should be Donnie, the only man who had ever really loved her, whom she should find herself in need of now. Need is what it was. She shifted her purchases back to her other hip. She was giving up a lot for this. And she knew the end would come. But she felt, as deeply as she had ever let herself feel anything, that he was now her destiny and her fate.

"I'll take the French porcelain, but I want to look at the guarantee," Erica Hess proclaimed.

On the Fourth of July at a little after seven in the morning, Janie Jamieson, who had had one of her bad nights, rolled over and felt with her foot that her husband was gone. Softball, she thought dopily, the sleeping pill still in effect. She turned over and fell back into a heavy half-sleep. Several thoughts bobbed up and down, cruising on the surface of her sleep. *Gina's birthday barbecue, gotta buy the corn before the stands run out of . . . Big Ben's taking the kids fishing . . . gotta find out when Donnie is going back to the city. Wanna go in with him for a couple of days, just get away from all of the mess—a vacation from my vacation house.*

She tossed, inching over onto Donnie's side of the bed, her arm hitting something. She opened her eyes and raised herself on one shoulder. An envelope was pinned to his pillow with a single red tulip, her favorite flower. Janie sat up, stretched and smiled. What a sweet gesture.

What she expected to find inside was some version of hundreds of similar notes he had left for her in various places over the years. *Good morning, darling. Went for a run meet me at Cosmo's for coffee at ten. . . . Hi, sweetheart! Just missed you. Meet me at Gino's at seven.* That is what she expected to find inside. That is not what she found.

At nine o'clock that same morning, the rusting doorbell at the Harts attempted to ring, and Harry who was still half asleep and Arturo who was more than half asleep, stumbled down to answer it.

Janie Jamieson stood on the porch, her face hidden behind her enormous horn-rimmed sunglasses, her nose bright red from blowing.

Before Harry could open his mouth, Janie thrust the note into his hand and said in a tiny, trembling voice:

"Donnie's gone."

My darling beloved wife. If I had figured out another way to do this, please believe I would have chosen it. There is something happening to me; in me; that I cannot make myself tell you or anyone that I love. I must leave you now, until I am able to see clearly how to handle what is happening to me. Bringing you and Owen pain is the last thing on earth I wish to do and I am choosing a road that at the moment, seems to be a way of ultimately causing the least pain. I may be entirely wrong. I have always been so self-righteous about being "good in a crisis," but now, I am in a crisis, so to speak, and I am not being at all "good."

A HOUSE IN THE HAMPTONS

It seems to me at this moment, that the line between weakness and strength is highly overrated. Arbitrary almost. Maybe those of us who pride ourselves on being strong (and you, my darling girl, are certainly among the strongest) are just those who have been forced by life to cope. Maybe strength is no better than weakness, but rather like a muscle that grows with use. If life has not required its use it stays flaccid, through no fault of its owner. Maybe this is all just a giant cop-out. I don't know yet. I am only trying to say, my Janie, that life has made you strong and that strength will help you deal with this. Life has not made me as strong as I thought or I would have found a better way to protect the people I love.

I have to go away for a while and I cannot tell you why or where or when I will contact you. I just cannot do that, yet. Please, I beg you, don't try to find me. Please trust that I must do this in my own way and time. And please know I love you and I am trying to do the right thing. Show this to Harry and Gina, because it also applies to them and to my dearest boy. I love you all.

Donnie.

They sat at the Harts' pine table, playing with their coffee all morning. There was nothing to say and everything to say, but they were all too stunned to say anything much. It was as if the most steady and dependable thing in their lives suddenly disintegrated before their eyes.

Donnie had vanished. Without so much as a warning tremor. A change in the wind, or a premonition of danger.

247

PART THREE

8

Rikki Bosco paced back and forth across his corner office, which looked out at the Statue of Liberty and the World Trade Center, his impatience growing. Sexual obsession had definite downsides. His work was going to hell and so were his households. To top it off, he was giving a dinner party for Katarina's parents, who were coming into town for the week and spending the weekend with them in the Hamptons. Florencia was not up to this and so he had spent the morning on the phone with his cousin, who owned an employment agency in Hempstead, trying to find a backup helper for her.

Usually his secretary would handle something like this or The Match, but his secretary was out with the summer flu and he was trying to find a way around inviting The Match down this weekend.

How he was going to pull that off, since he had long ago stopped actually inviting her, rather, it was an understanding that she was always invited, he didn't quite know. She was behaving very strangely. He knew she suspected what was going on with Katarina, but so far no confrontation had taken place. Just a lot of sullen sarcastic remarks and attitude.

251

"Yo. Rikki. I got someone. She's good. Great cook, very well trained and she's available."

"Great. What is she? Latino? Filipino?"

"Lemme look. Naw. Chinese Jamaican."

"What the fuck is that?"

"I dunno. It's that."

"Okay. Send her over, this I gotta see."

Most men with a fortune such as Rikki Bosco possessed would have butlers and a staff of help, but the whole scene made him intensely uncomfortable. That, he felt, you had to either be born into or marry into. Somehow he couldn't do it for himself. For Katarina, maybe. He knew she thought Florencia was a joke as far as help went, but she had been with him for years. She was family.

Rikki slunk down in his Knoll black leather desk chair and put his feet up on his hand-carved ebony desk. Thank God having a company to run gave him some perspective. If he stayed out at the beach during the week, he would be lost.

But, there was the matter of August. August he would be out there full-time. Every August he brought his top three people, and moved them into the office guest quarters he had built down by the pond. It had been a perfect setup. But now, he was edgy. How would he be able to juggle Katarina, The Match, Joey, and his work on a daily basis?

Well, he could break it off with The Match, that would eliminate one huge area of stress. Rikki swallowed. For some reason, as wild as he was about Katarina, he hadn't been able to cut The Match loose. Part of it was that Joey was nuts about her company and so was Katarina. She kept all of them entertained, took the hosting pressures off of him, that was for sure. He'd look like a shit sending her away and it would blow his cover. Joey was not stupid. He had no proof of anything, they had been super cool, but suspicion was oozing from Rivers and The Match.

A HOUSE IN THE HAMPTONS

Also, there was the highly obvious fact that Katarina was a married woman and the subject of her becoming an unmarried one had not been broached. Rikki wasn't sure about that one, either. The thought of having to take on a woman like Katarina full-time, forever, was more than unnerving.

But if Joey Rivers could handle her, and handle her without fucking her worth a shit, then what was he afraid of? If he told The Match not to come in August, he would have to tell her why. Not that she didn't know why, anyway. But, he would *really* have to tell her. He rubbed his eyes and stretched.

No more Match. The thought made him deeply sad and this confused him even more. He knew she loved him. He did not know if Katarina did. I mean he had been "out to dinner," so to speak. He was a big boy and he knew that great sex did not mean great love, as a given, anyway.

Had she told him she loved him? No. But then, he hadn't told her, either. Big words. Big stakes. Big odds. Well, he was used to all three. He had to get himself together and keep looking at this love shit like business. Then he'd be okay.

If Katarina's parents could handle Joey and his crazy relatives, they could probably handle The Match. So, okay. Maybe he shouldn't rock the boat just yet. More important was how he and Katarina would be able to get away from the others this weekend.

God. His cock hardened just thinking about her. He had uncorked her and she had turned into a fucking Aladdin's lamp. Now she couldn't get enough. She looked at him like he was some sacred sex guru. She told him she had always felt dead "down there." Not once in memory had she ever come close to feeling anything, let alone passionate lust.

Joey had been so mesmerized by her that he didn't seem to care, at least not at first. But there was no doubt it had caused a breach. Rikki's fear had been that she would take all of her new toys back to Joey and wouldn't need him any-more. But she had sworn to him it hadn't helped with Joey, only with him. He smiled thinking about her face when she told him that. It made him feel godlike, mighty and superior.

There was really only another month and then they would leave and she would forget him. That's why he had offered to finance Joey's fucking movie. Indebtedness. Continued con-nection. She needed his cock and her husband needed his cash; if that didn't give him the upper hand, he didn't know what would.

So, okay. He'd let it go for this weekend. Take his chances with The Match behaving herself. Then he'd see where he was. Sooner, rather than later, he and Katarina were going to have the big conversation.

Rikki lowered his long legs and stood up, facing the Statue of Liberty and seeing across the river to his hometown. He knew that he could lose this one. She was the Bayfront Club magnified a thousand times. He had too much riding on this deal to make a mistake.

As often is the case with men like Rikki Bosco, who have grown rich outsmarting the other guy, there comes a point when they begin to underestimate the competition. This is always a dangerous mistake and if they are lucky, they catch it before it becomes too costly.

So it was, that when Rikki arrived in his stretch Mercedes limo, having picked up Katarina's parents at Kennedy and driven down with them, he was greeted by a giant and to-tally unanticipated pie in the face.

At first glance, everything seemed in order. He had buzzed Katarina in the guest house and begun his nonchalant but highly orchestrated tour around the main house. The way Florencia was giggling in the kitchen and the Chinese Jamai-can was running around making sausage sandwiches, something he never ate, might have tipped him that things were out of whack, but at the moment, he paid no attention.

"And this is the pool deck," he said, stopping cold, struck dumb by the swack of banana cream in his metaphoric puss. There by the pool, lounging in a tiny string bikini, was The Match. Beside her, spread around a wicker table and chairs, in matching print housedresses, white cotton sweaters secured with sweater clips, and identical black lace-up orthopedic shoes, playing canasta with cigarettes dangling in their fish-puckered lips, were all seven of The Match's old maid aunts. The Gargoyle sisters in person.

The Match stood up, all six feet, huge almost naked white breasts and black punk sunglasses, and offered a long, purple-nailed hand to Katarina Rivers's stupefied parents.

"Hiya. I'm The Match and these are my beloved aunties. Yo! Girls! Show a little manners."

The seven sisters, disgruntled at the interruption, but making an effort, wiggled off their chairs, with some effort, considering their feet were nowhere close to reaching the ground, and lined up. The sight, with The Match beside them, creating the image of either Snow White and the Seven Dwarfs Go Hollywood or a sinister version of the Rockettes, was almost more than Rikki and the dour and refined Mr. and Mrs. Karlson could handle.

The Match, clearly enjoying every single second of Rikki's intense discomfort, began the introductions. "Gee, I was gonna have name tags made, but time got away from me, you know how it is. So, here we go. End to end, we got, Winnie, Minnie, Euturpe, Eunice, Olga, Pearl, Myrtyl. That does it. They caught the train and came down for the weekend. Rikki's so nice about my aunties. They never been outa Brooklyn before. Right, girls?"

"Right," they said in harmony, not bothering to remove the cigarettes from their mouths.

"Yo, Winnie, tell the Karlsons what the train conductor said to ya when you got on at Penn Station."

Winnie, knowing what was good for her, pulled her cigarette out of her wrinkled dry lips and stamped it out on Rikki's immaculate granite pool deck. "I asks the conductor, 'cause I ain't never been on the train before. I says, 'Does this train go ta the Hamptons or do we have ta change in Queens?' And he says, 'Naw. You can wear what ya have on!' "

The aunts found this hysterical and slapped their tiny legs and held their stomachs. Rikki and the Karlsons remained stunned into silence.

From somewhere behind them all, male laughter joining the aunts began, growing louder as it moved closer.

Joey Rivers was jogging toward them in a sweaty sweatsuit, a towel around his neck. He stopped beside The Match and laughed until he cried. She blushed. He knew what she was doing and she knew his laughter was at that.

"All right, girls. Back to the cards. Social duties are over."

The Gargoyle sisters curtsied spontaneously to the still stunned audience and returned to their game. The Match returned to her lounge. Joey Rivers got control of himself and turned to his tight-mouthed in-laws and Rikki Bosco went up to his room to take a long hot shower and wait for The Match to come in for a showdown.

It was Joey Rivers who insisted The Match and her aunts join the dinner party for Katarina's parents. Not even The Match would have pushed her luck that far. She had changed in the poolhouse, not ready to risk a confrontation with Rikki, and was herding "the girls" into Jakie's old Chevy station wagon for a tour of Montauk when Joey intercepted her and talked her into staying.

"God, you are the fucking greatest chick I have ever met. This was a world-class effort," he said, leading her around the side of the garage out of the seemingly insouciant but eagle-eared presence of her family.

Tears filled her eyes. "Yeah, well the cashmere look didn't work, I thought this might send the Royalty packing."

Joey laughed and kissed her cheek. He leaned against her and she could feel his penis responding. "God. God. What have you done to me. I can't stand this. This is fucking crazy. We should just all change partners and get on with our lives."

She moved away slightly and looked at him. She had stayed as far away from him as she could since the Cowans' party, more because she didn't know what to do with him, his feelings or her own, than because she didn't want to be with him. He had, in fact, scared the shit out of her. She had never counted on tenderness. On him caring about her.

Sex with Rikki had always been much more distant and so had sex with everyone else. She had sought him out to get even using the only possible tool at hand, but the tables had been rearranged on her. She did not know what to say, let alone do.

The Gargoyle weekend had come to her in what she thought was a flash of demonic brilliance. She knew Rikki didn't want her to come this weekend, so she had just played hard-to-get all week, not returning his phone calls or picking up messages.

It had seemed like a really hot way to let him know how really pissed she was—another paying back. But like with Joey, it was not working out as she had planned. At least her aunts were having a high old time, as oblivious to the undercurrents and emotions of other people on the earth as ever, and Rikki had backed off. Why? Why hadn't he thrown them out or stormed after her and demanded an explanation? Well—she would find out soon enough. Maybe he was just too cheap to give up his in-house masseuse. That was the only service she was performing. Sex had stopped weeks ago. At least he had that much integrity. She looked across at him —entranced with the Kunt's babble. He was hardly even pretending anymore.

Joey Rivers knew, in the way creative people often know things, that someday he would film a dinner scene based on, as he later came to call it, "The Gargoyles Who Came to Dinner."

He had convinced The Match to stay, not because he wanted to embarrass or compromise her or her surreal aunts, but because he was trying to help her hold on to her grit. If she had chosen to go this far out on the spiny limb, no point in copping out now. They were both street kids and so he knew how she thought and how Rikki thought, funny that none of them had a clue how Katarina thought. He looked at his beautiful wife across the table, her cheeks warm with French wine and the spotlight. This was her group of admirers, after all. Her adoring husband, her cockeyed lover, her devoted parents, and the Gargoyle sisters, who had read all about her in the fashion magazines and were impressed. Being impressed with Katarina was also a subtle but highly effective way for them to deny and demean The Match, which had been their recreation since her childhood arrival.

Joey saw this too and saw the pain in her eyes, beneath the pouty, fuck-you angle of her head while she listened to Katarina drone on and on about Gustave Courbet. "He was a nineteenth-century French Impressionist who painted the most divinely erotic nudes. He managed to capture a sensuality, especially in his rear views of nude women, that just overwhelmed me. I would love to see his drawings next time I'm in Paris."

Joey smiled. Hearing his wife use words like *erotic* and *sensual* was a dead giveaway of what he already knew was going on. What he couldn't quite figure was why it wasn't

bothering him. I mean not only was she boffing his old boyhood pal, but she was obviously liking it. Something he had
never been able to achieve. But then, that was a two-way
street. She didn't turn him on, either. What a joke. Everyone
had always assumed that since they were such an unlikely
match, it must be wild sex that kept them together. When in
fact, it was Hollywood that had created them and bound
them.

He felt ashamed of himself. What kind of a man had he
become? What could be more of an ultimate sellout than, in
addition to letting your "peers" determine your clothes, ad-
dress, car, and taste in art and people, letting them choose
your wife. Or rather, you chose a wife to impress them, to
gain cool and clout and increased status regardless of your
real needs and feelings. Horrifying.

It was not that he had been unattracted to Katarina. He
had been knocked out by her, or rather the fantasy of her.
But he knew, well before he married her, that it was wrong.
They didn't connect anywhere, in bed or out.

He had always prided himself on being honest with himself and with his friends; but he had come to Hollywood and
created a world in which he had no friends, only associates,
and he had lost his awareness and his respect for the truth.
His work was fucked up now because of the lies of his sup-
posedly hip life. He had gone to Hollywood and it had taken
adultery and this incredibly real woman from Brooklyn to
bring him back to his senses.

Maybe he wasn't jealous of Katarina and Rikki because it
had nothing to do with the real Joey. It was that phony piece
of Tinsel Land that was being cuckolded. Not him. Also, he
knew his marriage was over. That it was endangering his
spirit and his work. If he could manage to get out without a
mess, with Katarina leaving him for Rikki Bosco—perfect
Hollywood ending.

Joey caught The Match's eyes and winked at her, causing a deep purple blush to move up her pale white throat and across her cheeks. There was the fly in the aspic. She was scared to death with him. Rikki, she knew. She knew how to protect herself with him—knew the boundaries of that kind of love. Unequal and not very nice. But he was stripping her of her defenses, with every wink, every touch of caring.

It made him so sad for her. He wanted to hold her in his arms and comfort her. He wanted to make her know it was safe to let him in. She was like a virgin. Though she would have scorned such a view. She had never been entered, never touched inside, so high were the walls around her heart. In a way, Rikki and Katarina had made it possible for her to open to him. They had hurt her. The pain had torn into her— raped her of her armor—allowed a flow in and out.

Joey had been patient long enough. Now it was time to shut his wife up and give The Match a little support.

"So, Winnie," Joey addressed her, since she seemed to be the official spokesperson for the girls, "You ever heard of this Courbet? What kind of art do you ladies like?"

Winnie's eyes widened, startled to be plucked out into the center. The sisters shrank back, not sure what was going on. Winnie put her cigarette down and crossed her arms over her narrow sunken chest.

"Art. Shmart. We don't go in for that stuff. Though there was a time we used to paint by the numbers. Did some ships and a couple a clowns, got 'em on the walls. Hurt our eyes, though, so we stopped."

Katarina's face tensed. It was a clear attempt to make her look foolish. Her mother shot her a look. Her father smiled pleasantly, revealing nothing. Rikki looked stricken with embarrassment. The Match beamed.

"We did read something about them makin' replicates or whatever they're called of the Shroud a Turin, once they decide if it's the real McCoy or not. We'd buy one a them and pin it up. We go in for church pictures. Got a lot of the Lord and the Virgin and some cute crucifixes made outa plaster. Got em in Coney Island. Amazin' how they paint all those colors, where the nails went in, with blood drippin', just like the real McCoy."

The aunt called Euturpe sat forward, excited by all the attention. "Did youse people read about those nuns that been barricaded in their convent for months now protestin' the new Reverend Mother, bringin' in TV and junk foods? Such a big deal over nutin'. Who's to make 'em turn it on? They don't gotta watch it. They don't gotta eat no Tastee Cakes. I don't get it. To each his own, we always says."

Round and round they went. Like the bashful child who does his shy two-step for company and hears the roar of his first applause, out of the clown car they poured. Story on story gathered during years of radio call-in shows, television talk programs, Merv, Oprah, Donahue—decades of opinions borrowed from magazines, tabloids, and media news.

For the very first and most likely last time in their narrow and shuttered lives, they were in the limelight. Eating on golden plates, drinking French wine from crystal goblets, sitting on real leather seats and being listened to by rich famous people.

They talked on. One by one coming forward, and as they spoke, something happened between The Match and Joey Rivers, something that neither of them had counted on. They merged. They linked hearts. They fell in love.

"Tomorrow Geraldo's gonna do 'Teen Diet Horror Stories.' The promo said some of these girlies don't eat for weeks. One a them took two hundred laxatives in one day and dropped over nearly dead."

"Coffee's served in the living room," the Chinese Jamaican

announced, setting them all free to ponder what had happened.

Katarina Rivers lay back in the sunken Italian marble tub filled to the brim with bubbles, and looked up through the skylight into the stars. She yawned, feeling exhausted but far too restless to sleep. What she really needed was a massage. She smiled. Maybe she could ask The Match. She'd probably strangle her on the table.

She laid her head back and breathed deeply, trying to loosen her tension. What a horrible evening! She had thought it would never end. She hadn't even been able to speak to her parents alone afterward and apologize for bringing them into this.

What must they think? Of course, they were far too polite to be rude, though they had excused themselves rather abruptly, before coffee, but having just flown in, that was perfectly acceptable. How could she send them back to the city early without offending Rikki? Well, she would worry about that tomorrow. There were suddenly so many complications in her life, so many worries—all of the smoothness and order she so cherished had just vanished.

She sighed and ran her hands up and down her body, under the water, massaging herself. She paused at her pubis and stroked herself. Nothing. That was still too difficult for her, though Rikki kept promoting it as a wonderful way of releasing her inhibitions. She felt quite uninhibited enough for now. The thought embarrassed her, even when she was all alone.

Well, one thing was certain. Things could not go on like this. The Match would have to be sent away. It was becoming too unpleasant. She was so desperate, it was pathetic. First, trying to copy her look and now, bringing those bizarre people down just to embarrass Rikki. It was all so obvious. What could she possibly have hoped to accomplish?

Katarina closed her eyes and let the water seep into her pores. She knew Joey found The Match amusing and she had to admit, she had too, but now she was endangering them all. What could Joey say anyway. The Match was Rikki Bosco's girlfriend and if he didn't want her around, it was no business of Joey's. Besides, he was working on a financing deal with Rikki, which was certainly more important than some New Wave city slut.

She opened her eyes. The harshness of her judgment startled her. She never got used to this part of herself. She wanted to be inside the way she was outside, serene and elegant. But she was really a snobbish bitch. She just was—though as far as she knew nobody saw that about her, not even her parents. Certainly not Joey or Rikki. She kept up the front. It was so low-class not to be kind. But, when she was alone and thinking about people, she was almost never kind.

And now, she had no time for niceness. She was going to have to come to some sort of decision. After all, they would be going back to California in a month. She couldn't very well keep running back to New York to get her rocks off, as Rikki would say.

One thing she knew. She was not about to outsmart herself and end up alone. No way. She had seen too many of her friends make that mistake. Play around with a workman or acting teacher and blow their marriages. They all ended up the same. Desperate, trying to find another winner to give them back their lost status. Becoming psychologists or decorators. God forbid. She was at her peak, but she was smart enough to know it would not last forever, there was always a new crop, fresher, smarter, and more luscious, just waiting for their buds to pop.

She was pretty sure she could have Rikki Bosco as a husband and as soon as legally possible. He was lovestruck—that she knew. But what did it mean? Her family would be aghast. Joey had been bad enough. But Joey had learned the packaging, had bettered himself, become more sophisticated about society and behavior and also, more importantly, Joey was an artist. A great talent, and that her father respected. Her parents were used to Movie People—crude and otherwise.

His talent had been his calling card. He and her father had so much in common. They both loved the movies. And now that her father was retired, Joey had provided a way for him to stay involved. It had worked out rather well.

Rikki Bosco was a horse of another color. He was still so crude. He had money. Tons more money than all of them put together, and she had to admit, she loved that! With her, he would grow. She would teach him about real art, film, music, literature. She loved the idea of all that money to spend on anything she wanted. What great fun! But what he made it from was so boring. He wouldn't fit in with any of her friends or family.

Joey did. Joey *was* "in." Of course, she had lived in Hollywood long enough to know that Joey could be "out" just as fast, and if his next film did as poorly as his last one, he certainly would be.

She sat up and stretched her long slender legs, flexing her feet. What a nightmare that would be! Married to a fading director, watching him become an object of ridicule and pity. Not for her. Money was always respected. The only failure was losing it, and Rikki was far beyond that stage.

The perfect solution would be to get him into Hollywood. Maybe he could buy a studio or at least start an indie production company. She could put that together for him, after all she had fantastic contacts and a great eye. She had found

A HOUSE IN THE HAMPTONS

Love Notes for Joey and that was still his biggest success. Katarina smiled. She liked the way that sounded. That would solve all the problems.

She stood up and reached for her Turkish bath sheet. She felt better than she had in weeks. She had found a way to have this great sex, heaps of money, and not lose her status. It was perfect. She looked at the clock on the bathroom counter. 2:00 A.M. Everyone was long asleep. She was meeting Rikki in fifteen minutes at the office quarters. She was sure now of what to do. She would let him know he could have her for real and let him decide the details. He was the kind of guy who liked to take care of things. How silly men were. They really believed they were in charge, when any smart woman was always ten blocks ahead of them.

Katarina slipped into a huge white T-shirt and after checking to see that Joey was asleep, tiptoed through the bathroom's French doors and out across the lawn to meet her lover.

At five A.M. The Match woke up and saw Rikki was gone. She lay there, feeling the sea breeze on her body, trying to figure things out. It amazed her that she wasn't jealous anymore. She didn't fucking care. Something had happened at dinner that had lifted her over the fence on which she had been perched, straddling the cold metal links, twisting in discomfort for endless weeks. Warm, helping hands under her, lifting her over the top. She felt free.

She got up and made her way across the vast, cool, sleek beauty of Rikki Bosco's summer palace to the kitchen. She would make coffee, clear her head of too much champagne and too many emotions. Insomnia had always felt kind of romantic to her and tonight especially.

She didn't hear Joey come in. Rikki's prize macaw

squawked, and she turned. Joey was standing in the doorway smiling at her.

She stood up and walked back to the counter to pour him some coffee and he came up behind her and gently, but very firmly, raised her nightgown. The guy was a quick study. She liked that. Something was happening to both of them that had never happened before and they were allowing it.

Two hungover insomniacs and a macaw. A cartoon bird with one-dimensional eyes.

That's the trouble with being a houseguest, anyway, she remembered thinking as he bent her over the French bistro stool, the kind that cost hundreds of dollars in New York and about twenty francs at any Parisian flea market, and pushed himself inside her. God. Oh God. Virginal entry. It felt like that. Like it had never been entered before. Strange bird. Someone else's kitchen. Someone else's Braun coffee maker dripping hot in the background; someone else's husband dripping hot in the foreground. Being a houseguest—it disorients you, she thought, tightening her muscles and coming like crazy with two silent witnesses taking it all in.

They did not see or hear Katarina and Rikki enter, in search of leftovers, hungry after their own lust. The bird said, "Take a load off," but they didn't notice and they didn't stop. It was only when Rikki, overcome with a feeling of betrayal so powerful, it caught him completely off guard, yelled out, "What the fuck is going on here!" Only then did they come to and float back to the kitchen.

The coffee gurgled, the bird said, "Buy low! Buy low!" and the four of them faced one another and the new dawn, compromised and together.

A HOUSE IN THE HAMPTONS

July 25

Okay. I haven't written because I've been really, totally upset. I mean, I wanted to keep this stupid diary to record my feelings and thoughts and stuff, but I didn't have a clue what I was getting into. I may not want to be a writer after all—I mean it's really scary to have to think about all of this stuff so much. So first. I may be pregnant.

Okay. I said it. I am so freaked, I haven't slept in two days and I'm sure the only reason the Cowans haven't fired me is that everyone here is in worse shape than I am. I haven't told Kenny yet. I want to be really sure. I'm only three weeks late, so I'm going to see my mom tonight and tell her. I know she'll understand. I mean, she was my age when she had me, so she's *got* to understand! But then, I mean, after I see the doctor and all, if I really am, then I don't know what to do.

I mean, I love Kenny so much, but getting married and having a kid! I'd have to quit school. But in another way, it would be nice. Kenny makes good money and Frankie is going to make him a partner someday. Maybe I could finish college at Southampton; it's pretty low-key out here for kids and I can write anywhere. But he doesn't even know, yet. I mean he hasn't mentioned anything about marriage. The whole thing is really, totally freaking me out. I mean I was wearing a diaphragm! I really was.

So that's my melodrama for the week. But the real heavy news is that Dr. Jamieson's disappeared! I mean he has totally vanished. Janie is like completely hyped out of her brain. So are Gina and Harry. Harry is so hysterical, you would think that *he* was married to him. Well, they have been friends since they were little. Anyway, he left this note, that

267

Owen told me was really sad and very mysterious and no one has seen him since!

I know everyone suspects he's run off with Fritzi Ferris (Kenny says she dumped Frankie Karsh and he's been wandering around in a daze for weeks. Kenny's practically running the whole business and working on all the cars himself!).

Gina, Janie, and Harry actually went over to Fritzi's to confront her. But, I mean, they didn't have a search warrant or anything, so I don't know exactly, just what Owen and Jeremy overheard and have been able to pry out of them. God, parents can be so stupid! I mean they think we can't handle stuff, and guessing and not being told the truth is so much worse!

Anyway, she told them Donnie wasn't there and she seemed genuinely shocked and offered to help, so then they were all totally lost again.

Owen said his grandfather had hired a private detective! So, I'm telling you, this is really getting to be like a writer's dream (or nightmare).

Poor little Louie is really upset. Mrs. Cowan is still in the rehab, and Big Ben hasn't been spending enough time with him. Janie's trying, but, I mean, like her husband's disappeared!

Louie even had an accident and wet his bed last night. He's totally moved into Owen's room. Owen quit his job because his mom really needs him here. He's wiped out too, but he's been terrif with Louie.

So, that's that. Actually, I don't think I'm going to wait until tonight. My doctor's appointment is in an hour and I think I'll just drive over to my mom's afterward. It's her day off, so she should be there. This is sure not the easygoing summer I had imagined.

A HOUSE IN THE HAMPTONS

China O'Malley *was* pregnant and it was with this news and tears clouding her view so she could hardly see the Highway, that she drove the Cowans' extra car to her mother's neat little house in the Springs, the only house she had ever lived in, let herself in through the kitchen door, called to her mother, wandered through the parlor, turned the knob on her mother's bedroom door, opened it quickly onto the riveting sight of Ben Cowan's face, frozen in shock. Her mother's head was under the sheets, down somewhere that no young woman ever expects to see it, caught in the act of love by another of its victims.

One hour later China O'Malley pulled into Vintage Classics and found Kenny the mechanic and sat with him at the back of the lot in the backseat of an old Rolls-Royce and told him about her mother and Big Ben and about the baby. Shortly thereafter, Kenny asked her to marry him and China O'Malley, who now had $1,500 in the bank and a very nice tan to show for a most difficult summer vacation, said yes.

"Fuck you, Donnie. Fuck you forever!" Harry Hart was crazed. He panted along Georgica Pond, his calf muscles burning with pain. He had started running again, just to work off some of his hysteria. For a control freak, there could be nothing worse than this! His best friend for life, the person closest to him in the entire world, even including, many times, his wife, had gone off into the wild blue without *telling him anything about it*! He couldn't sleep. He couldn't eat and he couldn't concentrate on his work worth shit. His whole life was out of control because of Donnie!

Of course, Harry had run every scenario possible and the only one that made sense was a major acting-out midlife crisis, a fuck of a lifetime with Fritzi Olsen Ferris. But he wasn't there! And Fritzi was showing up at the shoe repair, at Sapore Di Mare for dinner with friends, stopping by to see Aaron, calm as a cherrystone.

Could there be someone else? Some entire other person Harry knew nothing about? The thought almost burst his brain open. He told the fucker everything! What kind of a best friend would be having an affair so passionate that he would vanish into thin air without a trace and not tell him?

It was quite simply inconceivable. It was not in Donnie's character to behave like that. Unless he had been completely misled by him for forty years! Like one of those British thrillers when your best friends turn out to be KGB agents and you never had a clue. Maybe that's it. Maybe Donnie was CIA. Undercover all these years, sacrificing his own happiness to save his country. Get serious! You watch too much television, pal.

Harry stopped, gasping for breath. Where was he? He had lost track of time. He wiped his face with his sweatshirt. Lo and behold. His inner compass had led him right to the foot of Fritzi Ferris's driveway. Well, well, well.

Okay. So was he a man or a mouse? When they had all tromped in to confront her, she had graciously (if with more than a hint of amusement) taken them on a tour of the house. Donnie had not been hiding in any closets or cupboards or bathrooms. Harry had wanted to look inside the walk-in freezer but Gina had practically yanked him out of the pantry by his neck. But who was to say there wasn't a secret room? They had figured that if he was there, he'd be in her bedroom. Being there at all was weird enough; I mean, she was free as a bird and if he wanted to vanish into an illicit love nest, why stay three miles away from his family and best friends? Why not go off to Positano or Portofino or any of those Italian *P* places that people in love always flew off to? So, at some point they had all realized how silly they looked and left. But still, who the fuck knew. Now he was

270

accepting the hard fact that he really didn't understand anything about anyone. Everything was a mirage. So much for
control.

Harry got his second wind and moved slowly and carefully up Fritzi's long, lushly landscaped driveway toward the
house.

The place was dead quiet. Only the sound of the gulls and
the ducks. A faint sea whisper and the wind. It was so quiet,
it was almost Swedish. One of those island openings, when
Bergman pans, someone steps on the rocky pebbles near the
shore. Some bony Swedish legs. Crunch. He felt the gravel
on Fritzi's driveway beneath his Nikes.

So. Where to look? He crouched down and hobbled
around the side of the large white house toward the pool.
There was no dog and no security system at the pool entrance. The house, he knew, had a rather elaborate alarm,
but so far, he hadn't seen anything outside.

Nothing. Just a large tile pool, some tables and chairs, a
barbecue and counter next to a small changing and storage
room. He turned, facing the house. Nothing. He had seen
her room, Aaron's room, the guest rooms, even the maid's
quarters. Not a trace of Donnie—no telltale pair of his black-
rimmed glasses, no copy of Freud's *Interpretation of Dreams*.
Zip.

And then Harry saw something. Reflected in the sliding
glass doors to the house, he saw, way back beyond the trees
and the pool, a hedge and behind the hedge the tip of a chimney. A shiny white chimney.

Harry's heart was pounding. He was still wet with sweat.
He took a long deep breath, bent down, and ran on tiptoe as
nimble and quick as a field mouse, back down toward Georgica Pond to the chimney behind the hedge.

He had found something. A cottage. Cozy and white. An
old barn restored. It faced the pond with a wonderful view

271

of the water and the sky. Smoke puffed from the chimney. As Harry eased his way to the window he thought that if Fritzi had not painted the chimney white, to match everything else, he never would have seen it.

Big Ben Cowan waited in the visiting room for his wife to see him. He had talked to her doctors and they had given him the okay. He had been waiting for weeks to tell her the truth, and now he could wait no longer. A searing blast of self-loathing washed over him. The look on China's face when she had opened that door. Too long, Ben.

Maybe too late. Now other lives had been directly bashed by his cowardice. Clovis was hysterical and God only knows where China had gone or how it would affect her. He may have lost them both, before he ever had a chance to do the right thing.

"Hello, Ben." His wife stood in the doorway wearing jeans and a sweatshirt, looking relaxed and clear-eyed. He had never seen her dressed this way. She looked younger, almost girlish.

"Hi, babe. Can we talk?"

She smiled and closed the door. "That's all we do here."

He cleared his throat. It had been so long since they had faced each other, clear, sober, and without the party masks that covered them from their lies and resentment. It felt almost as if they had never met. Strangers coming together for some reason—jury duty, hostages. Fellow inmates.

Delores sat down and curled her legs up under her. He had never seen her do anything remotely like that. A Janie posture. His wife did not move like that.

"I have to tell you something, he said. "I know it's something you've suspected for a long time, but, it seemed that every time I got up the courage to tell you, something happened and I just couldn't hurt you so—"

A HOUSE IN THE HAMPTONS

Delores Cowan raised her hand and stopped him.

"Ben. Ben. It's all right. I know. You're in love with some-one else and you want a divorce. There. We did it."

Their eyes locked. They had traded places. He put his head in his hands and his broad muscular back shook with grief. "God. I'm so sorry."

Delores watched him. Amazed at her own growth. She felt no bitterness. No hate. No love. Just melancholy. She was free. "I was a lousy mother and a terrible wife and you weren't much better on your end. I was punishing you for not wanting me—not needing me the way I needed you. I look at that poor woman now, and I hardly recognize her." She smiled. "We never really had a chance, you know. Go on, Ben, and get your self-respect back. Funny that only you and I ever knew you'd lost it."

They were silent. The feeling of loss passed between them like an electric shock. A jolt of release. It was almost like leaving oneself.

Delores stood up. "One favor. Since I drove myself so crazy guessing. Tell me who it is."

He swallowed. This was the hardest part. "Clovis O'Mal-ley."

"I was right," she said softly, and was gone.

Janie Jamieson was exhausted. She put her head against the window of the Hampton Jitney and tried to sleep. She could hardly remember the last real sleep she'd had. When she got back to the beach she was going to take two big fat sleeping pills and collapse.

Janie had been in the city for a week trying to find Don-nie. She had exhausted everyone and every hunch she had. No one had seen him and no one knew anything. Because of his note the police were not about to help and the private detective had come up with nothing but a former patient,

273

who thought he had seen him in a disco on 14th Street. Janie had laughed, rather hysterically at that. The only way she'd find Donnie in a disco on 14th Street would be dragging Owen out of it. God! God! God! It was all she could do to keep from screaming it out loud.

Unless the note had been written at gunpoint, the only person she had ever completely trusted had betrayed that trust and she did not believe at this moment that she was strong enough to survive it. Or even, if she wanted to be.

She sighed, wiping at the tears that fell, almost spastically now, from her eyes. Some JAP. My mother's in the detox ward, my father's off fucking some strange woman, and my husband's vanished from the face of earth. So much for a privileged life.

She tried to clear her head. The couple across the aisle from her were having a marital chat. She had noticed them when they got on with her at 70th Street because they looked like extras in a "Smug, Aging Preppies of Manhattan" sitcom. The wife was small, plump, slightly porcine-faced and lighting her cigarettes with a Cartier gold lighter while they waited for the Jitney. The husband had the puffed florid face of the noontime tippler, a large pot belly, Brooks Brothers sportswear, and the slicked-to-the-side hair and wire-rim glasses of a New York man of clubs and commerce.

"I thought we'd have a little dinner weekend after next."

"Grand. The group's so low."

"Exactly. And everyone, because it's Greenwich, well, they're all so glad to come out."

"I think we should send invitations, though."

"Exactly. I have some left from the brunch."

"So much nicer than calling. Who are we thinking of?"

"Peter and Sally. Peter and Laura. Rex and Kathy. Peter and Buf. Gordon and Kate."

274

"Fine. They're all so down."

"And we don't have to do Peter and Sal alone. Too depressing, but it still shows we care."

"Right. I do feel I've let him down. My only brother and all. We've just been, you know what the office has been like."

"Yes. Sure."

"I don't even think I've had a Scotch at home in the evening in what? Three weeks?"

"Could be."

"What the hell. So we're tired. We should start seeing the gang more. I do think I've let them down."

"Work hard, party hard."

"Right. We're so lucky. I mean everyone's marriage is so bad."

"It's a good group. A fun group, though."

"Exactly. It'll give them all a lift. You've got the little embossed invitations left?"

"Think. If not, I have to get the lighter fixed at Cartier next week, I'll pick up some more."

"The pale blue."

"Exactly."

Janie opened her eyes and snuck a look at the couple. She was riveted. It was far more fascinating than watching them fuck. They were married, obviously for some time, and they were really having a private conversation like that. It reminded her of one of those old radio programs. *Breakfast with the Tweedledums* or something. No married people really talked to each other like that. Did they? Well, maybe, just no Jewish married people talked to each other like that.

It was like reading a John Cheever short story out loud or something. How could they live like that? Like overbred robots. And she knew, she just knew that it was lousy in bed. He looked to her like the kind of guy who has prostitutes come up to his hotel room. How could they live that far away from each other? Public conversations in private.

A piercing loneliness for her husband hit her, making her pull her knees up against her self in the small seat. The tears again. God, how she missed him. They were so close. Or at least she had thought they were. Maybe the entire concept of closeness was a crock. Maybe they had been in no more intimate alignment than the yuppie marionettes beside her.

The thought, that their relationship had not been real, was simply unbearable. Hang on, kiddo, she told herself. She was not about to lose it on the Hampton Jitney and give the Humanoids from Greenwich something else to be smug about. She sighed. One more hour and she would be safe.

How ironic, that on the very tip of her decision to leave her parents' house and reclaim her own life, she had lost the one person whose support had given her the courage, at this late date, to cut her family loose. Well, she was going to do it anyway. So there, Donnie Jamieson, wherever and whoever you are. Just as soon as she got some sleep, she was moving out.

"The thing you must never forget about New Yorkers," someone in front of her with a southern accent was saying, "is that they are all pretentious and they are all crazy."

Janie released her legs. Maybe that was it.

When Janie stepped off the Jitney at the Bridgehampton stop, Gina Hart was sitting on the bench waiting for her. It was totally unexpected, but she had never been so glad to see anyone in her life. Gina stood up and Janie walked right into her arms and they held each other not thinking or caring what it looked like to the cheerful weekenders around them.

When they had both stopped crying, Gina took Janie's bag in one hand and her hand in the other and walked her to her Volvo wagon. She helped Janie in and got behind the wheel. They sat for a moment, not speaking. Then Gina turned and took Janie's small tan hands in hers and looked right through her dearest friend's enormous dark glasses.

"Janie sweetheart. We've found Donnie."

When Harry Hart had peeked into the window of the hidden barn at the edge of Georgica Pond, the first thought he had was an image of the old *What's My Line* game show. All of those glittery New York sophisticates with their oh-so-ironic, patronizing patter, staring some poor sucker down while trying to figure out what he did. "Are you in show business, Mr. Smith?" Arlene Francis would inquire, grinning her best party grin.

"Nope," Mr. Smith would reply, pleased for the moment to have the upper hand with such a fancy, famous dame, who, he just knew, was never gonna guess that he was an equestrian taxidermist.

That's how Harry felt. He had been totally and completely hoodwinked by Donnie Jamieson.

The inside of the cottage was immaculate and cozy. Even though it was hot and muggy, everything was sealed, it was centrally air-conditioned and a log-burning fire was roaring.

There was a stereo system and a giant screen TV and two pretty friendly chintz-covered couches, hand-hooked cloth rugs on the floor, bookcases filled with books, a pair of over-stuffed armchairs in the same fabric—all unlike the main house but seeming, to Harry, much more like Fritzi.

There was a small kitchen, which looked fully stocked, and then, at the back against the wall was a daybed. Beside it was a card table filled with medical supplies, pill vials, syringes, disposable gloves, I.V. fluid bottles, and jars of swabs and sterile cotton.

On the bed wearing light blue pajamas, an I.V. tube dripping into his arm, his face so thin and pale, that for a moment Harry did not even recognize him, lay his oldest and closest friend, Donnie Jamieson.

Fritzi Ferris sat in a chair by his head, her eyes half on the television screen and half on Donnie. Every few minutes, she leaned over and looked at his I.V. He was clearly her patient.

It was more than Harry could handle. He ran around to the barn door that served as the entrance, slid it open, and burst into the room, gasping for breath.

"I'm hyperventilating," he wheezed, and Donnie opened his eyes at once.

"In my bag, Fritz. Give him the I.V. Valium." Harry sat down in Fritzi's chair and put his head between his legs.

Fritzi moved with the starched snappy efficiency of the well-trained nurse. She handed him a paper bag and quickly prepared the shot. "Easy, Harry," she said, as calmly as if they had been expecting just such a visitor.

Harry felt the shot kick in. He sat up and took a long deep breath. Donnie smiled at him. He seemed too weak to do much more, but he motioned to Fritzi to raise his bed.

"Are you sure?" she said, making Harry crazy, that she should be here, in this position of highest trust and intimacy. A stranger. It should have been him.

"I wanted to fucking kill you!" Harry said, and burst into tears. "What's happening here? What is this, you crazy fucking bastard! How could you do this to us!"

Donnie reached out for Harry's hand. Harry shook his head, unable to receive him. "I'm sorry you had to find out like this." Donnie paused, trying to regain his energy. "I was trying to protect you all, but I think I've made it worse." He looked at Fritzi Ferris, who was standing behind Harry, waiting for Donnie to tell her what to do.

"Hey, Fritz. How about letting me talk to Harry alone. I'm fine. Really. The I.V. helped. I'm okay." Her lovely face darkened, but she just nodded and left them alone to try to undo the terrible damage that had been done.

"Just listen, Harry. I'll try to tell you everything."

Harry crossed his arms over his chest like a child sent to the cloakroom. Listen was all he could do anyway. He was as disoriented and confused as a drunk in a funhouse. He only hoped he would be able to take it.

In the years to come they would always refer to the week before Big Ben's party, that week when everything began to change forever, as "The Aaron Week" or "The Delores Week" never, however, as "The Donnie Week," because, although what happened to Donnie Jamieson that week was far worse, they did not know about it till so much later.

What they meant, was the beginning of the unraveling. The first threads in the tapestry of their relationships loosening. It had all seemed more than enough at the time—having one's mother arrested in a drug raid and one's unknown son unveiled. More than enough, it would seem. But in that awful way of superstition, which says bad things come in threes, there was a third thing that week and it happened to Donnie Jamieson.

The day after Donnie rescued Harry Hart from his fainting spell at the Various Varinofskys', he had left early in the morning not to see a patient but to see his own doctor. His goddamn ulcer was really acting up and, though no one else seemed to notice, he knew he looked like shit.

When Marty Haber, his old med school buddy and long-time physician, finished examining him, before a word had passed between them, Donnie knew something was really wrong.

"Donnie," Marty said, his eyes lowered. "I don't like what I see. I'm not getting ulcer from this. I don't like the way your abdomen feels; I don't like the urine and your color sucks. Could be hepatitis. I want to check you in to NYU and run some tests."

"I've got a crazy week, Marty, and some personal stuff. Can it wait?" He knew the answer before he asked the question.

Marty put his arm around his shoulder. "Call me an alarmist, you know what a cautious fuck I am. Tomorrow."

Donnie nodded. "Okay. One thing. No one knows. I mean no one. Janie, Harry. No one."

Marty watched him. "You sure?"

"Yes. I won't go in unless you promise."

"You got it. Makes sense, anyway. Why worry them when it's probably nothing. But with your family history, kid, I want to be sure."

Donnie had gone back to his office and done what he would do in any crisis. He canceled his appointments, speaking personally to each patient and offering him or her a colleague in an emergency. He made up the Washington story for his family and his secretary, made arrangements with his super for the mail and the papers, packed a small bag, and checked himself into NYU.

It was familiar. Too familiar. He had sat in that waiting room many times before. He had sat in the same seat when he checked his father in and in the seat across from himself when he had checked his mother in. He had filled out all the forms and carried their bags and held their hands and offered reassurance and he had waited for their tests and he had taken them the bad news one by one, five years apart; and he had checked them in and out as they weakened and he had helped them die. Cancer. He hated the vile word. The word was attached to the faces of two people that he had loved deeply and who had died in agony, decades before their time.

He was not surprised that it was his turn. In some way, he

felt he had been waiting for years for the tap on his shoulder
—for his fate to find him. It was almost a relief.

"With your history," the doctors had always said. His parents had both died of stomach cancer, one of the rarest
forms, beating all kinds of odds. It was eerie. Almost as if
they had willed it. So the ulcer was watched. The ulcer had
come and gone, not taking him with it. Finally, he had begun
to relax, to embrace the scar tissue inside him as his penance.
His trade-off. Okay, I'll take the ulcer now and again, God,
as a reminder, not to get too cocky about being here.

In the dark, in the middle of many long, sleepless nights,
he would wake from a dream of his parents, his mother sitting in her favorite chair asking him a question from his
childhood, but addressing it to his man self. "Did you wash
behind your ears, Donnala? Have you clean socks for the
weekend?" He would wince in terror. They were in him and
they would come back and claim him.

He often wondered if this foreboding, this shadow of mor-
tality that followed him everywhere, just behind his conscious mind, was the reason he was so reticent, so stoic in his
life. "Don't get too involved. You won't be around long. The
more you embrace it, the harder it will be to let go."

Whatever the reason, he had remained somewhat aloof
from his own journey. Not uncaring. Certainly not uncaring. Just unemotional. Forcing an evenness, and acceptance,
over his head like last winter's turtleneck; too tight and
itchy, but protective in the storm.

He did not have an ulcer and he did not have stomach
cancer. He did not have hepatitis or gastroenteritis.

Donnie Jamieson had something worse. The worst something he could have. "Metastasized pancreatic cancer and it's
all over your liver. The thing looks like the lunar surface.
I'm amazed you feel so good." Marty Haber was his friend

and he told him straight truth because, like everyone else in Donnie's life, Marty thought he could handle anything.

There was nothing they could do for him and he would probably not have much pain. Being a doctor, he would know when it was time to come back.

"What I said before, Marty. No one is to know. No one."

Marty started to protest, but the look on Donnie's face stopped him.

"How long?" Donnie asked, his voice calm but thin as smoke.

"We can never be sure with this pisser. Miracles happen. But from what I saw, Donnie. Oh God! Donnie! I'm so fucking sorry!" Marty Haber was sobbing, his shoulders shaking with grief. "Two weeks to two months," Marty sobbed, and Donnie stood up and put up his arms around his deliverer, offering him the comfort he could not take for himself.

In a little converted barn behind a fancy white house in East Hampton, later that same day, everyone who most loved Donnie Jamieson gathered like the relatives of crash victims. The truth now was for all of them.

The only time Donnie cried was when Janie came in. She stood in the doorway not even bothering to hide her anguish. She just stood, her small shoulders shaking.

He reached out his free arm, and she came to him and they held on to each other with the ferocity of two people who have loved deeply and lived together closely for a long, long time. Everyone left them alone and they clung together at the edge of their world, trying to keep from falling off.

When they were calmer, he tried to explain.

"When Marty told me, baby, I just couldn't deal with it. I mean, I swear it blindsided me. Maybe it was one of the only times in my life I wasn't half expecting something like that, so much was going on—your mother, Aaron, the party. Telling you, made it real." He stopped, fighting to keep his focus, trying not to frighten her with his wandering. His head was no longer totally under his control.

"I came down for the party and I had pretty much decided I wasn't going to tell anyone until I—was, unable to stand up. I . . . didn't want to be treated differently. I remembered my folks—how people were with them. How I was. I know it sounds crazy, but I somehow felt that if I didn't say it, it wouldn't come true. But I knew pretty fast it wasn't going to be that easy." Donnie stopped.

Janie's face froze. "Are you—what can I do?"

"I'm fine. Just tired." He tried to take a deep breath. "Dinner at The Palm, remember? Well, late that night—I was real sick, and the next day I went to see Fritzi. I knew she was a nurse, baby. I thought she might be able to help. She'd gone through watching her husband die. I knew she wouldn't be shocked. I just couldn't lay it on you like that. I wanted you all—to have as much happy time as possible." He moved his arm and the I.V. bottle jiggled.

"Fritzi said she had had this feeling we had unfinished business together, that she was back in my life for a reason, but that she had never imagined this was it. She said she wanted to help. The next day I called and asked her if I could come and stay, hide out really, for a few days—until I— found a . . . a way to cope with it. I needed the time. I wanted to be strong in myself.

"When I left you that note, darling, I swear to God, I thought I was just going for a few days, a week. But I got worse very fast and by the third morning I was delirious.

"See, the blood going to my brain isn't being cleaned properly, because of the liver damage, so I get, fuzzy, paranoid.

"Fritzi just took over. She called Marty Haber and explained, and he ordered everything she needed. She kept begging me to let her call you, she did, please don't think it was her idea, but I made her swear she wouldn't until I was ready. I think she was scared to death that I'd die on her and she'd have to call you up and tell you.

"I mean, people don't—just—suddenly fall over from terminal cancer. It's not like getting hit by a truck.

"I kept thinking, I was just hitting a rough spot—that I would rally . . . go into remission . . . and then I would come home. I wanted to tell you on my feet. Pretty dumb for a doctor.

"Janie. You know something? I was really okay until I went in to see Marty. After the tests, when he told me what I had, I went downhill really fast. I've seen that before. I know this sounds crazy—maybe it's just the morphine—but I keep having this thought that if you never went in to see the damn doctors, you wouldn't get worse. Somehow their fating you like that, just zaps your resolve." He was so tired, he could barely keep his eyes open.

"Janie darling, I don't want to go to a hospital, I don't need to and if I do—I'll die—faster. Please forgive me, baby. I was only trying to make it easier. I never meant it to—turn out like this. Each day I thought tomorrow I'll be strong enough to go home. I wanted to walk in and tell you on my feet. I wanted to be standing up for you and the kids."

After a while he fell asleep, and Janie lay beside him, grateful for this time alone with him, having him next to her like so many other nights of their lives. She watched the sun go down over the water, saw the swans and the ducks glide off, wherever they went at night. She understood why he had come to Fritzi. But it was time to take him home. In the morning, she would have everything moved to the beach. He was still her husband. He was still her Donnie.

Fritzi came in and she got up and watched her fuss over him, settling him down.

A HOUSE IN THE HAMPTONS

She motioned for Janie to follow her and they left him asleep and walked out into the warm, humid night.

"Is it all right to leave him?" Janie asked, feeling shy and uncertain.

"Yes. He's had his medication and he sleeps very well. He has a buzzer right by his hand and it rings all over the house. I'll teach you how to do everything."

When Fritzi said this, Janie stopped, grief and gratitude claiming her. She stopped and turned to really look at this silky golden woman. This dreaded adversary, turned now into a much-needed ally. "You *know* what I thought. I thought he had left me for you. Even when we didn't find him here, I believed it. You were his dream girl—his heartbreak. How could a mere wife compete with that? I know you would have taken him if you could have. But I don't hate you for it. I want to thank you for what you've done for all of us. I want to bring him home in the morning." Janie paused.

"Do you want—I mean, could we hire you to be his nurse? This is crazy. I don't know what to say."

Fritzi put her arm around Janie and they walked slowly toward the house. "Let me think about it, okay? He was the best friend I ever had and I didn't even see it. I was very stupid and I paid dearly. You were a much better choice and you've made him very, very happy. Believe me, I'm not noble; I don't have Donnie's Mother Teresa complex. I'm getting a lot back from this. I haven't been useful in a very long time. We'll help him do this, Janie. It'll be okay."

When they got to the house, Fritzi went off to change and Janie called Isabel and asked her to come and bring all the food she could carry. When Isabel arrived, they told her and they all cried together and then Isabel went off to do the most comforting thing she knew how to do. She cooked an enormous meal. Halfway through the meal, Janie stood up.

"Oh my God!" she said. "Gina's fortieth birthday! We

never had her birthday dinner!" They had forgotten all
about it until that moment, even Gina. Fritzi ran to her wine
room and emerged with bottles of Dom Pérignon and Isabel
whipped up one of her lickety-split chocolate cakes and they
sang "Happy Birthday" and toasted one another with the
kind of maniacal giddiness ignited by intense emotion and
unrelievable pain. Across the cool green lawn Donnie Jamieson slept on, covered now by the thick and misty weight of
their love. It was their turn to take care of him and it was his
turn to let them.

Three A.M. Fritzi Ferris's living room. She has gone to bed.
Big Ben has taken Louie and the boys back to his house for
the night. Gina and Harry and Janie are sitting or, rather,
slouching deep into one of the oversize white couches, working on the last bottle of champagne, unwilling to end the
intimacy.

Harry Hart, who is lying between Gina and Janie, an arm
around each of them, is thinking out loud.

"I know it's morbid, but if the doctor told *me* I only had a
month to live, I'd make a beeline for the nearest newsstand,
buy myself a carton of Marlboros, and smoke my fucking
brains out."

Gina laughed. "So much for ever really being cured of the
habit."

"Fucking A. I just abstain. I assumed I was cured, but
when I thought about what I'd do, if it didn't matter anymore, that was it." Harry tapped Gina with his fingertip.

"What would you do, Gin'?"

Gina sighed. "I'd buy the worst junk novels ever written
and get into bed with a twenty-pound bag of heavily salted
potato chips." She looked across to Janie—checking to see if
this was okay.

Janie leaned forward and smiled at her.

A HOUSE IN THE HAMPTONS

"Chocolate mousse cake and crates filled with Hershey with Almonds. Every Clint Eastwood movie ever made— shown at sea—on a yacht going nowhere. Just circling.

"I'd go up to that old Mohonk resort up at New Paltz and ice-skate across the lake at night—with candles lining the shore. All alone. And I'd have music playing. Mozart and Janis Joplin."

"I'd find the biggest most beautiful swimming pool on earth and have it heated as warm as I liked and swim naked all alone in the moonlight."

"I'd rent the Lunt-Fontanne and an orchestra and sing all my favorite songs, very, very loud."

"I'd do something I've always been afraid of. Hot-air balloon. Scuba diving. Maybe, hang gliding."

Gina sat up. "I'd never do another thigh exercise or eat another teaspoon of yogurt or pick up the dry cleaning or make my bed. No more shaving, waxing, or depilitating my body parts. No talking to Jeremy's Spanish teacher or cutting my toenails. No more deep pore cleansing, I'd never roast another chicken!"

Janie joined her. "I'd stop washing my hair. I'd stop cutting it, coloring it. Fuck hair. I hate hair care. Just bed and chocolate. Burn the Fonda tapes. Never return another phone call. No more lip-lining. Throw all that shit away."

Harry jumped up and drank down the rest of the champagne right out of the bottle. "No more dental hygiene! No more jogging, paying bills, running a business. No business meetings, business lunches, business calls! No more business suits! No more employees. No more *psychoanalysis*! (This is great!) I'd never have to go to the theater again! I'd never have to talk about current events and the greenhouse effect! I wouldn't have to be well informed, well groomed, well spoken or well intentioned! Endless Mets games and I'd fly to Stockholm and meet Ingmar."

Gina rose up on her knees, glass in hand. "No more PTA meetings, co-op association meetings, block protection meetings. *No more psychoanalysis,* electrolysis, dermatologists. No more dental floss, income tax analysis, cleaning people. Carpet cleaners—"

Janie interrupted. "Upholstery cleaners. Window washers. Having those creepy guys on the ladders outside your windows. No more self-improvement, the four basic food groups! No more oat bran muffins."

"I'd stop pretending I like French food."

"I'd tell Erica Hess to go fuck herself."

"I'd stop pretending I'm a 'people person.' "

"I'd stop holding my stomach in."

"Guilt. No more guilt!"

Gina held her glass high. "I'd throw away all of my sunblock and find myself the hottest, sunniest beach on earth and roll around like a pig in shit until I burned to a perfect crisp."

Janie stood up and put her arms around Harry. "I'd swim in the Grand Canal. I'd sleep with Harry. I'd sleep with that guy we keep seeing at the Soda Shack. The pool guy."

Gina laughed. "Jack Reed? Me too. A threesome!"

Harry blushed. He was such a prude at heart. He had started this and now the ball had rolled back into his court.

"I'd call up one of those really kinky escort services, or massage places and have them send over their sleaziest, most grossly slutty woman, with huge tits! Two of them!"

"Harry Hart!" Gina jumped up and the three of them danced around, hugging one another, an awkward, rumpled, inebriated human hero sandwich.

"Jesus," Harry whispered, and they all moved apart. "Jesus. Do you know what we've just done? We've made dying seem like a lot more fun than living our lives. Do you hear us? All of those things we do that we hate? All of that god-awful bullshit? Jesus!"

They all fell back on the sofa, quiet for a while. Each back in their separate sadness.

Janie got up first and paced back and forth for several minutes.

"What is it, sweetheart?" Gina said.

Janie moved off toward the back door. "Donnie's list. He never gave this to himself. I just thought of something I can do. Something he would have wanted if he had gotten to do this." She went outside, marching across the lawn to the barn.

Harry and Gina watched her go.

Harry yawned. "I hope God doesn't hear this, but it's almost disappointing. I mean if you thought you were dying and you just let everything go—and then you found out you weren't. You'd really be screwed up."

"You're tired, Harry. Let's not dwell on that one. "Come on, pal. We've got to sleep sometimes."

They linked arms and swaying slightly with too much emotion and too much champagne, they let the endless day end.

Fritzi Ferris's door was open and Janie stood in the doorway for a moment, trying to find the way into this communion.

Fritzi was sleeping on her back, her lovely breasts, just barely covered by a white satin gown, rising and settling so smoothly, so steadily; it was almost like watching snow fall.

Janie was enamored, in the way that little girls are enamored of fashion models and movie stars. A woman like this— like "Marilyn," as Gina called her—who slept like that, gracefully on her back in white satin. Sleeping Beauty come to the Hamptons.

Janie slept coiled in a tense little ball, lost in one of Owen's

extra large cast-off T-shirts. Lately the one that said JAPS ARE
A DEFINABLE WORLD BODY.

Janie felt the loss already. As much as she had protested,
she had seen Owen's teasing of her princess origins as loving
and part of their family myth. She knew he would never do
it again, knew it as sure as she knew that everything she held
around her, her invisible picket fence of stability and security, had been trampled. It was all ending and what was
replacing it was not yet clear.

She sighed and Fritzi opened her eyes and saw her. It
seemed perfectly natural, somehow, that Janie should be
standing in the doorway of her room, watching her sleep.

Janie moved quietly across the threshold, just barely into
the small white room.

"I'm sorry. I know how tired you are. I have something, a
favor, something important to ask you."

Fritzi sat up and reached for her robe and Janie came forward, closing the door behind her. Fritzi motioned for her to
sit beside her and Janie climbed onto the silky French sheets,
curling her legs up under her.

Those feelings of being the oldest and wisest and the
smallest and scariest, feelings she had carried all of her re-
coverable life, were melding together now, a weld forming,
making them fit, making them all right together and not the
source of inner doubt and endless conflict; a battle between
them for control of her, that had sapped her energy and
thwarted her growth.

They sat together on the narrow bed, facing each other in
the dark. The only light came from a small dormer window
above them.

"I want you to know, Fritzi, that what I'm going to ask
you, this favor . . . I'm not good at this. I'm not a good
favor asker. I never ask them, even of Gina. Almost never.

And you have no obligation to say yes. I mean it's, well, not your usual kind of favor.

"You see, after you went to bed, Harry and Gina and I were talking—and chugging down the champagne a bit—anyway, we were talking about what we would do if we found out, like Donnie, that we were going to die soon. I know it sounds creepy but it wasn't. Anyway, most of it turned into what we would *stop* doing, which was interesting in itself, but during it, I thought about Donnie. He never gave himself that. One wild night. A trip to Disney World, whatever. He wouldn't have even thought that way. Poor Donnie. He's always been so self-denying. I'd be stuffing down the Milk Duds, puffing up the butts, never Donnie. Good father, good husband, good friend, good son, good doctor—good luck. What a joke! Okay. I'm heading to it. I am." Janie looked into Fritzi Ferris's fluorescent blue eyes, trying to see all the way into her.

"So I was thinking. I know what Donnie would have said, if he had been up there with us and not down here in that awful bed like he is. I know his one unfulfilled dream, was, you."

Janie swallowed hard and tried to catch her breath. All of a sudden she wasn't sure she was brave enough for this. She blinked and tears fell, running through her freckles and down onto her neck. "Fritzi, is it still possible? I mean, could he, if you tried? Could he make love with you? Could you, would you do that for him? I don't want him to—I don't want him to die without having one absolutely sensational memory from right this minute. You're the only thing I can give him. Believe me, I wish there was something else. But the bum doesn't even like chocolate."

They were both crying now. They sat, not speaking, not touching, just facing each other for a while. They could hear the crickets and the light summer rain beginning to fall on the roof.

"Are you sure?" Fritzi Ferris whispered, and touched Janie's knee.

Janie nodded, not trusting her voice.

Fritzi wiped a tear from her cheek. "He won't, you know, even if he can, unless he thinks it's all right with you."

Janie tensed. "Oh, no! Oh, no! Then he'd misunderstand! He'd think it was charity. I want him to feel it is coming from you. Not from me. I want it to be real, you know. Not like a favor. Like a dream coming true."

Fritzi smiled. "Janie. You are something else. I see why he loves you so much. He'll know, anyway, but he'll also know it's not a favor. Do you read me?"

Janie wrinkled her nose and sniffled. "Yep. I do. I don't want to, but I do. Okay. Well, if that's the only way. If you're sure about that. I'm sure you're much better at all of this seduction stuff than I am. But, try to just slide it in. Sort of subtle. No stripagram with a great big 'From Janie' card. I couldn't take that and neither could he."

Fritzi laughed. "You're right. I know a lot more about it than you do. Trust me." Fritzi got up and tiptoed to the door, she put her fingers to her lips and motioned for Janie to stay where she was. Fritzi disappeared down the hall. Janie waited. Her heart pounding, not quite sure what to do next.

Fritzi reappeared in the doorway, "Why don't you go on up to the house, take a nice hot bath in my tub, take a pill and sleep in my room. He wakes up for his shot about now. This is a good time for him."

Janie's eyes widened. "Right now?"

"Janie, honey. Right now is all he has."

Janie stood up and followed Fritzi out of the back way. Fritzi opened the small side door and Janie stepped out into the last of the night light, the moonglow and the rain covering her gently.

"Thanks, Fritzi," she said because she didn't know what else to say.

"Thank *you*, Janie," Fritzi Ferris said, blowing her a kiss and closing the door behind her.

If a perfect gift can be defined as one that fills the specific need of the bestower and the bestowed; the entwining of the content with the needs of giver and getter, then what Janie Jamieson and Fritzi Ferris gave Donnie Jamieson that pre-dawn summer morning was the perfect gift.

And he accepted it for what it was. He received it in the spirit of its offering; which is also a requisite of the perfect gift transaction. For the first and only time in his forty-four years of life, he just fully let something happen to him. Without judgment, analysis, trade-off, or thinking about someone else. It was his present and he was going to have it all for himself.

His dream had come true. Not how he had imagined it or, God knows, how he would have wanted it, but as his father had said to him long ago, "You gets what you gets." He got it.

His Dream Girl carried him off into the misty magic of his boyhood, with all of that fresh lust, energy, and pain. She fulfilled his fantasy. They were not really young and they brought to it so much more respect for the gift that it was and because he knew that somewhere inside it was his wife's love, too, it was even more majestic—a Magi's offering.

"God!" he shouted out, holding his Dream Girl tight against him, feeling the fluid, silken roundness of her. "Thank you, God," he whispered, his gaunt face washed with sweat and tears, his heart full of his life force.

He felt it in him; the power of his will, coming back. She

had infused him with life; with joy. And when she was gone, leaving him to sleep again, the morphine floating him off on this cloud of hope, he knew he would rally. He would not die so fast. He just knew.

Janie Jamieson marched down the hall of the Sea Oaks Clinic, her arms swinging, her legs as stiff as an Alabama drill sergeant's. She knocked at the door to her mother's room, but without hesitating or waiting politely for a response, she opened it.

Her mother was sitting in a chair by the window reading *The Dance of Anger.* Apt, she thought. Her mother turned, smiling hesitantly. It was not like Janie to come without calling. They had not had one private meeting since her admittance. She started to welcome her, but the look on Janie's face stopped her.

"Donnie has cancer. He's dying," her daughter announced, holding her head high, chin up, the way she had done as a child, always bracing against invisible blows.

Delores inhaled so sharply, her vision blurred.

"Oh, my God! Oh Janie! What can I do?"

Janie's chin held, but her lower lip was shaking so hard, she could barely control it. "Nothing! Like always, Momma! Not a *fucking* thing!"

The word hung between them. It was not a mother–daughter word. Janie had never said it before and neither had her mother.

Delores put her hands to her throat. She had known, in some unconscious way, that this scene was waiting to be played but she had never thought it would come so soon. She wasn't ready for it.

"Please, Janie. Don't hate me."

"Why not?" Janie flung her tote bag onto her mother's

carefully made bed and then flung herself down after it. A teenage move. Acting out, her shrink would probably say.

"Why shouldn't I hate you? What have you ever done to earn you anti–child-hate immunization? You never cared about me. All you ever cared about was *him*. Great God Cowan! We could all have gone to hell in a Saks box for all you cared.

"Put your head in the oven. Pass out on the beach. Run your car into the bay. Never ever comfort me or look at me or ask me how I was, what I was, who I was! What kind of mother were you? Why shouldn't I hate you?"

Delores's hands were shaking so hard, she put them under her thighs. Just when she thought she was over the worst of it. She was right back on first. She would kill for a drink. She had no idea how to help her daughter. She could see her rage, but she could not reach out to her. She could not mother it away.

"Janie. I never did it on purpose. I never wanted to hurt you. I'm sick. I've been sick for a long, long time. I'm so sorry. So, so sorry. I've only wanted the best for you. You know how many times I've told you how lucky you were to have a husband like Donnie. A man who really loved you, not like it was between your father and me."

Janie grabbed all the pillows on the bed and threw them on the floor. "Great! Fucking great, Mom! Perfect! Is this the price I have to pay for all this luck? Okay, I'm paying. He's going to die! See, I'm no luckier than you are. We're even. End of contest!"

Delores burst into tears. Her whole body was shaking. "I can't take this, Janie. I'm not well enough."

Janie jumped up. It was too late to rethink this. This was a truth tantrum. It had a life of its own.

"Tough. Tough shit, Momma! You've dished it out, plenty. In your own genteel way, you've piled the platters pretty high. Poor little Delores. Everybody tippy-toeing around. So frail. Can't be her fault. Must be mine. Well, guess what? I don't give a fuck if you're sorry! You were supposed to be the mother! I was supposed to be the child. Simple! If you can't take it, fake it. Works like a charm. Gotten me through the first fifteen years of Owen's life.

"You never even tried! I did it for you! I took care of you and Cowan. I don't even remember the last time I felt like the child! 'I can't take this Janie–Ben world. So I will just drink myself stuporous and pill myself senseless and inject myself into oblivion and the hell with all of you!'

"And don't give me any horse shit about alcoholism being a disease and you not being responsible. You *are* responsible! You weren't forced against your will! You knew you were sick and you thumbed your nose at it and us! You abdicated. Well, guess what. I'm a mother, too. And I have *insider* information. I have every right, to, to . . ." Janie doubled over and fell back on the bed. The words *hate you* refused to come. The rage fell away from her. Rage held against her frightened, fast-beating heart, a bird heart, easily seen through her skin.

She could not say it. It was no longer true. She didn't hate her. She mourned her. Because in releasing her rage, she was releasing her hope. Her mother had done the best she could. It had just not been enough. It had not given her a firm, grounded wire to receive the current of her new reality.

Her husband was dying and she needed her mommy. But the truth was . . . the truth. She did not have one. Some things are lost when they are lost and cannot be retrieved ever again.

She raised her ravaged face and met her mother's terrified blue eyes. She loved her. And she forgave her. But she also knew, in the most profound sense of knowing anything, that the damage done was done. They could go on, but they could never forget. For some things, it is too late.

9

August is to the Hamptons what April is to Paris, moon-light is to Miami, Christmas is to Wales.

Mythic. The essence of summer. The height of its power. A clenched fist of expectation. This time we'll do it right. We'll squeeze every last drop of time and place from its nippled teat. This one will be the warmest, the most relaxed, filled with the best friends, tastiest food, evenest beach weather, most engrossing books, sweetest corn, funniest movies, and longest naps.

Each summer comes around faster and deserts us sooner. Each one is another chance to grasp it, clasp it to us, hold it tight, extend its precious moments.

The cars can barely move on the weekends and the farm stands empty earlier, the restaurant lines form faster, and the beaches are filled with sun paraphernalia. Camp chairs and terry cloth, coolers and umbrellas, soda cans and portable radios. Bodies lying, swimming, walking, strolling, running, sunning. Voices rising, falling, laughing.

People in August, reaching for the magic promise of sea and shore. Ignoring the perils of sand flea, deer tick, floating waste, radiated light, perilous thunder, jellyfish, and undertow. They have come to find the glory of it, the freedom of its promise.

School is out for everyone. August is the grown-ups' only recess from reality. Sand under your city toes and melting ice-cream cones in your hands.

New York people in August in the Hamptons smile more. They stroll. They whiz around their chosen villages in trendy convertibles, radios blaring, taking risks with their bodies and their possessions that would be unthinkable in the City.

They still read *The New York Times* and *The Wall Street Journal* and they still socialize for business, though no one really admits it. But then again, for most of them, that is the only socializing they have ever done, so interwoven are the two in their lives, so folded. Other kinds of people do not come to the Hamptons. They find other places.

Gay men come in elegant pairs, and trios of working girls who rent rooms in restored guest houses and August renters who want to make the most of their month and wear themselves out entertaining and sightseeing.

And then there are the summer home owners old and new, rich, super rich and not so, who have been out there for a while—have come in fall and spring and winter. Have watched leaves change and snow fall and seen the towns deserted, as fine and exquisite as any very old town whose dignity is never touched by those who pass through it. "Founded in 1656—45—78" announce the signs at the entrance to each village.

The graveyard is the first sight the tourist has of East Hampton, a graveyard reflected in the vine green pond, marking entry to the prettiest town this side of the Cotswolds. The markers let you know, in the quietest, least obtrusive way, that the town is on to you. It is not just a repository for boogey boards and beer bottles. Lying beneath it are the corpses of its founders. A reminder, lest you forget, that someday you tourists, too, will follow them. To someplace far less beautiful no doubt, but someplace for sure.

This is not just about snow cones and beach balls, this is about respect for the places we invade, respect for the time—the racing summertime, that can never be caught, never held. It will leave us as it left them, dead and cold, watching the insolent hopefuls year after year trying to outrun it.

The Hamptons were there before it was a summer place. Before anyone ever thought of junk bonds and best sellers. Farmers and fishermen, and people with nowhere to go, came to the end of this island and forged a living. They built houses close to the road so the weather would not thwart them; churches to pray for the strength to carry on and the graveyards to house their loved ones.

The churches and the graveyards have stayed, reminders to some, fodder for tourist snapshot to others. But they have stayed through it all. As the land was parceled and sold to city folks looking for a tie to a past they could not even comprehend; they have stayed. Silent witnesses to the truth of the place. And to August. To the cycle of life and death that will go on summer after summer, leaving its nicks and ice-cream sticks—leaving its mark on the future, but not on their past.

It was Parents Day at Louie's day camp, but there was no parent available, so The Match had offered to go and represent the Cowan/Jamieson tribe. She pulled Janie's station wagon into the narrow overgrown driveway leading to the Sleepy Cove Summer Camp, passing the long lineup of New York status cars until she found a space. This was a first for her. She had never been to camp.

Because she had no idea what Parents Day at such a place might involve, and also because she knew how depressed

Louie was and how embarrassing it was for both of them for her to be filling in as his generic parent, she had probably overdone things. She swung her endless legs out of the car and gathered up her gear. Cameras, both video and Instamatic, folding chair, cooler with all of Louie's favorite drinks and snacks, first-aid kit (he could fall down in a race or get hit by a ball, slip by the pool, who knew what they had in store for them). A towel, two changes of clothes (one for him and one for her in case they had a Parents Party later). There was also her radio, an umbrella, a copy of *Vanity Fair* (just in case it rained and they had to wait for a while or between events if Louie wasn't doing something that required her undivided attention). Binoculars and sunblock (she had read an article in *People* about how black people get sunburned the same as white people). She had done her best.

Louie saw her struggling down the path and came running. He smiled and waved at her and she was glad she had come.

"Hey, my main man, help your old mother figure, here."

Louie ran to the car and pulled the cooler out. "What *is* all this stuff?"

The Match hobbled forward, wishing she had worn more sensible shoes.

"Supplies. I don't want any of those little turkeys thinkin' we weren't supportin' our camper."

Louie laughed. He liked her. "You're so funny, Match. It's just a stupid Parents Day. Hardly anyone even comes."

"Oh, yeah? Check out the driveway. Looks like a parking lot at a Southampton disco. This is happening. Come on."

It took three trips, but finally The Match was settled in, Louie was sunblocked and refreshed, and The Match, camera ready, sat poised on her beach chair, waiting for Louie and his team to take on the drippy-nosed squirts on the other side in some kind of leapfrog game that made absolutely no sense to her.

So this is what I missed. Weeks and weeks of this shit. She lit a cigarette. What a joke. Maybe bein' poor wasn't so bad after all. She looked around. The camp ground was seedy and run-down. The parents all looked like grandparents. So this was what all the mags were talking about. White-haired guys and wrinkled dames in fancy sportswear, cheering on the One Child of their middle age. Just what every kid longs for, a pop who'll probably croak before he hits double-number grades.

Some of the old guys had young wives. The young wives all seemed to The Match to have that kind of Katarina attitude. "Look at me, I've got this old prick wrapped around my diamond-covered fingers." Some of the fathers were sitting in fancy porta-chairs talking on their cellular phones. All of the parents had an au pair or Latin girl or, as The Match liked to call them, "yuppie slavettes," who did all the dirty work. Wiping noses, holding dry T-shirts, watching the few younger siblings present but not too connected to the occasion. The mothers mostly talked to one another, comparing child-rearing techniques, no doubt. The Match smiled. She could feel the devil in her. She would just love to take on one of these broads.

Two blond women wearing riding clothes sat down next to her. They waved to their kids on the field, who looked sullen and ignored them.

"I'm doing Terence's room over in primary colors and geometric shapes. My decorator says it will stimulate his visual sense, bring forth his own creativity. It's costing a fortune because we have to take off all of the trompe l'oeil, but it's worth it. I think he may have artistic gifts. His finger painting is exceptional. I'm having my art consultant look at it."

"Funny, but we've been given exactly the opposite advice.

We took all of the color out of Lowell's room. It's now absolutely stark. Just white and black. Our child psychologist told us we shouldn't interfere with his own process—not impose our tastes and interests on his imagination. This way, he has a clean slate on which to make his own visual and intellectual imprint."

The Match lit another cigarette. The Gargoyle sisters were looking better by the minute. No *wonder* the whole world was so fucked up. Okay, so letting little hutz futz sit on a golden potty was probably better than sending him for crack pickups or throwing him out of a window 'cause he wet his bed, but these bitches were supposed to be the *good* mothers. Something was wrong with the whole fucking thing. It almost made her want to have a baby, just to stay in the game.

Louie was on the field now. She flipped on the video camera and jumped up, causing the blond mothers to stare at her with distaste. Louie was first, hobbling across the brown, weedy field, his feet tied together. Hop, hop, hop. He was winning.

"Hey, yo! Louie! Take it home, dude! Right on!" She was shouting and jumping up and down, forgetting that the video camera requires a steady hand.

Louie could hear her all the way across the field. No one else's mother was cheering. But then The Match wasn't like anyone else's mother. She wasn't like his mother, either. He didn't mind. It made him feel good. He had felt so bad about her coming. I mean, what a boring thing for someone who's not even related to you to have to do. *He* hated it here and *he* was a kid.

He didn't want to be here. He wanted to be home where he was needed, but they didn't understand. They thought they were protecting him, but they weren't. Being with his family was the only protection in his life. No matter how sad it was at home right now. Kids were mostly mean. He was sure about that. There were a few nice ones who usually got picked on by the mean ones. Mostly they just weren't very kind. Or friendly. They hit and swore, some of them made fun of his skin, pulled his hair. One kid stole his lunch right in front of him, trying to see if he would be a baby and run and tell the counselor. Fat chance. But today was the end. Janie had promised. His most terrible dream was that Dr. J. would die while he was at stupid Sleepy Cove and he wouldn't even get to say good-bye.

He could see parents staring at The Match, but he didn't care. He wasn't embarrassed. He thought it was great. He was almost at the finish line. He was different, like The Match, but he was the winner.

When it was all over, they packed the car together and headed back down the Highway for home. The Match was elated. "Hey, Lou, I gotta thank you! I never been to somethin' like that. I mean the parents were a little, you know, 'who do we think we are,' but all those events! I never knew they had all of those things for kids to beat ass with! You were too much! You are like some athletic midget superkid or something! You won every fucking, excuse me, I got a bad mouth, don't tell your parents I said that. You were like the hero of the whole thing! I am impressed. I am blown away, dude!"

Louie was trying to be cool. "Oh, Match. You're just trying to make me feel good, 'cause of everything, you know. You don't have to say that stuff. But thanks."

The Match pulled the car over to the side of the road and turned toward him. "Hey! Forget that shit. I don't do that. Okay? I'm not one of those blond types. I mean it. You're hurtin' my feelings now. I'm out on a limb here."

He felt his lip start shaking. He didn't want to cry. "Oh, please, Match. Don't. Don't feel bad. I'm sorry. I guess, I was just kind of, you know, it feels funny to get compliments. It's sort of embarrassing."

The Match leaned over and kissed his cheek. "Oh, yeah? Well, let me give you some very big advice. Take every single one you can get, kid, 'cause they don't come often, not the real ones, and they gotta last a long time between shit. You read me?"

He laughed. She talked weird, but he understood everything she said. "Yeah. I read you."

She started the car and they drove for a while in silence. He could hardly keep his eyes open. He didn't want her to know he was tired. She'd make him get in the back like a baby.

"Hey, Lou? You gettin sleepy?"

He shook his head, trying to wake himself up. "Nope." He felt like crying again. They were almost home. What if. He swallowed hard and rubbed his eyes.

The Match saw. "You okay? We're almost home."

He nodded. "I'm fine. Sometimes I, I worry . . . it's nothing."

She smiled. "You worry that you'll come home and Dr. J. will be gone, don't you?"

He was wide-awake, his eyes so wide, they glowed in the twilight. "How did you know that? I never said that to anyone."

"I keep telling you guys. I'm a witchy chick." She reached over and patted his hand. "How do I know? Well, maybe because I'm an orphan, too, kid. Maybe us orphans are just kind of more nervous about people we love leaving us. Dying or just leaving. Maybe it's part of the orphan's creed or somethin'. I remember when my mother was dying. I was younger than you, but I hated to go to school, to the store, church, anywhere. I couldn't stand the idea that she could pass while I was gone—without me. So I just took a wild guess that maybe that's what's on your mind, too."

Louie moved closer to her, making his seat belt dig into his chest. "That's exactly it," he said, and leaned his head against her side, feeling less alone than he had all summer.

10

North of the Highway on the Sag Turnpike, the winding, misnamed road that connects the bay and the beach, the Hamptons proper, and Sag Harbor, there is a shabby roadhouse bar called Nellie's. It is not on any visitor's list and is known only to the locals and old-timers.

To many it is just "the Bar" because it is the only one they frequent. To others it is "the Duck Hunters' Joint" because it is popular with the husky, rifle-carrying men who stop by in their pickups and four-wheel-drive vehicles filled with camping gear and often, in season, with slaughtered deer or game fowl tied to the gun racks.

It is a rough, no-nonsense place for people who want to drink and people who want to talk and drink and no one who wants to do neither would like it much.

In the back there is a pool table and a video game machine and a jukebox and often, very late at night, people break loose and dance, rather wildly by themselves or with one another. There is also a sing-along machine and Nellie, the stringy, wiry barkeep and owner, will turn it on when requested and let the musically inclined tipplers serenade one another.

It has been in the Hamptons for a long time and it is not alone and if it closed, there would be another Nellie's because of the need it serves to the real people who live there.

Frankie Karsh had, without realizing it, crossed the line to the Other Hamptons—had traded in the Nellie's of his past for the trendy discos and nouvelle restaurants of his present —but it was to Nellie's that he returned to swab his wound, to try and heal his broken heart.

"Hey, Frankie! Long time," Nellie greeted him, as if he had been gone for weeks instead of years. It made him feel better. This was a place where he would not have to pretend. That was the function it had served for all of the wounded and lonely who supported it with their hard-earned money. It never changed and it always welcomed you back.

A very old, always slightly drunken lady known only as Mouse smiled at him and touched the brim of her large straw hat. "Hiya, Frankie. Your old man was in last night."

Frankie smiled back. "Yeah. Good. Glad to hear he's still hanging in there. I was afraid he was slowing up a little."

The Mouse wrinkled her nose in cartoon mouse fashion, and took a dainty sip of her martini. "Naw. Not him. He's too mean to get old. Even gave me a dance."

Frankie settled in at the end of the bar and ordered a beer. It was bad tonight. Really bad. He could hardly control the shaking of his hand when he lifted the bottle to his mouth.

He sat by himself, trying to calm down, conversations moving around him, zooming in and out like Formula One cars around one of his favorite tracks—close, then far away. He ordered another beer and a bourbon chaser.

"You notice the way those new summer people try to kiss up to ya?" An old-timer who had worked in the Southampton Hardware Store for twenty-five years or more was telling Rose, an enormous fat blond manicurist who ran her own shop.

"Nope. I don't do newcomers." Rose stirred her daiquiri daintily with the end of a maraschino cherry.

"Well, I don't like it. They want me to recognize them, not because they care about knowin' me, but so's it looks like they're not renters. I'm on to them."

Rose patted his hand. "Maybe they're just tryin' to be friendly. Don't be such a fuddy-duddy."

"In the old days it weren't like that. Even the famous writers used to look me in the eye, knew my name. Called me up for advice with their property."

"Yeah. It was nicer then. Had a woman from a magazine call me up last week, said she'd heard I used ta give Truman Capote manicures, wanted to know about him. Some dirt, I s'pose. I said, 'As a matter of fact I gave Mr. Capote *pedicures*. He'd come by before he met his pals at Jimmy Vale's. I told her, 'I did his toes two days before he went to L.A. and croaked. Always a gentleman,' I said. Can you imagine me dirty-mouthin' a customer, from the grave?"

The Mouse was listening to a sad-faced frizzy-haired woman in tight shorts and a tank top. "So I got this job with this celebrity P.R. firm so I thought, here's my big break, get into a real inneresting field. So, my first assignment was to find someone who looks like the Statue of Liberty."

"Someone's always on the way up and someone's always on the way down," a red-faced hunter type in a cowboy hat announced to no one in particular.

Two workmen in painter's overalls were chain-smoking and tossing back straight shots of single-malt Scotch.

"So's the fuckin' air conditioner falls on my fuckin' leg and I'm history. Like after ten years of runnin' the whole fuckin' building for these guys, I don't exist. Workman's comp is givin' it to me up the ass. My pop's dyin' in the hospital and I ain't got the money to take flowers to his funeral."

309

If misery loves company, then Frankie Karsh had chosen well, he let the misery of his fellow strangers wash over him, bathing himself in its comforting warmth. Was that why this had happened to him? He had reached too high, forgotten his roots, his place? Shame flooded him.

His stomach tightened in a knot of fear and nausea. The feeling was familiar. He had had it every day since he had left Fritzi Ferris standing in her room in her white satin robe.

At times, he felt like he was dying. Dying of love, of longing. It was unbearable, this feeling. It was driving him out of his mind. The word *lovesick*, a word he had never even thought of before, kept crossing in and out of his mind.

He couldn't sleep. He couldn't eat and he couldn't fuck. He had tried. Oh boy, had he tried. That was his first shot at exorcising her demon from his head. He could not. Even pretending it was her didn't help. The frustration of his need was driving him mad.

There was no one to turn to, nowhere to go. He was just too ashamed to ask for help. He was humiliated. He had never been rejected before and neither had any man in his family, as far as he knew.

He had almost confided in Kenny, but before he could have made a serious mistake (he was Kenny's boss, bosses do not show weakness to their employees), Kenny had come to him with his own problem. He had pulled himself together and had given him (he thought) very good advice. "Don't run away and do something crazy. Take China back to her mother and ask for her hand, like a man. If that's what you want to do, marry her and father this kid, then do it like a man."

Kenny had listened, tears in his eyes. He had been grateful for the guidance. Well, he was trying to follow his own advice. Do this like a man. Don't run to her and whine and plead with her to take you back. He would rather die than have her see him like this.

But it had been three weeks and he was no better. He was worse. He was a junkie, an addict. A fucking Fritzi Fiend. And it was affecting his work, everything he had worked his balls off for. God. It had to stop!

The bar was quiet. It felt as if the room had suddenly lost its power—radio plug ripped out of the wall by a frisky cat. Silence, severing his connection to the others. Forcing him back into the bleak smoky coarseness of the place.

Two people who did not belong there had come in, causing the regulars to freeze as if a blast of arctic wind had just blown the door off.

Katarina Rivers and Rikki Bosco stood in the doorway, smiling woozily, looking like two rebellious teenagers sneaking out in their mother's car.

Rikki saw him and waved. "Hey, Frankie, I was looking for you!" The regulars took it as permission to relax their guard, that these two summer people knew Frankie. The mood lightened. Someone started the jukebox going. Frankie sat up and moved over, making room beside him.

"Where the hell you been? I've been at the lot three times this week. Kenny said you might be here. I love this place. This is so much better than all of that other bullshit."

Frankie smiled. "Well, it's nice to have a choice. But be cool. These guys don't like, how should I say it, outsiders comin' in and acting like it's a novelty."

Katarina opened a slender gold cigarette case with one of her graceful, lightly tanned hands and held one up, waiting for Rikki to light it. "I've never been in a place like this, a real bar before. It's great fun."

Frankie smirked. Something about being almost out of control really lowered his tolerance for women like her. Maybe it was simply that he had known too many of them—

serviced too many of them, professionally and personally. He seemed to have o.d.'d on socialities. "To each his own," he said, trying not to be too rude, because Rikki was his friend as well as his client. Or at least he thought he was. He wasn't so sure about anyone, anymore. "Sorry, Bosco. I've had some . . . personal stuff to tend to. What can I do for you?"

"I wanna sell the Porsche. I left it with Kenny."

Frankie met his eyes. Katarina was pretending to look around the room, but he knew better. "The Match's Porsche?"

"Two white wines," Rikki shouted to Nellie, who stiffened slightly. Frankie smiled. White wine was not a highly popular beverage in places like Nellie's.

"Yeah. I mean it's my fucking car. It's registered to me, right?"

"Wrong. You gave it to her. I remember, because it took longer. It's in her name."

Nellie handed over two beer mugs filled with some suspiciously yellow-looking liquid. Rikki looked at the wine, obviously upset with the information. "It's either sauterne or some fuck pissed in the glass."

"Could be a combination. Sort of a workingman's kir," Frankie said, surprised he could still make a joke.

"Well, anyway, she gave it back. We've split. She doesn't want it. So sell it for me, okay?"

"Sure. But I've gotta talk to her. She's gotta sign and I've gotta give her the money. What she does with it is between the two of you. Sorry, Bosco, it's the law."

"Yeah. Sure. We'll work it out."

Frankie was curious. Part of misery loving company, no doubt. Though as far as he could tell, Rikki Bosco did not look too miserable.

312

A HOUSE IN THE HAMPTONS

Katarina had her shoulder turned. Frankie thought that she was flirting with the duck hunters.

"Jeez, I'm sorry to hear that. I really liked her."

Rikki took a long sip of the yellow liquid. "Yeah, well, that's life. I didn't want to hurt her. I like her, too. But, man, when love hits, it hits." He lowered his head onto Katarina's bare shoulder and nuzzled her. She turned her head and blew him a kiss.

Frankie watched, envy choking him. So that's how it was. He thought of Joey Rivers, whom he hardly knew. Poor guy. Maybe he should call him up. "Where is she? I'll call her about the car, if you want." The Match. He'd go talk to The Match. That was even better. She was smart about life. Maybe she'd have an insight into why Fritzi did it.

"She's staying at Big Ben Cowan's place. Here's the number." Rikki reached into his perfectly wrinkled linen jacket pocket and pulled out a piece of paper. He really had been looking for him.

Frankie took it. "How come she's there?"

Rikki shrugged. "She's got clients out here. She's gotten buddy-buddy with the daughter, Janie. And the whole scene is all fucked up. The daughter's husband disappeared, right into thin air. The daughter and her son are alone, so she told The Match she could stay there."

Frankie's chest tightened. Jamieson. God fucking damn it. That was it! That was why! She was with him! She had told him all about it. The whole high school saga. "We were like that old French film *Jules and Jim*," she said, and he had been too embarrassed to admit he'd never heard of it. He hit the video store the same night and rented it. It told him everything he needed to know. Jamieson. She was with the fucking shrink.

Frankie motioned to Nellie for a refill. The pain was excruciating. He tried to fight his way back to Bosco. The Match. He would call her now. He would ask her for help.

Frankie leaned in close to Rikki, away from Katarina, who seemed to be in her own elevated world, anyway. She *was* flirting, the bitch. "What about her husband? How's Rivers handling all of this?"

Rikki's face tightened. He suddenly seemed a little too uptight for the hopelessly in love. "Rivers? Rivers is with *her*!"

Frankie's chest felt like someone was inside of him, twisting it like pizza dough. "The Match?"

Rikki nodded his head up and down. "Fucking A. Funny? I traded up, that's for sure."

Somehow Frankie didn't quite think so. He moved back and tossed down his double shot in one gulp. Socialites. He hated them. All of a sudden he was filled with hate for all those shining spoiled tormentors. He had fucked them, but he had never liked them.

Fritzi was different. She came from working people. She had been a nurse. She didn't fit in either. She was on the outside like he was. The way she had clung to him at that party he had helped her give. So shy and scared. Like a little girl, really. She had needed him. She wasn't like this rich cocky twat, trading men like marbles. Or was she? Maybe she was just better at it. Older, more sophisticated. Maybe it had all been an act. She was new here and she had this phantom kid and the father to handle and the doctor was married.

She had needed someone while she got her shit together. So she used him for a while and then she dismissed him like a male hooker or a servant. Maybe she was the worst of them all.

He felt rage filling him, mixing with the bourbon and shooting through his brain. *Oh, God. Help me.* The Match had been his last hope. But she was with Rivers. Everyone was with someone. He was the only one left outside in the cold.

A HOUSE IN THE HAMPTONS

Frankie stood up and threw some money on the bar. Rikki reached out and put his hand on Frankie's strongly muscled shoulder. "Hey. You okay, Frankie? Where you going? Why don't you hang out with us tonight?"

"No, thanks. Something I gotta do. Don't worry about the car. I'll take care of everything."

He waved to Nellie and without breaking his stride, he stormed out into the heavy summer night.

One A.M. Nellie's is packed. Duck hunters, plumbers, off-duty security guys, waitresses, carpenters, townies. The pool table is hopping and the dance floor is so packed, no one can do anything but bounce up and down in place.

Rikki Bosco is smashed. Getting smashed is not something he does often or well. Control is his interest. The edge. Diet Coke, his drink of choice. Never can tell when the phone's going to ring; it's always nine o'clock in the morning somewhere. Always a commodity coming up for play. He tries to keep a clear head. But Katarina had really gotten into this place. The two of them were like Republicans in Harlem. They were having an adventure. So, what the fuck. Besides, she had that look on her face. The look from the first day, the day he let her drive his car. It was the same turned-on, slightly dazed look. He knew what that meant. It meant great sex. It was worth it, to keep her looking that way.

He watched her. She was dancing with one of the construction machos. He laughed to himself. What a sight. She had probably never been anywhere near that close to a guy like that before in her entire life.

The macho was wearing a sleeveless T-shirt, stretched across his overpumped chest muscles. He had a black tattoo of a lion's head on one of his deltoids. Beauty and the Beast, he thought.

315

"Hey, sir. You're Mr. Bosco, right?" Rikki turned. A pink-cheeked slender young man stood next to him, smiling shyly.

"Yeah. Do we know each other?" Rikki motioned for him to sit in Katarina's seat.

"Sort of." The boy lowered himself slowly onto the stool. "I helped build your house, Mr. Bosco. Remember? Scotty Daniels. I did all the special carpentry. The detailing."

For some reason, not recognizing this boy made Rikki feel like crying. He had been in his house for months. Rikki had seen him hundreds of times. Looked at his sketches, shown genuine respect for his work. He had watched the kid's joy build as he gave him more to do. A chance to work on something so special. They had popped beers together and shared cigarettes. And he had forgotten him.

"Oh, boy. Scotty! Of course, I remember. Jesus. I'm sorry. I'm a little splashed tonight. How's it goin'?"

"Okay. I'm doin' a couple of jobs in Georgica with my old man. You know, Mr. Bosco. I always wanted to tell you. That time I spent at your place. That was the best time of my whole life. I take out the pictures and just look at them sometimes. Most people aren't so nice to work for. How's it look with everything finished?"

"It looks great. Scotty, why don't you come by and see it, with the furniture and everything. I'm there all of August, just come to the gate and buzz."

"Gee. I'd really like that. That'd be great. Can I, would it be all right if I brought my mom? I've told her so much about it."

"Sure. Bring anyone you want." Rikki stood up. His head hurt. He had the Lamborghini with him. He didn't want to drive it drunk. "I gotta find my girl. I'll see you soon, Scotty."

The boy grinned as if Rikki had just handed him the keys to the car. "Great. Thanks, Mr. Bosco."

A HOUSE IN THE HAMPTONS

Rikki made his way through the smoky overcrowded front room to the dance floor. Katarina was nowhere in sight. He was pissed. Enough was enough. Where could she be? The bathroom. Only place left to try.

Rikki pushed his way to the back of the bar and out through the door marked PRIVATE. There was a small storeroom and a unisex bathroom. The door was open. Shit. He turned to leave, but then he heard something. A scuffling sound. Coming from outside. My God, maybe she was sick. Or in trouble. That big ape could have hurt her!

Rikki ran to the back door and tore it open. No one. Nothing. He shook his head, trying to sober up. A large black pickup was parked under a tree several yards from the bar. Rikki walked toward it. He heard the scuffling again. Louder. And he moved faster. Then he heard someone speak one word. "More."

He walked to the truck and looked up into the back. On a blanket up against the rear of the truck was his Dream Girl, her dress over her waist, the macho and a clone crouched about her like toads on a lily pad. One was inside her and the other was waiting to be.

She opened her eyes and saw him. "Hi, honey," she said, and closed them again.

He turned and walked away. He waited in the shadows until they were finished. He had no idea at all why this was his choice of action. But it seemed to him, even then, no more bizarre than her choice. "Hi, honey," she had said, as if he had walked in on her in the shower or polishing her nails. He was too confused to act. He was far too good a poker player to freak out and get pounded in a roadhouse parking lot by two muscle-bound he-men, who were certainly not forcing their attentions on his childhood buddy's wife.

He breathed in and out, trying to think this through. And he saw it. He got it. A new toy. A bauble. Like a sable coat or

317

a diamond ring. She was practicing. Showing off. She could come now, but would it work with just anybody? She was exploring. Because to her—this mysterious, beautiful, unattainable woman he thought he had conquered—sex had absolutely nothing to do with her or with love. Love was not what her relationships with men were about. Some men were investments. Some were vanity mirrors reflecting the world's view of herself. A perverse businesslike way of calculating the valve of her stock on the open market.

He could get to it, because he was, above all else, a businessman. She did not even know she was doing anything wrong. She did not even care. Katarina Karlson Rivers had lived her entire life having anything and anyone she wanted. She had no basis for comparison. It was a kind of amorality bred in ignorance. And to Rikki Bosco, who did know what the world was, what people could do, what the consequences were for each and every action of his life, it was the most terrifying idea that he had ever encountered.

"Hi, honey," she had said, and had frozen his heart.

Two A.M. Fritzi Ferris is gliding silently, in the star-dotted blackness, back and forth across her pool. Her favorite time to swim. With the pool lights off, the water takes on the shape and texture of a lagoon. A silent ebony lagoon, settled into the summer-sweet thicket of her lawn. She swims on her back, floating, stroking, turning over and over. Thoughts pass through her mind, like raindrops.

Donnie was better. It amazed her still. He had been strong enough to sit in the sun and finish his letters to his patients. It was a miracle. It really was in God's hands, all of it. She rolled onto her stomach and did the breaststroke, pulling herself along, her face smiling under the water.

Janie had taken him home and set up the most unsick-like sickroom ever seen. She had put Donnie in the front window

318

where he could see the ocean and covered his adjusta-bed with designer sheets. A good scout, "her nurse's aide"—she liked to call her—soon she would be able to do it all herself. Soon, Fritzi would leave them and let the Jamiesons finish alone together. Tears filled her eyes and disappeared into the silky black water.

Louie followed them around like a lost puppy, asking thousands of questions, as if that would help him cope with what was coming. Harry and Gina were doing everything but sleeping there and she knew that was coming, any day. Jeremy stayed most of the time, keeping Owen's spirits up.

It was like Turkey or somewhere, where the entire family moves in to care for their loved one. Donnie called them his "groupies" and they all liked that. It was as if, being away from him, left them out of what was happening and that was more unbearable than watching his suffering. So when he rallied, when they saw him stronger, had him back, they grabbed at it, at him, with the frantic, desperate hope of the doomed. She had seen it before as a young nurse but it still wrecked her. The truth was, he had bought some time. Thanks to Janie and to her, too. She stopped swimming, rolled over and floated again, her breath coming fast.

Frankie. She had asked Donnie if it would be all right for her to tell him. They had parted so badly. She missed him so much. How strange that she should find herself falling in love with someone like Frankie Karsh. A baby. Not much older than Aaron, for chrissakes. The hell with it. It was real and it made her feel so safe and so good. She would call him tomorrow and make a date to see him and try to explain why she had been so mysterious. She could only hope it wasn't too late.

Well, if it was, then she had been wrong. And she would probably look back on the whole thing with relief.

Fritzi pushed her naked body with her arms, leaving her

319

legs limp, bobbing in the still water, until she reached the side. She stopped and tossed her head back, her silver-white hair glowing in the dark.

An arm reached out and grabbed her by the neck. A man's arm pulled her up out of the water. She couldn't see his face. She could hardly breathe.

"I can't take it! I don't care anymore! I know why you left me! I know it was Jamieson! I thought you were different but you're just like the rest of them! You could have told the fucking truth! You . . . you're killing me!"

Frankie. She tried to turn her head to tell him. She had to tell him, somehow. He was so strong. She couldn't move.

He was crying. "Look what you've done to me! Look! You've turned me into a fucking animal! You've driven me crazy! Crazy! I can't . . . I can't . . ."

Oh God. It was all her fault.

"Please!" She gasped.

Her voice calmed him. He shuddered. His arms relaxed. She moved, ever so slightly.

Now he would be able to listen. It would be okay now. He seemed almost unconscious of her. She was almost free. She pulled one leg forward and tried to walk. Two arms and one leg.

She grew bolder, the shock hitting her. She was cold. Her teeth was chattering. Her robe was on the pool edge, on the ladder. She pushed against his arms. For a moment he let her go, but she moved forward too quickly, startling him. Like a wounded animal in an ambush, he lashed out, grabbing at her, and she slipped, falling forward and hitting her head on the side of the pool. She fell hard and she did not get up again.

Four A.M. Rikki Bosco is lying on his pale yellow leather-covered Art Deco chaise. He is drinking Perrier from a tall

crystal goblet and washing Extra-Strength Excedrin down
with it. Katarina is asleep in his bed. He is in his study. He is
trying to figure something out but he is not even sure what it
is. He has never felt anything remotely like this mood before. He is bemused, because even though he should feel
truly miserable, enraged, and heartbroken, he doesn't. What
he feels, in fact, is not altogether unpleasant.

The phone rings. Rikki looks at his watch. *His father.*
Whenever his private phone rings late at night, his first
thought is always that something has happened to his father.
It's Sunday. So, who? The Match. She must be really fucked
up to pull something like this. He answers.

"Yeah?" He is whispering, even though Katarina is dead
asleep at the opposite end of the house. He wonders to himself why it is people always whisper if the phone rings late at
night.

"Rikki?"

"Yeah!"

"It's Frankie Karsh."

"Frankie? What is it? It's four fucking A.M.!"

"I. Something's happened. I gotta, I gotta talk to you. I
don't know what to do. Can I come over?"

"Sure. Sure. Come over. I'll turn off the alarm. I'll meet
you at the end of the driveway. How long?"

"Five minutes. I'm close."

Rikki got up, tightened the belt to his Armani robe, and
went to meet his guest. Somehow it fit, it was a night like
that. A night when life was meant to veer, to zag off its usual
course. In business Rikki had always believed it was at those
moments that change occurred. Risks were taken, points
scored, lessons learned. But in his personal life, all of this
was new.

Except for the night in the diner when he had first met
The Match, not much had ever happened to him that re-

321

quired his surrender or his sense of irony. He picked up the Perrier bottle and carried it with him, some primitive rescue instinct leading him, like the St. Bernard to the avalanche victim. He shut off his alarm system and went out through the front to wait for Frankie. He was flattered that he had been chosen by this kid, a guy in his life, but not close. He hoped he would be able to help.

When Frankie Karsh screeched to a stop at Rikki Bosco's security gate, Rikki was waiting for him. He pushed the button raising the bar and got into the passenger seat of Frankie's Ferrari.

The only face he had ever seen that looked like Frankie's was on a figure in the Wax Museum on the pier at Coney Island. Waxy. Ashen. Shiny wet. He could barely sit up. Rikki got out, helped him move over, and drove him up to the house. They sat in the car, letting the silence quiet them.

"Jesus, Frankie. You look like the last survivor in *Nightmare on* fucking *Elm Street.* What the fuck happened to you?"

Frankie put his hands over his face, sobbed, shaking his whole body. "I lost it, man. I lost it. I think I may have killed her. Oh God! I don't know what to do! I didn't mean to! I didn't want to! She was trying to run away from me and I just wanted to stop her and she fell and she stopped moving."

Whatever Rikki had expected, this was not it.

"Who? Who?"

"Fritzi! I think I killed her!"

Rikki took a long deep breath. Here was the heart of the irony that had been escaping him. Choices and how they turned your life. One night. Two lovestruck men. Two women. Two choices. He had waited in the dark for Katarina to finish and he had driven her home and put her to bed. He had not done it to be cool or kinky or cowardly. It was just a by-product of his mental training. Count to ten, check it out, don't let emotion run you, too much is always on the line. It was why he was rich and, like being a marine, it had infiltrated all his other behavior.

So, he was home in his mansion, in his six-hundred dollar robe, his wanton feckless woman safely asleep upstairs and Frankie, poor Frankie, who had been at almost the same place on the ledge, had made another choice and now sat beside him, quivering in terror—facing the possibility that his choice of route home might well have ended life's wide-open path. The yellow brick road may have turned into rubble. Silently he thanked his whatever-it-was, that he would never call God.

"Frankie. We're going into the house and get you together. I'm gonna get you a 'lude or something and you're gonna take a sauna and calm down. Okay? Then, maybe, we're going to call someone."

Frankie grabbed his arm, squeezing tight. *"Who?"*

Rikki covered his hand. "Hey, Frankie. You called me. You gotta trust me. Come on, now. First things first."

When he was clean and calm, Rikki had him tell the story again. The only missing detail, and it was not a small one, was whether Fritzi Ferris was, in fact, dead or simply unconscious.

Frankie was pacing back and forth. Rikki knew he wasn't going to like what he had to say. "Frankie. We gotta go back and see if she's, you know. If she's okay or what. Then we'll decide what to do next."

"But if she isn't. They'll see us."

"Hey. Frankie. Hear this. If she's dead, we are going immediately to the police. I am calling you the best fucking criminal attorney in New York, you are going to tell the fucking truth and most likely walk in a year. Crime of passion, second-degree manslaughter. You would be the only fucking suspect. You run, when they find you, we're talking murder one."

"No. I'm not. Jamieson! She's with him. He could have."

"Get real, Frankie. You're scared, but I know you. You're a good man. You gonna let some innocent person walk this mile for you? Forget about it. You're gonna do what's right. You loved her, she left you; you went nuts. A nice guy, a kid in over his head with a fucking sex goddess. Everyone who saw her knew that. The biggest cocktease I've ever seen anywhere."

"She wasn't like that. That was just her mask. Her protection. She was so nice. Kind. She was scared—she was just trying to get away from me. The cops will think I'm a fucking monster."

Rikki stopped him and held his shoulders. "Are you? Are you, Frankie? Are you a monster?"

Tears streamed down Frankie Karsh's face.

"No." He could barely say it.

"Then don't worry about it. I'm getting my pants and we're going."

Six A.M. Harry is dreaming. In his dream his mother and father are alive and sitting at his country pine kitchen table playing cards. His mother is smiling, which is one way Harry knows he is dreaming.

"Maybe the hips are stiff, but the lips are still soft," his mother says.

"Get me Mr. Rockefeller on the phone," his father replies.

"I want to tell Harry about my cancer," his mother says.

"I've got my own problems," his father says back.

The phone is ringing. Gina moans and nudges him. The phone is on his side. Harry fights his way awake, still hearing his parents as he goes. "Hello?" Fear comes with consciousness. Donnie.

A HOUSE IN THE HAMPTONS

Janie Jamieson is crying. She can hardly speak. *Oh God, no. Not yet.* Harry sits up and turns on the light.

"Janie? What is it?"

"Harry. Oh, boy. Harry. It's, it's . . ."

"He was better. He was—"

"No. No! Donnie's okay. It's Fritzi. She's, Harry. Please come. The police are *there* and paramedics, Donnie's still asleep. I don't want to leave him alone. I don't know what to tell him when he wakes up!"

Gina was watching his face. How was any of this possible? They were not the kind of people who had lives like this! They read about people like this. The guy who ground his wife up in the wood-chipper; the woman who gave birth to a baby girl in an airplane rest room, put her in the trash container, and returned to her seat; four siblings burned alive playing with matches; Coma mom; Hedda and Joel; teen suicide pacts; preppie murder; subway rapist; remote macabre urban Muzak, passing over them like subway steam and auto exhaust; whatever part of it that is potentially deadly remaining invisible, impersonal, and most certainly not applicable to them.

They were upper-middle-class Jewish liberals, for chrissakes! He edited stories called "Mallards on Ice." His wife had never smoked pot or read *The Story of O*! Somehow, angst and anxiety aside, Harry had always believed he would get what his parents had gotten (at least). Some unwritten guarantee from God, promising eighty years and a condo on Collins Avenue. And that offer extended to all their friends.

Donnie had ripped into the magic sheet of plastic wrap that Harry had created to protect himself and stripped his defenses bare. But cancer was one thing. Violence was something else entirely.

325

"I'm on my way." Harry dropped the receiver and leapt out of bed, searching frantically for his sweatpants.

Gina followed, handing him his clothes. "What is it? What's happened?"

Harry hobbled toward the bathroom, pulling the pants on as he went. "You won't believe this. Something's happened to Fritzi! I don't even know if she's alive! Janie said the police were there! Her maid called Janie."

Gina stopped dead, her eyes and mouth open wide. Harry stumbled around her into the bathroom.

"Gina. Turn into Lot's wife later, get moving! Janie needs us! We're going to stay there. I can't take this back-and-forth anymore. Pack a bag. No, never mind, we'll come back later and do it."

"My God!" Gina could barely speak.

From the bathroom, she heard Harry. "No! Oh, no! Not now!"

She shook herself, as if someone outside her was taking over. She ran to the bathroom. Harry was kneeling beside Arturo, who was lying in a heap on the floor, his eyes rolled back in his head, his tongue hanging out. She screamed.

"What is it! Is he dead?"

Harry had his ear to the beagle's chest. "No. No. He's breathing. But he's unconscious. Oh, Jesus. Maybe he's had a stroke. What'll we do?"

Gina clicked into automatic pilot, the mother's conditioning pulling her together. "You go to Janie. I'll take him to the vet. The clinic opens at six-thirty. Go! It's okay. Oh, God! Harry, Aaron! Better take him, just in case she's, you know."

"Right!" Harry threw on his 92nd Street Y T-shirt, grabbed his running shoes, and ran downstairs to Aaron's room. Gina threw on her shorts and yesterday's mustard-stained sweatshirt, grabbed her purse and tried to lift Arturo off the floor.

A HOUSE IN THE HAMPTONS

Dead weight. She couldn't move him. She was already damp with the humidity and it was barely dawn. She looked around. Nothing. She tried again. The damn dog must weigh fifty pounds! His paws were turned out like Charlie Chaplin as the Tramp. Hysteria rose in her throat. She burst into peals of hysterical laughter. She had never seen anything as hilarious as the bloated beagle spread-eagled on the bathroom floor, looking like an old drunken floozy. My God! It was all too much. She was obviously stressing out.

She ran out of the bathroom. She ran back. She grabbed Arturo's hind paws and tried to pull him. But the stairs! She couldn't bounce him down the stairs! She ran to Jeremy's empty room. In the corner pushed against the wall she saw his skateboard. She grabbed it and ran back to the bathroom. Foam was running out of the sides of Arturo's mouth. Oh God! Please. She would never say another mean thing about him, ever again, please don't let him die. Not now. Not like this. Please!

Gina stood over him, bending her knees the way she had been taught in some lifting-for-the-back class she had taken five years ago. Somehow she managed to get enough leverage to pull him onto the board.

She rolled him across the bedroom, down the hall to the stairs. What now? She left him, looking like Snoopy on his doghouse on a very bad day, and ran back into Jeremy's room. She grabbed his basketball hoop, the sash to his bathrobe and a handful of safety pins used for his T-shirts and ran back to Arturo. She slipped the basketball hoop netting over the front of the skateboard and pinned the opening shut to keep him from sliding off. She tied the sash around the rim, crossed the ends over Arturo's chest and knotted them under the board—an animal version of a ski patrol rescue sled. She threw her purse down the stairs, climbed down in

327

front of him, and slowly lowered the skateboard. Bump. Arturo slid forward, but the net held.

"Come on, chowhound. Hang on. It's going to be just fine. Just a few more." It seemed as if she would be crouched backward on those creaking ancient stairs on her knees, forever. Every once in a while the laughter would start again, and she would stop, leaning against him to keep them both from toppling all the way down and releasing herself from all absurdity, past and present.

She rolled him outside and opened the back door of her car. Using all her lower body strength, she pushed the front of the board down, raising the back wheel so that it stood against the door frame. Arturo slipped forward. His head rolled loosely to the other side. Using both her arms, she pushed forward on the board, flipping it and Arturo over backward onto the floor of the backseat of the Volvo. The board was now on top of him. All that could be seen of her dog were the pads of his paws and his ears.

She slammed the door, jumped into the front, and took off as fast as a woman in her condition could go, straight toward the East Hampton Pet Hospital.

"Help. Please. Help me! Something's wrong with my . . ."

The plump, friendly vet assistant recognized her. "Arturo? What is it this time? I hope it's not another thermometer."

The cheerful briskness of the young woman calmed Gina. She sighed.

"I don't think so. I think this time he may really be sick. A stroke, my husband thought, maybe it was a stroke. He's unconscious. Can someone get him?"

"Sure. I'll get one of the guys."

Gina sat down. When they took him out of the car, she did not want to be anywhere nearby. First, they would think she

328

was some kind of animal abuser and worse, she might start laughing again. She could feel the giggles moving back up her throat. I bet it's the first beagle to arrive impaled on a skateboard and tied down with a basketball hoop and a terry cloth bathrobe sash. She lowered her head into her lap, trying to control herself. The attendant came up behind her.

"Don't cry. I don't think it's as bad as it looks. When you feel better, I need you to sign a consent form."

Gina sat up. Her face was so red, she looked like she had been crying. She signed the form and handed it back.

"Coffee's on. Relax. We'll be back soon."

There was a radio on the table next to her bank of folding chairs. Gina flipped it on. There was nothing to read and she was too restless to just sit there speculating on the fates of Arturo and Fritzi Ferris.

A talk-radio interviewer was interviewing a member of Fundamentalists Anonymous. Former fundamentalists who now protested First Amendment violations and such. Gina made a mental note. What a bizarre example of the American need to belong.

Did members crawl in, begging to be stopped from spouting literal prophecy? Please help me! I started to believe in Adam and Eve again last night. What? Gina took a long deep gulp of coffee. It was too hot and it burned her insides. Tears sprang into her eyes.

"Still crying?" The cheerful pink-cheeked young woman was back, making Gina feel like a terrible fraud.

"No. I'm okay. How . . . is he? Is he . . . ?" Gina swallowed. She was scared.

The girl laughed. "He's fine."

"What was it? He was, I mean. I was sure he was dying."

"We pumped his stomach and he came right around."

Gina jumped up. "Pumped his stomach?"

"Mrs. Hart. This is a first for us, I gotta tell you. Arturo o.d.'d."

"O.d.'d? You mean like drug addicts?"

"Just like. Looks like Valium or sleeping pills."

"Oh, God. We did have a bottle of sleeping pills. We've been going through a lot of stress and our friend, he's a doctor, he gave my husband a bottle, just in case. But I looked all over the bathroom. I would have seen the container. There wasn't anything there."

"That's because he *ate* the container. We found big slices of plastic in his vomit. O.d.'d. Probably the first dog in history. We did have a Siamese in one time who swallowed her owner's birth control pills, but this is the first narcotics episode. Want to see him? He's a little groggy, but he's fine."

Gina followed her numbly into the surgery. Arturo was lying face forward, his head resting on his paws. He looked up at her when she came in and Gina could swear she saw remorse on his face.

The girl left them alone and went to see about the bill. Gina stood facing him. They looked at each other. It had always been a love–hate relationship and she knew now that it always would be. She took back her promise to God. "Arturo, next time. No skateboard. Next time, the window. I bet you're hooked. I bet you'll end up in some crack den in the Bronx as a courier. Sick, Arturo. You are one sick character. Come on. Your Sex Goddess is in worse shape than you are."

Arturo slid down off the table and weaving slightly, he followed Gina slowly out to pay for his folly.

It was left to Harry to tell Donnie about his Dream Girl. Harry sat beside his bed waiting for him to wake up. He had been so much better, they had even lowered the hospital bed and thrown a quilt over it. He looked almost normal. Thin, but almost like himself. Harry watched him sleep. He felt an overwhelming urge to just pick Donnie up and carry him off. Take him someplace warm and safe and protect him from the world. Harry snickered. This *was* someplace warm and safe and protected from the world. So much for fantasy.

Aaron. Fucking amazing! Two months ago he didn't even know Aaron Ferris existed and now, he could turn out to be his sole living relative.

He sighed. Of course Dr. Wexel was away. That was chapter one in the secret Big Book of Psychoanalytic Sadism that patients never saw the shrink. God saved all the bad stuff until August, when every therapist on earth was away. Eleven months, you sit there, nothing much happens; a dream here and there, a lot of kvetching. Thousands of dollars trade hands. Vacation comes. *Boom!*

So how did he tell his best friend, who had been kept from the edge of the Valley by their recently rediscovered first love that she had probably been attacked by her young lover. Jesus!

Frankie Karsh and Bosco had still been there when Harry arrived. The kid was shaking so hard, he couldn't stand up. In a way, he could identify. She was a woman like that. If she hooked you, you stay hooked. Look at Donnie.

Now they were all Donnie had to get him through. Janie felt confident. Fritzi had taught her to do everything, even give him his shots. Marty Haber was coming out to see him. They would be okay. The main thing was for Donnie to feel they were okay. If he saw fear or distaste, he'd do something crazy. What, Harry didn't even want to think about. The way the summer was shaping up, it was anyone's guess. It was all more than he could comprehend.

The police had taken Frankie in for questioning. No one knew what had really happened. Rikki Bosco had called some hotshot attorney and had stayed so close to Frankie, the cops had to physically move him when they took Frankie downtown.

"Don't say anything to anyone," Rikki hissed into Frankie's ear, and jumped into his Italian fantasy car to follow them in.

Janie was on her way to the hospital with Aaron. Fritzi was gone by the time they arrived. No one knew how bad she was or even what had happened.

Donnie turned. Harry moved closer. Donnie seemed to be smiling in his sleep. Maybe it wasn't so bad after all. Dying. Maybe it was one great big fucking relief. I mean he watched the *Today* show. Willard Scott and his Polaroids. One-hundred-year-olds grinning through their bifocals at the television audience from various wheelchairs in various nursing homes across America. Who really wanted that? Harry had decided from years of *Today* show viewing that the only people who lived past ninety anyway were all named Eula Belle or Amos and shared a passion for bingo. Bingo seemed to be the key. Someone should do a study charting bingo passion and longevity.

Harry's throat seemed to swell, pushing the tears against the sides of his eyes. He didn't believe a word of it. God! Please, take it away. Not Donnie!

He realized he did not even remember being on earth without Donnie. Donnie had always been there. In the next bed, at the next desk, beside him on the tennis court, beside him in the dugout, next to him in one car or another. Double dates. Double marriages. He had spent more of his life with this man than with anyone else on earth. His wife, his parents, anyone.

It was quite inconceivable that he would not always be there, that they would not wobble off into old age together, complaining about arthritis and gumlines. Harry hyperventilating, Donnie calming. God!

A HOUSE IN THE HAMPTONS

He remembered when Donnie's mother died. After the service Harry had wanted to visit his grandfather's grave, which was in the same cemetery. Harry, Gina, Janie, and Donnie, all newly wedded, had tromped around trying to find the grave. Finally, in despair, they asked the gardener. The old man scratched his head. "Well, now, let's see." He reached into his pocket and pulled out what looked like a Rand McNally road map of the dead. "Looks like you go straight through those trees, past Babyland and turn left at Mabel Katz." They had all stared at him, not daring to look at one another.

"It's a little tricky. If you get to Ethel, that's the wrong Katz. Go back to Mabel."

Off they had gone, heads down, not wanting to laugh, but filled with the profoundness of the absurdity. Of course. It was really so simple once you took the Grim Reaper and put him in his proper place. If you get to Ethel, you've gone too far.

They all sat cross-legged in a circle around Harry's grandfather's grave and told family jokes. Harry told his favorite story about his grandfather claiming to be "The First Jew to Exercise. Only they didn't have exercise then. No health clubs, no jogging. He invented everything."

Gina told a story about visiting her grandfather after his prostate surgery. "I'm so depressed, darling. I lost my manhood this year. But I heard about a doctor in Arizona, has had some terrific luck with the elderly. So I set up an appointment, booked the plane and then your grandmother, she says to me, 'What's with you? Flying to Arizona to see specialists? Enough already. Fifty years of sex with you is enough.' "

Harry told his favorite. "So when my parents first moved to Florida, my mother's going to everything. Hula class. Ice-carving demonstrations. And one day, I'm down there visit-

333

ing and I'm sitting in on my father's poker game and my mother comes in all dressed up. 'Jacob, I'm going to the recreation room to hear a lecture, I'll be back later.' My father is humoring her, 'Wonderful, darling. What's it about?' 'Something about romance and the mature adult.' 'Great. Great!'

"Well, off she goes and about thirty minutes later she's back, looking all bent out of shape. 'So, what happened?' *'Feh. Feh,'* she says. 'Disgusting. You wouldn't believe what that man said. Romance, smomance. He talked about oral sex! I got such a headache. I left. I'm gonna take an aspirin and lie down for a while and take a nap. *Feh. Feh.'* So my father, he never looks away from his cards, got his cigar stuck in his teeth, he says over his shoulder. 'Hey, Bea. Do me a favor, dear. Sleep with your mouth open.'"

They all laughed. They sat together around the grave and laughed and laughed in a hearty, loving way about the flawed and missing loved ones they had lost or would lose. They were so young and so far away from what all of it meant. This graveyard. The end of the line. They sat in the cool still grass and celebrated life together. They were just on the road toward maturity. They had so far to go. So much to do. So much time for everything.

Harry tried to swallow. There was no longer so much time.

Donnie opened his eyes and saw him. For a moment, Harry thought he saw fear or maybe just surprise. Then Donnie smiled. "Hesh," he said. That was what his father used to call him. Harry got up and moved his chair closer. He took his best friend's hand and leaned over him.

"Donnie. There's something I've got to tell you."

11

August 17

Well, here I am again! I bet you thought I'd given up the diary-writing business forever. Not so! In fact, I think I may just keep writing in you for the rest of my life, something to leave my grandchildren. If the rest of it is anything like this summer's worth, I may even have a best seller!

So much has happened. I'm going to have a baby! I can hardly believe it! Kenny has been so wonderful. Things just keep getting better and better for us. He went to see my mom and he asked for permission to marry me, just like in an old movie or something. My mom just cried and cried. I know she thinks I'm making a terrible mistake, but after finding out about her and Mr. Cowan, well, she's hardly the one to judge.

I still feel upset about that. But, I can understand how it happened and why she couldn't tell me. I'm trying to be grown up about it and see her side.

The funny thing is that I'm also kind of happy about it. I mean, he really loves her and she's had such a hard time all her life. Also, it makes me a real part of the Cowan family.

That's really neat, since I feel like that anyway. I mean, I'll have a dad. Kind of.

He's been really, really nice to me and Kenny. Frankie Karsh has been great, too. He's been through a lot because of Mrs. Ferris (I know you don't know about all that, but it's too depressing for this entry). Frankie made Kenny the manager and gave him a humongous raise. I've been working there, too, helping out. Big Ben is buying us a condo in Hampton Bays as a wedding present. I mean, really nice! I've made arrangements to transfer to Southampton College and I *am* going to finish school! That made my mom happy. I know she thinks I'm repeating her mistakes and I'm too young and all, but Kenny's different. I've never been this happy. A baby. Imagine.

It's been really hard because of Dr. Jamieson. I mean finally, Big Ben and Janie told me what was going on! They've all moved into the beach house, so it's been like camp around here. The Match and Joey Rivers and me, and the Harts most of the time. Big Ben has been staying with my mom (which is really weird) but I can understand why she wouldn't come here. The house is up for sale and some Japanese billionaire is interested. Mrs. Cowan is getting out of the clinic next week and she's rented another house in Water Mill. So, the fairy tale ends, I guess.

Big Ben told my mom that the hardest part was telling Janie. I mean, the poor woman has really a lot to deal with and on top of everything, she has to find out her father is in love with *my* mother (who is just about her age!). Well, he finally did it. My mom said she took it pretty well. Janie came home after he told her and gave me a big hug and told me she knew and she was glad that I was now "almost officially family," is how she put it. She was really sweet. I'd do anything for her.

Anyway, I've been helping as much as I can. The Match

has, too. She's been giving Dr. Jamieson massages, which seem to help him keep his circulation going.

Owen has turned into this medical missionary. His room is filled with books and he's always reading one, making notes, following Janie around with treatment suggestions. It's so sweet and so, so sad.

There was some talk about trying chemotherapy, but they did some more tests and decided against it. That was really depressing. I was there that day, when his doctor came to tell him. Dr. J. had said he wouldn't do it, because he had seen what the treatments did to his parents, but Owen got so upset and ran around gathering books and reading his father about this miracle here and there and finally Donnie said he would try it. When the doctor said no, Owen just collapsed by his bed and sobbed his heart out. We were all in tears.

Poor Louie. He's really too young to deal with this. He woke up one night and marched himself down to Dr. J.'s bed and crawled in with Donnie and wouldn't leave. Since then, he's slept there every night. It's really funny, because first the Harts moved into the main house. Then after Mrs. Ferris's accident—when Janie took over, one by one, they all moved into the Jamiesons' little house. They're all sleeping there now. On the couches, taking turns in the bedrooms. I think it's really good for Dr. J., but he's not doing very well. He's really skinny and kind of yellow, even his eyes. Owen says that's jaundice because of the cancer in his liver.

Owen keeps making these enormous health food drinks and herb teas, but poor Dr. J. can't get anything down. They keep him on I.V. pretty much all the time, now.

Janie is really like Miss Head Nurse. She's amazing. She just totally took charge. She hardly sleeps and I can tell she's tired, but she never lets on. She has a part-time nurse—but Dr. J. doesn't like her so much. What I think is, he misses

Fritzi. She was so cheerful. He was always trying harder when she was here.

Harry and Gina have been super, too. Harry and Donnie watch television and make fun of all the talk shows. Harry is always making up bizarre subjects for Geraldo and Oprah and it makes Dr. J. laugh. Yesterday I was there and Harry was doing it and he came up with "Anorexic, transsexual Hassidic crack addicts and their mothers, the subject of tomorrow's *Geraldo!*"

The hardest thing is the way Louie sits for hours asking Dr. J. questions. Dr. J. always tries to answer him but he kind of drifts in and out, he never gets impatient, though, even when he's really tired. "Are you going to go where my mother went? What does cancer look like?" On and on.

So, anyway. That's what's happening now. The Match told me she had this patient once and the first time she came to see her the woman was wearing a full-length mink coat and it was like July and she had long blond hair and dark glasses on, like a movie star.

Well, she took off the coat and The Match said she was really skinny, then she took off her hair and she was bald and she took off her glasses and her eyes were all sunken. She had cancer and she was dying, too. The Match said she massaged her every day until her bones were too fragile to stand it. She said that working on Dr. J. keeps bringing it back to her. She's good for him, always telling him funny stories. But when she comes out, she just sits down and bawls.

I've gotten to know her and Joey Rivers really well. Boy, who would ever have thought I'd know someone famous like that! He and The Match are really good together, I think. He just adores her.

He's had kind of a hard time because Katarina is all bent out about The Match. It's like she can't believe any man could reject her. She calls and screams and carries on and says she's going to take everything he has. He doesn't seem too upset about it.

Rikki Bosco was going to finance his next movie, and that fell apart, but he told us last night that he's put a new deal together with one of the studios and he's going back to Hollywood soon. I don't know if The Match is going with him or what. She seems kind of mopey.

Well, that's about it for now. I said I'd stay and house-sit until they find a buyer. Kenny is moving in, too. We're going to get married in September before I look like one of those shotgun brides. With school starting then and the baby and all, I guess a honeymoon will have to wait. Well, I'm not going to worry about it. I'm just grateful for what I've got.

I don't know where Big Ben and my mom are going to go. I have a feeling they're going to move away. But no one is going to do anything while Dr. J. is still sick. Oh boy. That sounds really gross; like everyone's waiting for him to die so they can zoom on with their lives. It isn't like that. Really. It isn't. But it is kind of like, everyone's on hold.

I don't know when I'll write again, but I know I will.

12

The very first thing Fritzi Ferris saw when she regained consciousness was the very last thing she had seen before she lost it. Frankie Karsh's anguished, tear-stained face, searching hers.

She tried to smile. Her head felt as if it were stuffed with cement.

She tried to speak, but her mouth felt funny. No sound came. She moaned. Frankie shot up out of his seat and leaned over her.

"Oh, God! Oh, Jesus! Oh, please! Forgive me! Please, please!" His whole body shook.

She reached out her hand, causing a searing pain to shoot from her temple down her arm. Why should she forgive him? Her mind was blank. She must have a concussion, she thought. She had all the symptoms, including amnesia. She had no idea why she was in the hospital. Or what Frankie had to do with it.

"I'll get the doctor. Don't move. I mean, please, stay awake for a minute. I'll be right back."

She was trying. She had no idea how long she'd been out. Her eyes felt so heavy. She would try to help him.

341

The doctor came and took her pulse and shone lights in her eyes and asked her some questions that she was not able to answer and went to get the neurologist. She closed her eyes again and when she opened them, Frankie was back, looking, she thought, as if he had just had a death sentence commuted, though not knowing at the time how apt the metaphor was.

She was going to be okay, he sobbed. She had a pretty bad concussion, but now that she was awake and they had done some more tests, they said she would be just fine. What happened to me? she asked, and he started to cry again and told her. Then he left her alone.

She slept and after some time, she had no idea how long, Janie came and she asked about Donnie, and Aaron came in and he held her hand and cried and cried and then she slept some more. Deep, dreamless sleep, not deep enough to escape the pain in her head or the heavier, deeper one in her heart.

The next time she woke up, two detectives were there and they asked her if she remembered what happened and she said she had been playing around with her boyfriend and she had slipped and fallen. This did not seem to be what they wanted to hear, but they accepted it and when they asked her if she was sure she didn't want to press charges against Mr. Karsh, she had gotten upset and said, "Absolutely not, it wasn't his fault," and the nurse had come in and made them leave.

And as far as she was concerned, that was the truth. Whatever had happened, and since she could not remember any of it and had only Frankie's tortured confession to base her information on, she had told the truth. It was not his fault. She had driven him crazy. It had just never occurred to her that he cared for her so much. She had always thought men wanted her for sex—something she knew how to deal with.

A HOUSE IN THE HAMPTONS

But that kind of obsession, *that* she did not believe herself capable of triggering. She had shoved him out of her house, out of her life, without so much as an explanation. He was hardly more than a child. She knew better, or at least she should have. When Donnie called her that morning, asking for help, she pushed everyone and everything else out of her heart. And she had hurt someone who loved her.

She had come back east to tie up the loose ends left dangling for almost half of her life. She had come to try and give her son back his real father and to give herself some sense of worth that she had lost between two boyhood buddies who had never quite left the edges of her memory. She had come back to find something and to lose something, and she had done that. She got lucky, too. She hadn't died trying.

She felt lighter, somehow. She would try to be with Frankie and not be afraid of the future. Not spoil it by waiting for him to tire of her, abandon her for someone younger. Her whole life had been based on the care of her outside, a fantasy image she had created as carefully as if she were made of wax. No one had ever gotten close enough to melt her. Not even her own son. Maybe now she could change that.

Owen Jamieson and Jeremy Hart parked their bikes in front of the Bridgehampton Library. They were sweating and out of breath. Every morning since they had found out about Donnie, they set off in search of knowledge. They visited every library in the Hamptons, every bookstore, and bought all the counterculture self-cure books in the local health food stores. They took the train into the City and spent all day at the New York Public Library and attended seminar sessions at Mt. Sinai on alternative medicine. Most of this they kept to themselves. Their plan was to gather all the knowledge they could and then, when they had enough ammunition, propose a new form of treatment.

In back of it was Owen's belief that he could find a way to save his father. The truth was, that none of the news was good. None of the books, even the really far-out ones, offered any real hope except radical changes in diet and philosophy, which was a joke because Donnie couldn't eat anything, even his favorite things, let alone the kind of disgusting gunk that Owen kept bringing him.

Finally they had gone public, but it was clear that by then it was all pretty much wishful thinking. Still they kept on. A new book had just arrived at the library and the librarian had called and so off they went. It was better than doing nothing at all.

They settled in the reading room and leafed through the volume. It had something to do with the results of cactus extract therapy on stomach cancers among Southeast Asians. Their hearts were not in it. *Metastasized* was the dreaded word.

Jeremy poked Owen. "This isn't anything. Let's go."

Owen closed the book and followed Jeremy out to the book-return desk and back into the hot August morning. "Wanna get a soda before we ride back?"

"Sure." They walked across the street and over to the Soda Shack and settled in a booth. It was quiet, for a change. Owen worried about running into anyone they knew. It was like they had all moved to Mars. They still hadn't told anyone. For some reason his dad refused to let them.

Anger shot through him. It was so dumb. It was no crime to be sick! If people knew, maybe someone could help. He had carried the anger since the beginning. Since his mother had come to tell him his father was back. So dumb! Why had he gone off like that? Why had he gone to her? That big dumb blonde. She was up to no good. He was sure of it. First the mysterious son and then his dad. If Aaron hadn't looked exactly like Harry, he would have sworn it was all a setup.

What a way to find out your father is dying! No, he wouldn't say that word. All the books said to think positive, to believe in miracles. Great. Fine. But his dad didn't. His dad was giving up. After she got hurt. He just gave up. Good. He was glad she was gone! At least it gave his mother a chance to be with her husband. He wanted to shake him.

Jeremy was the only one who knew how he felt. His dad said he hoped he and Jeremy would be like Harry and him. Friends for life. He hoped so, too. He would never be able to handle all of this if it wasn't for Jeremy.

Jeremy smiled at him. "Penny for your twisted thoughts?"

"I was thinking about our situation. I was thinking that I'm glad Fritzi got zapped, if you must know."

Jeremy raised his eyebrows. "Now, now, son. Mustn't think like that. She is, after all, my half brother's mother." Jeremy watched him. He had screwed that up.

"You're right, Owen. I think about that, too. But it really isn't her fault. Your dad called her. I think she was trying to help. Aaron says she's really a fine person. That all of that sexy pinball-head stuff is just a front. She's his mother, he should know."

"Come on. Every guy protects his mother. She could have been a baby murderer and he'd still protect her."

"Jeez, you really are blowing steam. Chill, Owen. It won't make anything better."

"I know." Owen lowered his head and sucked his Coke with his straw. He emptied the glass and kept sucking, making loud suction noises that would have driven his parents crazy.

Jeremy laughed. "Get it out, boy."

Owen stopped and looked up at him. "I think this is the last library day. I think we'd better give it up now."

Jeremy watched him. "Yeah. I guess you're right."

"Your dad was the only person who yelled at him. I mean when they finally found him. My mom was mad, too, but she was too grateful that he was dying and not leaving her for Bazooka Boobs to say anything. My mom said Harry stormed in and just started yelling at him. 'I'm going to kill you, you stupid fuck!' I wish I had been there. I wish I had done that."

Jeremy felt like crying. He wished he was older and had had more experience with other people's feelings. He didn't want to make it worse for his friend. He didn't know what to say.

"Maybe you should tell him that, Owen. Your dad's a shrink, after all. He can deal with it. Tell him how you feel. You know how in all those movies we used to make fun of? Like Robbie Benson movies and stuff? The old man's always dying and the son has this big teary scene and tells him the truth and then it's okay when the father dies?"

Owen took one last long slurp with his straw. "Yeah. I think maybe I'd better try it. Let's go."

They paid their bill, trying not to make eye contact with anyone who might recognize them and ask personal questions. They put on their helmets like the good boys that they were and set off on the long ride down the Highway to the grandparents' house that had always been a safe summer haven but was, for now, haunted by the future.

When Owen arrived, The Match was sitting outside on the front step smoking a cigarette, her eyes were all red and Owen thought she had been crying.

"Yo. Owen, how's it going?" She smiled at him and winked. He liked her. He liked to watch her when she didn't know he was looking. She was unique, he thought. Though he had never used that word before. It fit her. She was always herself.

346

"Is my dad awake?"

She took a deep drag on her cigarette. "Yeah. Kind of. He's not good today. I don't think we can do any more massage. It's hurting him now."

Owen flushed. The anger was back, but he was also afraid.

"Can I see him?"

"Sure. Hey, Owen. I'm not the warden. He always wants to see you. He told me, 'If Owen comes, let him in.' He always says that. You're his main man."

"No. Louie and Harry are."

The Match narrowed her eyes and looked at him. "Hey. You forget who you're with, dude. Little dude. This is not Momma. I know that shit. 'Poor little Owen, the Unloved.' Forget about it. You know your dad is nuts about you. You *know* it. Don't start running those games. They really mess with your head. And most people aren't like me; they're more genteel. They'll let you take that scene right to the end. If you're going to go in and talk to your dad today, just lose that shit."

Owen crossed his arms in front of his chest, and stood up straight. No one had ever talked to him that way. He held on to himself, trying to let it sink in. She was right.

The Match watched him. She blew smoke rings. She seemed unconcerned with how he was taking it.

He felt his pride. It was hard to admit. "Well, maybe I should come back later." He lowered his head. It was a challenge and she knew it.

"So, Owen. You hate me or what?"

No. Of course not." He felt like crying.

The Match put out her cigarette. "Come here. Plant your butt for a minute. It's so pretty here. Look at the—whaddaya call those things?"

Owen sat down. "Egrets. I think."

"Yeah. Egrets. What a funny name. I never know how

347

they think of all those names for things. Mushroom. That's one. Imagine the first guys that saw them. So disgusto. I mean, they don't look like you'd wanna pop them in your mouth. So who was the first guy that saw one and said, 'Hmmm. I bet if you grilled that sucker with some olive oil and garlic, it'd be great.' 'A great what?' 'How 'bout *mushroom*?'"

Owen laughed. "You're funny."

The Match picked up his hand and turned it over. "Anyone ever read your palm?"

"No."

"Let me see here. I used to be good at this. I even did it for a living for a while. Wow! Look at that life line. You're gonna live to be a real old dude. Hundreds of years."

Owen let her hold his hand. Her hands were cool and soft. They calmed him down.

She looked at him. "I was sittin' here and I was thinkin' of this client of mine. She's a real nice lady. Just one of those real nice people that takes the world as it comes.

"Well, one day I was givin' her a massage and she starts to cry and, she was always real cheerful, so I was surprised. So I asked her what's wrong and she says that her father was real sick and they didn't think he was going to make it.

"Well, I never had a father. Never really had a mother, either, for that matter. I'm kind of like a mushroom. Sort of just sprung up onto the earth. So, when she said that, I really felt kind of funny. I mean like, I didn't understand how she felt. But then she started to tell me this story about how every time she went to see her father, it started to rain. Like some sort of mystical shit. Every time, it would start to rain on the way. She said, 'I never worried about it because my father always had an umbrella for me by the door when I left. I always knew there'd be one and I'd get home dry.'

"Well, you know, Owen, when she told me that I just fell

348

apart, started bawlin' like a baby. I understood it then. What she was losin' if her old man died. I always got wet. No one ever waitin' with an umbrella for old Ellen Mary. See? See my violins and poor-little-me shit? We all got it. But it's not good for us. Your father is really smart. He's your umbrella. He knows you're pissed at him and he knows you love him, too. It's okay. You can both deal with it."

Owen put his head down. "I don't want this to be happening to him. Why did this have to happen to him?"

The Match moved closer and put her arms around him. "Who the fuck knows, dude. Things happen. That's how it goes. Good things and crummy things. If we were supposed to figure it out, we'd have done it by now. I don't think we're supposed to. We're just supposed to go forward, keep our dukes up and keep on going. That's the way it is, from what I've seen."

Owen sat up and wiped his face. He felt better. "I think I'll go in, now."

"Good. Don't feel bad if he's a little, fuzzy. Janie had to give him an extra morphine. Don't take it personal."

Owen nodded. The Match watched him go in, wishing that Janie had given her a shot of morphine as well.

Donnie's eyes were closed. Owen tiptoed to his bed, not wanting to disturb his peace. He watched him, hoping he would sense he was there without his having to do anything. He was scared. It took all of his will just to look at his father like that. Weak and emaciated and helpless. It didn't even look like his dad anymore. He looked so old, so small. His dad was tall and in really good shape. It was like a trick had been played on them.

Donnie opened his eyes and smiled. The whites of his eyes were all yellow. Owen felt like screaming.

"I was dreaming about you."

"You were?"

Donnie reached out his dry, bony hand. Owen took it and sat down next to him on the bed. He could feel his father's hipbone right through the covers.

"Yes. Remember when you were two or three, you had this toy. It was called the Happy Hippo and it was a wooden hippopotamus on wheels with a string around its neck? You used to pull it behind you, everywhere you went. Round and round all day long. If we tried to take it away, you just cried and cried. I was dreaming about you and the Happy Hippo."

Owen smiled. "I remember. I was really overcome with that thing. I think I still have it. In the hall closet in the City."

"Save it for the next generation." Donnie watched his face. It was harder and harder for him to stay present. He hated taking the damn pain medicine. It altered the truth. It floated him off. He wanted to be there with them, until the very last second.

It was nothing like he had expected. The mind was so clever, so amazingly complex. He could feel himself tipping into paranoia, into blackness. He could watch it and identify it, actually feel the toxins climbing into his brain, playing games with his reason. That was the most frightening part. Reason had been his God, his strength. And he was no longer entirely reasonable. He fought the urge to let go and let the morphine carry him off on its magic carpet. He had been waiting for this. Waiting and praying that Owen would find his way back to him in time. He knew that if he pushed it, forced a conversation, it would not work.

He had written Owen a letter and he hoped that in it he had given him what he would need to heal without jagged psychic scars, scars he had spent his life trying to fade in his patients. But this was the best way. His son finding him.

"I'm not going to the library anymore." Owen squeezed

350

his hand, not realizing how weak he was. He was holding on to his source of courage.

"Oh?" Donnie tried to keep his gaze steady.

"No. I mean, I figure, you've given up, so why shouldn't I?" Owen swallowed hard. "I . . . It makes me mad. I know how terrible that sounds, but it does. It all makes me mad. You just went off and you didn't even let us help. You didn't respect us enough. You nearly drove Mom crazy and then, only by accident, we found you like this!

"I mean, if Harry hadn't snuck in there, we might have never even known! One day, we'd just get a call. 'Oh, by the way, your father's dead.' I mean, you were always Mr. Level Head and from where I sit, you just freaked out. Went to a stranger! Like how totally rude! I mean, you treated Mom and me like retards. Like we couldn't cope with this better than Balloon Boobs!

"It was like you didn't even care how we felt! You didn't trust us enough and we're your own family! I'm your son! I'm almost a man. You could have come to me. I'm the one that's going to be left to take over. To help Mom and Grandma and Louie. If I'm okay to do all of that, then I should have been okay to tell the truth to. You robbed me! You never gave me a chance to give you something back! It's like all of the love I had inside for you; all the things you gave me all my life; it was like a chance to give back and now all of those feelings are just stuck inside me. Like a big glob of stuff and it'll never come up now. You cheated me. You don't want my help. You just want to give up and die. So fine. So, go ahead and die!"

Donnie held his hand. His son's face was a mask of grief. He held on to him with all the energy he had left. He knew that if his grip loosened, Owen would stop, would feel that his permission to finish had been retracted. He held on.

The hardest part of all was, that listening to Owen pour

out his rage and terror and love, he knew that the reasonable man had blindsided himself. His reason had turned on him, and misled him. Owen was right. He had let them down. He had made a mistake. When Harry had first torn into the cottage and accused him, lashing wildly in his own disbelief and panic, he had not been ready to absorb it. It had come too fast. Too soon. Now, he was ready. Now he was stripped of all extra mental baggage. All the dead weight had been thrown over the sides of the life raft. Now he could hear it. He held his son's wet hands, hot with life, and let him empty his heart into him.

13

Delores Cowan came home to her castle on the sand on the last day of August. She was shaky and she was scared. She had never been called upon before, to be strong. Now, even though the only one calling upon her was her newly functioning self, the call was loud and clear.

Her therapist drove her and when she arrived no one was expecting her. They were all with Donnie or on the beach, somewhere else, anyway. The huge house was still. She took her bag upstairs to the room she had shared with her husband. He was gone. It was hers now. She put down her bag and took a long deep breath, waiting for the old desolation to claim her. Nothing came. She exhaled.

What did she feel? Something new. A kind of excitement. An anxiety. But not a negative kind. Anticipation. Not apprehension. A hopeful feeling. Almost what? Joyful?

She threw herself down on the vast creamy silk-covered bed and stretched. It was nice being here alone. It had never been her house. Not one single choice about any of it had anything to do with her. She had felt far too guilty to impose any of her needs on Ben. This was the house built to save his manhood. One gigantic ego trip, really, though she would never, ever had said that, even to herself. She had always assumed that she owed him the house as an apology for The Money. *My money ruined his life* was her party line. It had never occurred to her that he had equal responsibility in that chain of events. After all, he could have said no. It suited them both. He used it to cop out on himself and blame her, and she used it in reverse.

Now she had reclaimed it. She would stalk it, feel her power, and then she would sell the damn thing and never look back. She was a small woman. The entire house was scaled to the comfort of a huge man. A giant's house. No wonder she hated it. She could hardly reach the sink without standing on her toes. She rolled over and over on the bed like a child. She could do whatever she wanted now. She rested her head on her folded arms and thought about that. How did it feel? A little sad. But, mainly, pretty terrific.

Someone was in the room. She rolled over and opened her eyes. Louie was standing by the bed, his perfect little face grim.

"Hi, Momma." He was trying hard not to cry. His mouth wiggled up and down with the effort.

Dear God, she thought, tears popping out of her eyes and coursing down her cheeks. Is it conceivably possible that I was so far gone, I never even saw how much this child needed me! The truth of this thought was almost unbearable. Janie had been hard enough. To know that you had totally failed someone you loved so much. But Louie. Louie was like the house. He had been Ben's. Ben had found him, Ben had swept in with him. Ben had needed him to give his life a purpose and reaffirm his sense of himself as a great humanitarian. She had loved Louie with all of her heart, but she had never for a moment felt she had any right to him. She barely felt entitled to touch him, let alone guide, mother, comfort. He was Ben's. Another payoff for the massive injury she had done him. Give me a break, she thought, Owen's lingo fitting her well. She and Louie were the same. Orphans of the storm of change. Seduced and abandoned by Big Ben Cowan.

This was a second chance, standing before her, brave and scared like herself. A child who still needed her. Who loved her. Hope. There was hope. She could stand up and make a demand. She could demand Louie. She could even fight for him if necessary. Fight her husband and even her daughter. They had other things. She and Louie needed each other.

"Hi," she said. She sat up, her girlish legs dangling over the side of the bed, feet not touching the floor. She wanted to gather him to her and smother him with all of the hugs and kisses she had held inside her, doubting their value, not feeling entitled to intrude on him and her husband; all of the love she had denied them both swept through her, shaking her with its force. She was not sure what to do. She did not want to frighten him away.

"You're not sick anymore?" His eyes were almost closed, his face held down, trying to be a big boy.

"No. I'm better now. How about you, *baby*?" The word filled her heart. She had never called him that before. "How are you?"

He looked up at her, tears starting to move down his silky brown cheeks. "I'm cool," he said, not fooling either of them.

"How is Donnie doing?" She swallowed, unsure of her course. Moving ever so slightly closer, like Big Ben in the jungle. Not wanting to scare him off.

Louie shook his head. He crossed his small arms over his chest, trying to hold himself together. "He looks like the people in the pictures Poppa has from my country. 'Skin and bones,' that's what The Match says. He's going to die. He is. I can't sleep with him anymore, 'cause it hurts him. It hurts him if I even touch his arm. I don't want to hurt him, so I sleep in my sleeping bag on the floor next to him. He says he's okay, that I don't have to, 'cause he wants me to sleep in a bed and be more comfortable, but I don't mind. I think it makes him sleep better. I do."

Delores wiped tears from her face. *I am responsible for myself,* she whispered inside her head. It was time to risk something.

"You know how it feels to be the littlest? Well, that's kind of how I've always felt. Like the littlest. Unimportant. But that wasn't true. I was important to you, and I didn't even know it. You don't remember this of course, you were just a baby, but the day Poppa brought you home and put you in my arms you looked right at me, just looked at me so hard for a long time, as if you were trying to decide if I was okay or not, and then you reached up with this one tiny finger and put it in my mouth and gave me the biggest smile. You only had one tooth, so it was a pretty impressive smile. It was your way of letting me know that I had passed the test. I could have just eaten you up, I was so in love with you. But I didn't know how to show it."

The tears were falling again and she let him see them. He needed to see her cry over him. "Louie, darling, I am never going to leave you again, unless God takes me and I'm going to have a little talk with him, too. He's taken enough away from you already. So God, I'll tell him, piss off! Leave Louie and me alone for the next twenty years."

Louie was holding himself so tight, his fingertips were white. Delores opened her arms wide and the little boy ran into them and they held tight to each other. Two lonely survivors finding their missing piece. Putting the puzzle of the universe back on top of the coffee table. Organizing the pieces and finding the last one. The mast of the ship. The nose for the clown. The stack of the chimney. They rocked back and forth together, fitting perfectly.

A HOUSE IN THE HAMPTONS

Donnie Jamieson died on the first of September on the Friday before Labor Day, the last big weekend of the summer. No one was exactly sure when because he died in his sleep. So, even though his entire family was lying around him on couches and cots and sleeping bags, he died alone.

Many of their friends and acquaintances did not even know that he was sick until they read about his death in *The New York Times*. That was how he wanted it. That was how it was.

He was buried in a private ceremony beside his parents and then the people who loved him drove back down the Island in heavy traffic, smashed in between campers and station wagons filled with happy vacationers; cars loaded with tennis racquets and coolers, all lined up and heading for the same place, the tip of the island; the last grab at summer.

No one wanted to be at the Cowans'. They packed up their belongings and left the tainted palace to the realtors. They all went to the Harts', an exhausted, raggedy caravan of survivors. They wandered around one another, trancelike, while all around them, they could hear barbecuers searing animal flesh, and neighbors laughing; children splashing in pools, ice cubes rattling in plastic glasses. A robust farewell to another summer.

Delores was there, and Ben. Both trying to make amends to their daughter. But it was Harry and Gina who held Janie up. It was their loss, too. They had all been through it together.

Arturo broke out with psychosomatic eczema and that gave the kids something to hang on to. Hours were spent soaking the poor itchy beagle in warm water and rubbing ointment into his brittle fur.

The morning after the funeral Harry woke up at dawn sobbing so hard that for several moments he could not speak or breathe, he choked on his tears, strangling on his own agony.

Gina brought him a wet towel and a glass of water and sat beside him, patting his back and helping him through. When he could speak, he jumped up, squeezing the end of the towel with his fist and lashing out with it at the bed, the bedposts, the furniture.

"Not good enough! What the fuck is the matter with us! He needs more. *We! We need more!*

Gina watched him, absorbing his fury. "Like what?"

"Like what? Like, shit. A proper send-off. Like a wake— like the Irish do . . . like the blacks in New Orleans do. Something special. A tribute, or a, a celebration."

"You mean a memorial service?"

Harry beat the pillows with the towel. "No! No fucking memorial service! I hate fucking memorial services! So serious. So controlled. Donnie had that shit all his life. That's the last thing he would have wanted. Look! Look at this!"

Harry ran to the dresser and pulled out a legal pad covered with Donnie's clean, even handwriting. "He wrote a letter. He told me it was his good-bye to me and to do with it whatever I wanted. I haven't even read it yet, just the first page and I couldn't handle it. But I know what he did it for. I just know that he would never ask it, but he wanted it to be read somewhere."

Harry stopped. His eyes opened wide and a smile, a slow, wicked Harry smile spread across his tear-stained face.

Gina smiled back. "What?"

"I've got it. I know what to do."

"So? *What?*"

Harry grabbed his shorts and ran out of the room. "Gotta get Janie and the kids. Be right back."

358

14

The Soda Shack in Bridgehampton was Donnie Jamieson's favorite place. He loved it mainly because it was so unlike anything else in his life. And also because it was about his family. Ice-cream and children and all the food he loved but rarely allowed himself. It was a perfect place to say a proper good-bye to him and in the early morning moment of his own pain, Harry Hart had a brainstorm.

On Labor Day morning, on the front door of the Soda Shack, which was never closed, ever, no matter what, a hand-painted sign went up.

THE SODA SHACK WILL BE CLOSED TODAY FROM
ONE O'CLOCK ON FOR A PRIVATE PARTY TO
CELEBRATE THE LIFE AND TIMES OF DR. DONNIE JAMIESON.
THIS PARTY IS OPEN TO ALL WHO KNEW HIM, BRING
CHILDREN AND MEMORIES.

Harry Hart had not slept in two days. He had thrown himself into the planning of the celebration of his best friend's life with every last shred of his always considerable nervous energy. It was as if his own life depended on its success.

By noon on Labor Day, Harry had called just about everyone Donnie had ever known. The long soda counter was piled high with Donnie's favorite food. American cheese sandwiches, peanut butter and jelly, tuna fish on white bread, and chilled splits of French champagne stood next to the root beer float glasses. Raw french fries and cheeseburgers were piled high and ready for cooking. Whole pies lined the service counter. Harry paced. Gina and Janie sat on stools like two wistful extras from *Happy Days* and offered support. Because this was about Donnie and Harry, they were really just supporting players. This was Harry's goodbye. And they understood.

At twelve-thirty the entire Sunday softball team arrived, dressed in full seedy regalia, a statement that moved Harry to another round of choking sobs. The next arrivals, in character in a white stretch limo, were Owen's favorite relatives, the Porcinettes, all clad in matching black leather pantsuits and black fedora hats, adding a wonderful counterpoint to Sunday Softball.

By one-thirty, the entire Soda Shack was packed. Many of Donnie's patients were there, looking lost and heartbroken. Frankie Karsh wearing reflecting Ray-Bans and a Mets cap low over his face, and Fritzi Ferris—still weak, but smiling and holding on to his arm for dear life, snuck in the side door and stood against the back wall. The Match was working behind the counter flipping burgers and giving Owen, Jeremy, Aaron, and Louie prep-chef tasks to keep them occupied and cheered up. Rikki Bosco arrived alone and slouched against the front window as if poised for a fast exit.

China and Kenny were there and Janie's parents, who sat together but did not speak much, and Isabel and Ondine, who kept his head lowered and wiped tears from his eyes. Norman Gallo and his wife, and the Cuccis and Max Stiles wearing a white silk suit and a Panama hat. Tennis buddies,

jogging buddies, med school pals, and the owner of the hardware store and the lady at the pharmacy who always saved a
Sunday *Times* for him. On and on. Ones and twos, people
who had been touched by the genuine human decency and
kindness of Donnie Jamieson came and partook; lining the
room, sitting on counters and tables and the floor, gobbling
french fries and American cheese, licking chocolate cones
and sipping French champagne from split bottles through
plastic straws. Some laughing, some crying, some trying not
to do either. When as many as could possibly squeeze in had
arrived, Harry Hart stood up on a chair and brought them
all to attention.

"My name is Harry Hart for those of you who don't know
by now and—Donnie Jamieson was—my best friend." He
stopped and let the grief out and everyone waited with him
and helped him through his and their own.

"Donnie wrote a letter. He left it with me and he didn't
say anything about it except that I had to promise not to
publish it in the *Duck Hunter's Journal.*" Everyone laughed,
including Harry. It was such a Donnie thing to say. "That
was hard, but I promised. Also he forbade me to read it
before he—he was—gone. I still haven't read it. So bear with
me. I just hope I can get through it and do it justice."

Harry paused and took a long breath. He looked for Gina
and found her eyes and she winked at him and he was okay.
He began.

"Harry. I am addressing this to you because, since I have
shared almost my entire time on earth with you, I know you
well enough by now to know, that if I were to leave you here
without me and didn't write you a special letter, you would
spend the next ten years and thousands of dollars on Dr.
Wexel's couch trying to work through your feelings of betrayal, and that is not what I want you to concentrate on.
What I want is for you to have compassion for yourself. To

361

take a lot of long deep breaths; to watch over my beloved boys and my darling Janie and have some fun. Have a lot of fun, Harry. Time is short, as we have both discovered this summer. Have fun, my dearest friend. I have a feeling that in spite of my saying, no service, no fuss, you will not be able to stand it and will plan some memorial or something. It's okay, Harry. Anyway, I won't have to be there to see if anyone shows up.

"I want to tell you a story. You probably don't even remember this. But it's why I've never let you or Janie or anyone give me a party of any kind. I know you all thought that I did it to be selfless and modest, but that's not why.

"When I was going to be five years old my parents moved from New Jersey to the suburbs of Philadelphia and I started kindergarten and I didn't know one single person. I had only been in school for a week or so and it was my birthday, and my mother felt so bad about moving me and it being my fifth birthday (the beginning of mature life) and all, that she insisted on giving me a party. I was, to say the least, indifferent to the prospect, but I didn't want to hurt her feelings and so I went along with it. For hours she drilled me on each kid's name. She wrote out the invitations and called the teacher and arranged for me to hand them out in class. That was one of the worst mornings of my entire life, walking up and down the aisles, handing out the invitations to the appropriate (or sometimes approximate, I was terrible at names and faces) person. The teacher following behind and correcting me as I went. 'No, Donald, that's Sarah not Susan.'

"The party was the following week on Saturday afternoon and my parents spent two days, making cakes and cookies, hanging pin-the-tail games and dartboards and even setting up a cowboy and cowgirl cut-out that kids could put their heads in and be photographed like the ones at amusement parks. Bowls of Hershey's Kisses and peppermint balls were

362

everywhere. My mother was so excited, she could hardly stand still.

"I approached that Saturday afternoon the way you, Harry, approach dental visits. But I put on a good show for them. Finally it was time. The three of us lined up at the door, all dressed up and eager to begin our social life in our new neighborhood. My mother had thoughtfully made iced tea and homemade pastry for the friendly and eager parents who would arrive with their adorable offspring. We waited at the door for one hour. Bravely. Optimistically. I remember saying to my mother, "No one likes to be first, I heard that on the radio." Or second or third for that matter. No one came.

"My parents, trying to spare my feelings, recited a list of excuses beginning with the wrong date and ending with a rather feeble projection of a mass influenza outbreak that could have felled one and all.

"Finally we gave up and sat down together to eat the cake and open the presents, when, lo and behold, the doorbell rang. We all looked at one another, with the manic, nervous hope of the reprieved death-row inmate. My parents leapt up and raced to the door so fast, I was almost knocked off my chair. I followed, expecting the worst. Whatever that was, I was not sure.

"Two small boys stood on the doorstep, looking as uncomfortable as I felt. One was very fat and pigeon-toed and had a large and rather formidable booger at the entrance to one of his nostrils. The other, Harry. Was you."

Harry stopped. If it had not been for his own blind sorrow, he would have seen that almost everyone in the room was crying.

"That was, in hindsight, one of the best and worst days of my life and I was never sorry my mother had insisted on it. However, afterward, I felt I had gotten the one pearl in that

363

enormous oyster of mortification, and that I should not push my luck again.

Next time it might only be the fat kid with the boogers. Or no one.

"Anyway, that is why I have never had another birthday party or even anniversary party (maybe now, my dear wife, you will forgive me) but since for this one I will not be waiting heart in hand behind the front door—do it if you must, Harry.

"And if you do and no one shows up, it's okay. You showed up, again. And if you do and hordes of admirers (secret and otherwise) flock to say their fond farewells, then tell them for me that I am grateful. Very grateful to everyone who has touched my life. If my patients come, tell them they have helped me far more than I have helped them, and I love them and miss them and I am so very sorry to have to leave them. But they will all be fine. They are all fine. You have to have wonderful patients to be a good doctor and I did. We chose one another well.

"I hope wherever I am going I can watch you all. Keep me with you in funny stories and fond memories. I insist on keeping you all, too.

"Remember the time, Harry, when we all lived in that building on West 80th Street next door to the two drunks who never closed their door and Arturo got out, tore into their place while they were passed out on the couch and stole an entire leg of lamb right off their kitchen counter?

"Oh, God, I will miss all our laughter. Know how much I love you all. And how much joy you have given me. And have fun, Harry. Have some fun."

Harry bowed his head. No one spoke. One by one heads bowed, giving mourners a moment of privacy in the midst of the others. Some things cannot really be shared. Harry folded the pages neatly and put them in his pocket.

A HOUSE IN THE HAMPTONS

A new feeling began to build inside him. It built slowly in the silent crowded room. A twitching disquiet. A spark taking fire; a fidgeting, rustling ember. It built, bursting into flame within him. A foaming, fuming, ranting flare. A sizzling fuse racing toward his heart, running wild, boiling his blood. On the table beside him stood a fresh tray filled with champagne bottles and root beer floats. Harry bent down and grabbed a frothy, foaming mug of root beer and raised it high in his clenched fist. High over the bowed heads of Donnie Jamieson's friends.

He shouted out, releasing all the heat, passion, violence, and desperation inside him.

"Fuck death!" Harry Hart shouted. *"Fuck it to hell!"*

One by one the heads raised. He had released them. People jumped to their feet. They climbed up on tables and chairs, mugs and bottles held high, like an English pub portrait. One by one the voices joined him. A chant of life took hold.

"Fuck death! Fuck death! Fuck death!" Old and young. Hands clapped it. Feet stomped it. Louder and louder. Deeper and deeper. *"Fuck it to hell!"* All of the fear and rage and loss and passivity and false acceptance and pretense and denial that most of them covered themselves with like scouts in a thunderstorm, huddling under the fragile pup tents of their humanity—out they came into the lightning strike.

"Fuck it to hell!"

Harry jumped down off his chair and into the fray of chanting emotion. Jeremy, tuning instantly into the mood, slipped a Bob Marley tape into the portable player he had brought and turned it up full volume.

"Jamming, Jamming. Gonna have a party tonight!"

People went wild. Children whirled in circles wiggling to a beat too sensuous for them to feel. Max Stiles threw his hat into the air, followed by his Italian silk tie and shirt, and grabbed Esmeralda Cucci, knocking her backward and twirling her frantically back and forth. Everyone started moving. Dancing. Swaying. Uncorked. Decanted in the middle of a Bridgehampton malt shop by one sentence of truth.

As they undulated, eyes closed, lips parted, champagne wetting their necks, sweat dripping down their tan, attractive faces, now and then someone shouted it out. Renewing them.

"Fuck death!" A voice would swell and be swallowed by the crowd. Abandon. They experienced abandon. The New York sophisticates' version of a tent revival.

Owen, Jeremy, and Louie, who were too young, too far from the other side, to comprehend fully the force of the reaction, the frenzy of the release, stood quietly together behind the counter, dutifully performing whatever service The Match requested of them. They were amused. They were bemused. None of them had ever been to a funeral before, much less a funeral reggae party. The Match watched them out of the sides of her long green eyes. "Hey, dudes," she said finally, sensing their confusion. "Chill. Don't you know yet that grown-ups are crazier than kids? Give 'em a break. They need this. They're just real scared, is all."

They nodded solemnly. That was something they could relate to. Owen made his way through the rocking throng to his mother, who was curled up in a far corner booth looking small and lost. She saw him and smiled, reaching out her arms to him. "Lap. On my lap."

Owen groaned. "Mom. I'll squash you. I'm too big for that." He said it, but he did it.

"Never too big. I'll be doing this when you're eighty." She reached around him and put her hand on his neck, pulling his head down onto her shoulder. "My baby," she said. They sat like that, rocking gently back and forth. She knew he was crying, but she kept quiet. Patting his back softly, mothering both of them.

366

A HOUSE IN THE HAMPTONS

"Fuck it to hell!" Aaron Ferris shouted, moving from Fritzi's side toward Harry, mirror images of past and present—shouting their defiance at the future.

The party went on and on. Finally, Glenn Anderson, the owner of the Soda Shack, tied on his apron and started putting his place back together for the morning. The holiday was over. The summer was ending. The season was closing. But the daily life of the village, the six A.M. coffeepot that the Soda Shack provided for its members, would go on.

People carried their ecstasy out into the night, wandering down Main Street singing and swaying, no one willing to let the power of the experience end. Some went to the beach and continued. Some went home to make passionate love. Some simply sat up and talked, making plans for the fall. Endings turning into beginnings, once again.

The Harts and the Jamiesons left early and drove, without planning it, back to the giant empty summer house, now lying dark and deserted, waiting for the Japanese lord of commerce to claim her. Janie still had her keys and they wandered around, quiet and wide-eyed, in the vast, empty rooms. So many memories were held here. After a while they stopped wandering and sat in a circle in the middle of the giant glass-and-stone living room and reminisced about Big Ben's party and how long ago it seemed.

Louie stood up and ran to the window, looking far up into the star-crusted sky. "Look," he said solemnly, his small dark finger pointing upward. "There's Dr. J."

They all rose and followed him. A shooting star, or maybe just a plane far away, flashed across the sky. They chose to accept Louie's theory.

The day after Labor Day, Harry, who had hardly been in his office since the middle of July, left to go back to work. Somehow, that was the moment that everything became real. Donnie was gone and life must still go on.

The Match was packing. The Japanese zillionaire had finally written a check, all cash, for the Cowans' house and Janie and Donnie's wing still had not been packed. Joey had left the week before for the Coast and she was debating what to do next. To follow or not to follow, that was the question. The phone rang. She ran to answer it, figuring that it was Janie, who was coming over to help her.

"Yo. Janie."

A pause. She could hear someone breathing on the end. "Oh pa-leese, no weirdos today."

"Match?"

"Rikki?"

"Yeah. Listen, I gotta talk to you. Can we meet?"

The Match twisted the phone cord around her wrist, something she did when she was nervous.

"Well, it's a little intense over here. Is it about the car? I thought I signed everything."

"No. No. It's not. I just have to talk to you about something. It's important. It'll only take a few minutes."

"So. Okay. Come on over here. You remember the way?"

"Yeah. How about ten minutes?"

"Okay. Just come around the back, I'll meet ya at the side entrance. The one that leads down to the beach."

He was already there when she came down. Waiting behind the gate for her to let him in. They stood for a moment looking at each other. It had been over a month since they'd seen each other. She thought he looked tired.

"Come on. Let's go sit on the beach." He followed her. She liked that he followed. That had not been the way their relationship had worked. She had always been the one following. She flopped down on the sand and crossed her legs under her. Rikki did the same. The sun was in her eyes. She pulled out her dark glasses and put them on. It made her feel safer.

"So, what's the emergency?" She drew circles in the sand with her fingernail.

Rikki pulled out his Vuarnets and put them on. They were now fortified. "I don't know quite how to do this. So just be cool here. Give me a chance. Don't interrupt with some smart-ass comment, okay?"

"Who me?" She grinned at him.

"Yeah, you. Well, first. Katarina is gone. I sent her home to her parents. We had a talk and she, well, she flipped out. Just kind of went nuts. For someone so cool, it was really heavy. She made you look like Miss Mental Health."

"Hey. Bosco. Rules are rules. If I gotta sit here with my lips sealed, no cheap shots, okay?"

He smiled. "Okay. Sorry. Well, the thing was that I told her that maybe I'd made a mistake. Maybe what I'd felt for her wasn't love at all. Wasn't too cool for me. I, she—well, she was like a fantasy. But underneath, it wasn't there.

"You know, when Frankie Karsh lost it and almost killed Fritzi Ferris? Well, he came to me. I guess you know that. Anyway. It could have been *me*. She could have done that to me. See, she did something, and I realized that she didn't love me and I didn't love her. I loved *attaining* her. Like one of the paintings or the cars. Or the fucking Bayfront Club.

"The whole scene was messed up. And it got worse. She wasn't—she wasn't my friend. So, what I'm trying to say here is, I told her that. I told her it wasn't going to work. I couldn't marry her. Like she didn't even know me. She didn't even *like* me. Not really. Well, I don't think anything like that had ever happened to her before. I mean first she lost Joey to you and then she lost me to you."

The Match took off her glasses. "What're you saying?"

369

Rikki leaned forward, and spoke very softly as if he was afraid she would run from him. "I told her I loved you. That I wanted you back. I told her, you were my only real friend."

He had been right. The Match jumped up and ran down the beach. She was sobbing and shouting while she ran. What was with her! Twenty-five years, not a tear, and boom; all summer long she's like some fucking saline factory.

He caught up with her and threw his arms around her, knocking them both down into the sand. They rolled over each another.

"Fuck you. Fuck you forever, Bosco!" He let her go.

She sat up and wiped the sand, wet with her mucus, off her face. She was still crying.

"I'm sorry. I know I hurt you. I acted like an asshole. But you hurt me, too. I mean that kitchen scene was a little much. So we're even. We can go on from here. We can get married and start a family."

She looked at him. She reached over and took his glasses off, wanting to see into his eyes. This was the last thing on earth she had ever expected.

"You know, I've been wandering around here since Joey left, trying to make a decision. He wants me to come out there. It means giving up everything here. My work. All my clients. And he's not divorced. And, I mean The Kunt wasn't easy when she thought you were going to make Ivana fucking Trump out of her, so's I can imagine how it's going to be now.

"She couldn't even handle that *Joey* could want *me*. So, I really have been strung out about it. I didn't want to go until Dr. J. died, I felt like they needed me here. I guess I was scared. I haven't taken too many risks in my sordid little life. You were my first big risk and it didn't turn out so good. But now I know why I couldn't decide. I was waiting for a sign."

The Match leaned over and touched him on the cheek. "So

370

A HOUSE IN THE HAMPTONS

Bosco. I'm sorry. But I'm going to L.A. I may be fucking crazy, but I just decided. You helped me. You saying that, asking me to marry you. Every dream I had coming true. It's nice, to know that you learned somethin'. That you know I loved you. But, it wouldn't work now.

"See, I don't think I'm such a piece of shit anymore. I learned something really major league this summer. I'm valuable. Really wonderful people have become my friends. Just as I am. Joey fell in love with that. Right next to Miss Perfect Everything. You would always think of me as who you came back to. I'd never be the one you found first. When Joey looks at me, there's a glow in his eyes. Like he found me. A diamond in the rough, kind of thing. I can't describe it. But it makes me feel really special. I'd never have that with you. I'd go backward. I know it. So, gee. Thanks, Rikki. But it's too late. I'm really sorry."

She stood up and started back along the beach. Her heart was pounding and she put her hand over it and patted herself, calming herself down. She could hardly believe what she was doing. She did not turn around and he did not follow her, but she could feel his eyes on her back, watching her go, and she knew, even while it was happening, that she would never forget this moment, not even if she lived forever.

EPILOGUE

The Principal Sum. Payable for the following: loss of life, both hands or both feet, one hand and one foot, the entire sight of both eyes, speech and hearing, or the entire sight of one eye and one hand or one foot. One-half the Principal Sum: loss of one hand or one foot, the entire sight of one eye, or loss of speech and hearing. One-quarter the Principal Sum: Loss of thumb and index finger.

Janie threw the policy on the Harts' table and covered her face with her hands. Perfect. This was the way it would end for all of them. In a pile of paper insanity, compromising over body parts with lawyers and insurance agencies. On the bottom of the form, she wrote: *What if loss involves the loss of one thumb and one half the index finger and two toes and the sight of the left eye? That ought to muddle it.*

It was all really over now. The summer, the sickness and most of the loose ends. School started next week and they were going home. Home. How ridiculous that sounded. Her mother and Louie were staying out in a rented house and her father and Clovis were setting off on some European tour. Sort of prehoneymoon, she supposed. She couldn't really blame them. Or could she?

The Match had gone to California, Aaron had gone to

373

Washington to take the bar exam, and she and Gina were left to close up shop and finish with the legal mess. She was lucky. She knew it. So many women had gone through what she went through and were left broke besides. She should be grateful for that much. She sighed. Arturo waddled over and looked up at her with his mournful tired eyes. She knew how he felt.

The house was sold. She was taking her son back to the City to face life on her own for the very first time. Sounds pretty sitcom to me, Janie Jamieson.

She hugged herself. She was scared. She missed Donnie so much that sometimes it actually ached. Like cramps. Or rheumatism. Something like that.

She never had been any good with men. Donnie was the only man she had ever known who hadn't scared her half to death. She could not even imagine another man ever coming into her life. She had called her shrink after Donnie died and told him and he had asked her gently how she felt.

"Like I just climbed the side of the Empire State Building with King Kong on my back," she said.

"Well, it takes a pretty tough little cookie to do that," he said.

Mighty Mouse in Manhattan. She would see. There was a part of her she had found this summer that she had never known was there and she felt it inside her. A warm, full feeling. A wholeness she had never felt before. Whatever it was, it felt good. Wise and flexible. Not so afraid.

It was there. And it was new. And she knew it was Donnie's gift to her. And because of that, she would not lose it. She would wear it everywhere.